DreamWorks

She-Ra and the Princesses of Power

Legend of the Fire Princess

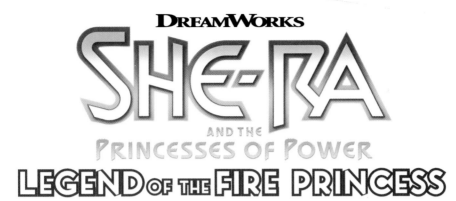

An Original Graphic Novel

Based on stories by Noelle Stevenson

by Gigi D.G.

illustrations by Paulina Ganucheau

colors by Eva de la Cruz

letters by Betsy Peterschmidt

graphix
An imprint of
Scholastic

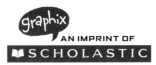

All rights reserved. Published by Scholastic Inc., *Publishers since 1920*. SCHOLASTIC and associated logos are trademarks and/or registered trademarks of Scholastic Inc.

ISBN 978-1-338-53895-3

10 9 8 7 6 5 4 3 2 1   20 21 22 23 24

Printed in the U.S.A. 40

First printing 2020

Edited by Chloe Fraboni

Book design by Katie Fitch

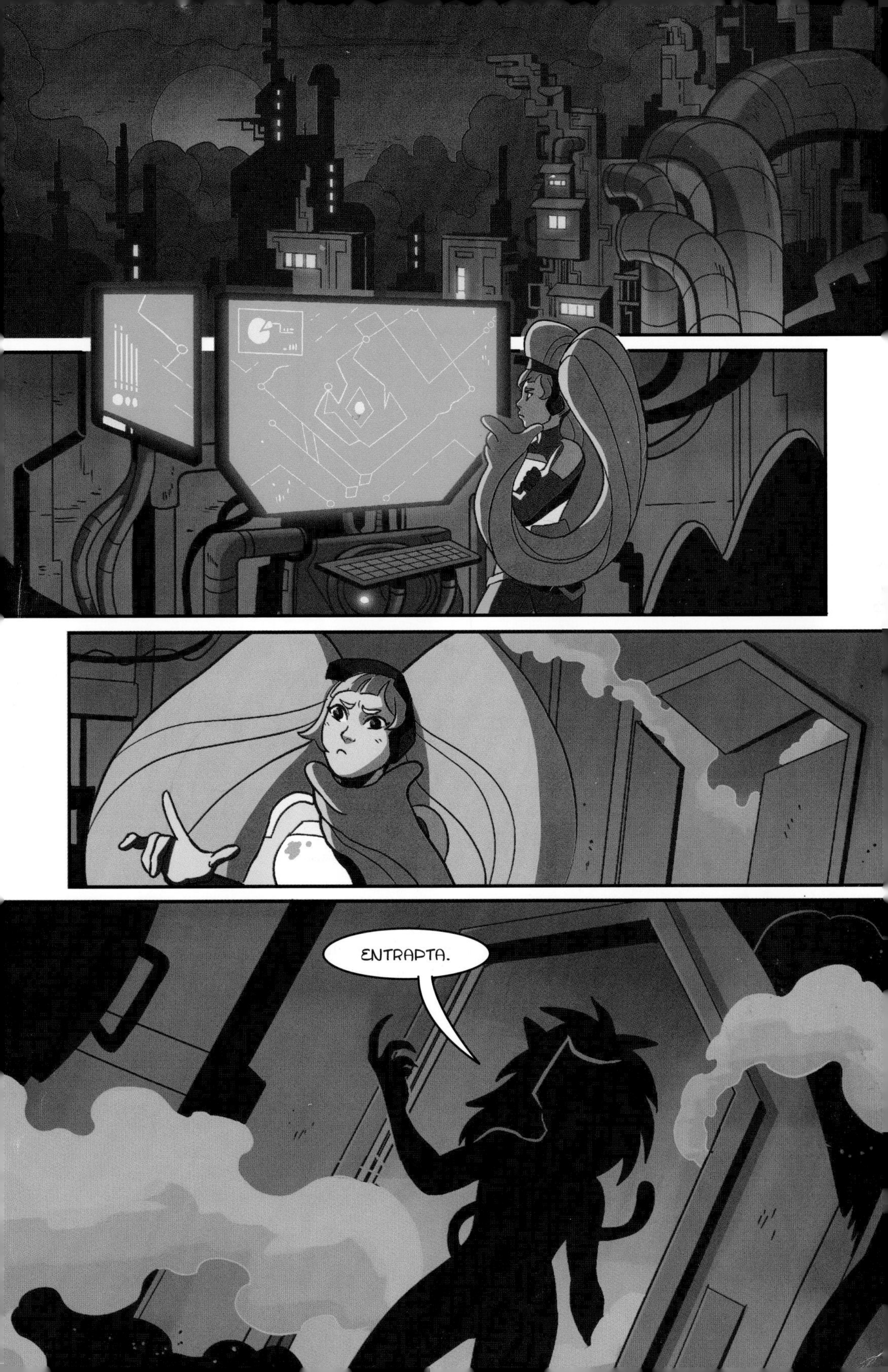
ENTRAPTA.

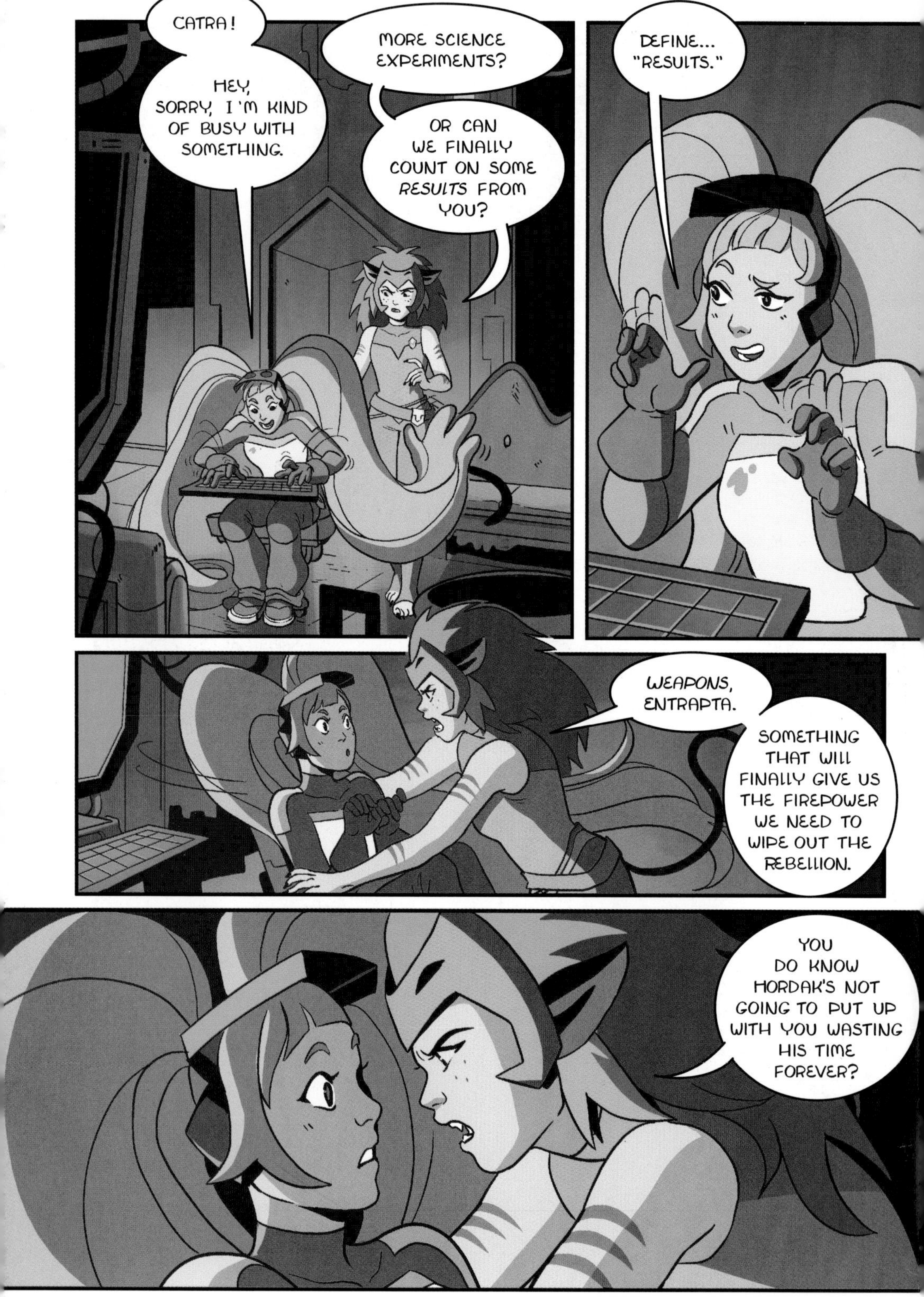
CATRA!
HEY, SORRY, I'M KIND OF BUSY WITH SOMETHING.
MORE SCIENCE EXPERIMENTS?
OR CAN WE FINALLY COUNT ON SOME *RESULTS* FROM YOU?
DEFINE... "RESULTS."
WEAPONS, ENTRAPTA.
SOMETHING THAT WILL FINALLY GIVE US THE FIREPOWER WE NEED TO WIPE OUT THE REBELLION.
YOU DO KNOW HORDAK'S NOT GOING TO PUT UP WITH YOU WASTING HIS TIME FOREVER?

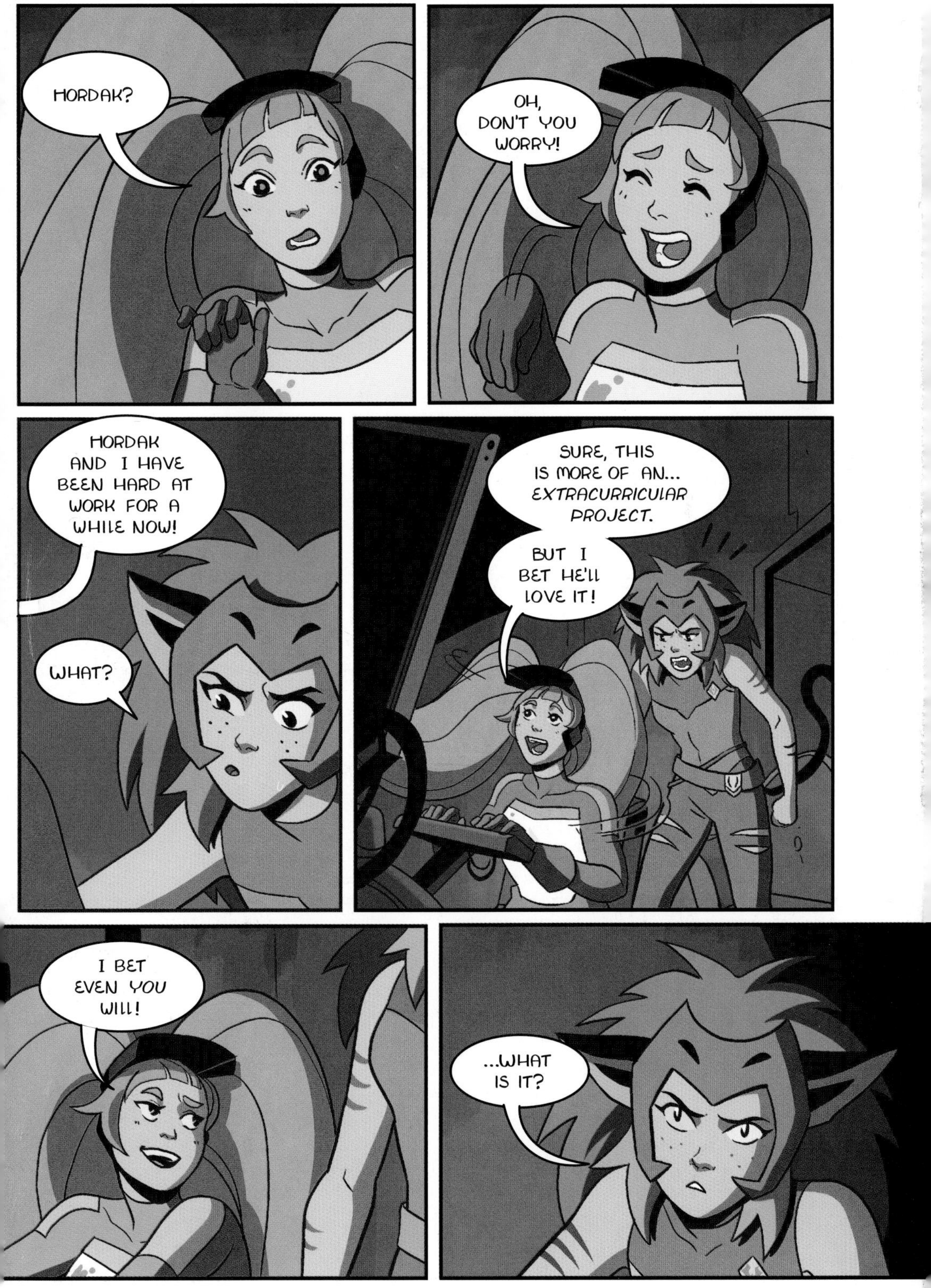
HORDAK?
OH, DON'T YOU WORRY!
HORDAK AND I HAVE BEEN HARD AT WORK FOR A WHILE NOW!
WHAT?
SURE, THIS IS MORE OF AN... EXTRACURRICULAR PROJECT.
BUT I BET HE'LL LOVE IT!
I BET EVEN YOU WILL!
...WHAT IS IT?

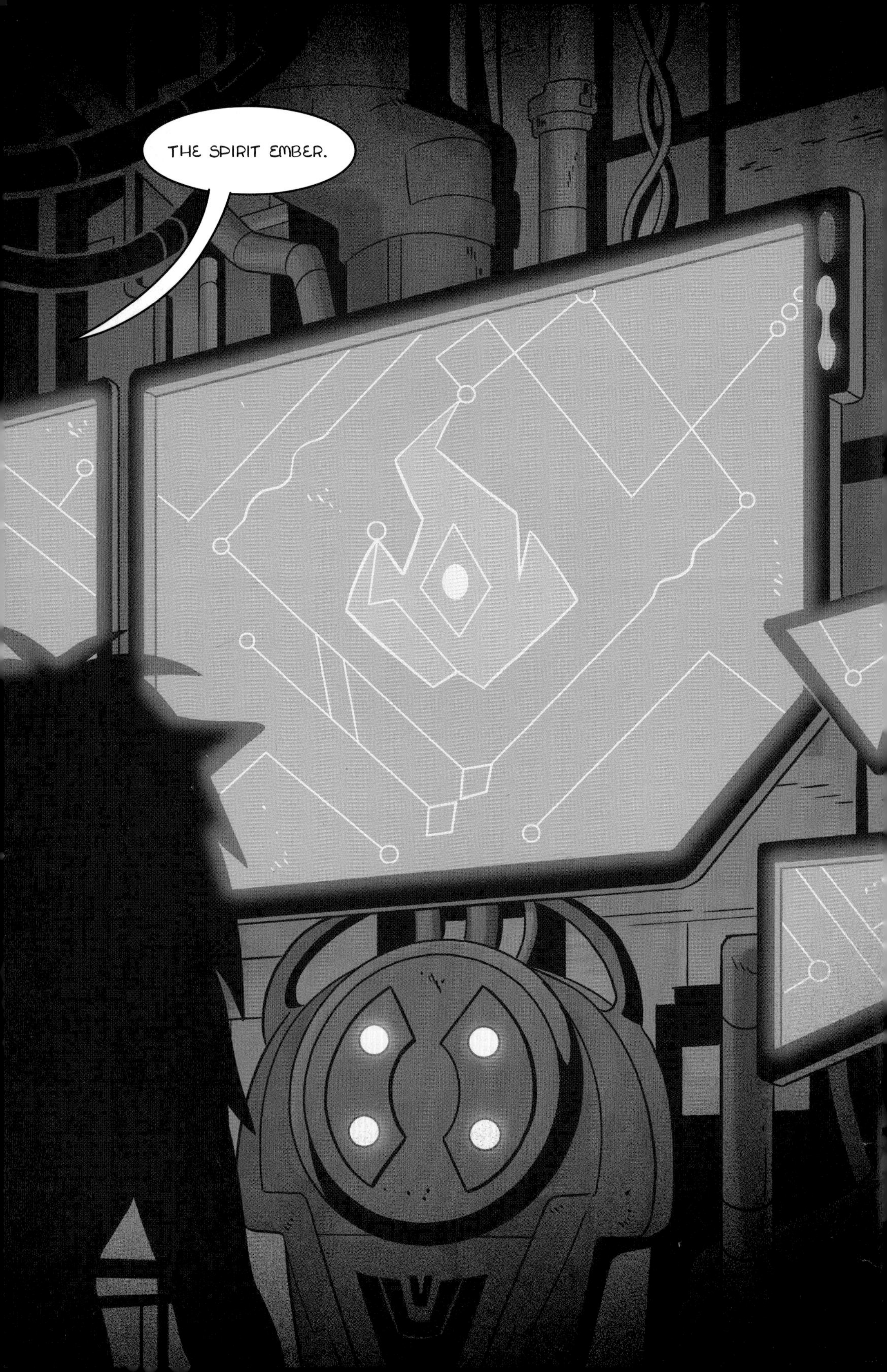
THE SPIRIT EMBER.

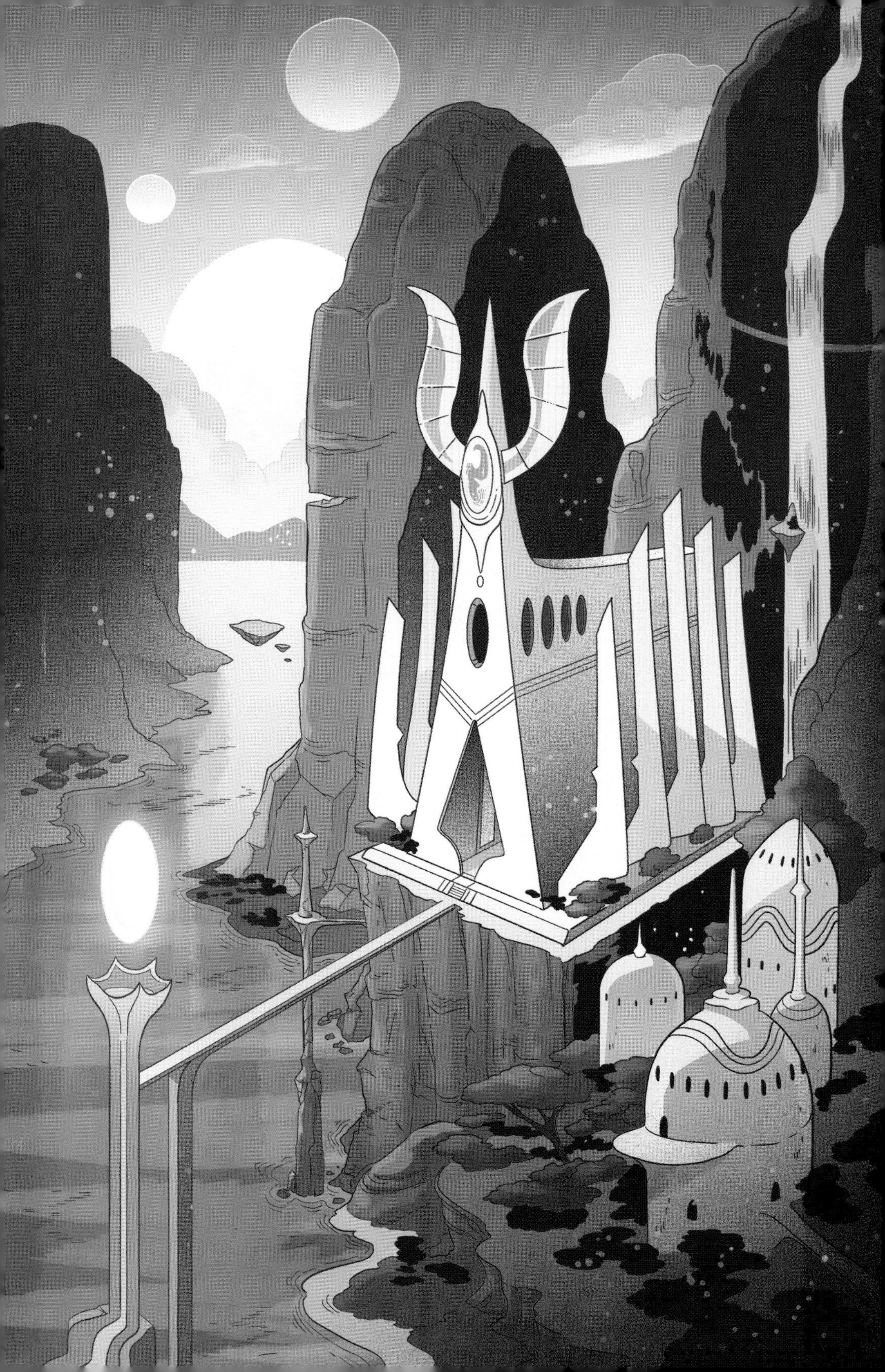

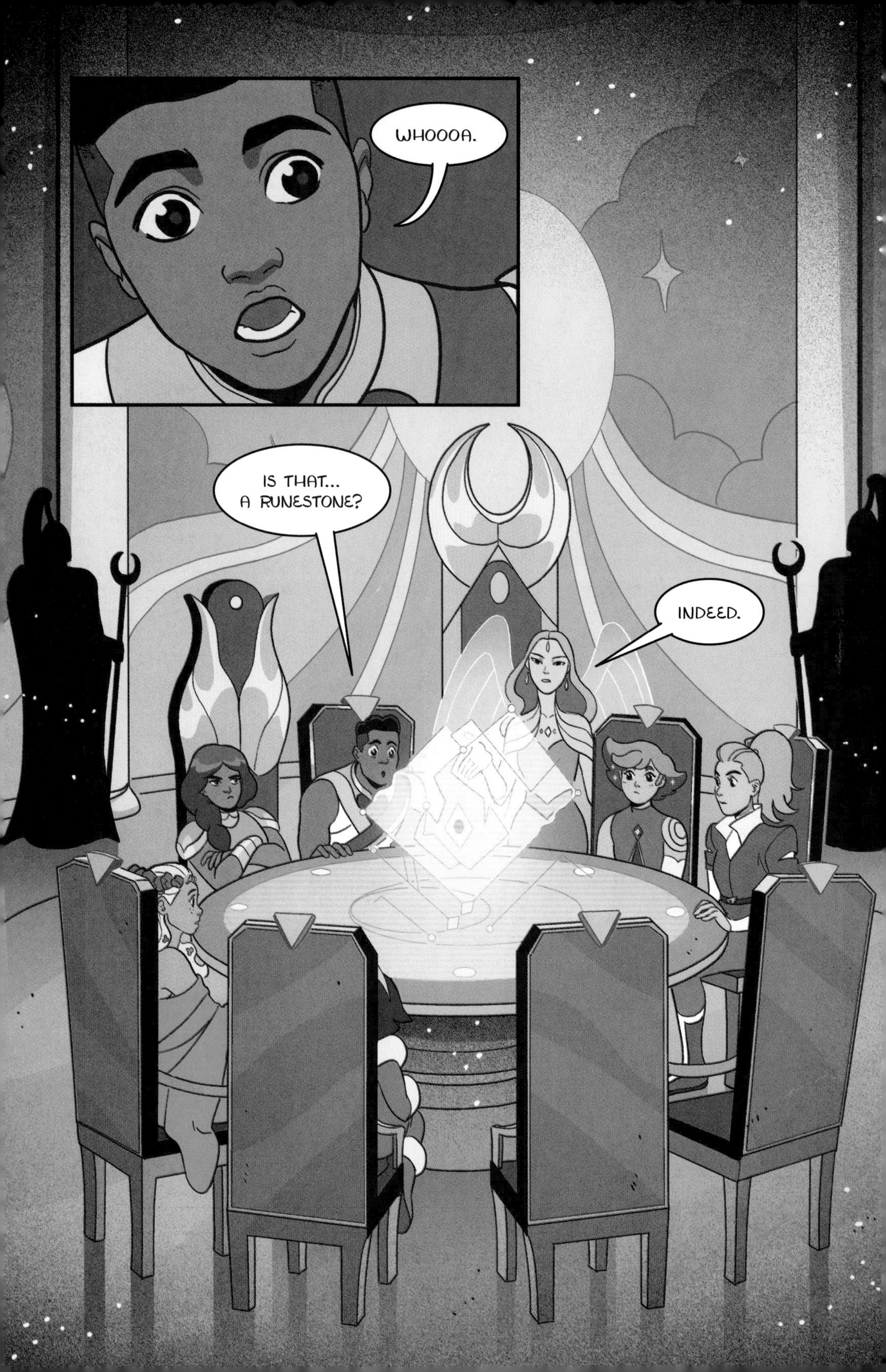
WHOOOA.
IS THAT... A RUNESTONE?
INDEED.

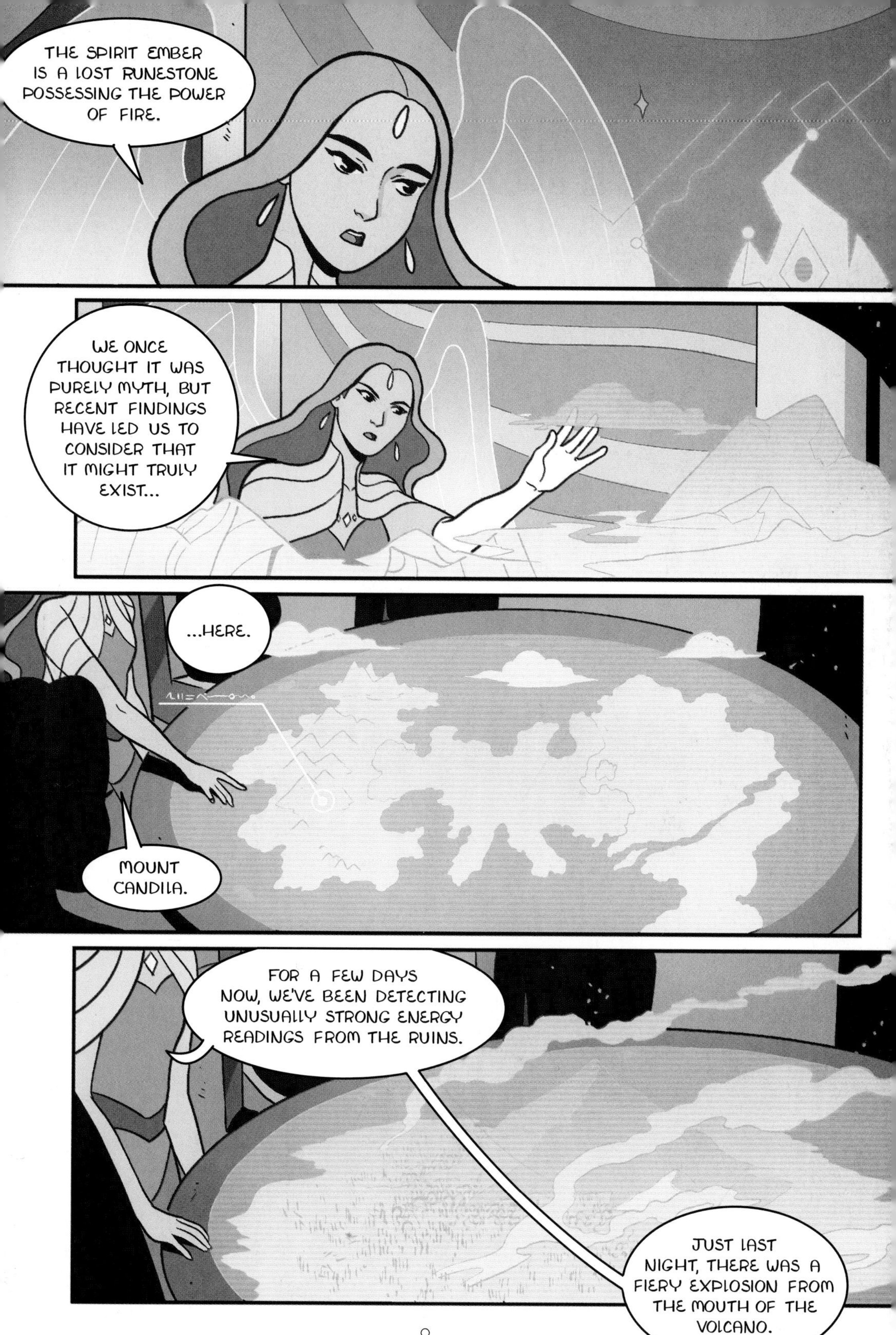
THE SPIRIT EMBER IS A LOST RUNESTONE POSSESSING THE POWER OF FIRE.
WE ONCE THOUGHT IT WAS PURELY MYTH, BUT RECENT FINDINGS HAVE LED US TO CONSIDER THAT IT MIGHT TRULY EXIST...
...HERE.
MOUNT CANDILA.
FOR A FEW DAYS NOW, WE'VE BEEN DETECTING UNUSUALLY STRONG ENERGY READINGS FROM THE RUINS.
JUST LAST NIGHT, THERE WAS A FIERY EXPLOSION FROM THE MOUTH OF THE VOLCANO.

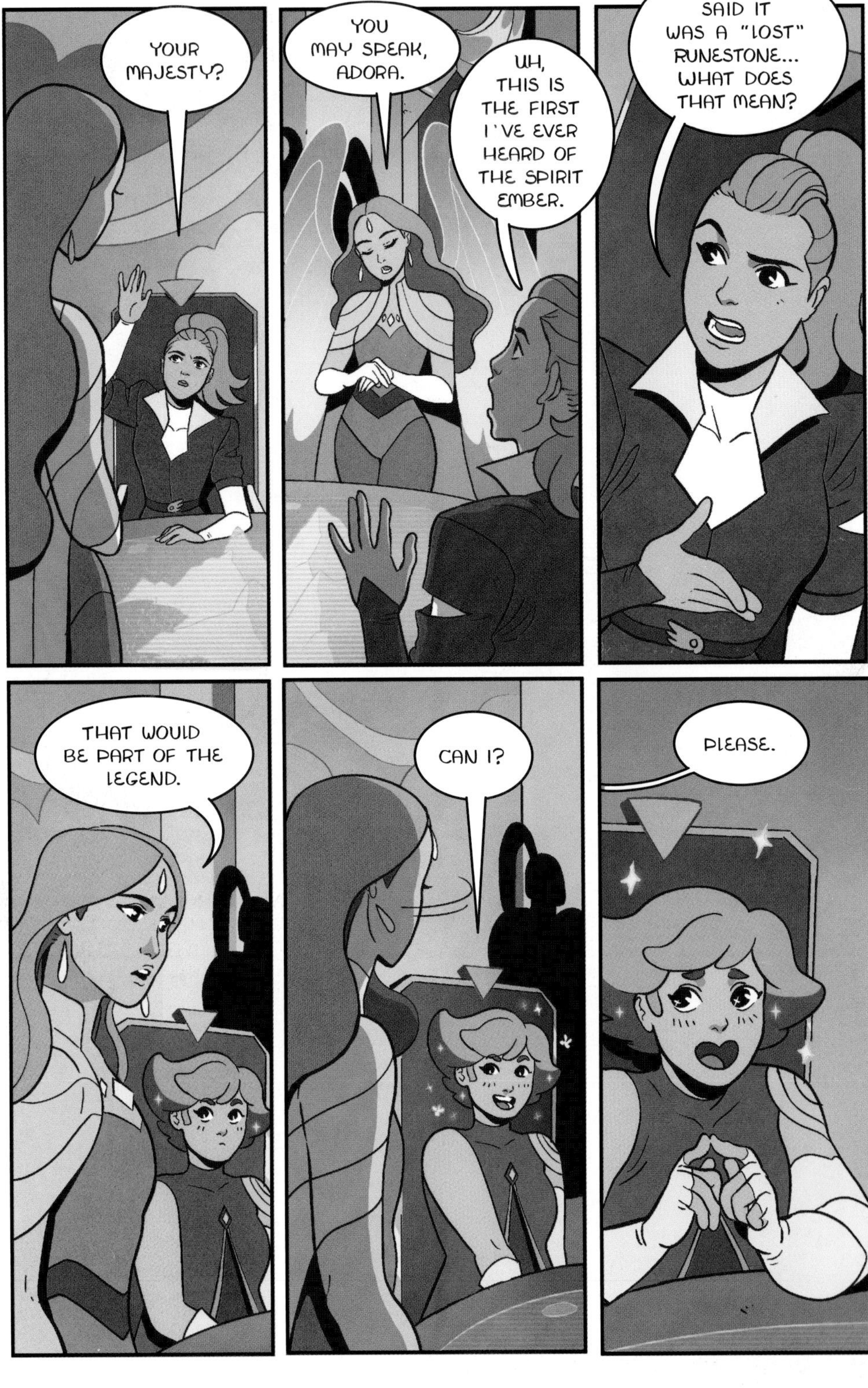
YOUR MAJESTY?
YOU MAY SPEAK, ADORA.
UH, THIS IS THE FIRST I'VE EVER HEARD OF THE SPIRIT EMBER.
YOU SAID IT WAS A "LOST" RUNESTONE... WHAT DOES THAT MEAN?
THAT WOULD BE PART OF THE LEGEND.
CAN I?
PLEASE.

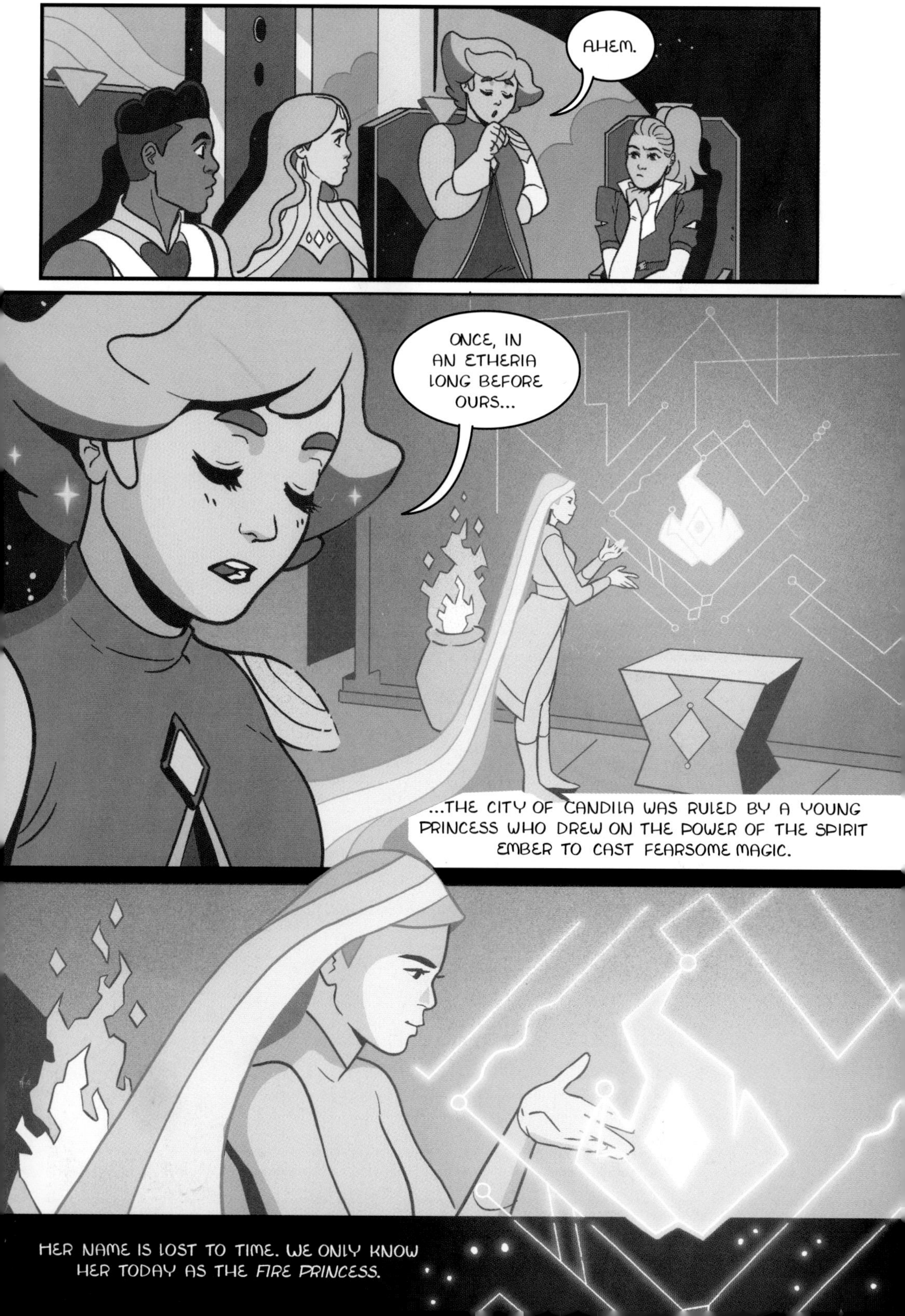
AHEM.
ONCE, IN AN ETHERIA LONG BEFORE OURS...
...THE CITY OF CANDILA WAS RULED BY A YOUNG PRINCESS WHO DREW ON THE POWER OF THE SPIRIT EMBER TO CAST FEARSOME MAGIC.
HER NAME IS LOST TO TIME. WE ONLY KNOW HER TODAY AS THE *FIRE PRINCESS*.

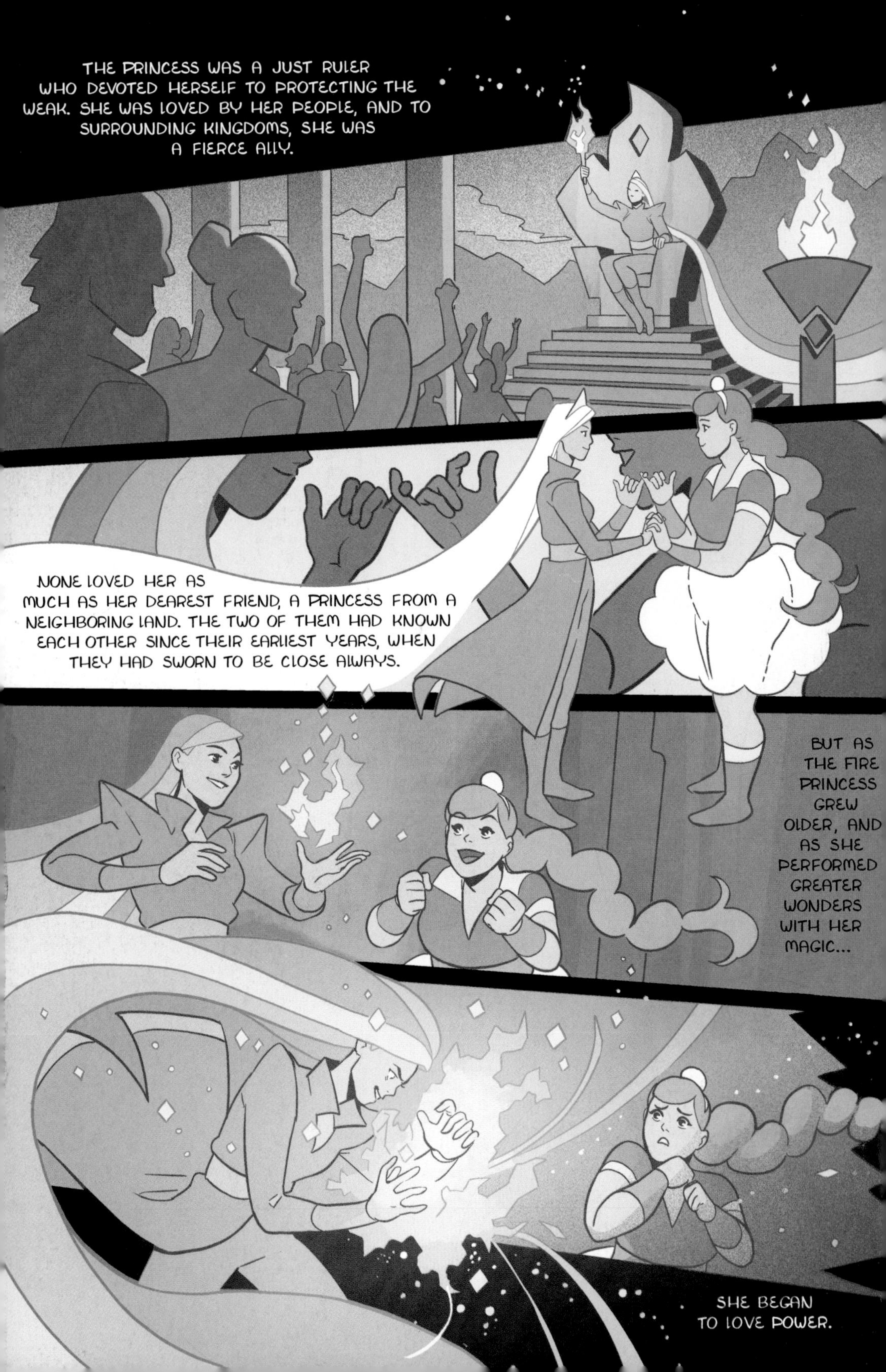
THE PRINCESS WAS A JUST RULER WHO DEVOTED HERSELF TO PROTECTING THE WEAK. SHE WAS LOVED BY HER PEOPLE, AND TO SURROUNDING KINGDOMS, SHE WAS A FIERCE ALLY.
NONE LOVED HER AS MUCH AS HER DEAREST FRIEND, A PRINCESS FROM A NEIGHBORING LAND. THE TWO OF THEM HAD KNOWN EACH OTHER SINCE THEIR EARLIEST YEARS, WHEN THEY HAD SWORN TO BE CLOSE ALWAYS.
BUT AS THE FIRE PRINCESS GREW OLDER, AND AS SHE PERFORMED GREATER WONDERS WITH HER MAGIC...
SHE BEGAN TO LOVE POWER.

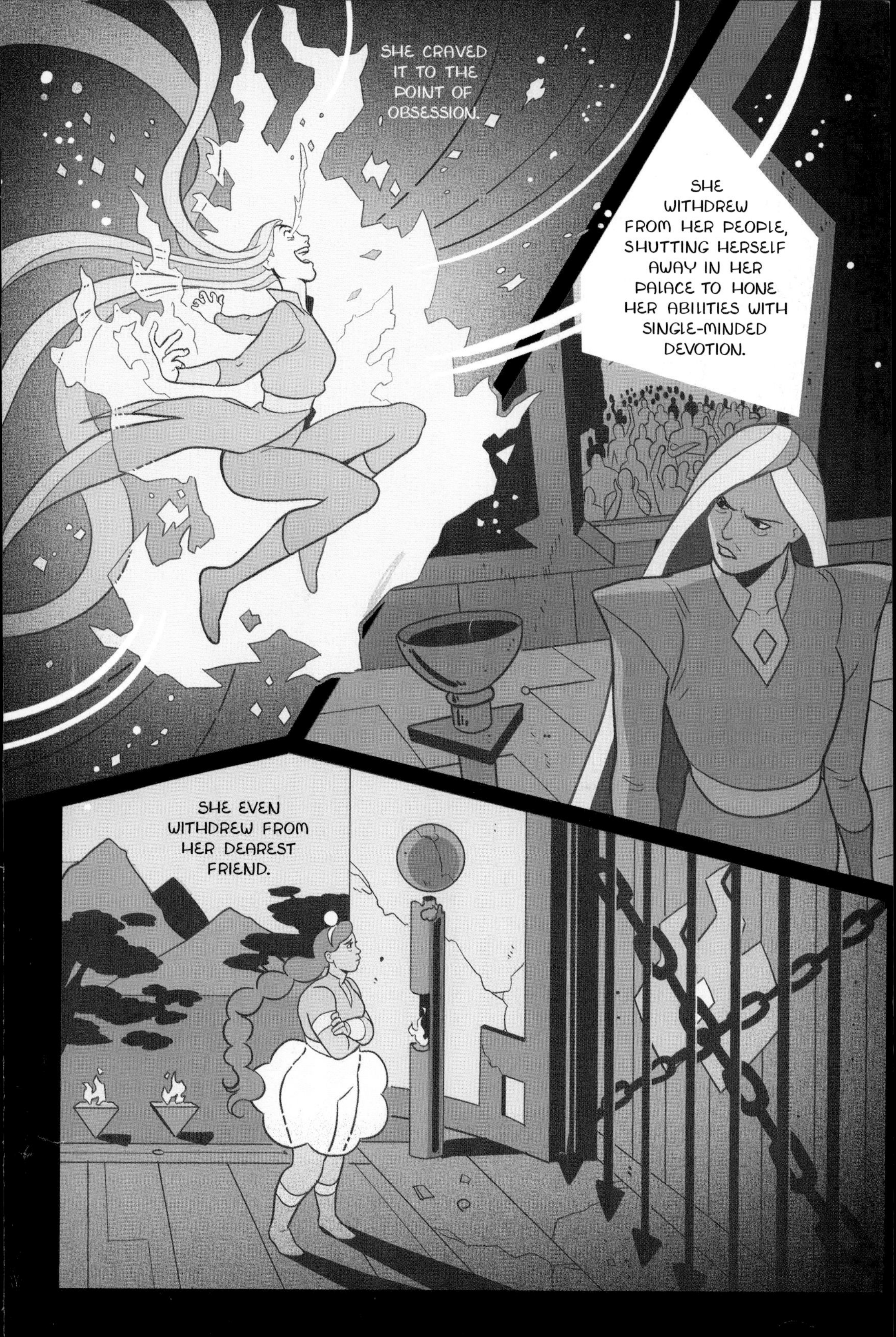
SHE CRAVED IT TO THE POINT OF OBSESSION.
SHE WITHDREW FROM HER PEOPLE, SHUTTING HERSELF AWAY IN HER PALACE TO HONE HER ABILITIES WITH SINGLE-MINDED DEVOTION.
SHE EVEN WITHDREW FROM HER DEAREST FRIEND.

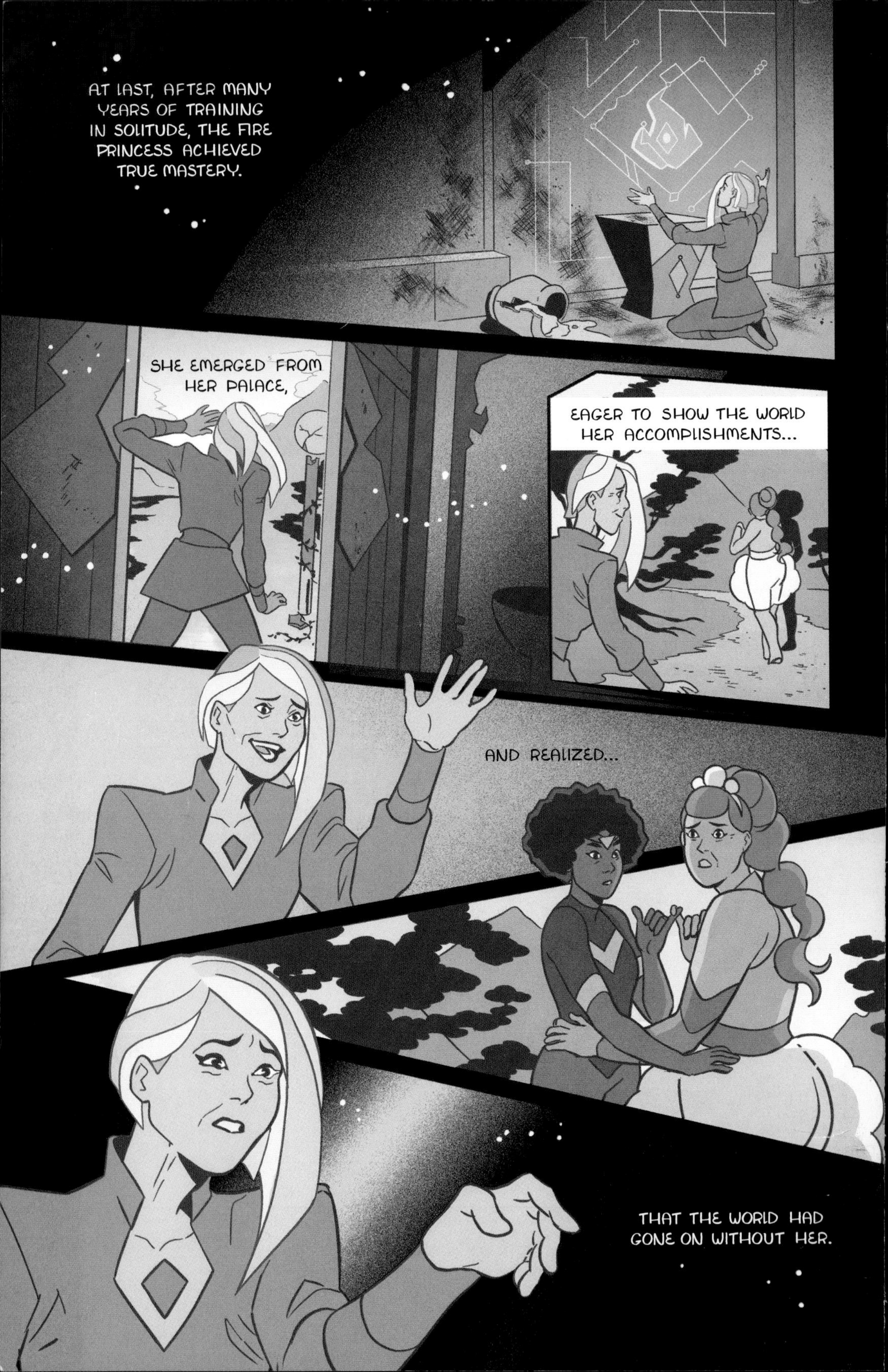
AT LAST, AFTER MANY YEARS OF TRAINING IN SOLITUDE, THE FIRE PRINCESS ACHIEVED TRUE MASTERY.
SHE EMERGED FROM HER PALACE,
EAGER TO SHOW THE WORLD HER ACCOMPLISHMENTS...
AND REALIZED...
THAT THE WORLD HAD GONE ON WITHOUT HER.

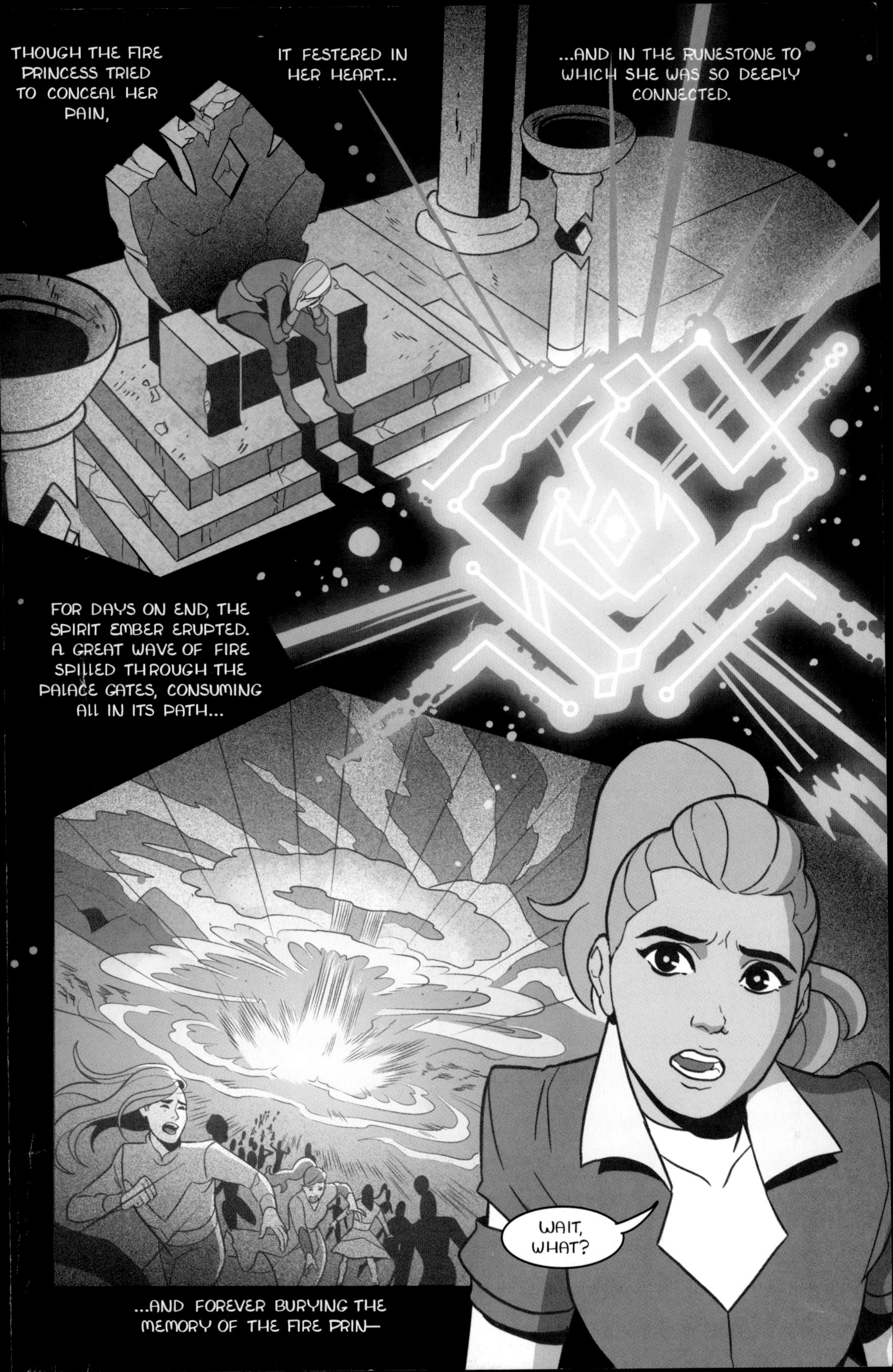
THOUGH THE FIRE PRINCESS TRIED TO CONCEAL HER PAIN,
IT FESTERED IN HER HEART...
...AND IN THE RUNESTONE TO WHICH SHE WAS SO DEEPLY CONNECTED.
FOR DAYS ON END, THE SPIRIT EMBER ERUPTED. A GREAT WAVE OF FIRE SPILLED THROUGH THE PALACE GATES, CONSUMING ALL IN ITS PATH...
WAIT, WHAT?
...AND FOREVER BURYING THE MEMORY OF THE FIRE PRIN—

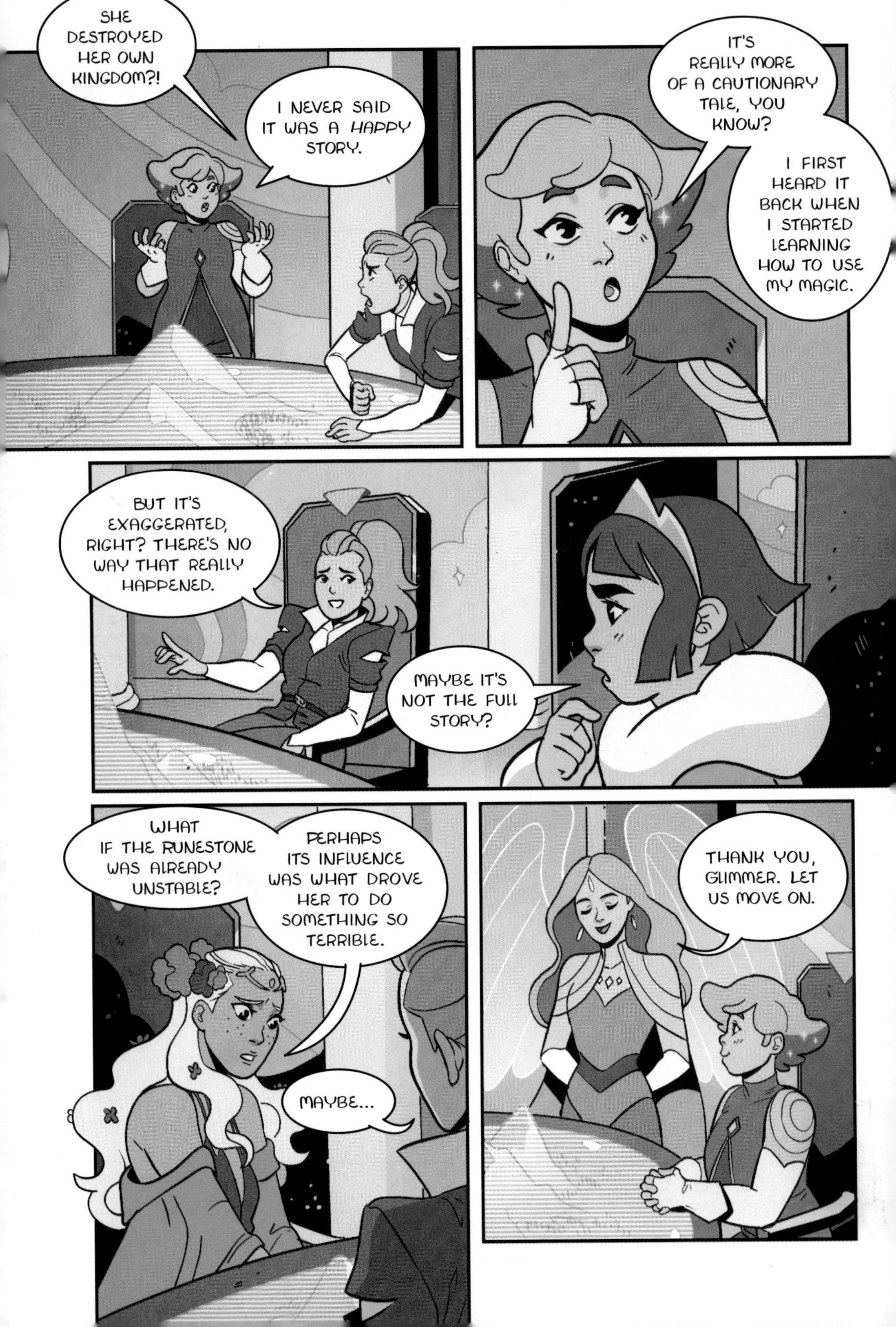
SHE DESTROYED HER OWN KINGDOM?!
I NEVER SAID IT WAS A *HAPPY* STORY.
IT'S REALLY MORE OF A CAUTIONARY TALE, YOU KNOW?
I FIRST HEARD IT BACK WHEN I STARTED LEARNING HOW TO USE MY MAGIC.
BUT IT'S EXAGGERATED, RIGHT? THERE'S NO WAY THAT REALLY HAPPENED.
MAYBE IT'S NOT THE FULL STORY?
WHAT IF THE RUNESTONE WAS ALREADY UNSTABLE?
PERHAPS ITS INFLUENCE WAS WHAT DROVE HER TO DO SOMETHING SO TERRIBLE.
MAYBE...
THANK YOU, GLIMMER. LET US MOVE ON.

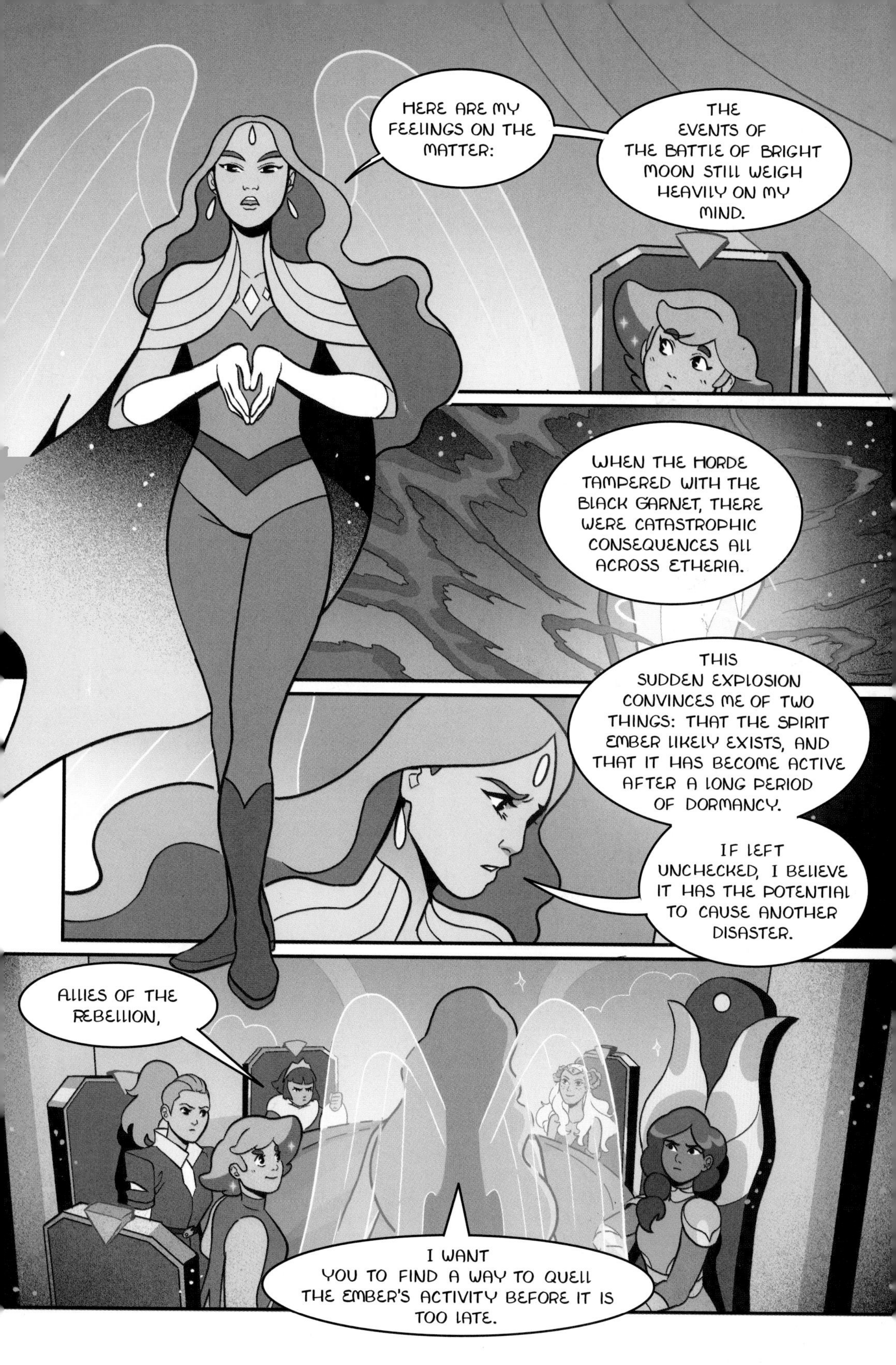
HERE ARE MY FEELINGS ON THE MATTER:
THE EVENTS OF THE BATTLE OF BRIGHT MOON STILL WEIGH HEAVILY ON MY MIND.
WHEN THE HORDE TAMPERED WITH THE BLACK GARNET, THERE WERE CATASTROPHIC CONSEQUENCES ALL ACROSS ETHERIA.
THIS SUDDEN EXPLOSION CONVINCES ME OF TWO THINGS: THAT THE SPIRIT EMBER LIKELY EXISTS, AND THAT IT HAS BECOME ACTIVE AFTER A LONG PERIOD OF DORMANCY.
IF LEFT UNCHECKED, I BELIEVE IT HAS THE POTENTIAL TO CAUSE ANOTHER DISASTER.
ALLIES OF THE REBELLION,
I WANT YOU TO FIND A WAY TO QUELL THE EMBER'S ACTIVITY BEFORE IT IS TOO LATE.

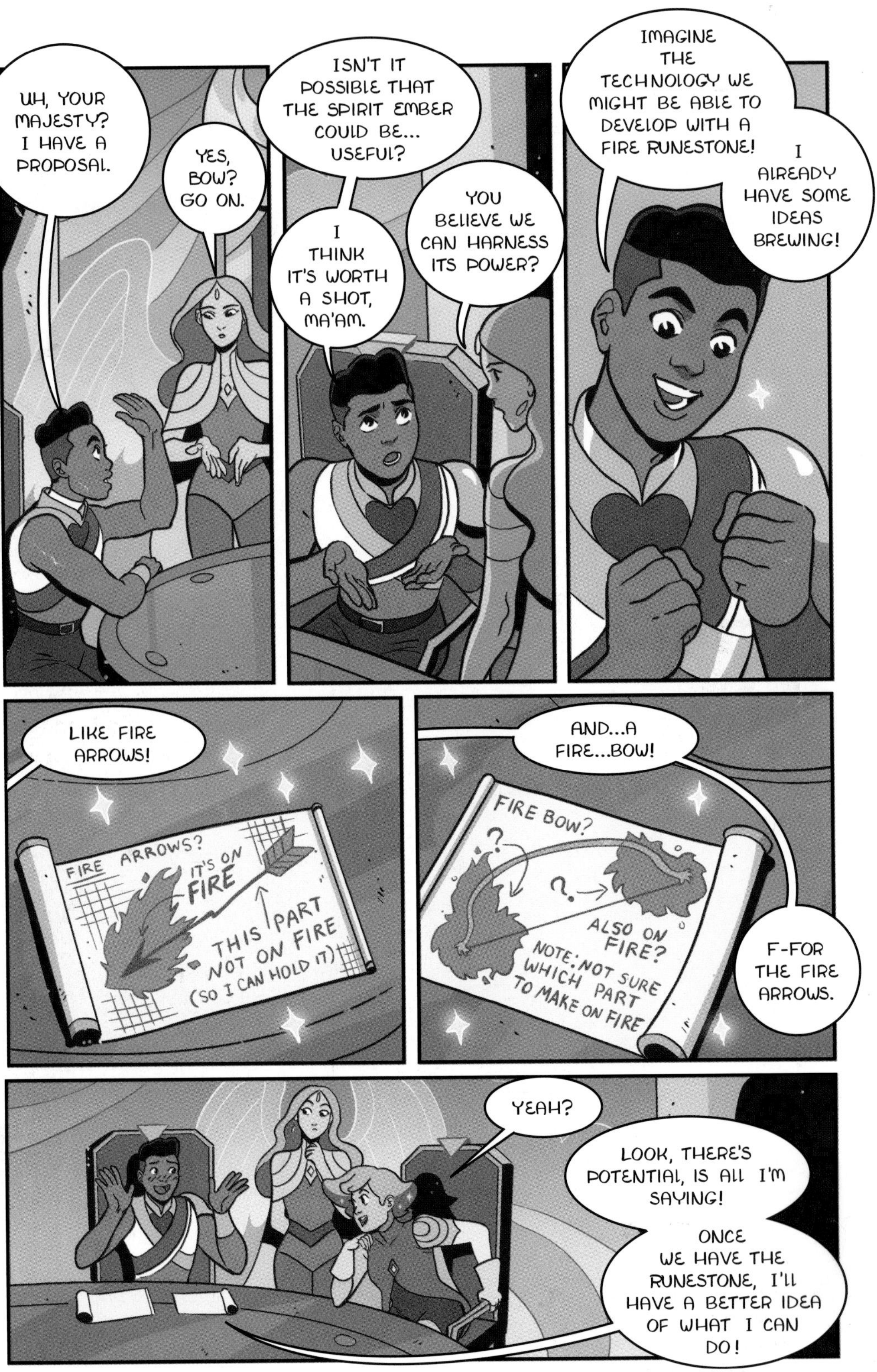

UH, YOUR MAJESTY? I HAVE A PROPOSAL.
YES, BOW? GO ON.
ISN'T IT POSSIBLE THAT THE SPIRIT EMBER COULD BE... USEFUL?
YOU BELIEVE WE CAN HARNESS ITS POWER?
I THINK IT'S WORTH A SHOT, MA'AM.
IMAGINE THE TECHNOLOGY WE MIGHT BE ABLE TO DEVELOP WITH A FIRE RUNESTONE!
I ALREADY HAVE SOME IDEAS BREWING!
LIKE FIRE ARROWS!
FIRE ARROWS?
FIRE
IT'S ON FIRE
THIS PART NOT ON FIRE (SO I CAN HOLD IT)
AND...A FIRE...BOW!
FIRE BOW?
ALSO ON FIRE?
NOTE: NOT SURE WHICH PART TO MAKE ON FIRE
F-FOR THE FIRE ARROWS.
YEAH?
LOOK, THERE'S POTENTIAL, IS ALL I'M SAYING!
ONCE WE HAVE THE RUNESTONE, I'LL HAVE A BETTER IDEA OF WHAT I CAN DO!

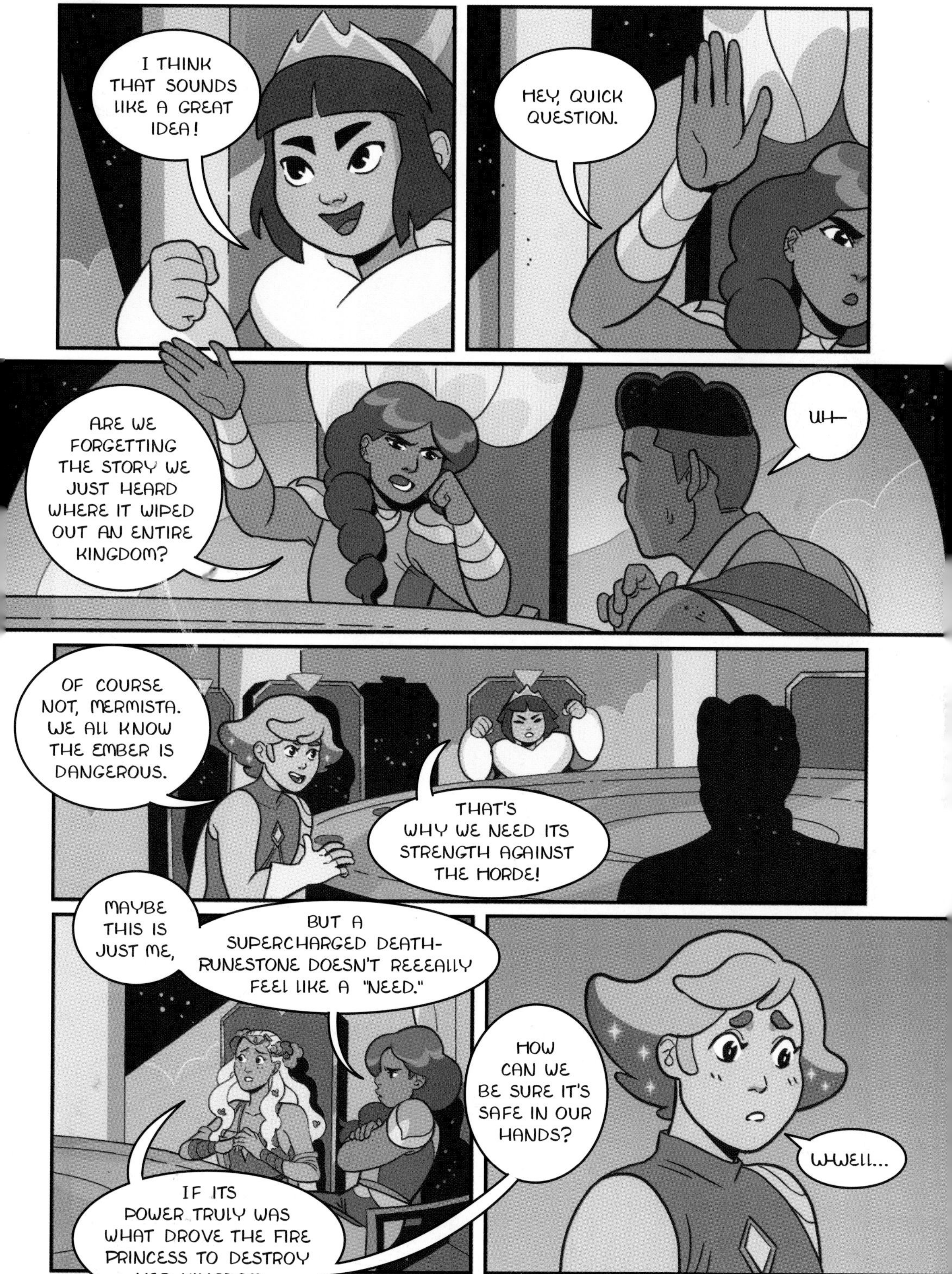
I THINK THAT SOUNDS LIKE A GREAT IDEA!
HEY, QUICK QUESTION.
ARE WE FORGETTING THE STORY WE JUST HEARD WHERE IT WIPED OUT AN ENTIRE KINGDOM?
UH—
OF COURSE NOT, MERMISTA. WE ALL KNOW THE EMBER IS DANGEROUS.
THAT'S WHY WE NEED ITS STRENGTH AGAINST THE HORDE!
MAYBE THIS IS JUST ME,
BUT A SUPERCHARGED DEATH-RUNESTONE DOESN'T REEEALLY FEEL LIKE A "NEED."
IF ITS POWER TRULY WAS WHAT DROVE THE FIRE PRINCESS TO DESTROY HER KINGDOM...
HOW CAN WE BE SURE IT'S SAFE IN OUR HANDS?
W-WELL...

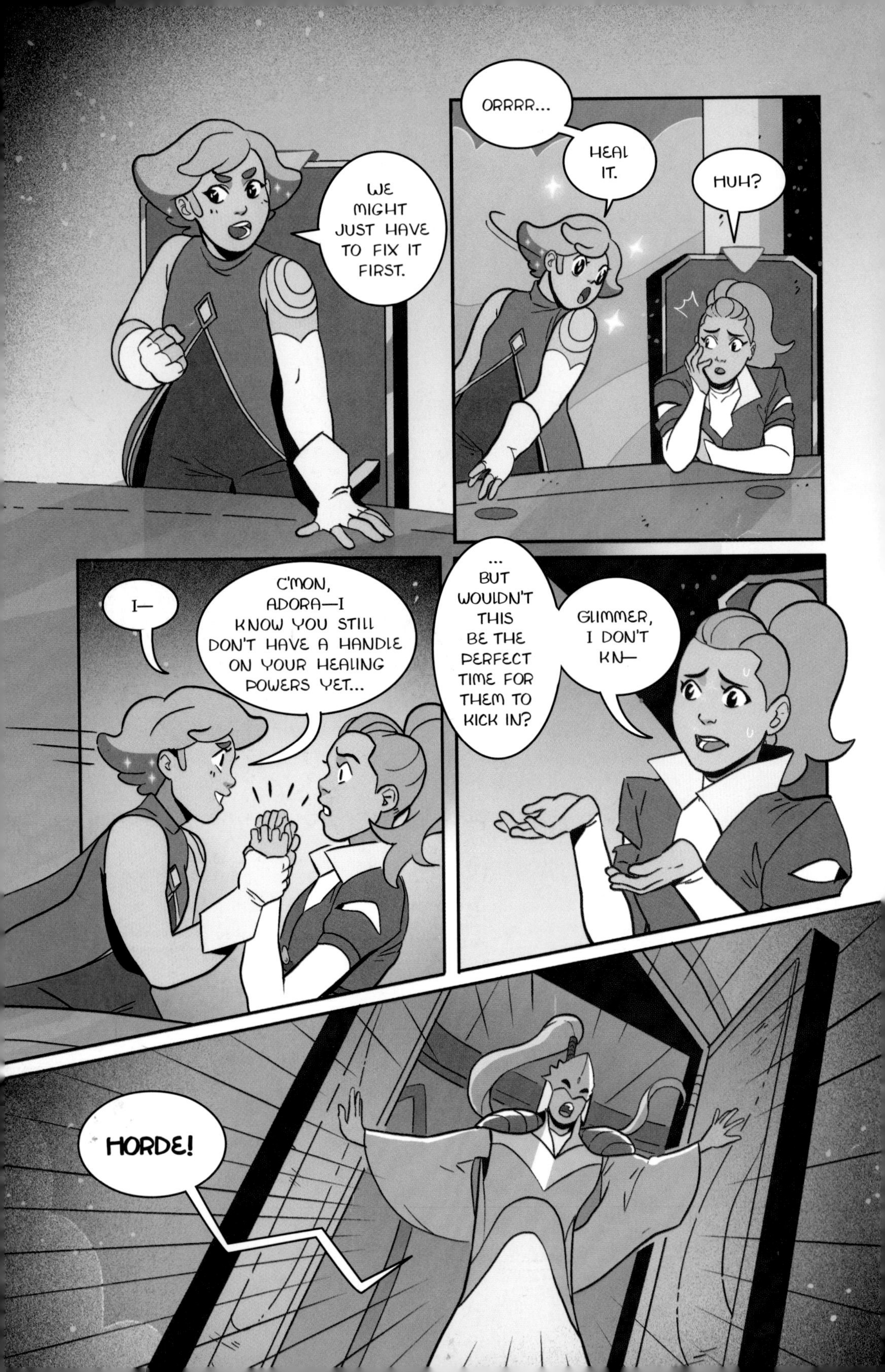

WE MIGHT JUST HAVE TO FIX IT FIRST.
ORRRR...
HEAL IT.
HUH?
I—
C'MON, ADORA—I KNOW YOU STILL DON'T HAVE A HANDLE ON YOUR HEALING POWERS YET...
... BUT WOULDN'T THIS BE THE PERFECT TIME FOR THEM TO KICK IN?
GLIMMER, I DON'T KN—
HORDE!

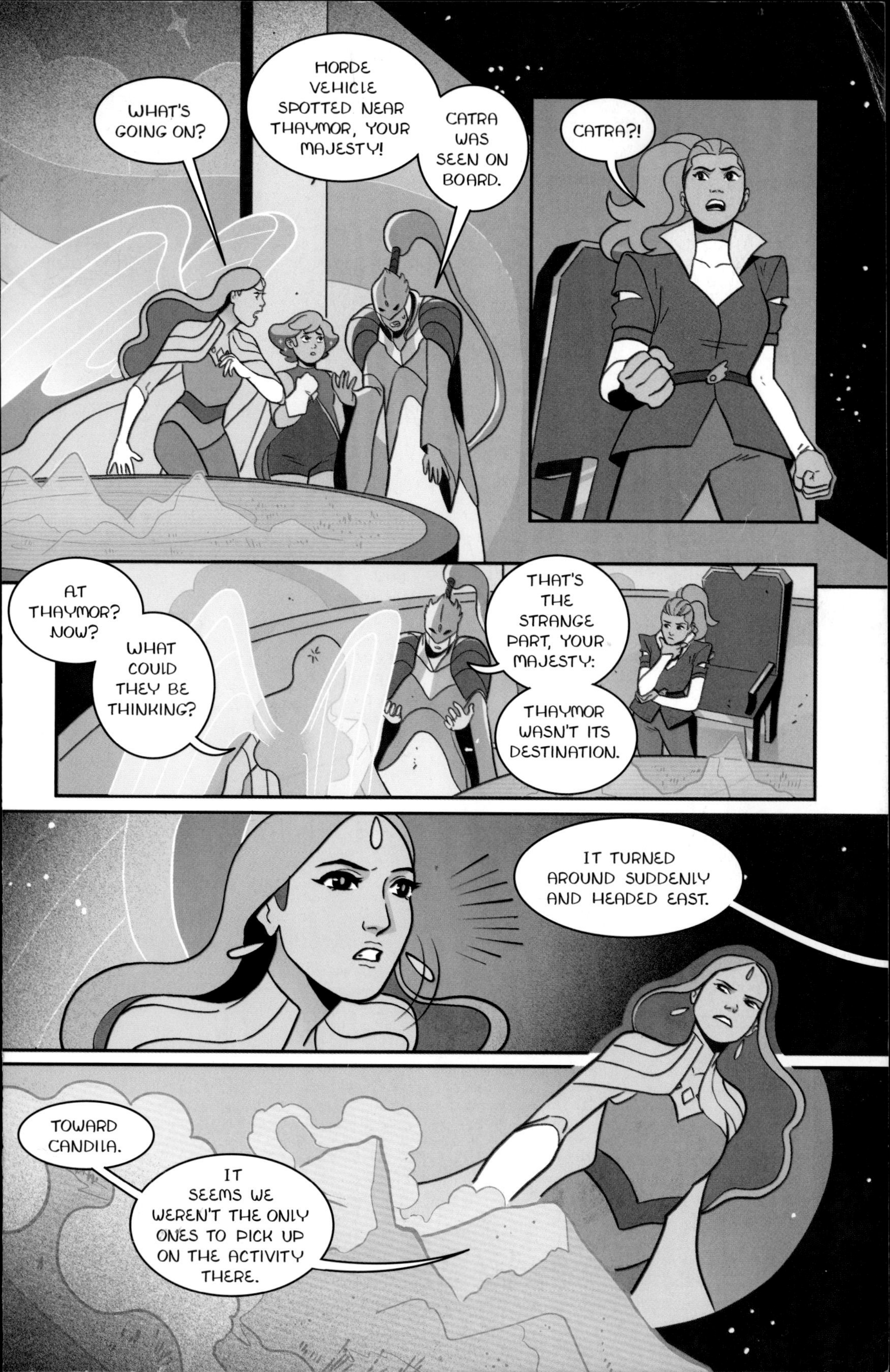
WHAT'S GOING ON?
HORDE VEHICLE SPOTTED NEAR THAYMOR, YOUR MAJESTY!
CATRA WAS SEEN ON BOARD.
CATRA?!
AT THAYMOR? NOW?
WHAT COULD THEY BE THINKING?
THAT'S THE STRANGE PART, YOUR MAJESTY:
THAYMOR WASN'T ITS DESTINATION.
IT TURNED AROUND SUDDENLY AND HEADED EAST.
TOWARD CANDILA.
IT SEEMS WE WEREN'T THE ONLY ONES TO PICK UP ON THE ACTIVITY THERE.

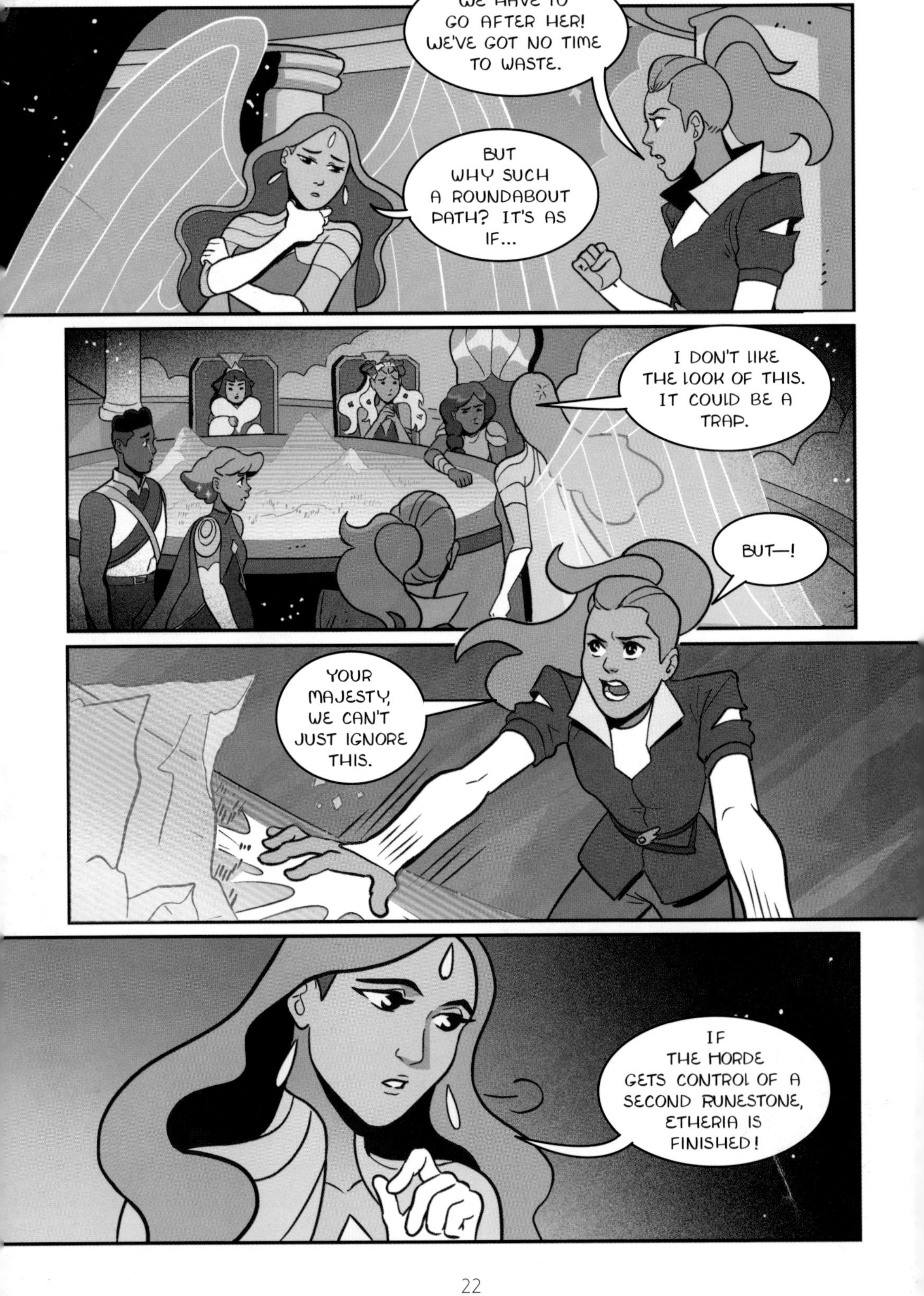
WE HAVE TO GO AFTER HER! WE'VE GOT NO TIME TO WASTE.
BUT WHY SUCH A ROUNDABOUT PATH? IT'S AS IF...
I DON'T LIKE THE LOOK OF THIS. IT COULD BE A TRAP.
BUT—!
YOUR MAJESTY, WE CAN'T JUST IGNORE THIS.
IF THE HORDE GETS CONTROL OF A SECOND RUNESTONE, ETHERIA IS FINISHED!

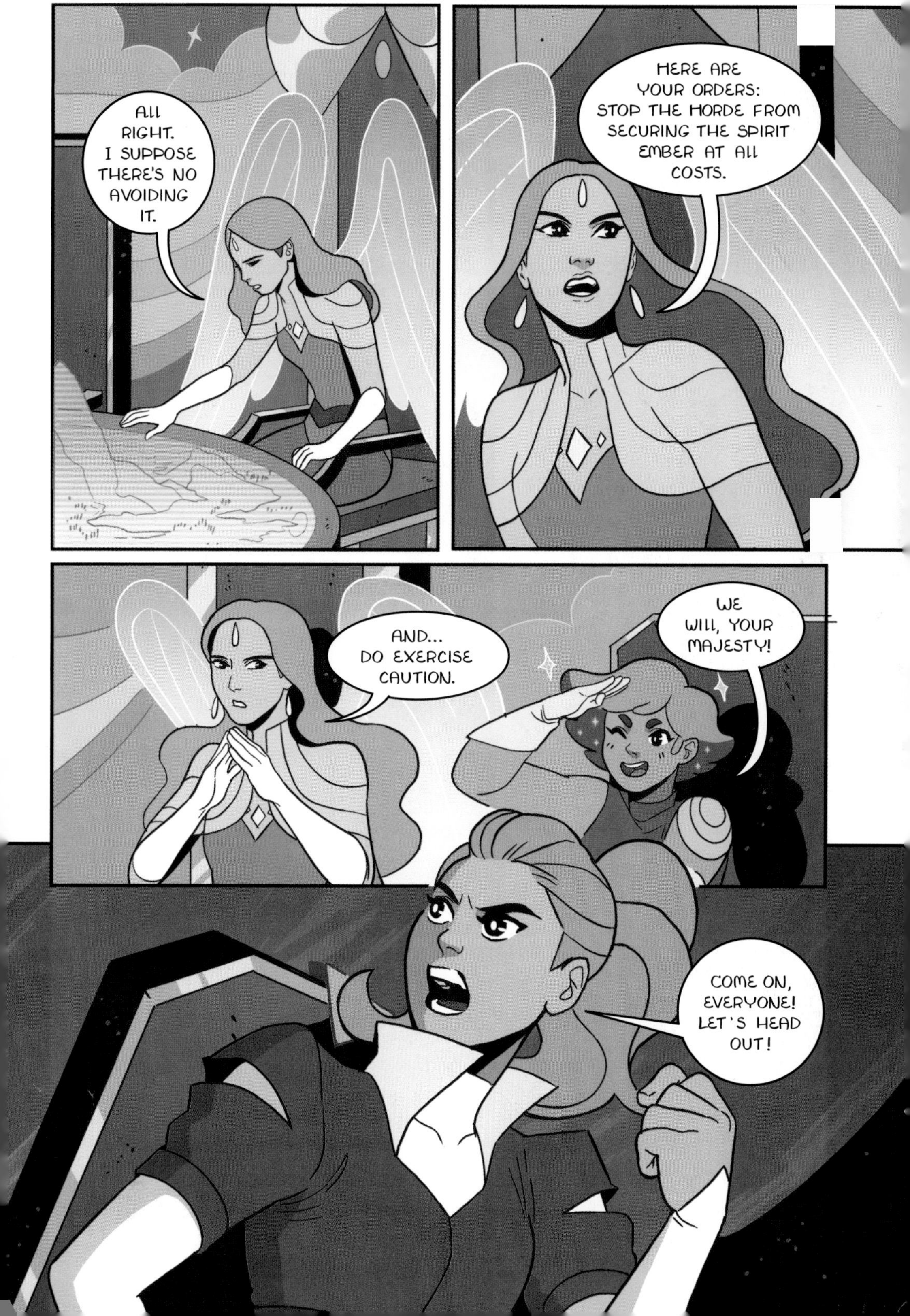
ALL RIGHT. I SUPPOSE THERE'S NO AVOIDING IT.
HERE ARE YOUR ORDERS: STOP THE HORDE FROM SECURING THE SPIRIT EMBER AT ALL COSTS.
AND... DO EXERCISE CAUTION.
WE WILL, YOUR MAJESTY!
COME ON, EVERYONE! LET'S HEAD OUT!

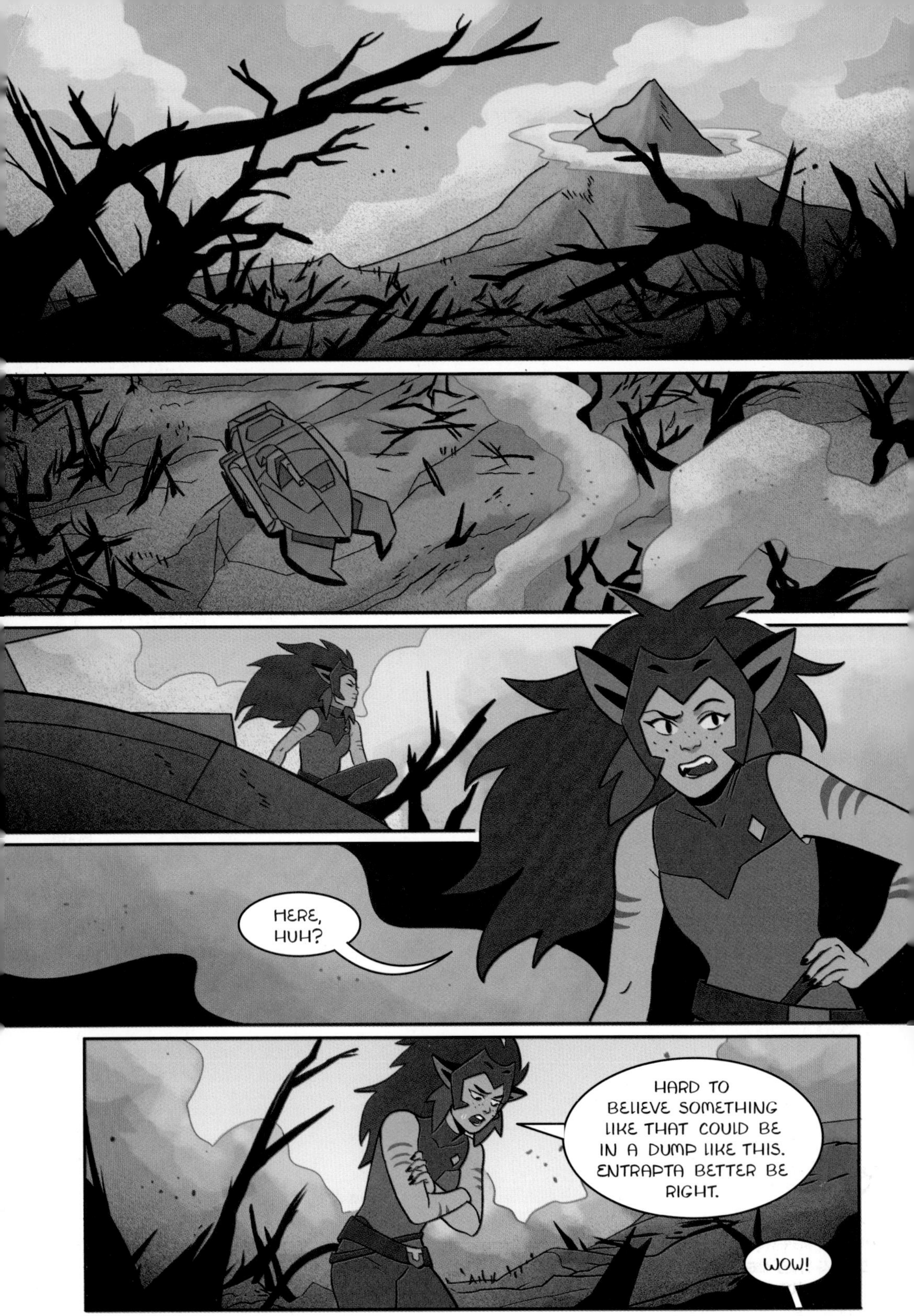
HERE, HUH?
HARD TO BELIEVE SOMETHING LIKE THAT COULD BE IN A DUMP LIKE THIS. ENTRAPTA BETTER BE RIGHT.
WOW!

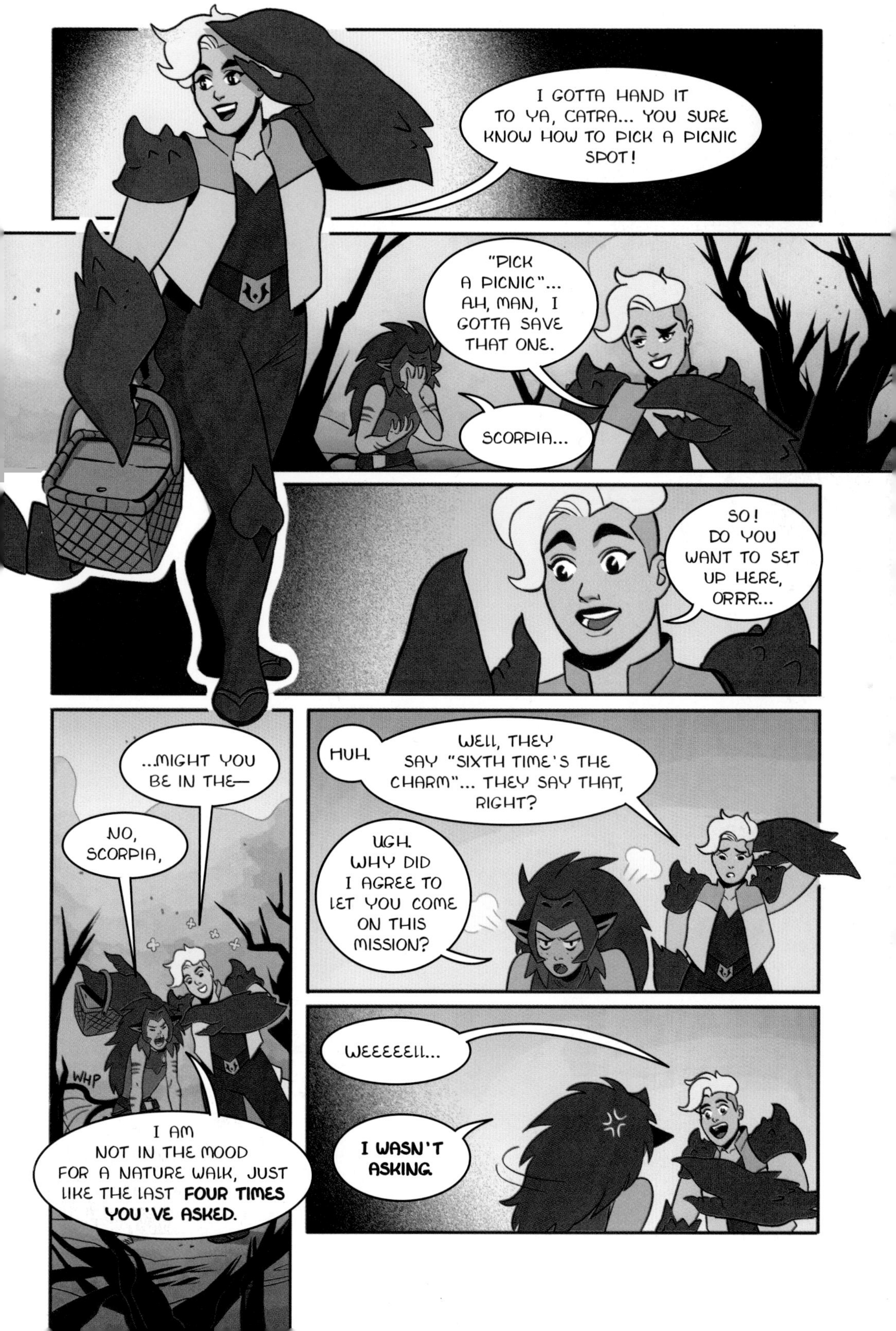
I GOTTA HAND IT TO YA, CATRA... YOU SURE KNOW HOW TO PICK A PICNIC SPOT!
"PICK A PICNIC"... AH, MAN, I GOTTA SAVE THAT ONE.
SCORPIA...
SO! DO YOU WANT TO SET UP HERE, ORRR...
...MIGHT YOU BE IN THE—
NO, SCORPIA,
WHP
I AM NOT IN THE MOOD FOR A NATURE WALK, JUST LIKE THE LAST **FOUR TIMES YOU'VE ASKED.**
HUH.
WELL, THEY SAY "SIXTH TIME'S THE CHARM"... THEY SAY THAT, RIGHT?
UGH. WHY DID I AGREE TO LET YOU COME ON THIS MISSION?
WEEEEELL...
I WASN'T ASKING.

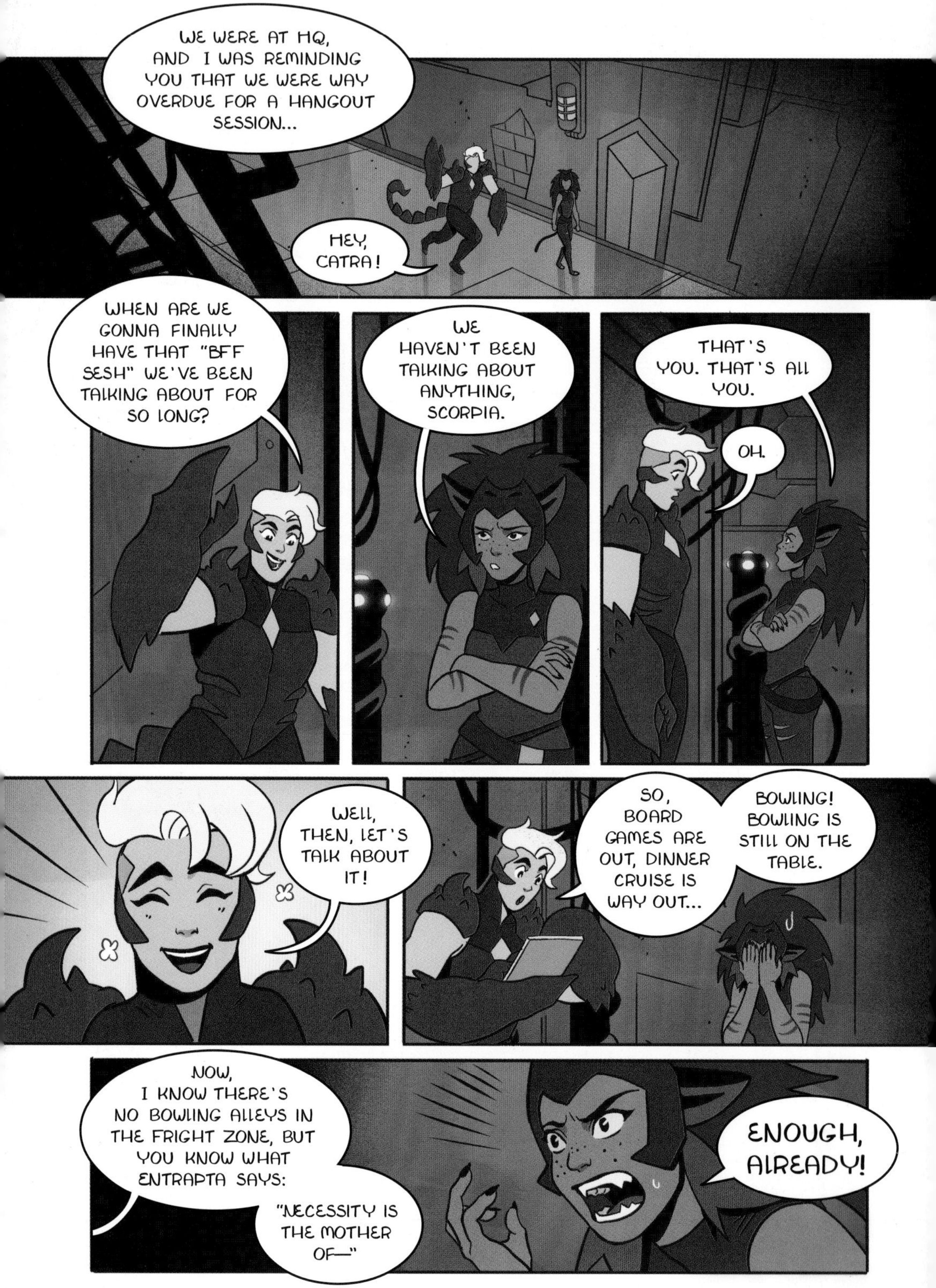
WE WERE AT HQ, AND I WAS REMINDING YOU THAT WE WERE WAY OVERDUE FOR A HANGOUT SESSION...
HEY, CATRA!
WHEN ARE WE GONNA FINALLY HAVE THAT "BFF SESH" WE'VE BEEN TALKING ABOUT FOR SO LONG?
WE HAVEN'T BEEN TALKING ABOUT ANYTHING, SCORPIA.
THAT'S YOU. THAT'S ALL YOU.
OH.
WELL, THEN, LET'S TALK ABOUT IT!
SO, BOARD GAMES ARE OUT, DINNER CRUISE IS WAY OUT...
BOWLING! BOWLING IS STILL ON THE TABLE.
NOW, I KNOW THERE'S NO BOWLING ALLEYS IN THE FRIGHT ZONE, BUT YOU KNOW WHAT ENTRAPTA SAYS:
"NECESSITY IS THE MOTHER OF—"
ENOUGH, ALREADY!

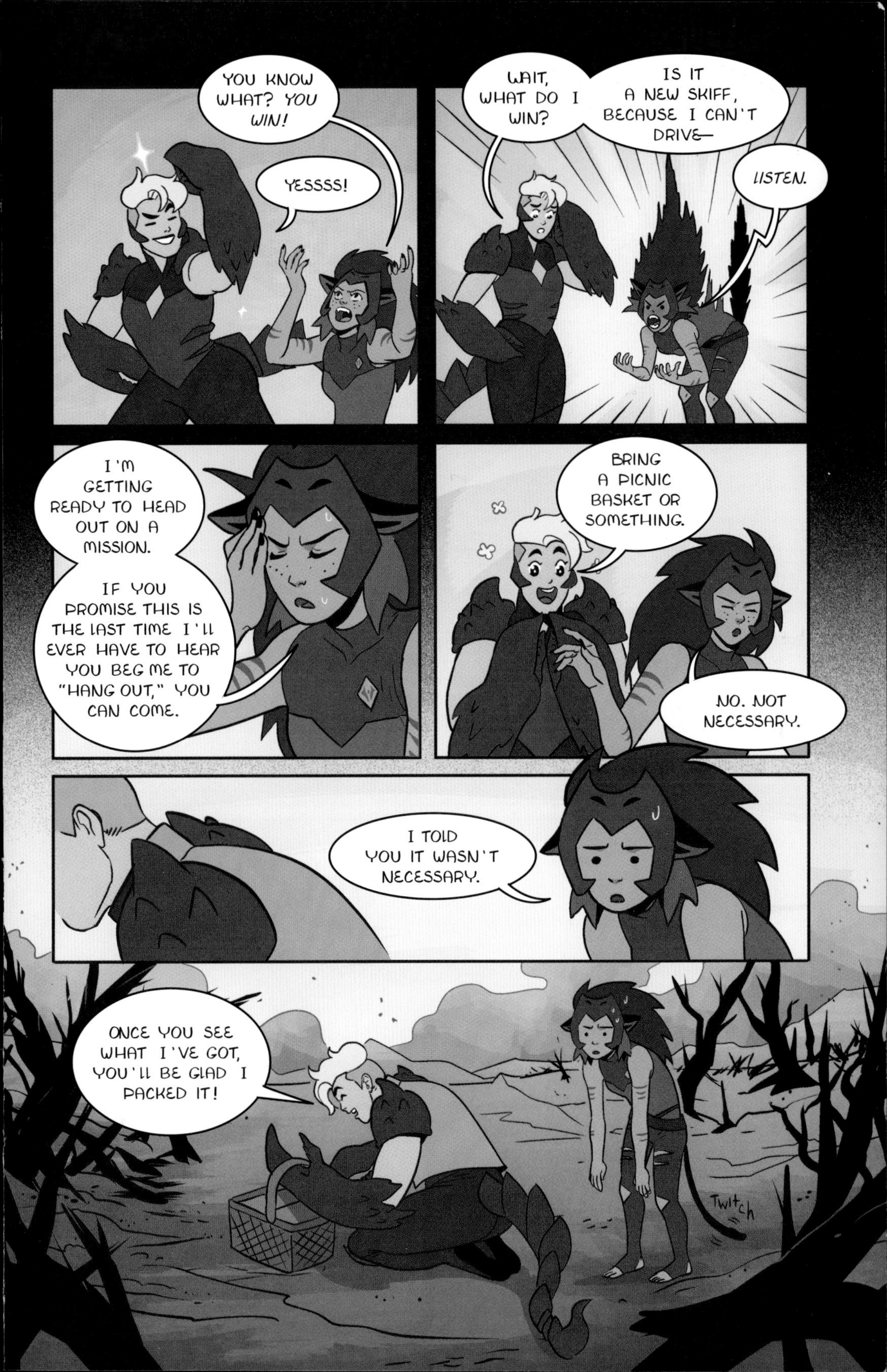
YOU KNOW WHAT? YOU WIN!
YESSSS!
WAIT, WHAT DO I WIN?
IS IT A NEW SKIFF, BECAUSE I CAN'T DRIVE—
LISTEN.
I'M GETTING READY TO HEAD OUT ON A MISSION.
IF YOU PROMISE THIS IS THE LAST TIME I'LL EVER HAVE TO HEAR YOU BEG ME TO "HANG OUT," YOU CAN COME.
BRING A PICNIC BASKET OR SOMETHING.
NO. NOT NECESSARY.
I TOLD YOU IT WASN'T NECESSARY.
ONCE YOU SEE WHAT I'VE GOT, YOU'LL BE GLAD I PACKED IT!
TWITCH

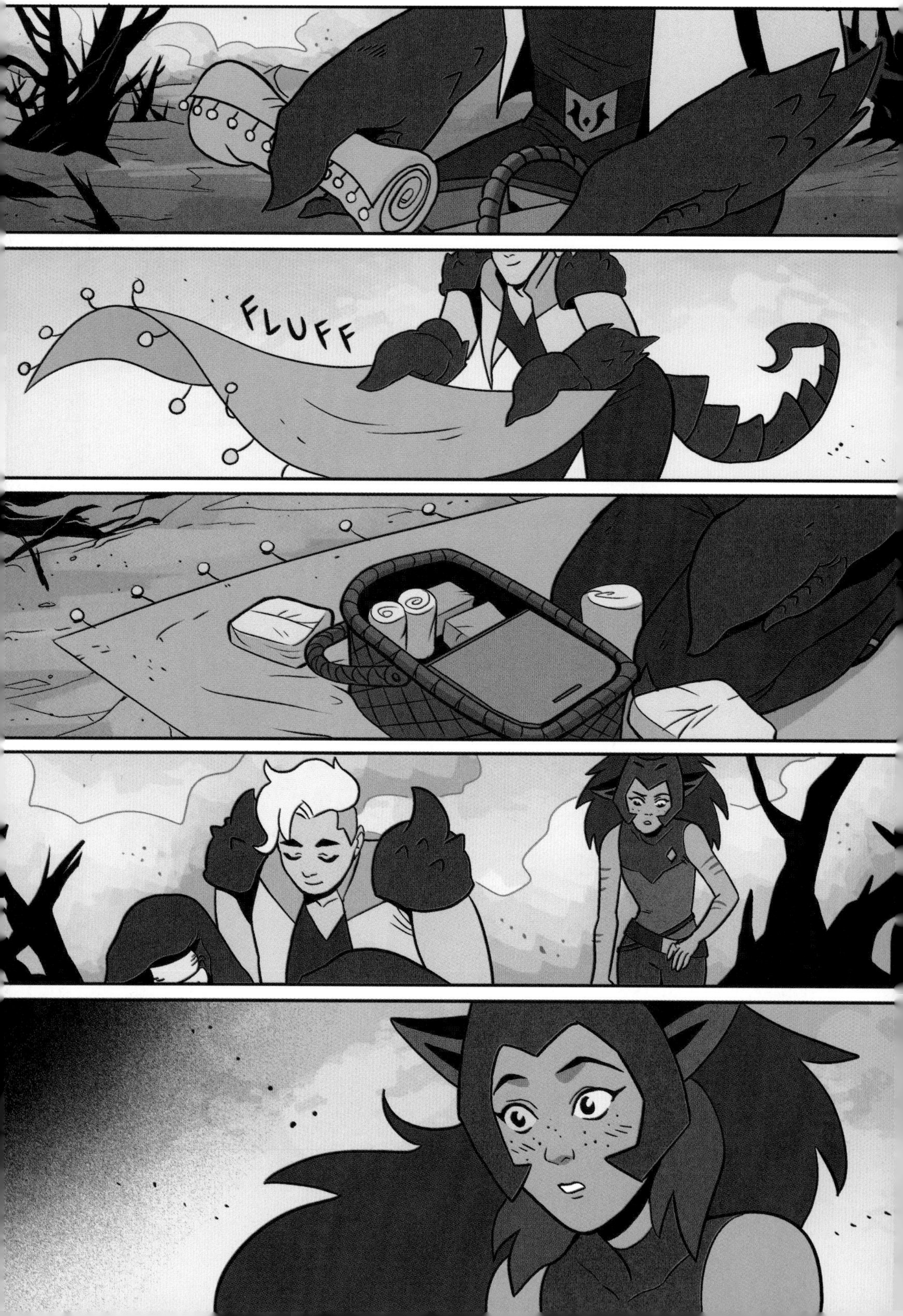
FLUFF

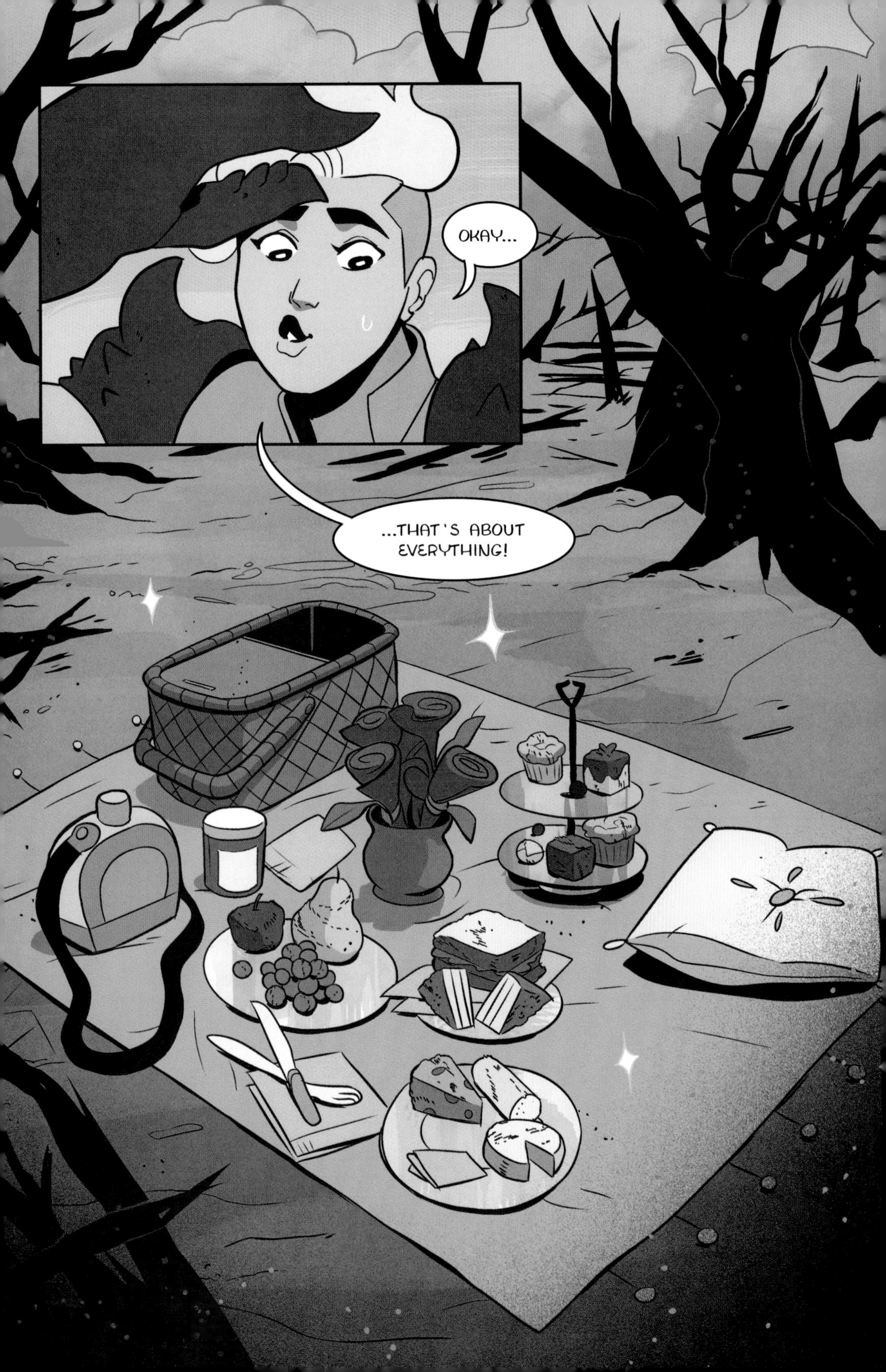
OKAY...
...THAT'S ABOUT EVERYTHING!

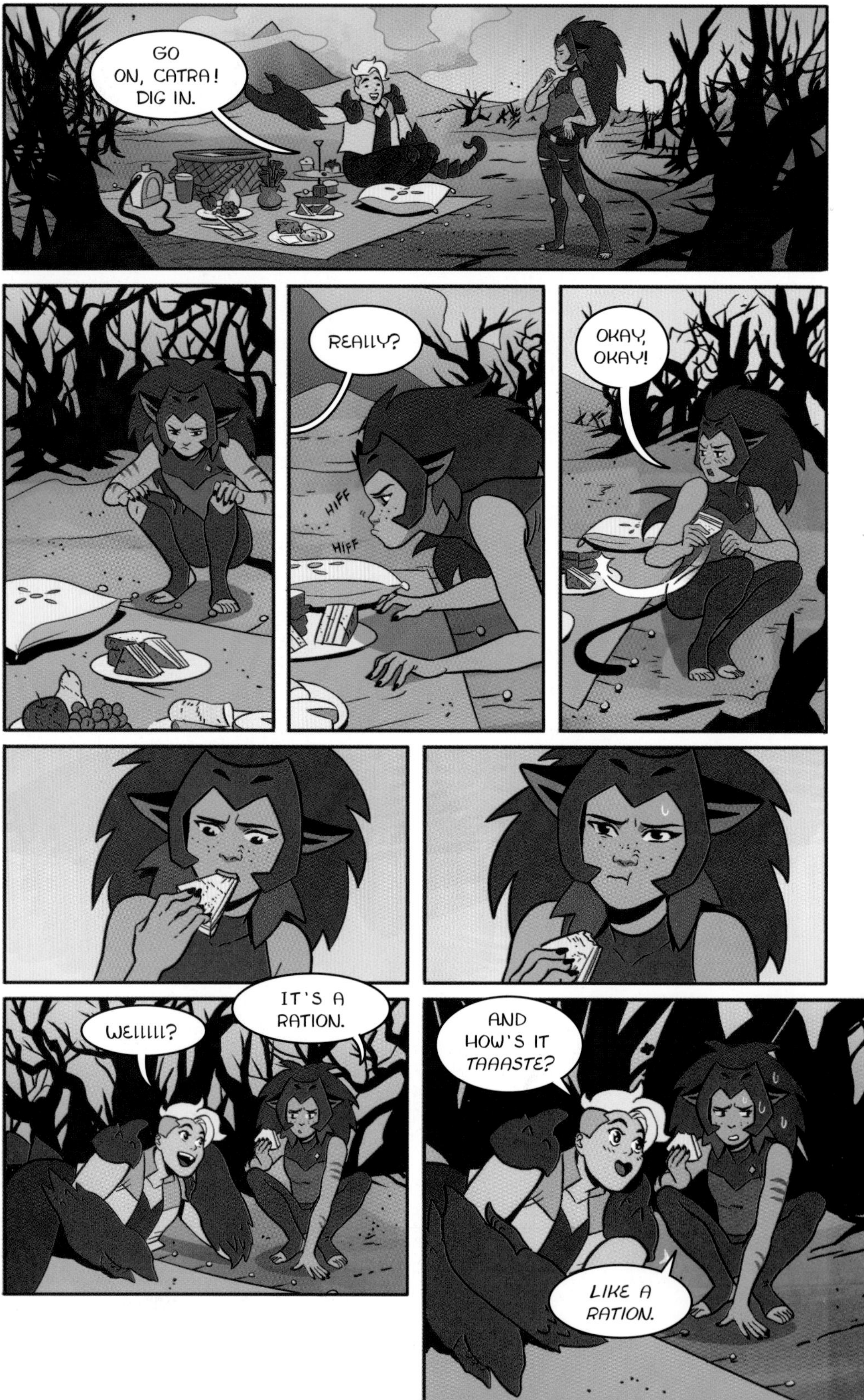
GO ON, CATRA! DIG IN.
REALLY?
HIFF
HIFF
OKAY, OKAY!
WELLLLL?
IT'S A RATION.
AND HOW'S IT TAAASTE?
LIKE A RATION.

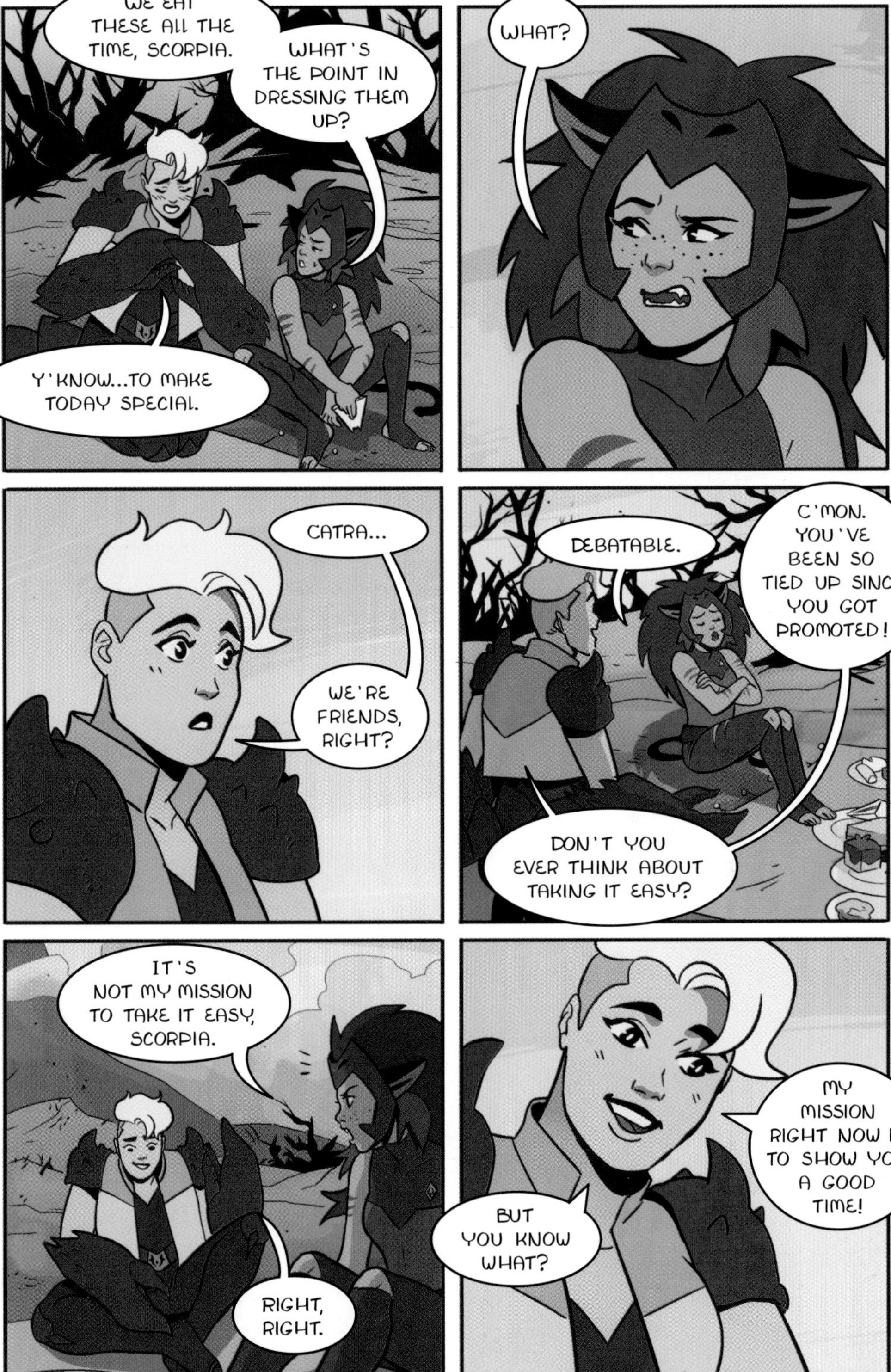
WE EAT THESE All THE TIME, SCORPIA.
WHAT'S THE POINT IN DRESSING THEM UP?
Y'KNOW...TO MAKE TODAY SPECIAL.
WHAT?
CATRA...
WE'RE FRIENDS, RIGHT?
DEBATABLE.
C'MON. YOU'VE BEEN SO TIED UP SINCE YOU GOT PROMOTED!
DON'T YOU EVER THINK ABOUT TAKING IT EASY?
IT'S NOT MY MISSION TO TAKE IT EASY, SCORPIA.
RIGHT, RIGHT.
BUT YOU KNOW WHAT?
MY MISSION RIGHT NOW IS TO SHOW YOU A GOOD TIME!

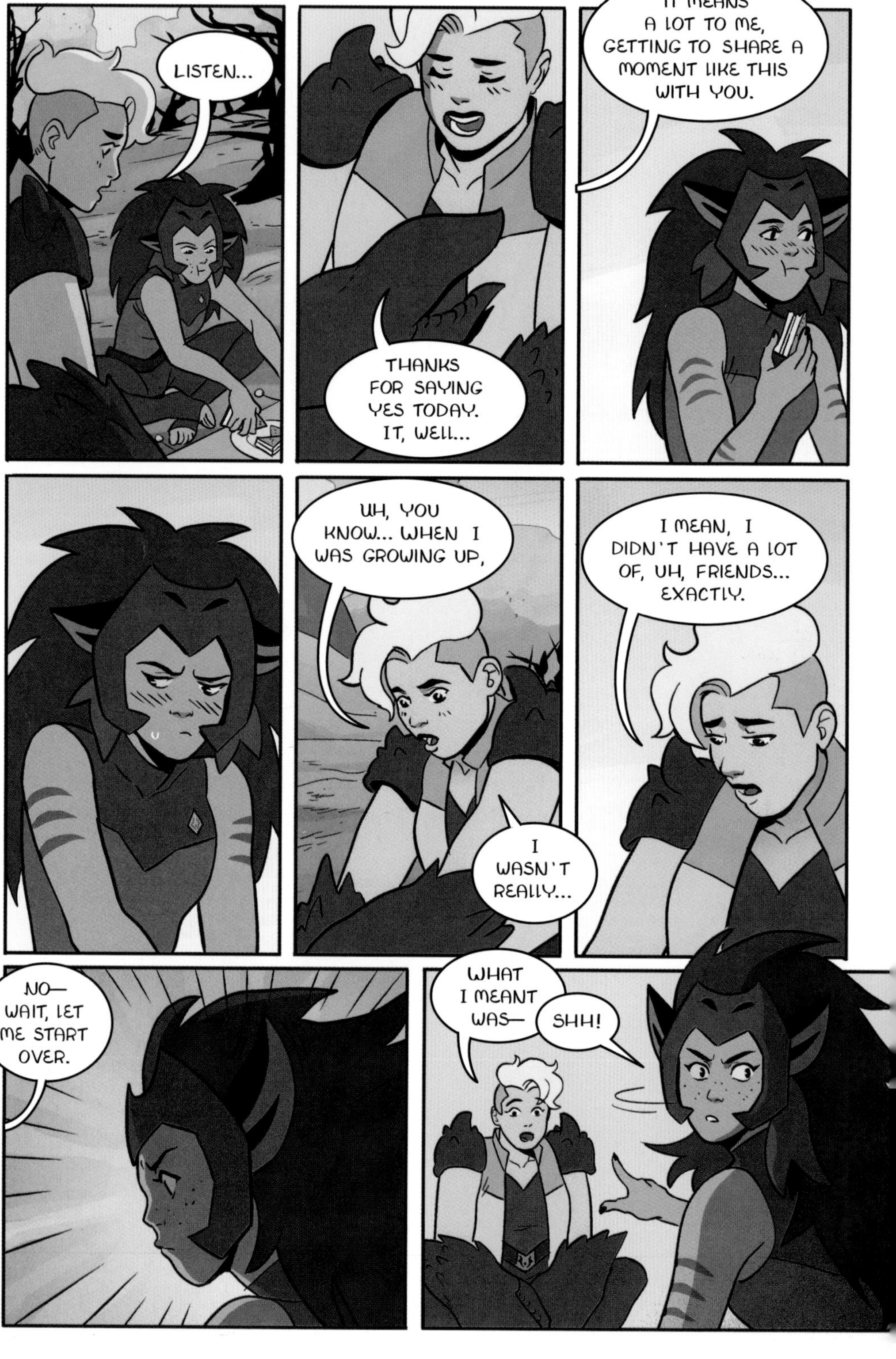
LISTEN...
THANKS FOR SAYING YES TODAY. IT, WELL...
IT MEANS A LOT TO ME, GETTING TO SHARE A MOMENT LIKE THIS WITH YOU.
UH, YOU KNOW... WHEN I WAS GROWING UP,
I WASN'T REALLY...
I MEAN, I DIDN'T HAVE A LOT OF, UH, FRIENDS... EXACTLY.
NO— WAIT, LET ME START OVER.
WHAT I MEANT WAS—
SHH!

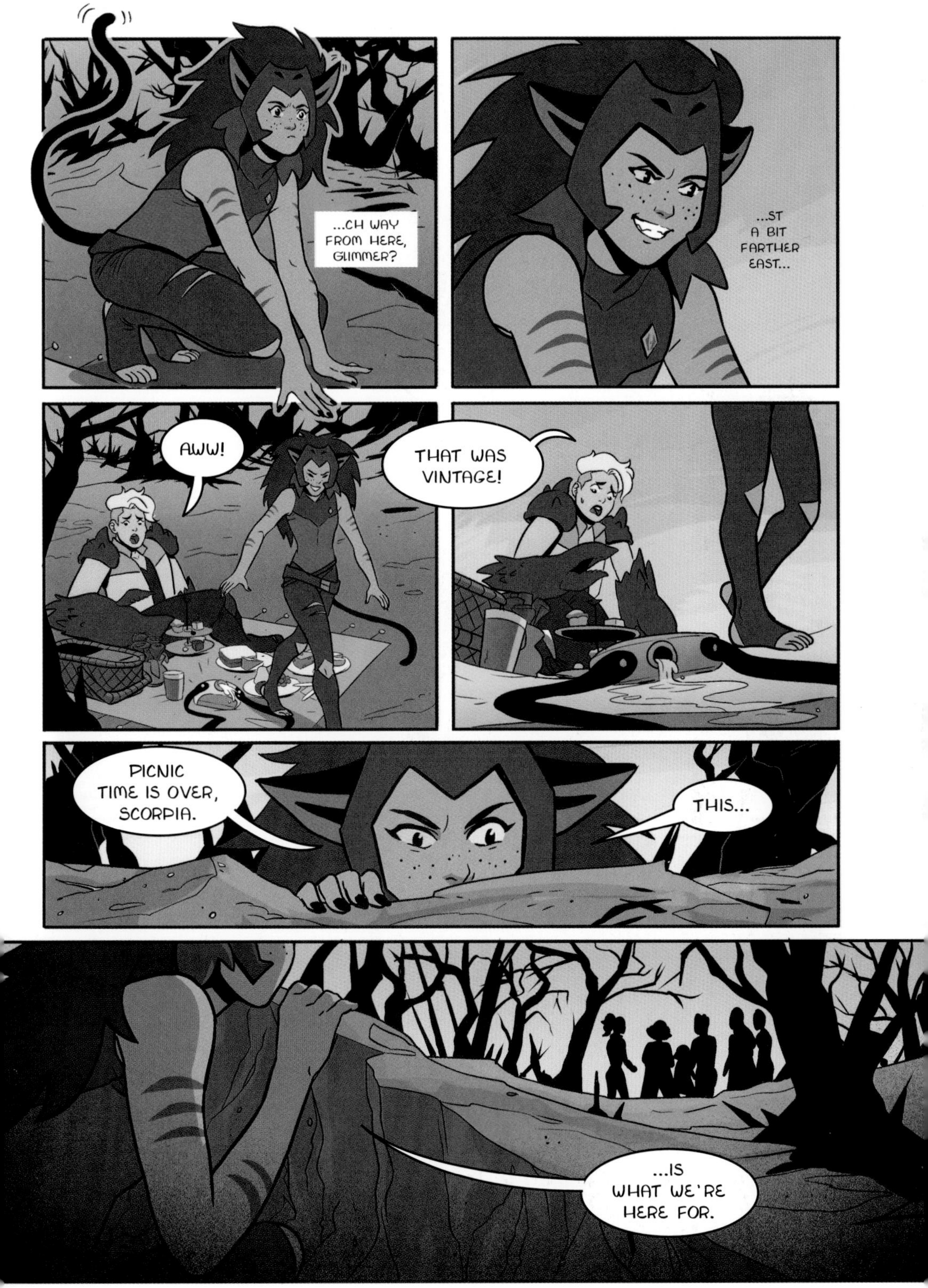
...CH WAY FROM HERE, GLIMMER?
...ST A BIT FARTHER EAST...
AWW!
THAT WAS VINTAGE!
PICNIC TIME IS OVER, SCORPIA.
THIS...
...IS WHAT WE'RE HERE FOR.

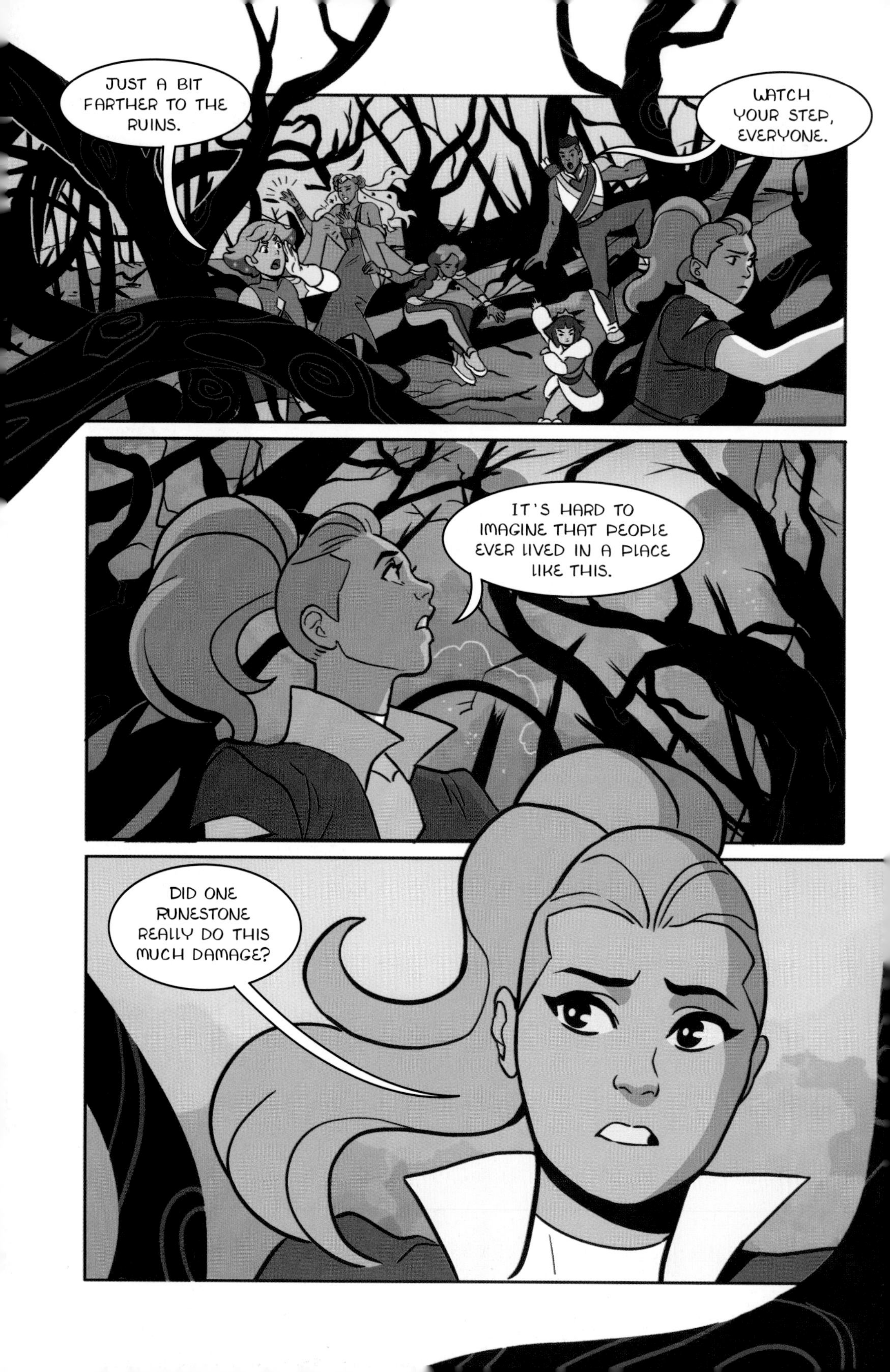
JUST A BIT FARTHER TO THE RUINS.
WATCH YOUR STEP, EVERYONE.
IT'S HARD TO IMAGINE THAT PEOPLE EVER LIVED IN A PLACE LIKE THIS.
DID ONE RUNESTONE REALLY DO THIS MUCH DAMAGE?

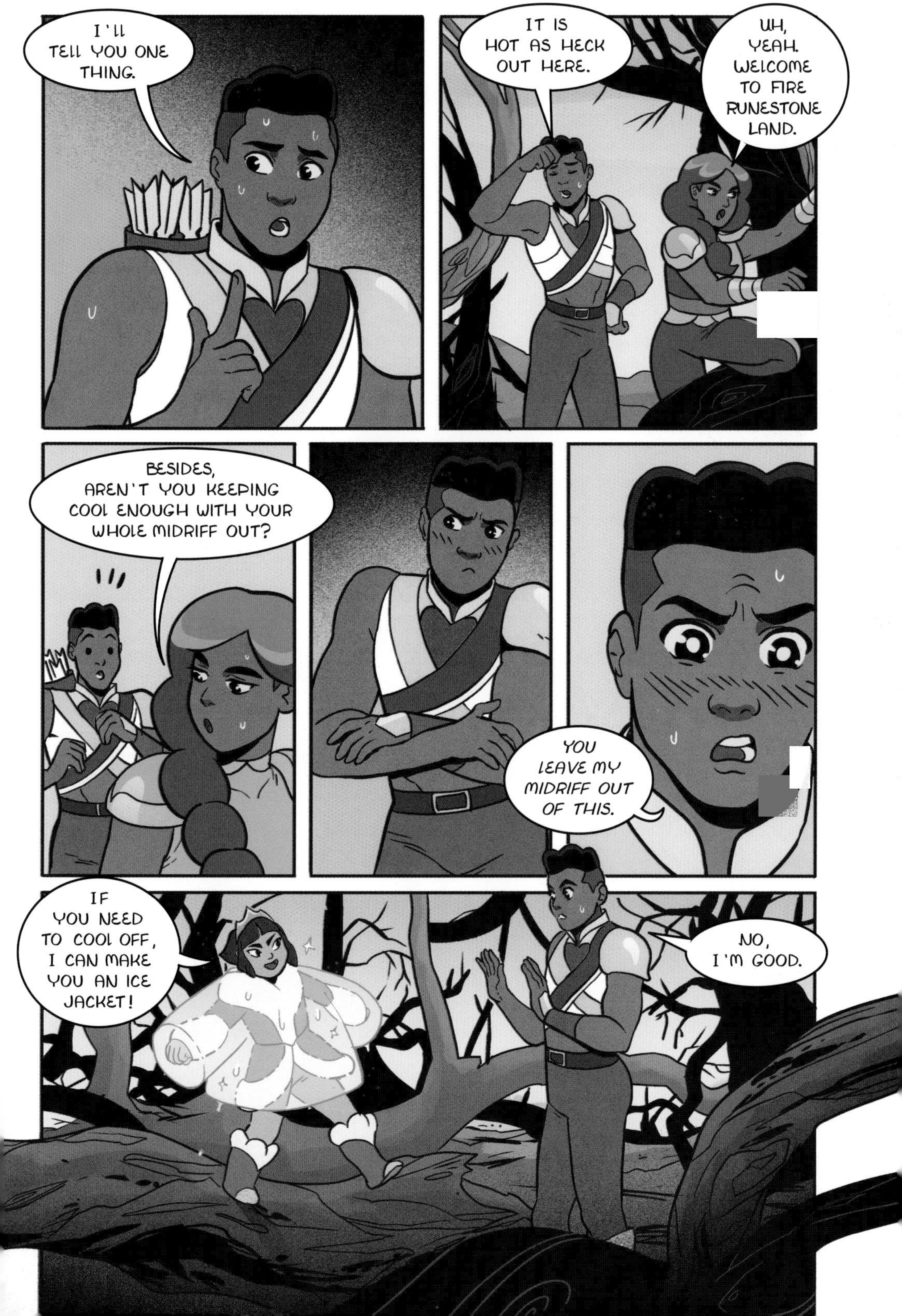
I'LL TELL YOU ONE THING.
IT IS HOT AS HECK OUT HERE.
UH, YEAH. WELCOME TO FIRE RUNESTONE LAND.
BESIDES, AREN'T YOU KEEPING COOL ENOUGH WITH YOUR WHOLE MIDRIFF OUT?
YOU LEAVE MY MIDRIFF OUT OF THIS.
IF YOU NEED TO COOL OFF, I CAN MAKE YOU AN ICE JACKET!
NO, I'M GOOD.

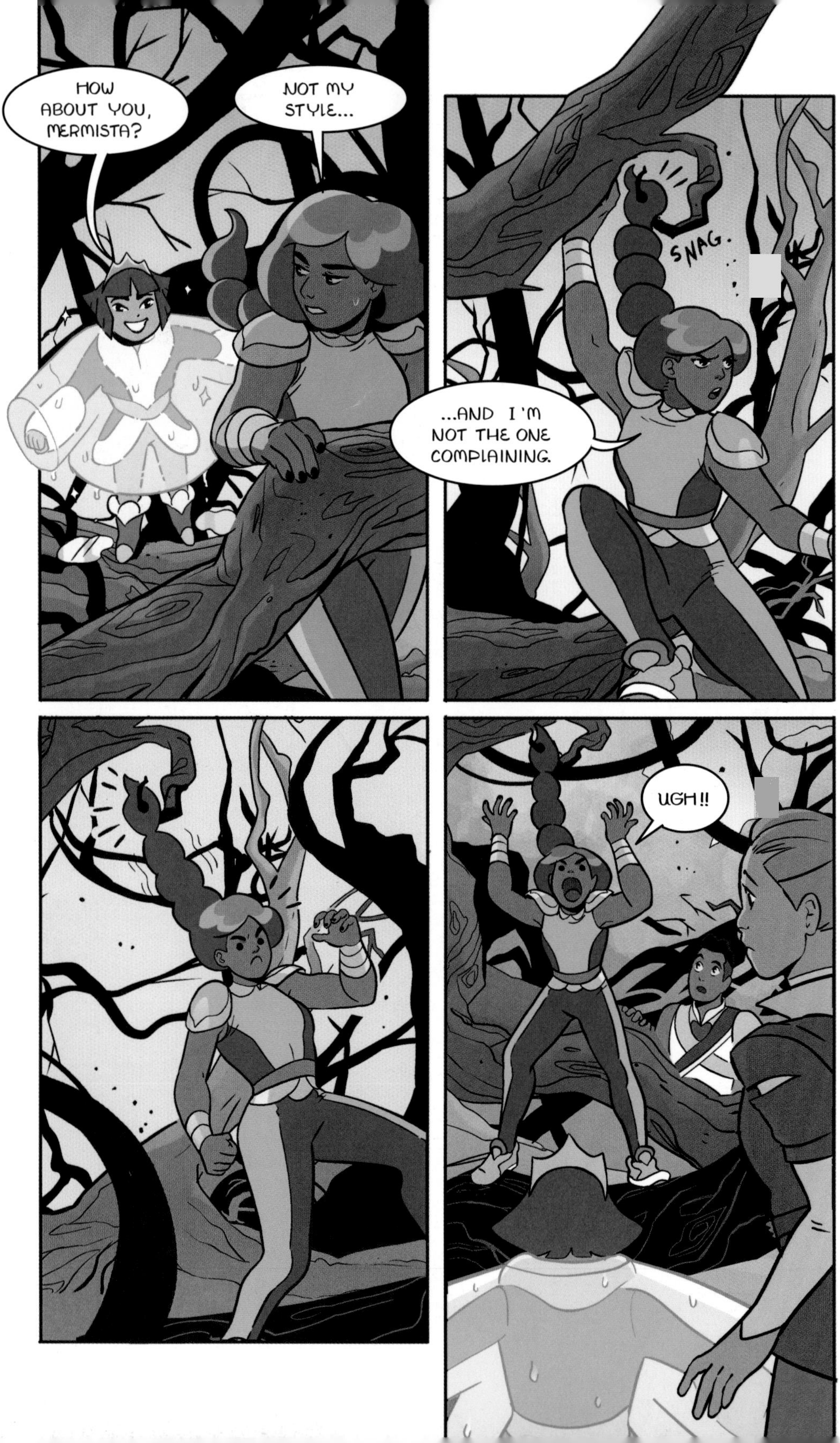
HOW ABOUT YOU, MERMISTA?
NOT MY STYLE...
SNAG.
...AND I'M NOT THE ONE COMPLAINING.
UGH!!

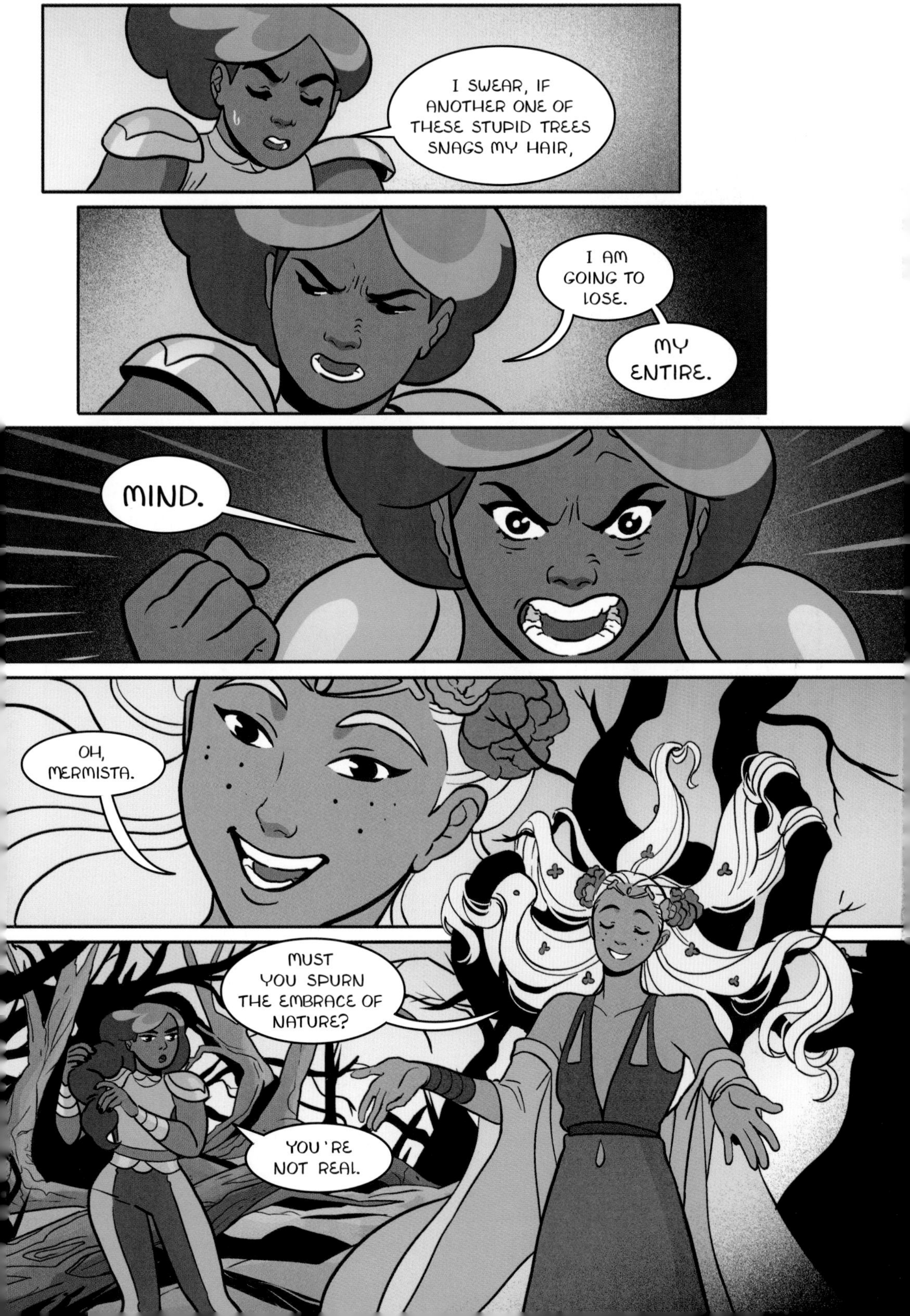
I SWEAR, IF ANOTHER ONE OF THESE STUPID TREES SNAGS MY HAIR,
I AM GOING TO LOSE.
MY ENTIRE.
MIND.
OH, MERMISTA.
MUST YOU SPURN THE EMBRACE OF NATURE?
YOU'RE NOT REAL.

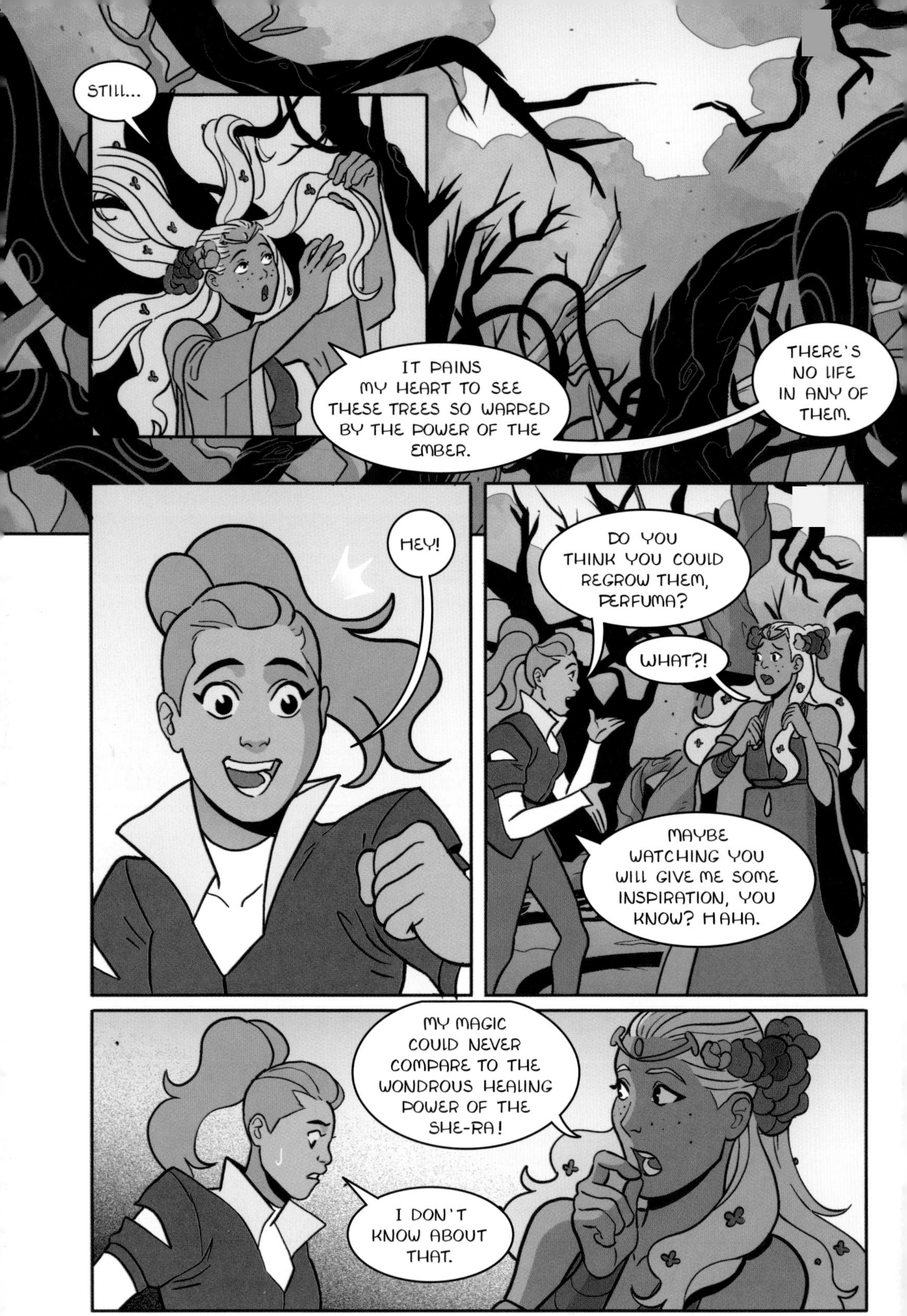
STILL...
IT PAINS MY HEART TO SEE THESE TREES SO WARPED BY THE POWER OF THE EMBER.
THERE'S NO LIFE IN ANY OF THEM.
HEY!
DO YOU THINK YOU COULD REGROW THEM, PERFUMA?
WHAT?!
MAYBE WATCHING YOU WILL GIVE ME SOME INSPIRATION, YOU KNOW? HAHA.
MY MAGIC COULD NEVER COMPARE TO THE WONDROUS HEALING POWER OF THE SHE-RA!
I DON'T KNOW ABOUT THAT.

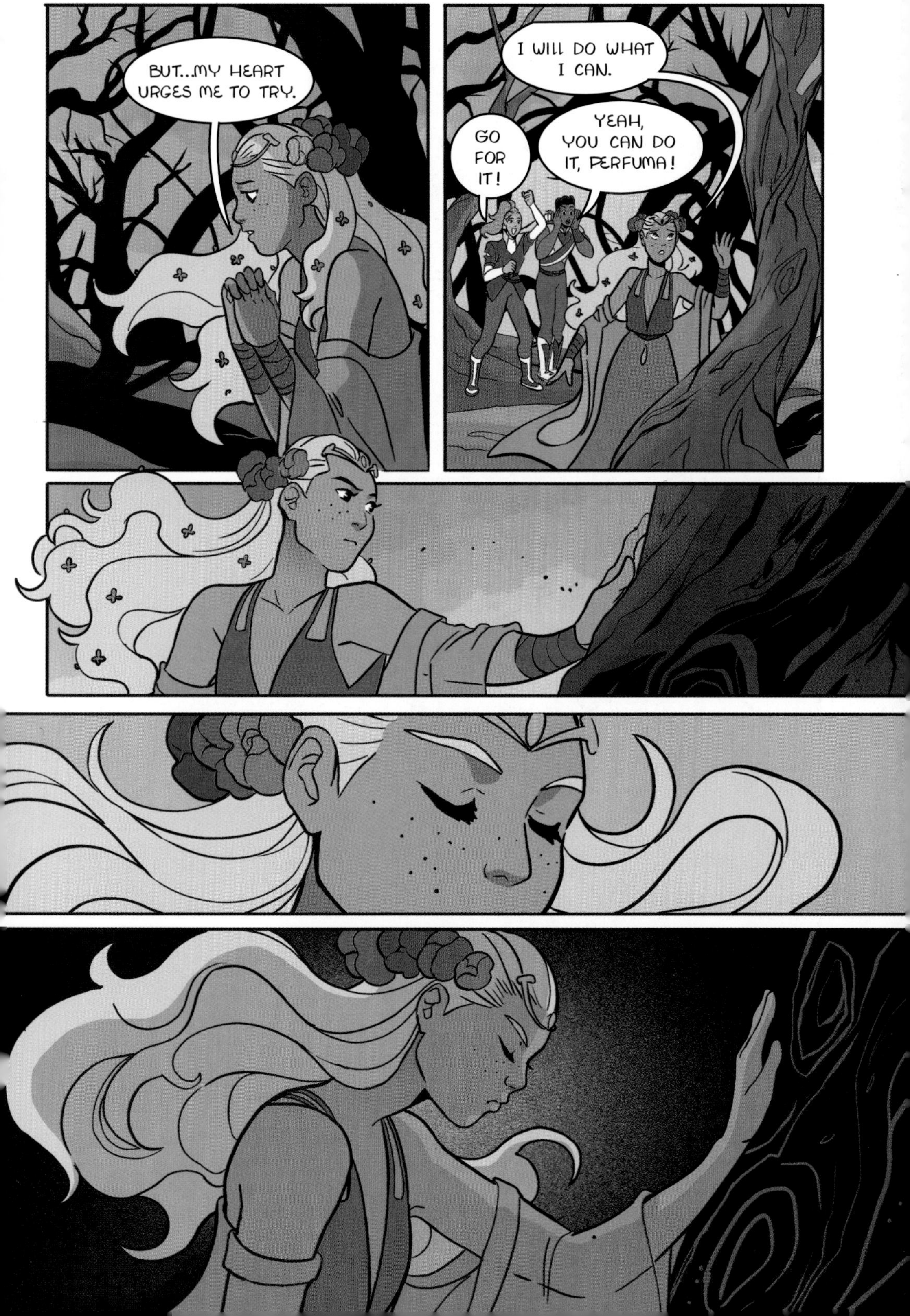
BUT...MY HEART URGES ME TO TRY.
I WILL DO WHAT I CAN.
GO FOR IT!
YEAH, YOU CAN DO IT, PERFUMA!

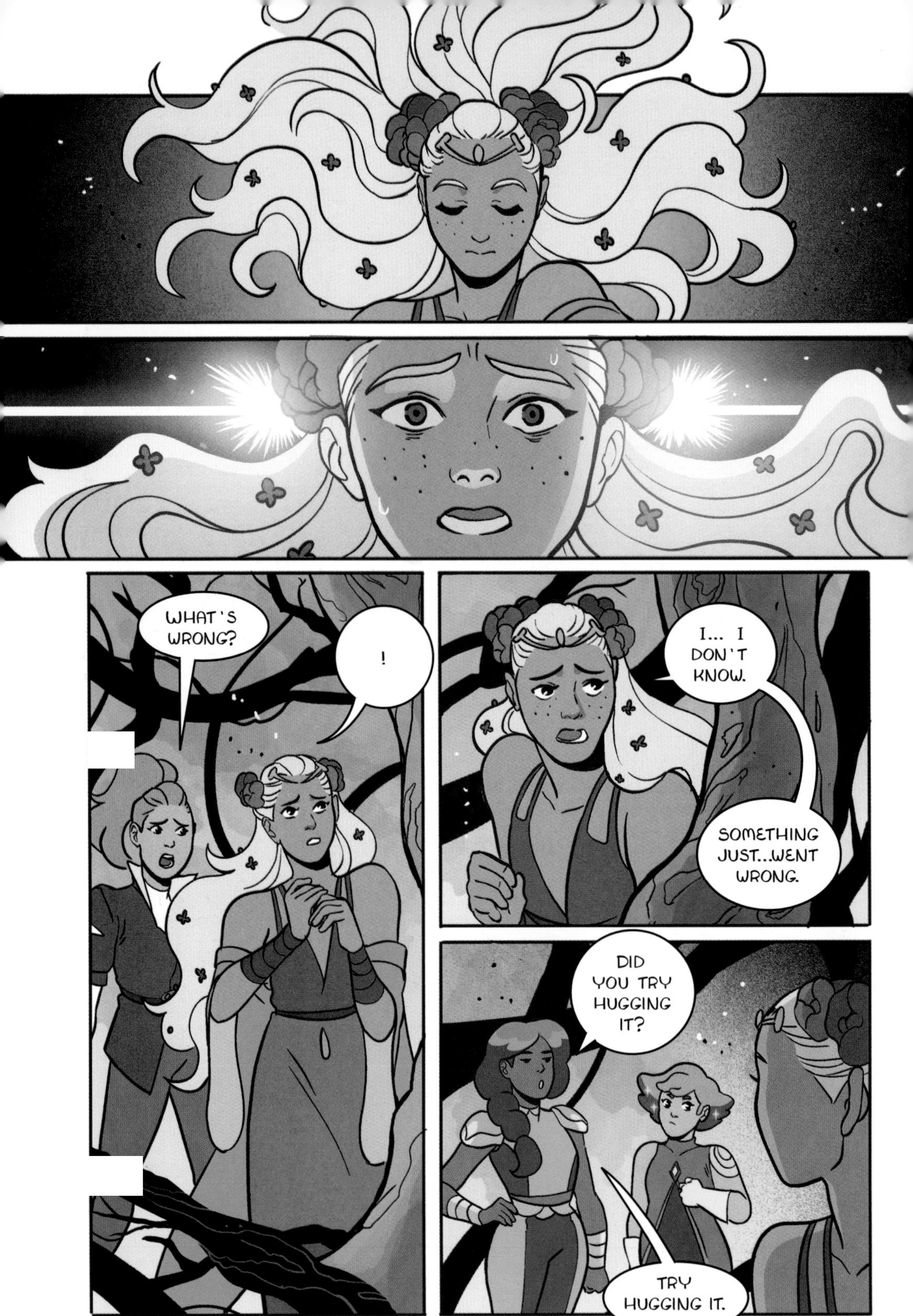
WHAT'S WRONG?
!
I... I DON'T KNOW.
SOMETHING JUST...WENT WRONG.
DID YOU TRY HUGGING IT?
TRY HUGGING IT.

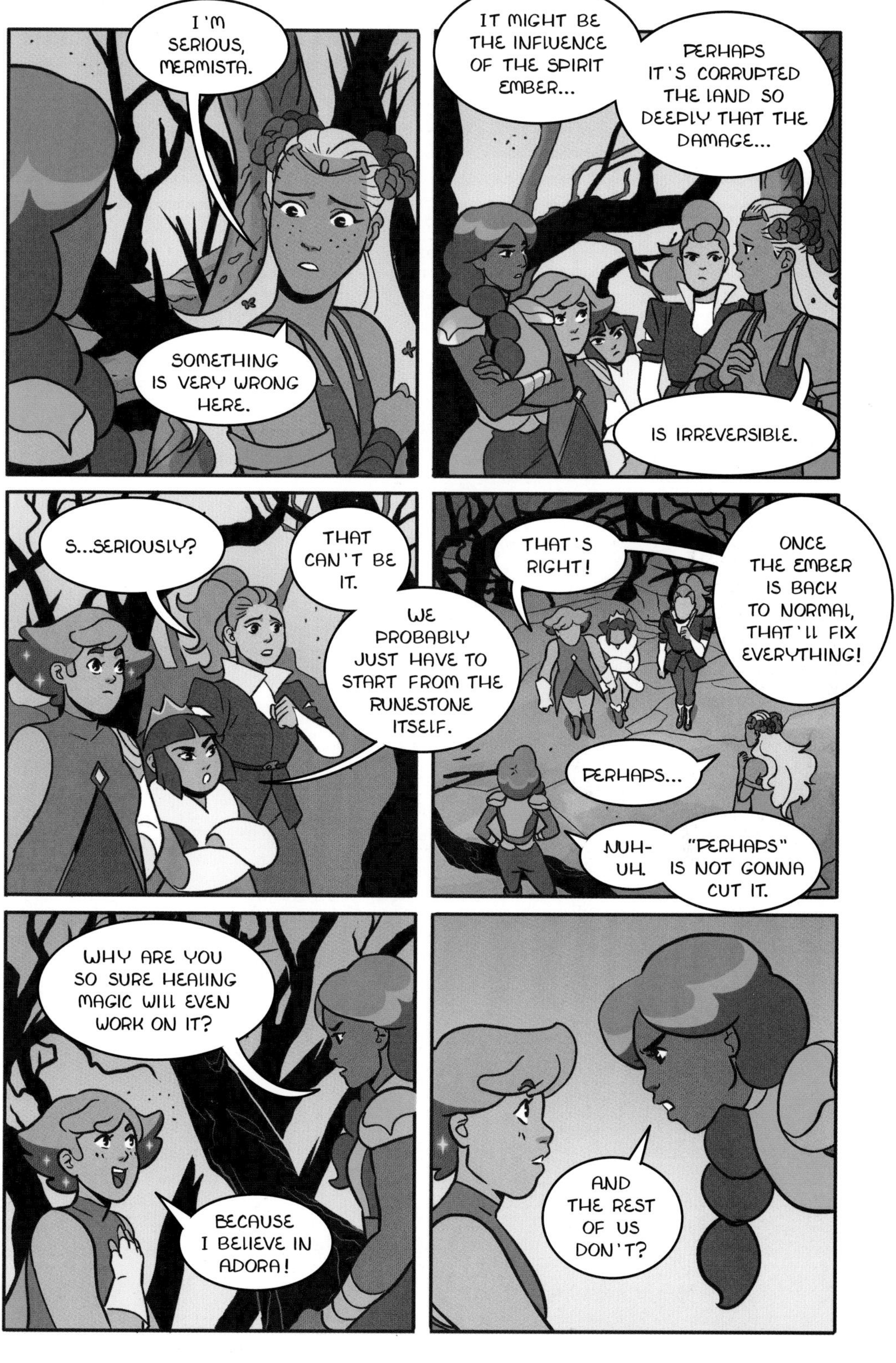
I'M SERIOUS, MERMISTA.
SOMETHING IS VERY WRONG HERE.
IT MIGHT BE THE INFLUENCE OF THE SPIRIT EMBER...
PERHAPS IT'S CORRUPTED THE LAND SO DEEPLY THAT THE DAMAGE...
IS IRREVERSIBLE.
S...SERIOUSLY?
THAT CAN'T BE IT.
WE PROBABLY JUST HAVE TO START FROM THE RUNESTONE ITSELF.
THAT'S RIGHT!
ONCE THE EMBER IS BACK TO NORMAL, THAT'LL FIX EVERYTHING!
PERHAPS...
NUH-UH.
"PERHAPS" IS NOT GONNA CUT IT.
WHY ARE YOU SO SURE HEALING MAGIC WILL EVEN WORK ON IT?
BECAUSE I BELIEVE IN ADORA!
AND THE REST OF US DON'T?

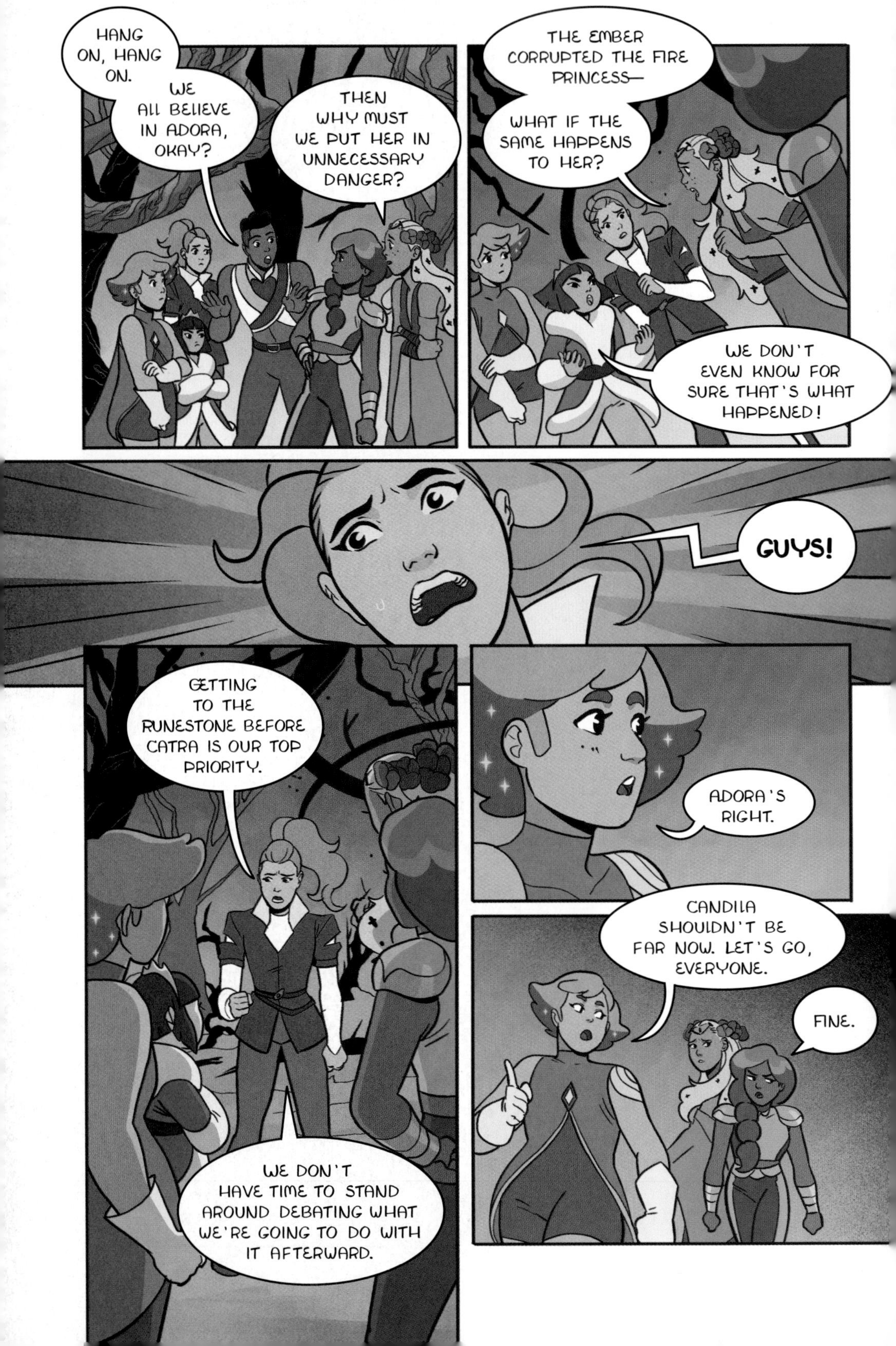

HANG ON, HANG ON.
WE ALL BELIEVE IN ADORA, OKAY?
THEN WHY MUST WE PUT HER IN UNNECESSARY DANGER?
THE EMBER CORRUPTED THE FIRE PRINCESS—
WHAT IF THE SAME HAPPENS TO HER?
WE DON'T EVEN KNOW FOR SURE THAT'S WHAT HAPPENED!
GUYS!
GETTING TO THE RUNESTONE BEFORE CATRA IS OUR TOP PRIORITY.
WE DON'T HAVE TIME TO STAND AROUND DEBATING WHAT WE'RE GOING TO DO WITH IT AFTERWARD.
ADORA'S RIGHT.
CANDILA SHOULDN'T BE FAR NOW. LET'S GO, EVERYONE.
FINE.

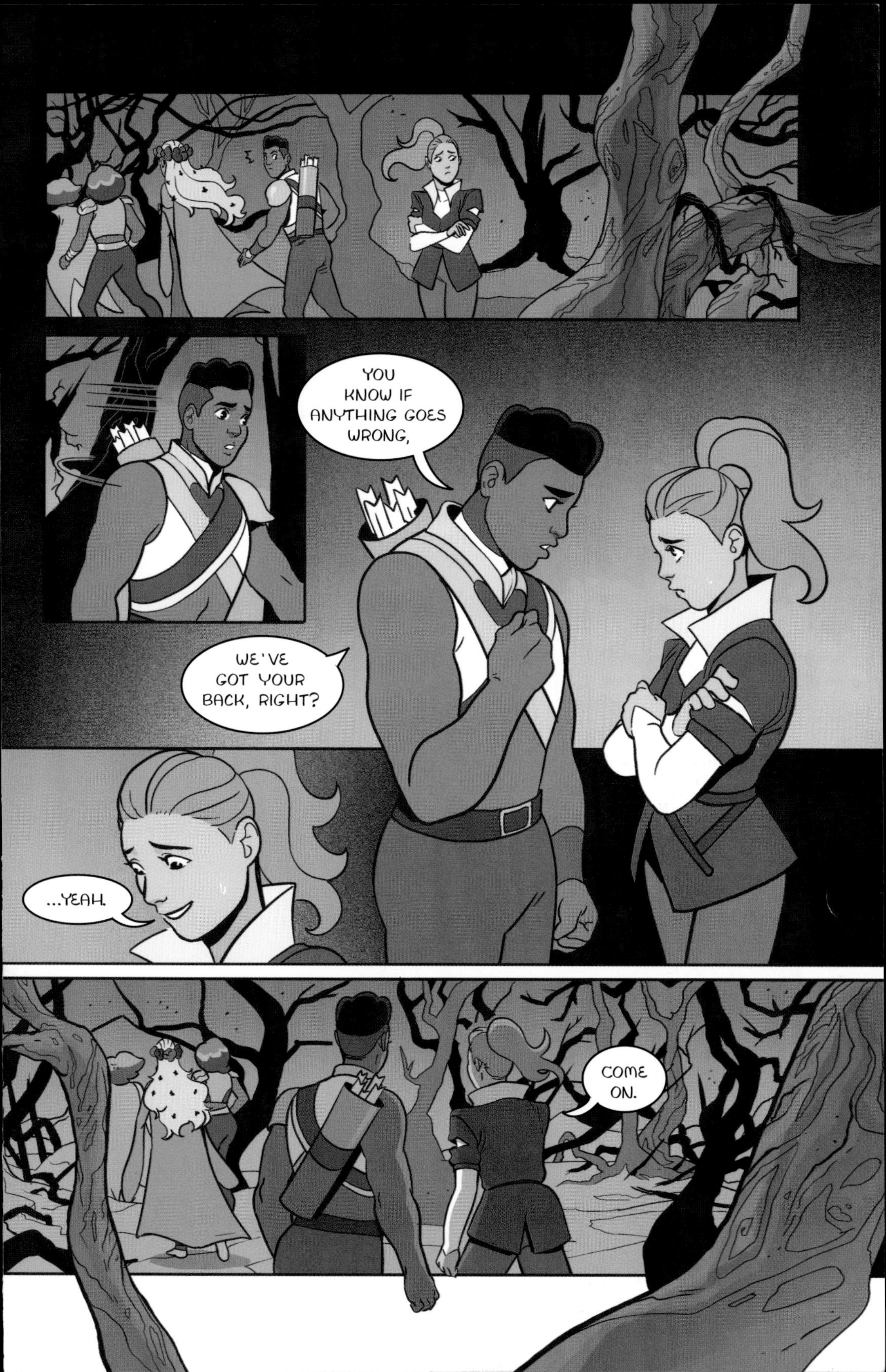
YOU KNOW IF ANYTHING GOES WRONG,
WE'VE GOT YOUR BACK, RIGHT?
...YEAH.
COME ON.

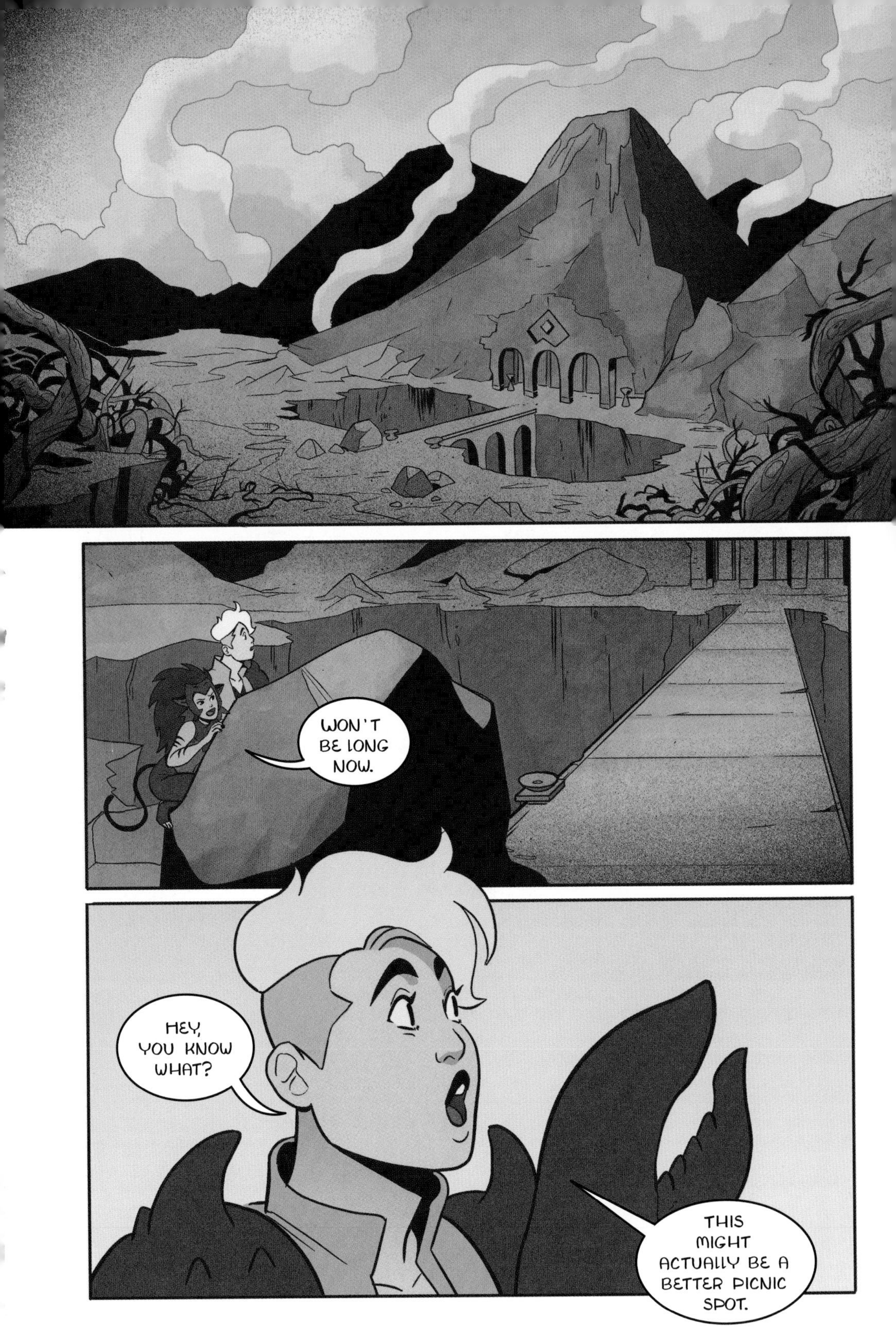
WON'T BE LONG NOW.
HEY, YOU KNOW WHAT?
THIS MIGHT ACTUALLY BE A BETTER PICNIC SPOT.

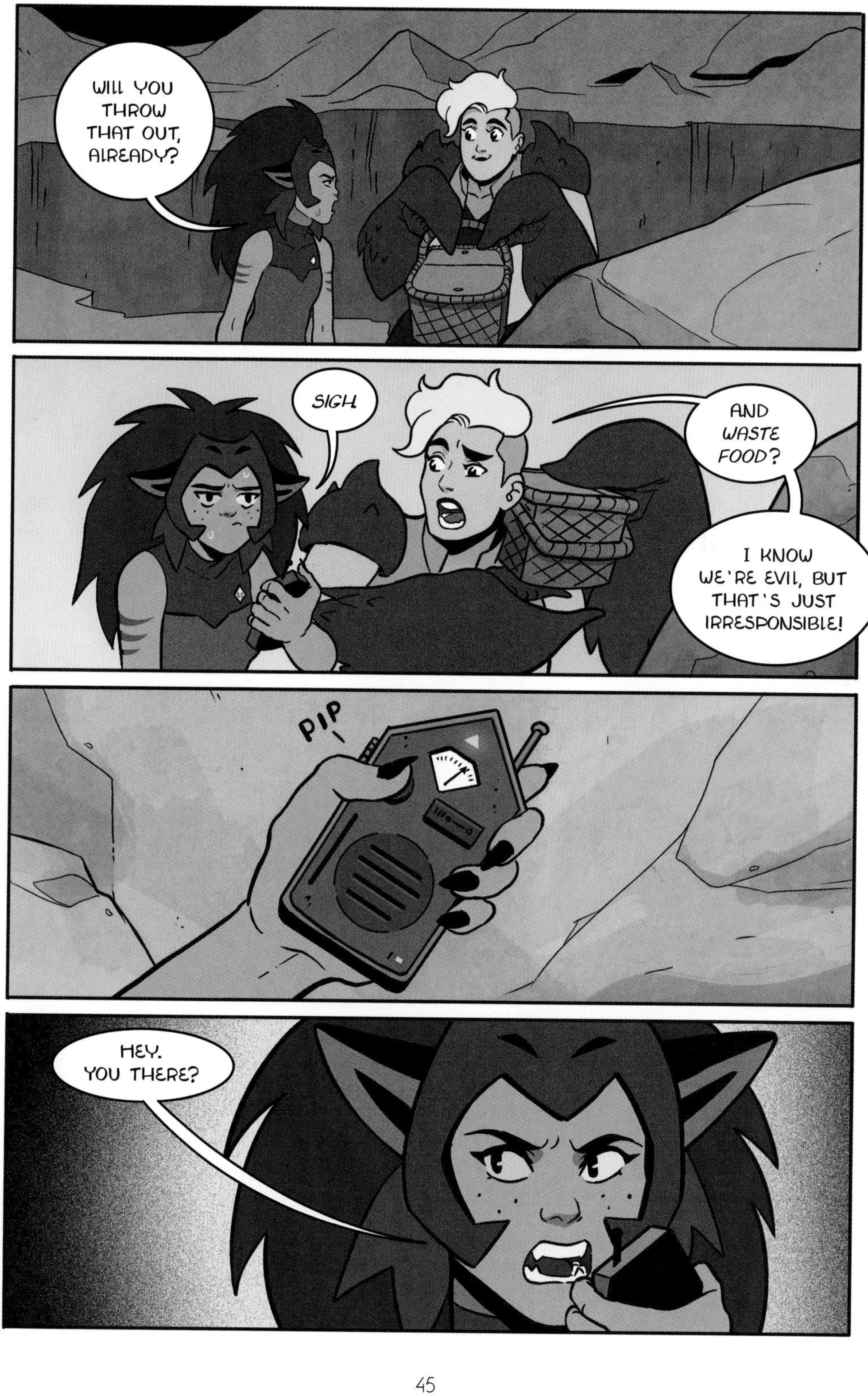
WILL YOU THROW THAT OUT, ALREADY?
SIGH
AND WASTE FOOD?
I KNOW WE'RE EVIL, BUT THAT'S JUST IRRESPONSIBLE!
PIP
HEY. YOU THERE?

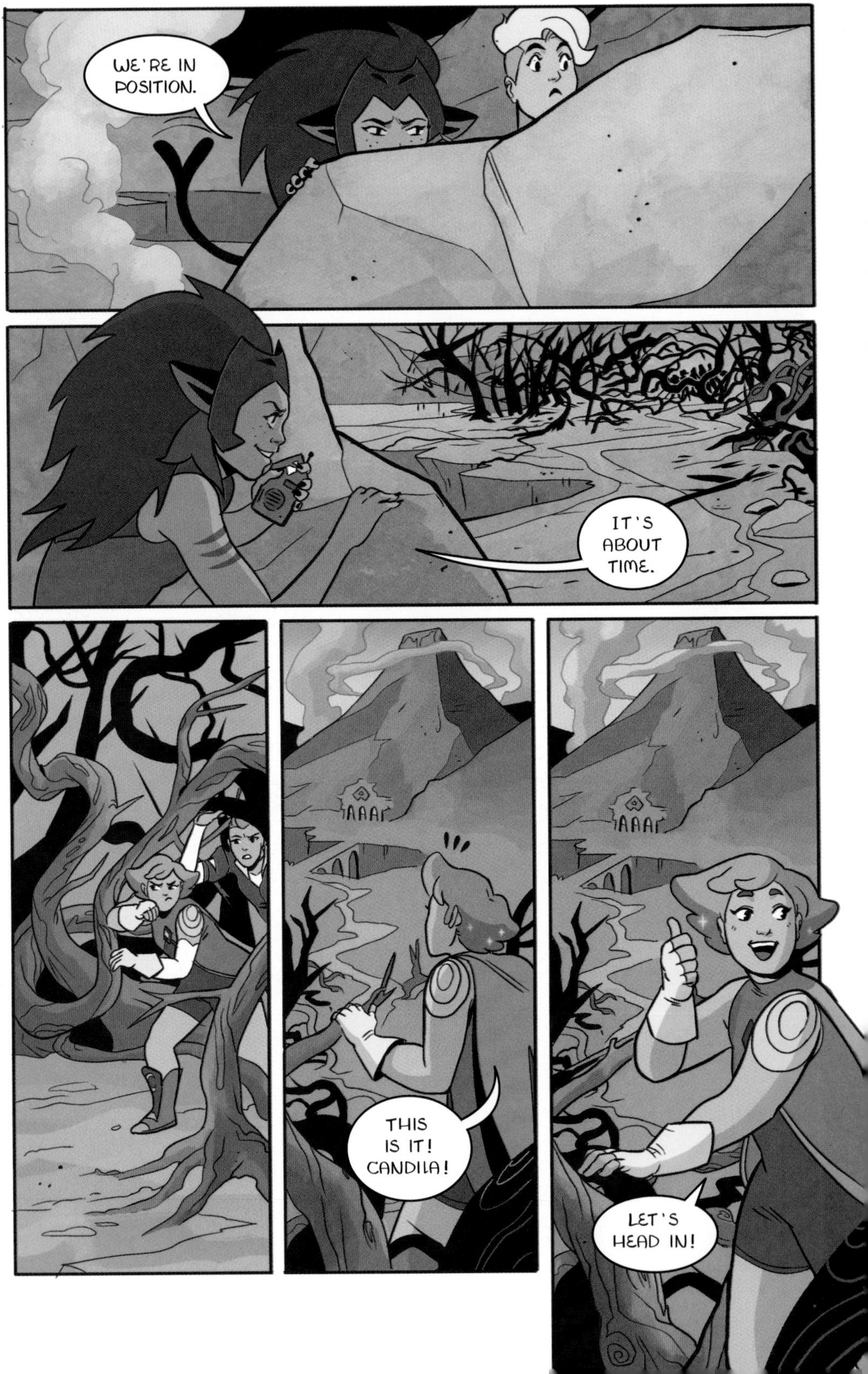
WE'RE IN POSITION.
IT'S ABOUT TIME.
THIS IS IT! CANDILA!
LET'S HEAD IN!

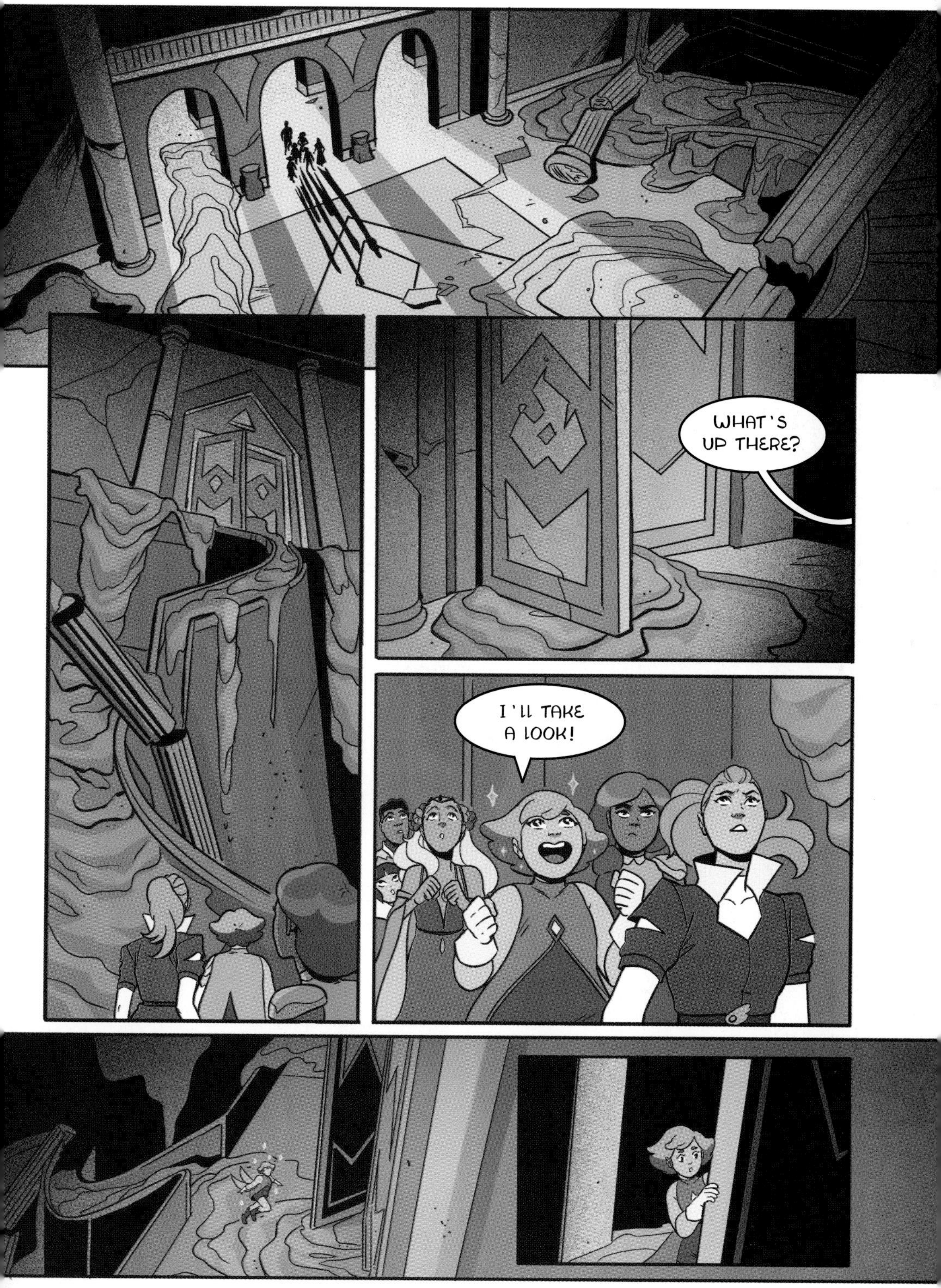
WHAT'S UP THERE?
I'LL TAKE A LOOK!

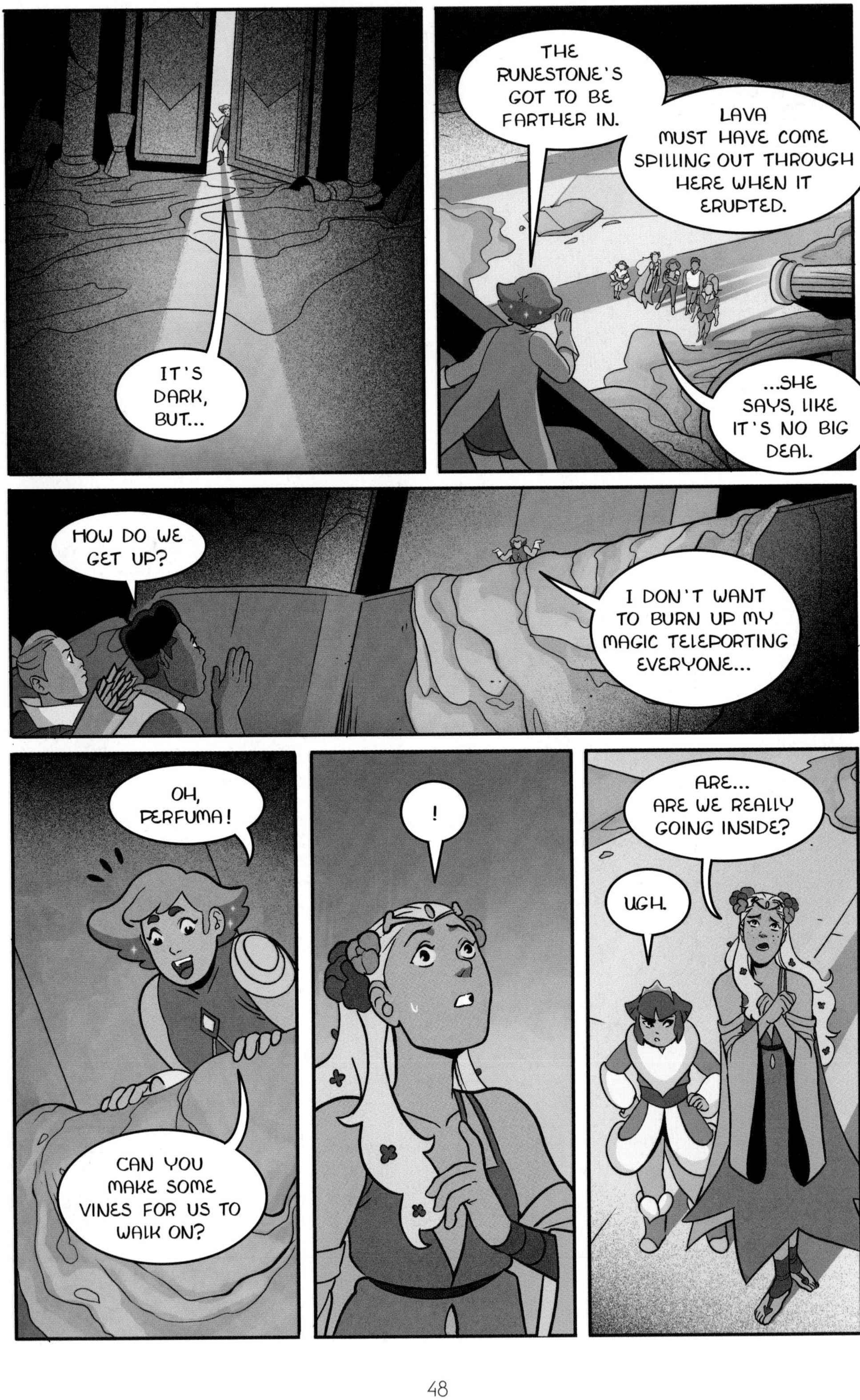
IT'S DARK, BUT...
THE RUNESTONE'S GOT TO BE FARTHER IN.
LAVA MUST HAVE COME SPILLING OUT THROUGH HERE WHEN IT ERUPTED.
...SHE SAYS, LIKE IT'S NO BIG DEAL.
HOW DO WE GET UP?
I DON'T WANT TO BURN UP MY MAGIC TELEPORTING EVERYONE...
OH, PERFUMA!
CAN YOU MAKE SOME VINES FOR US TO WALK ON?
!
ARE... ARE WE REALLY GOING INSIDE?
UGH.

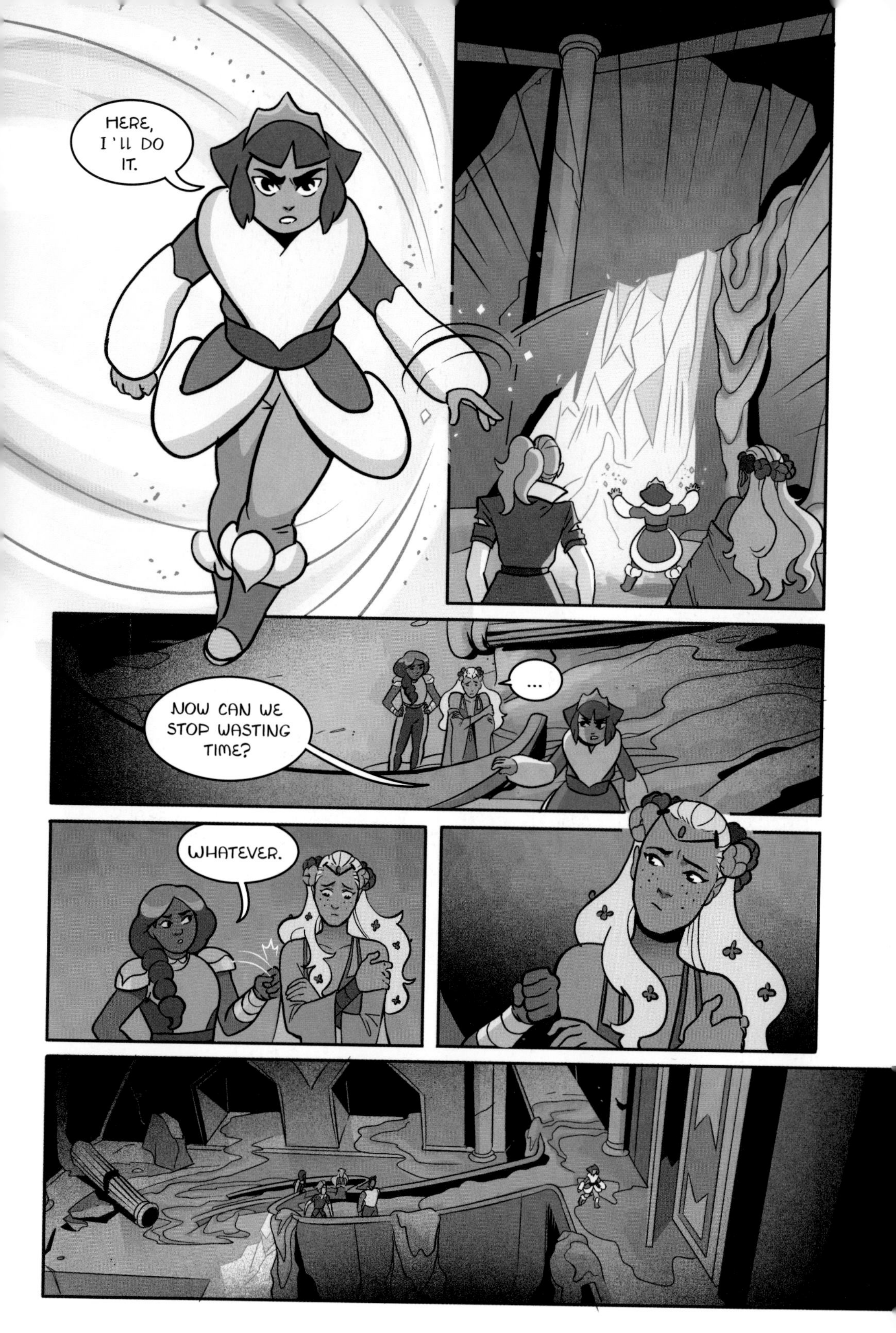
HERE, I'LL DO IT.
NOW CAN WE STOP WASTING TIME?
...
WHATEVER.

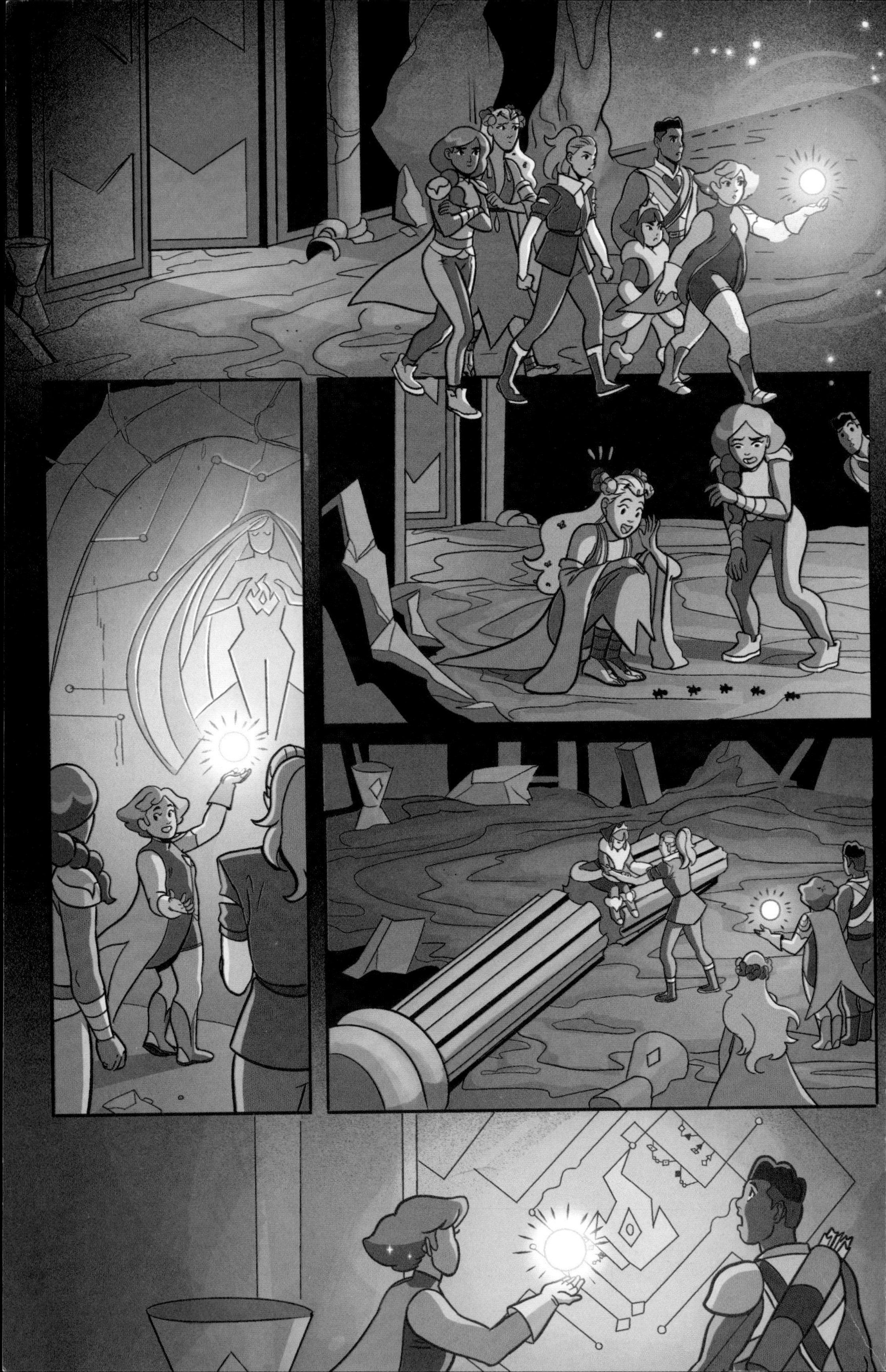

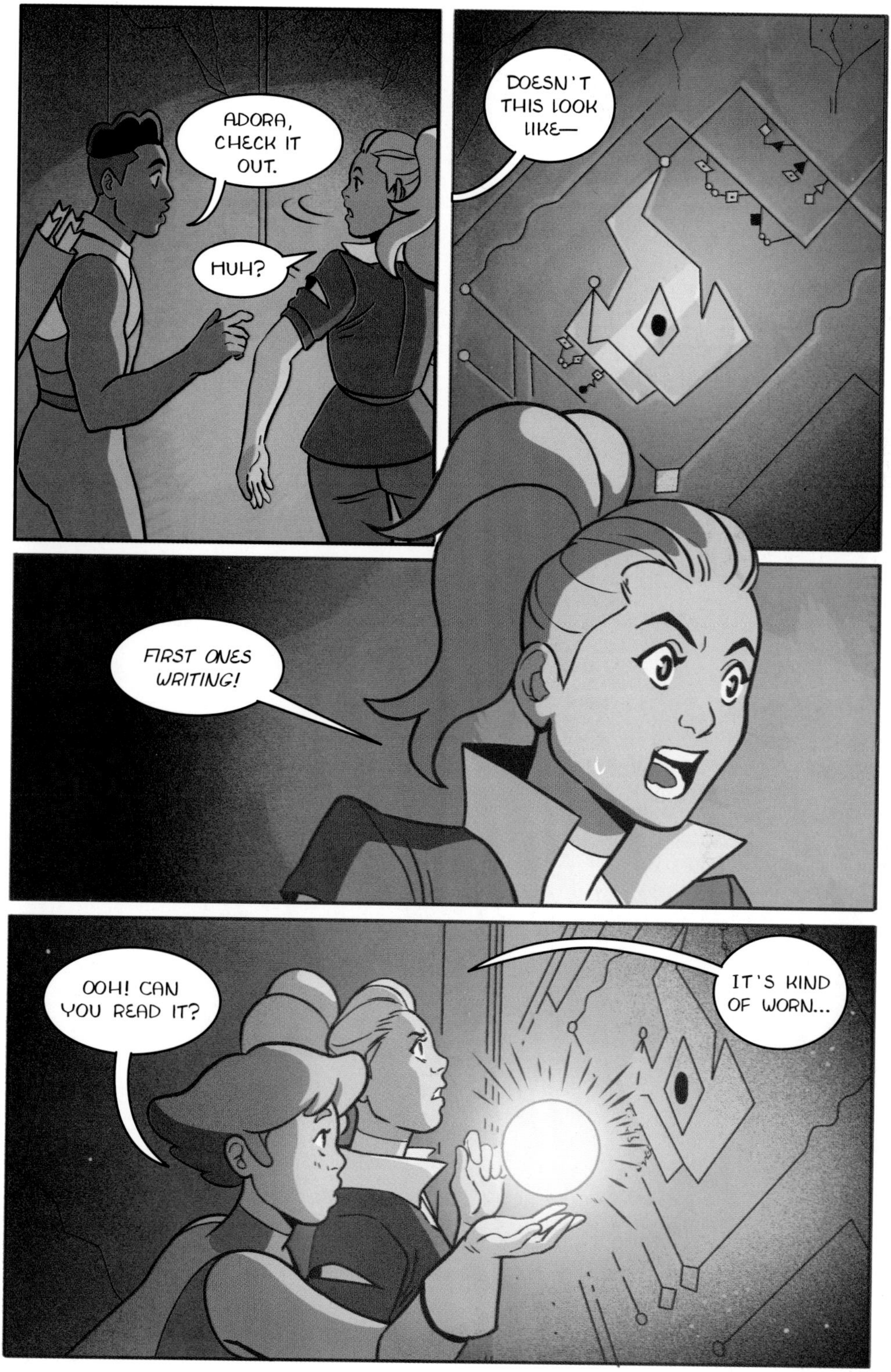
ADORA, CHECK IT OUT.
HUH?
DOESN'T THIS LOOK LIKE—
FIRST ONES WRITING!
OOH! CAN YOU READ IT?
IT'S KIND OF WORN...

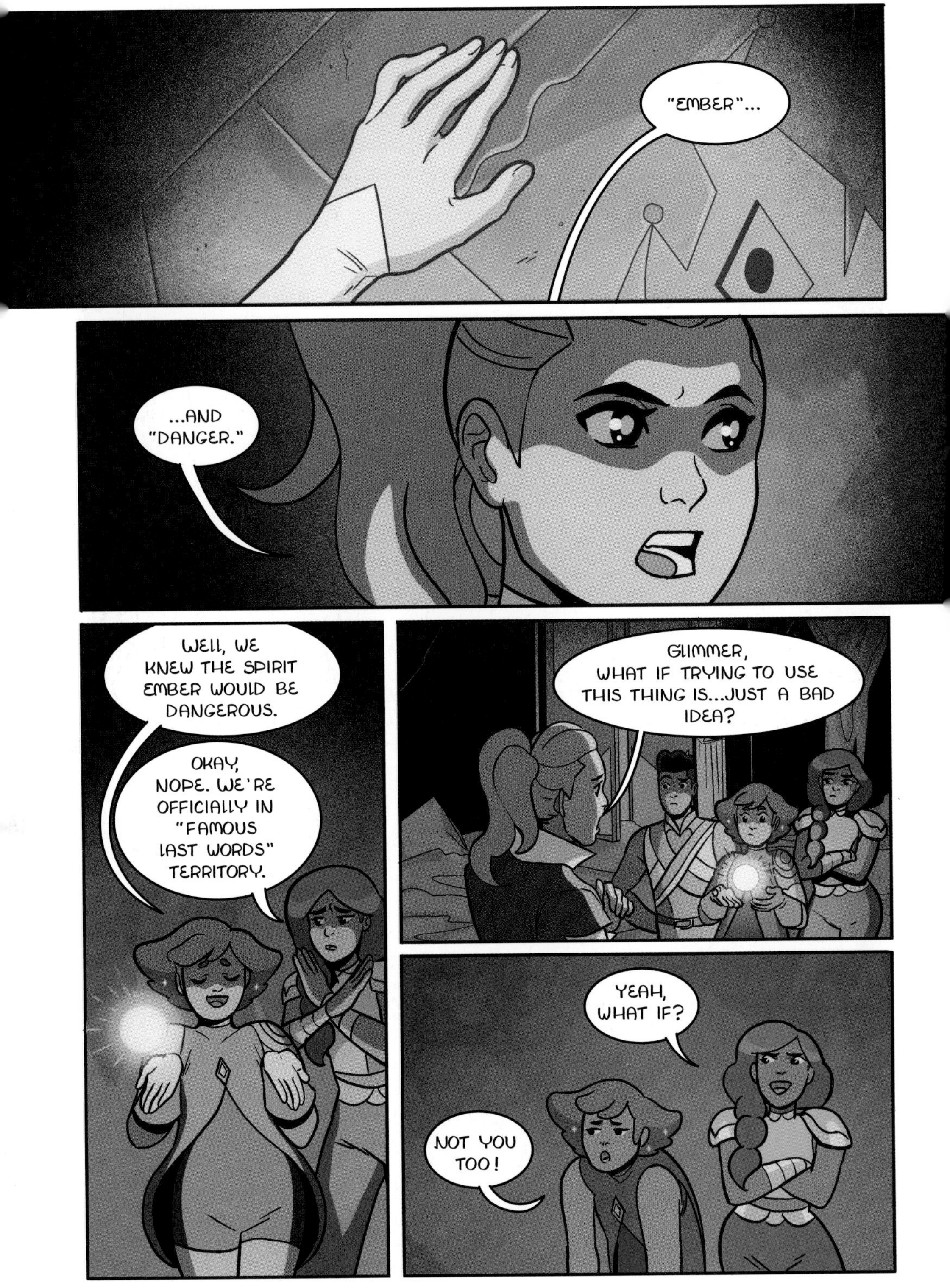
"EMBER"...
...AND "DANGER."
WELL, WE KNEW THE SPIRIT EMBER WOULD BE DANGEROUS.
OKAY, NOPE. WE'RE OFFICIALLY IN "FAMOUS LAST WORDS" TERRITORY.
GLIMMER, WHAT IF TRYING TO USE THIS THING IS...JUST A BAD IDEA?
YEAH, WHAT IF?
NOT YOU TOO!

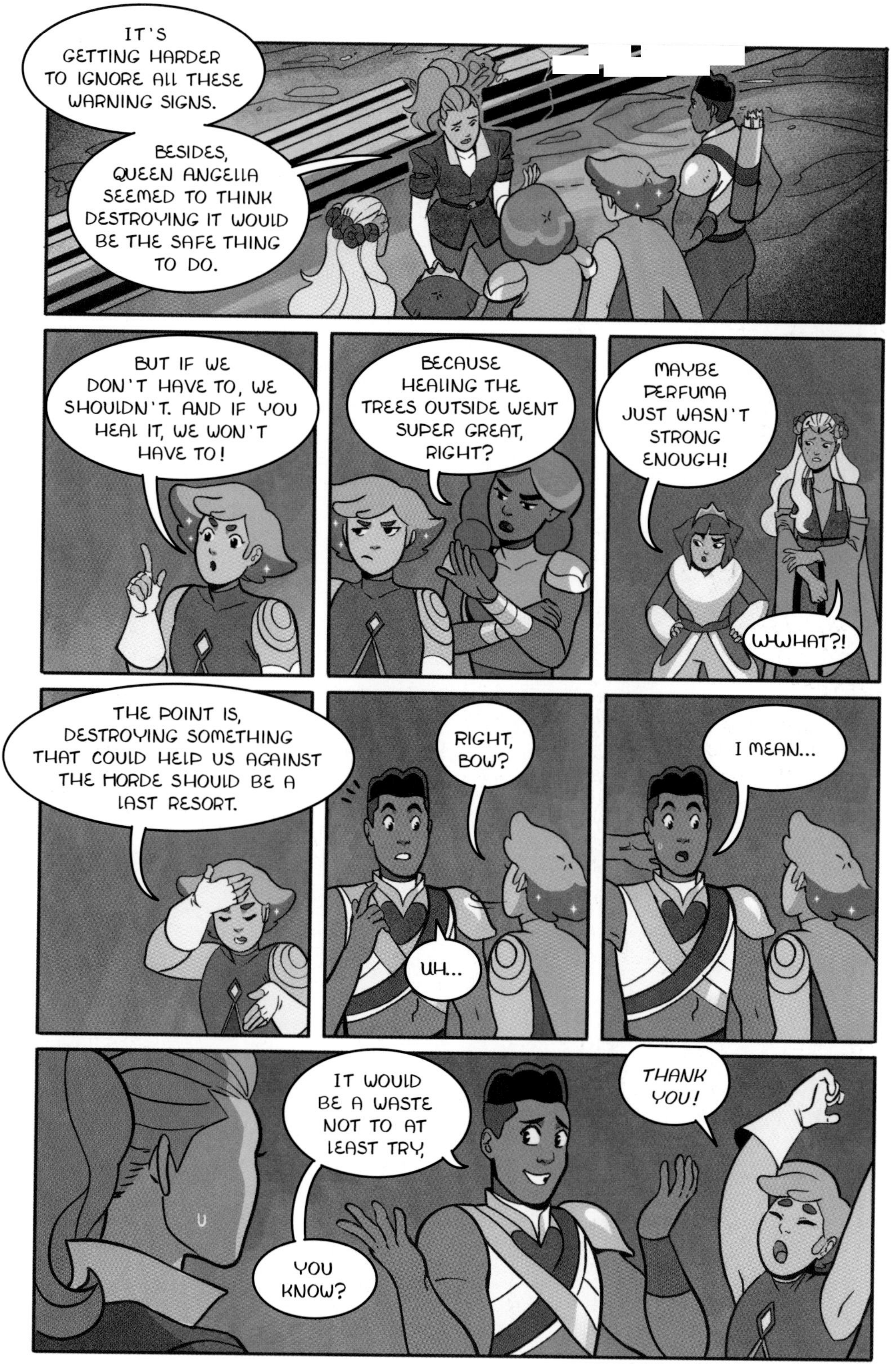
IT'S GETTING HARDER TO IGNORE ALL THESE WARNING SIGNS.
BESIDES, QUEEN ANGELLA SEEMED TO THINK DESTROYING IT WOULD BE THE SAFE THING TO DO.
BUT IF WE DON'T HAVE TO, WE SHOULDN'T. AND IF YOU HEAL IT, WE WON'T HAVE TO!
BECAUSE HEALING THE TREES OUTSIDE WENT SUPER GREAT, RIGHT?
MAYBE PERFUMA JUST WASN'T STRONG ENOUGH!
W-WHAT?!
THE POINT IS, DESTROYING SOMETHING THAT COULD HELP US AGAINST THE HORDE SHOULD BE A LAST RESORT.
RIGHT, BOW?
UH...
I MEAN...
IT WOULD BE A WASTE NOT TO AT LEAST TRY,
YOU KNOW?
THANK YOU!

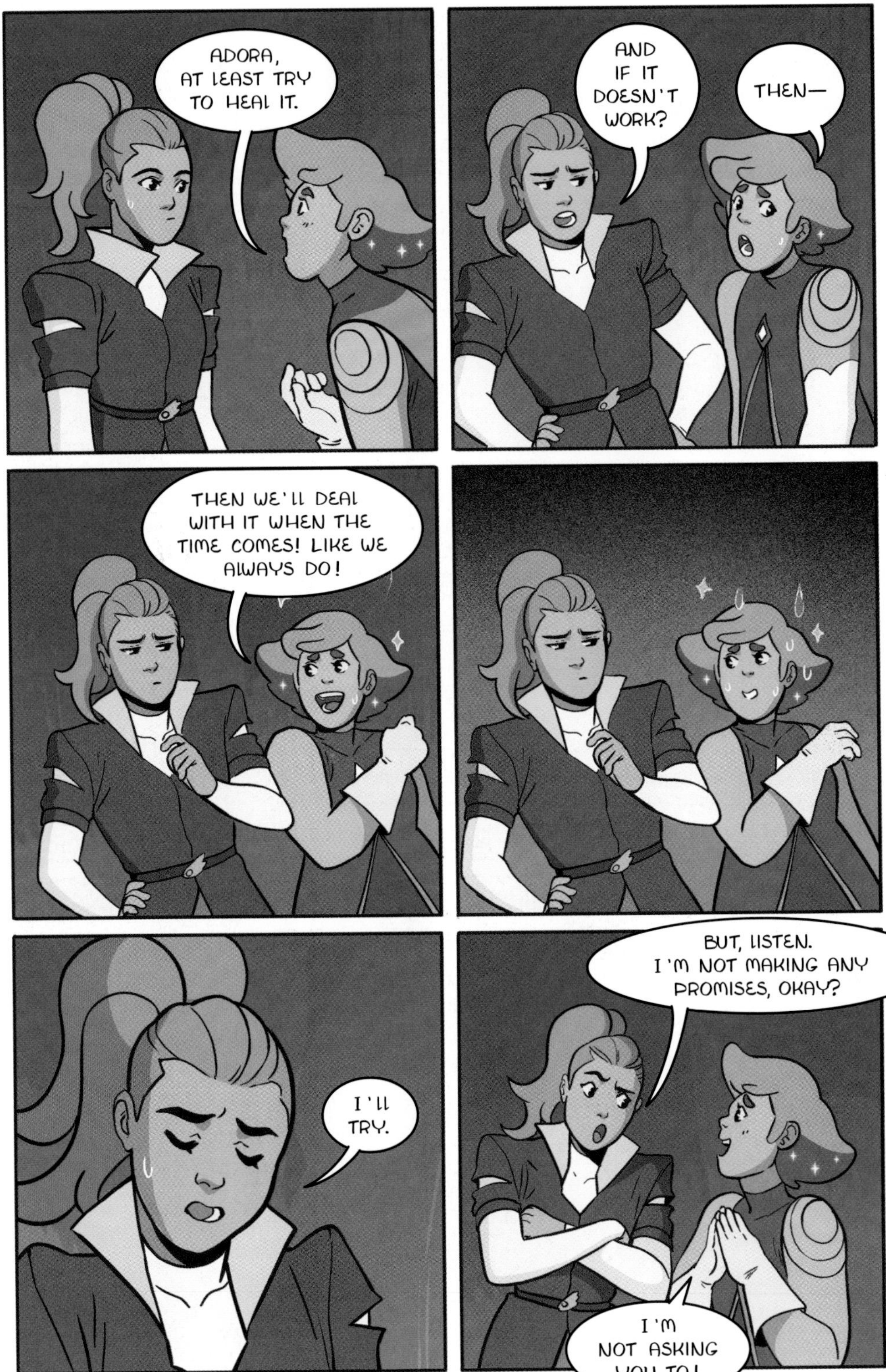
ADORA, AT LEAST TRY TO HEAL IT.
AND IF IT DOESN'T WORK?
THEN—
THEN WE'LL DEAL WITH IT WHEN THE TIME COMES! LIKE WE ALWAYS DO!
I'LL TRY.
BUT, LISTEN. I'M NOT MAKING ANY PROMISES, OKAY?
I'M NOT ASKING YOU TO!

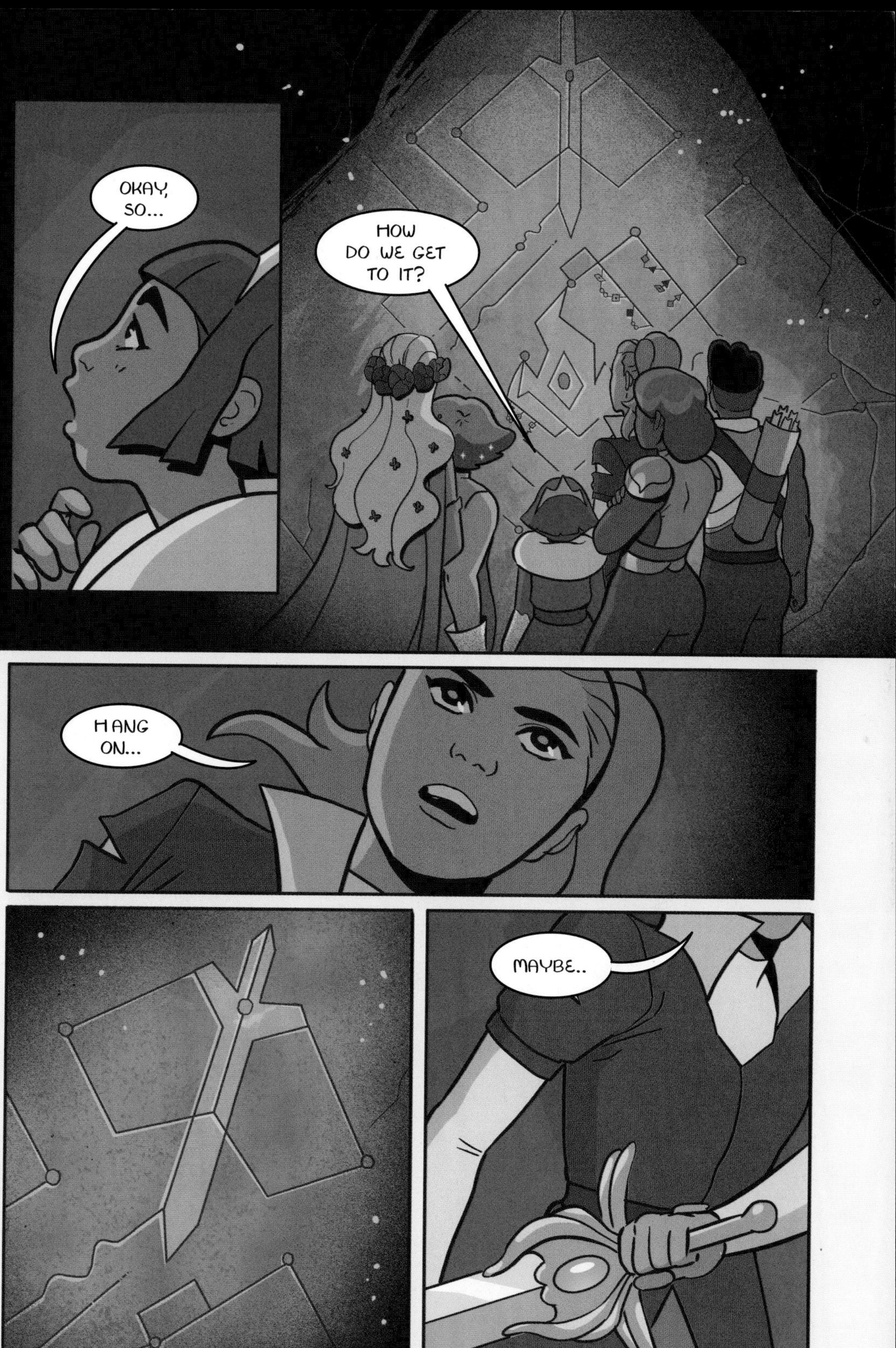
OKAY, SO...
HOW DO WE GET TO IT?
HANG ON...
MAYBE..

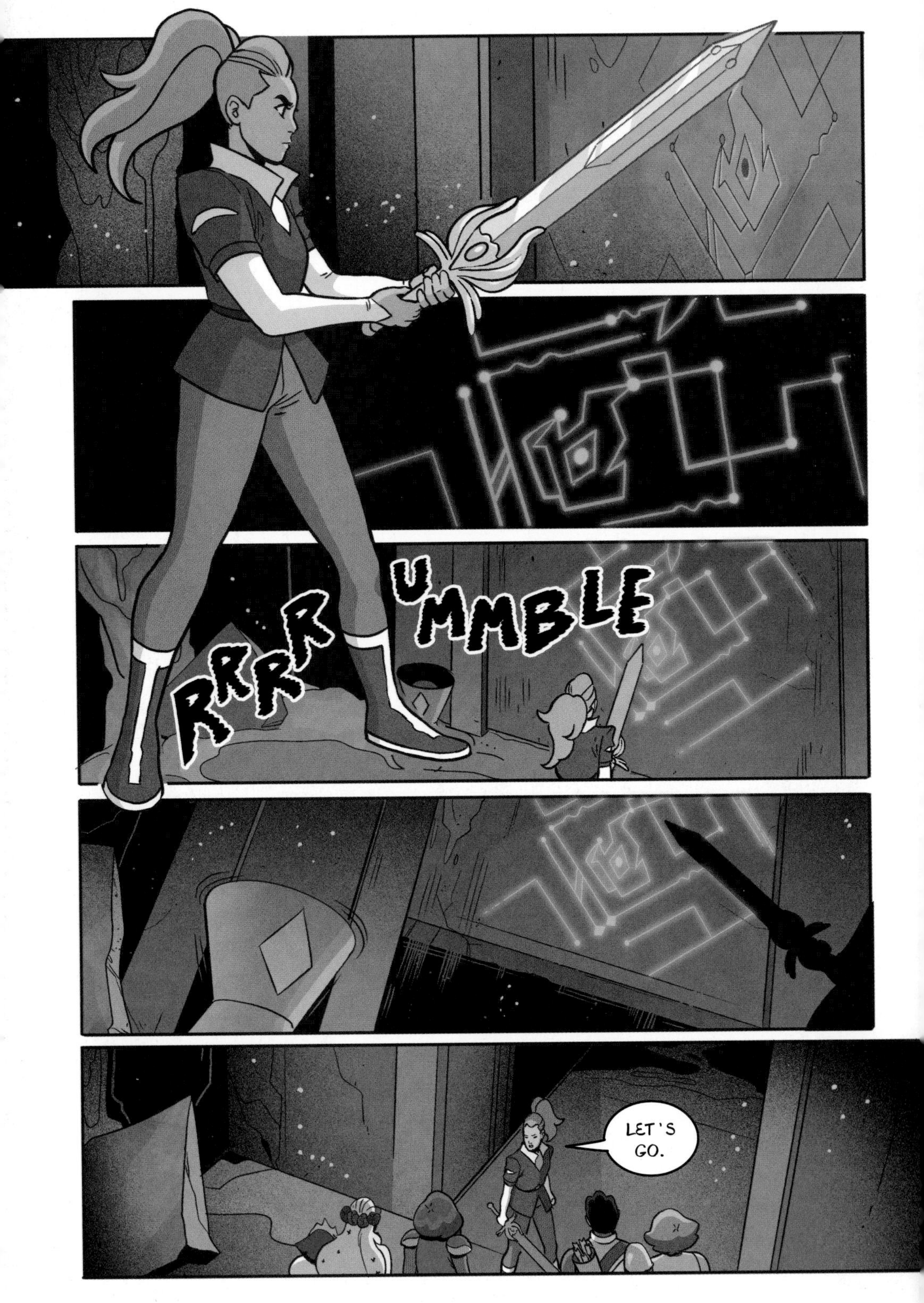
RRRR UMMBLE
LET'S GO.

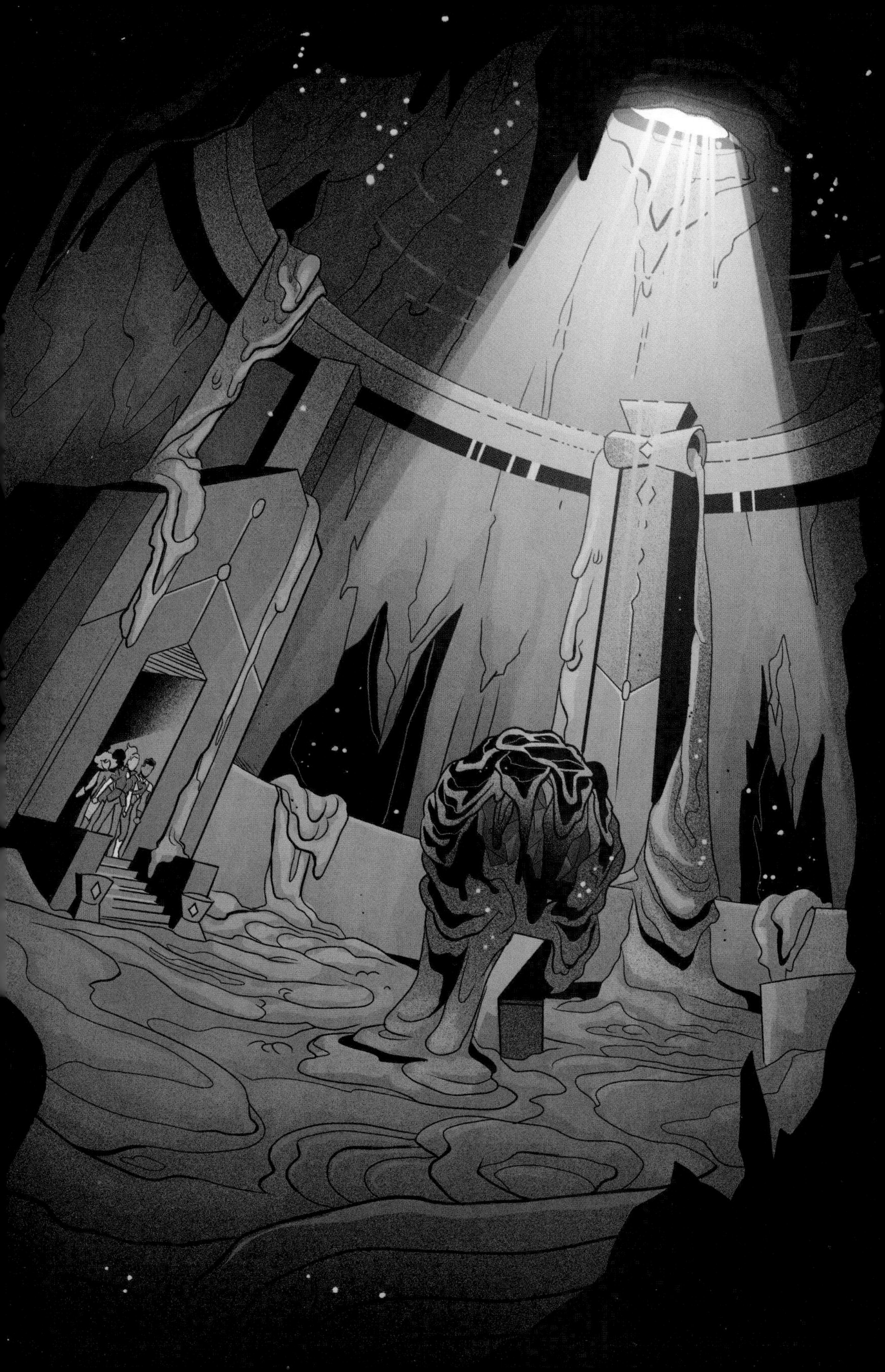

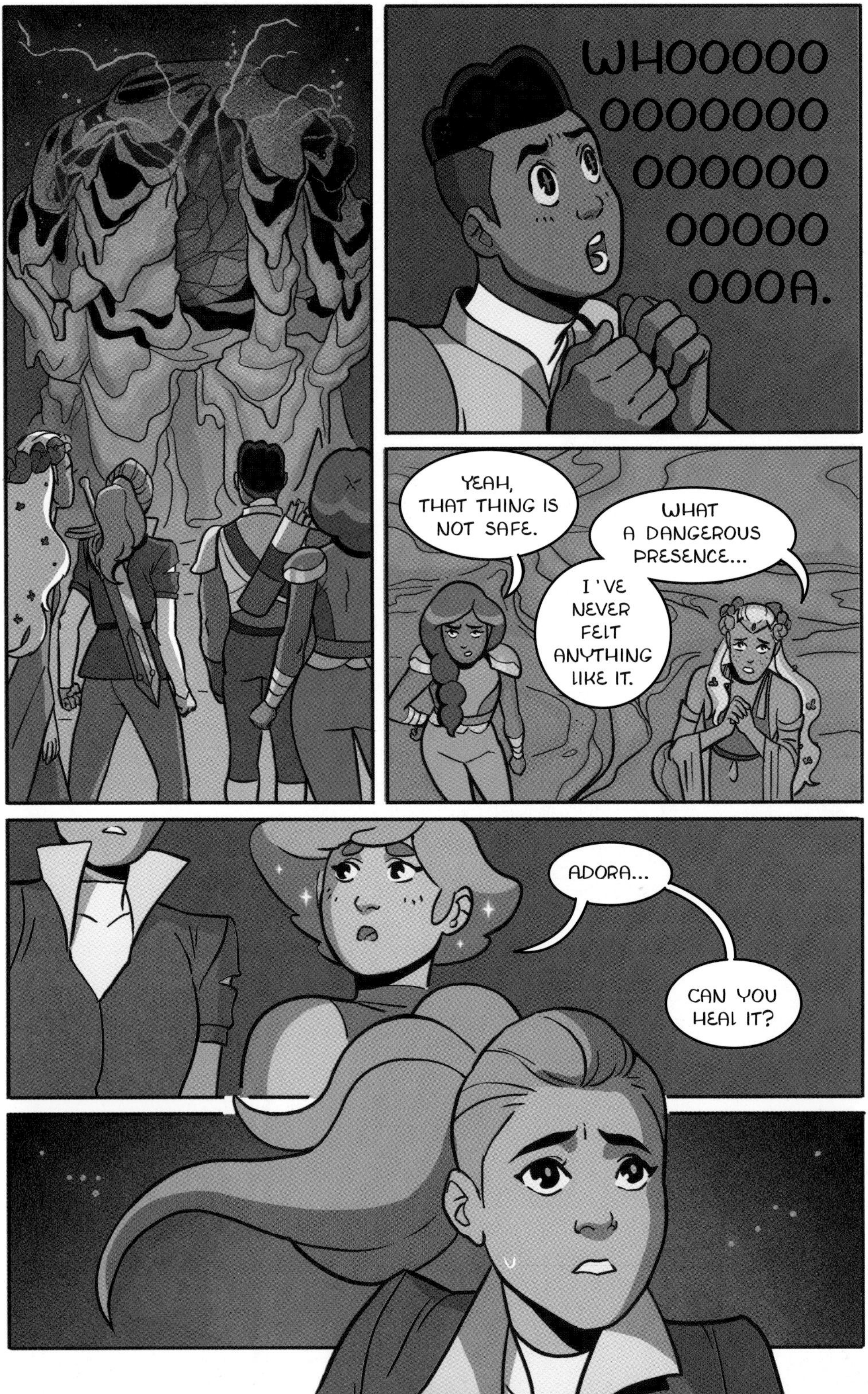
WHOOOOOOOOOOOOOOOOOOOOOOOOOOOOA.
YEAH, THAT THING IS NOT SAFE.
WHAT A DANGEROUS PRESENCE...
I'VE NEVER FELT ANYTHING LIKE IT.
ADORA...
CAN YOU HEAL IT?

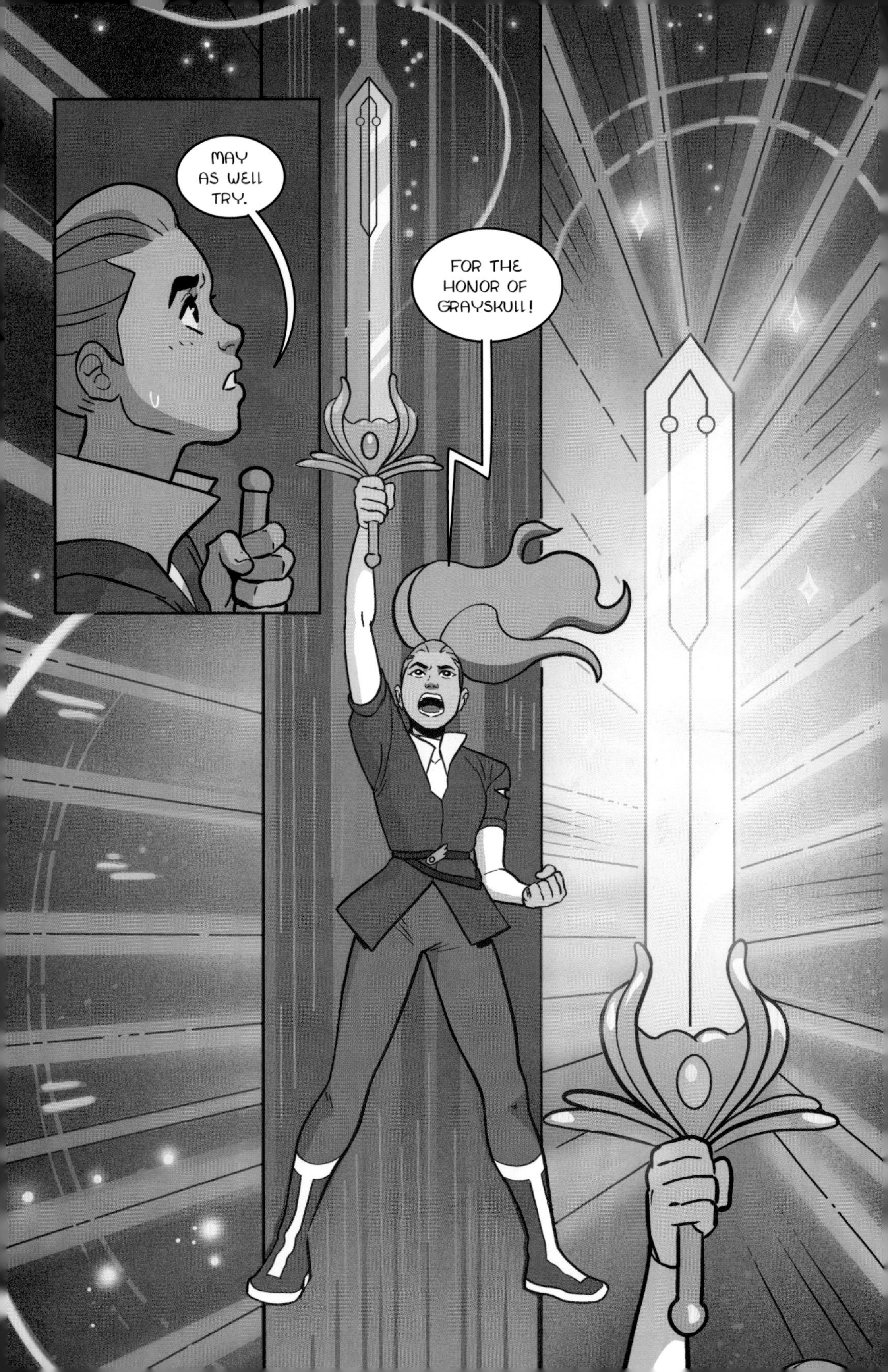
MAY AS WELL TRY.
FOR THE HONOR OF GRAYSKULL!

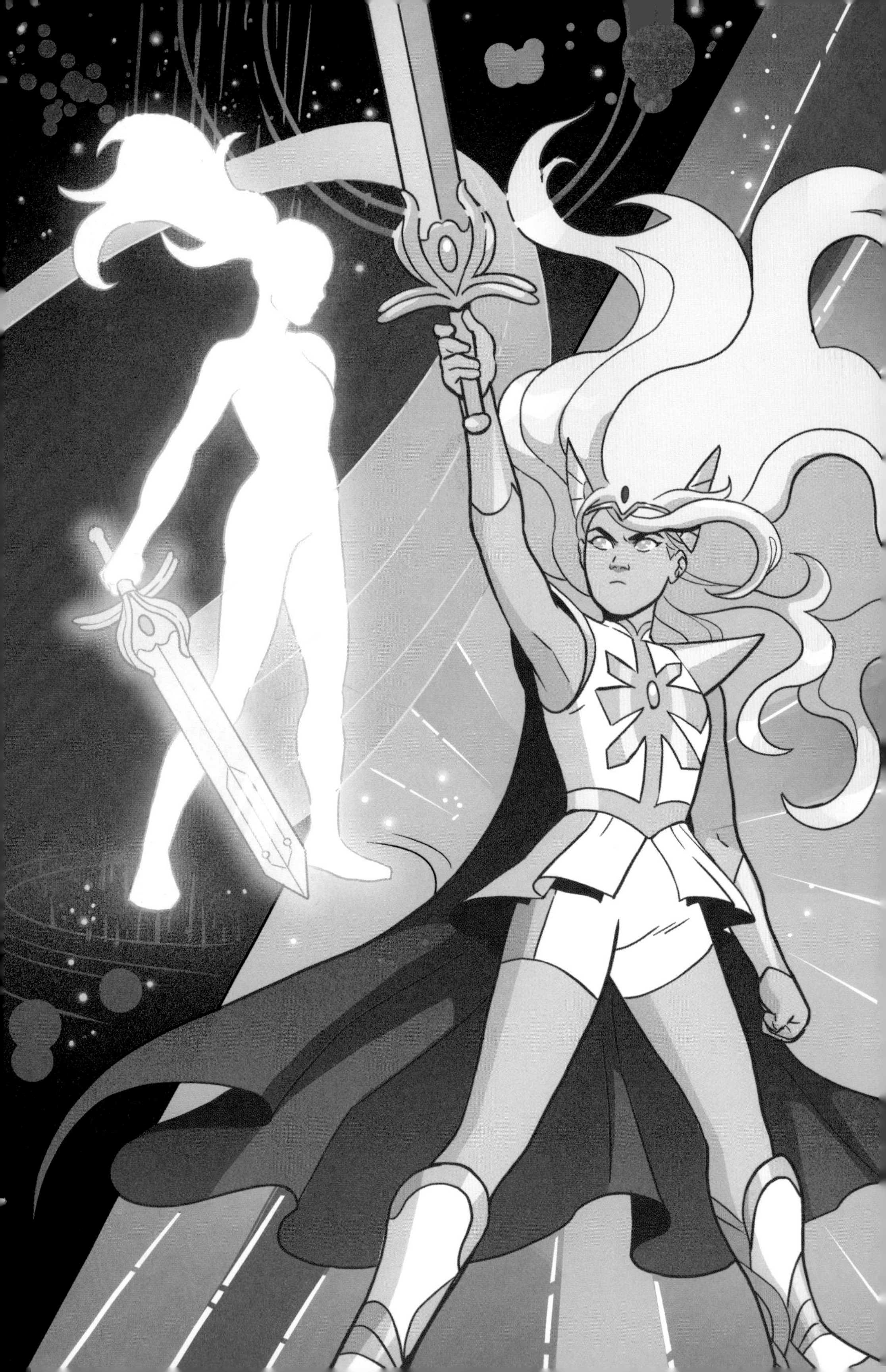

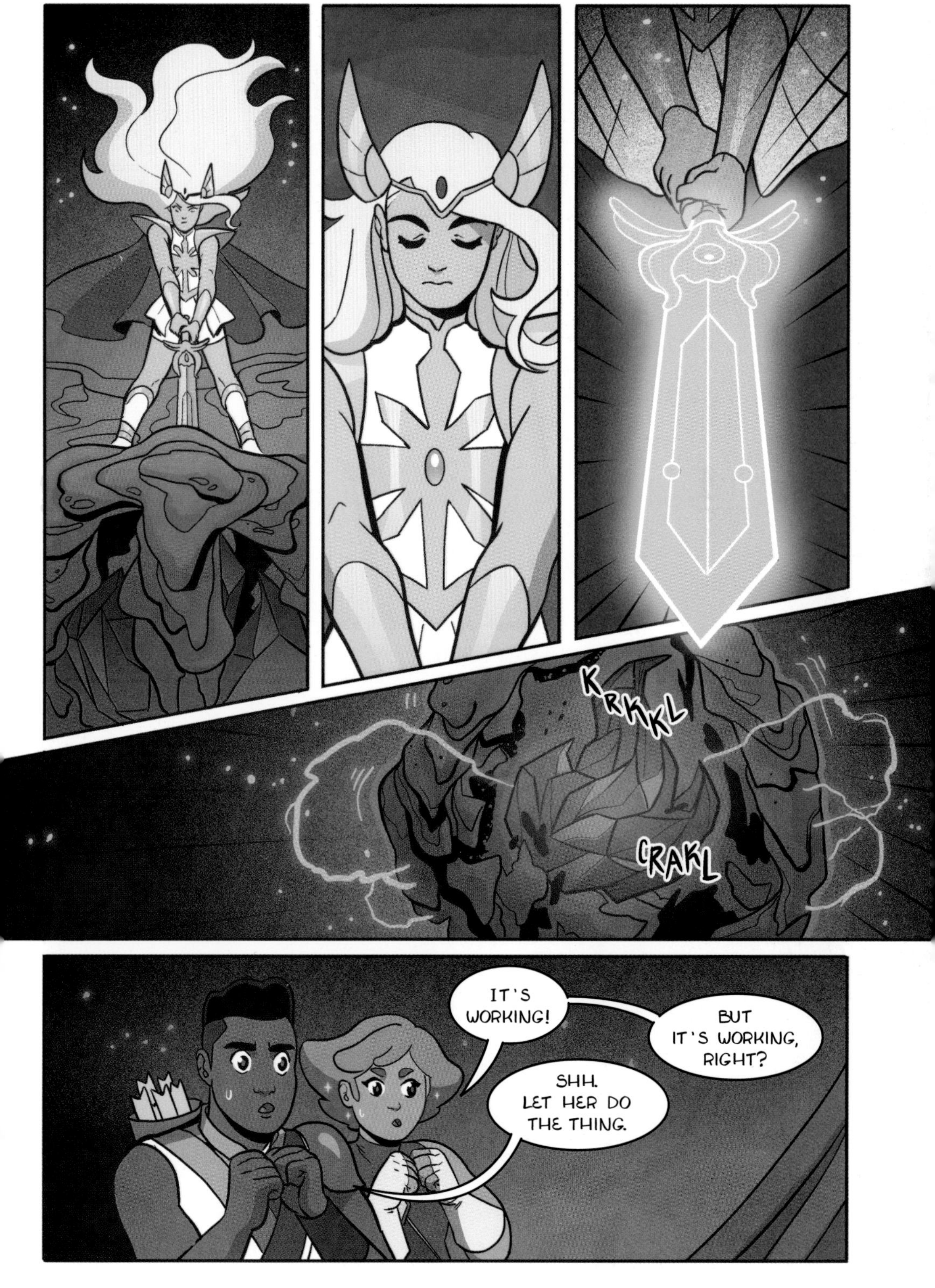
KRKKL
CRAKL
IT'S WORKING!
BUT IT'S WORKING, RIGHT?
SHH. LET HER DO THE THING.

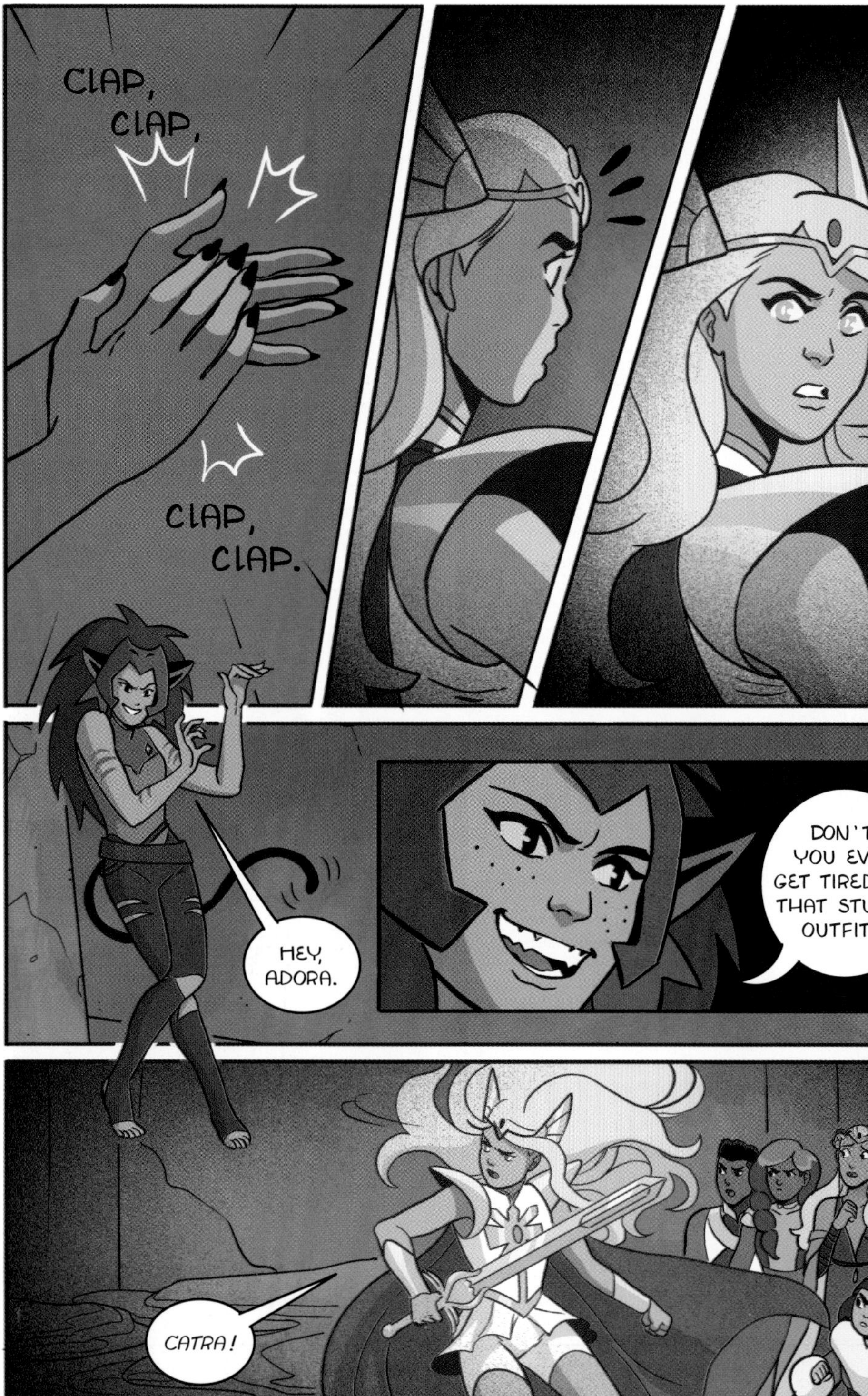
CLAP,
CLAP,
CLAP,
CLAP.
HEY, ADORA.
DON'T YOU EVER GET TIRED OF THAT STUPID OUTFIT?
CATRA!

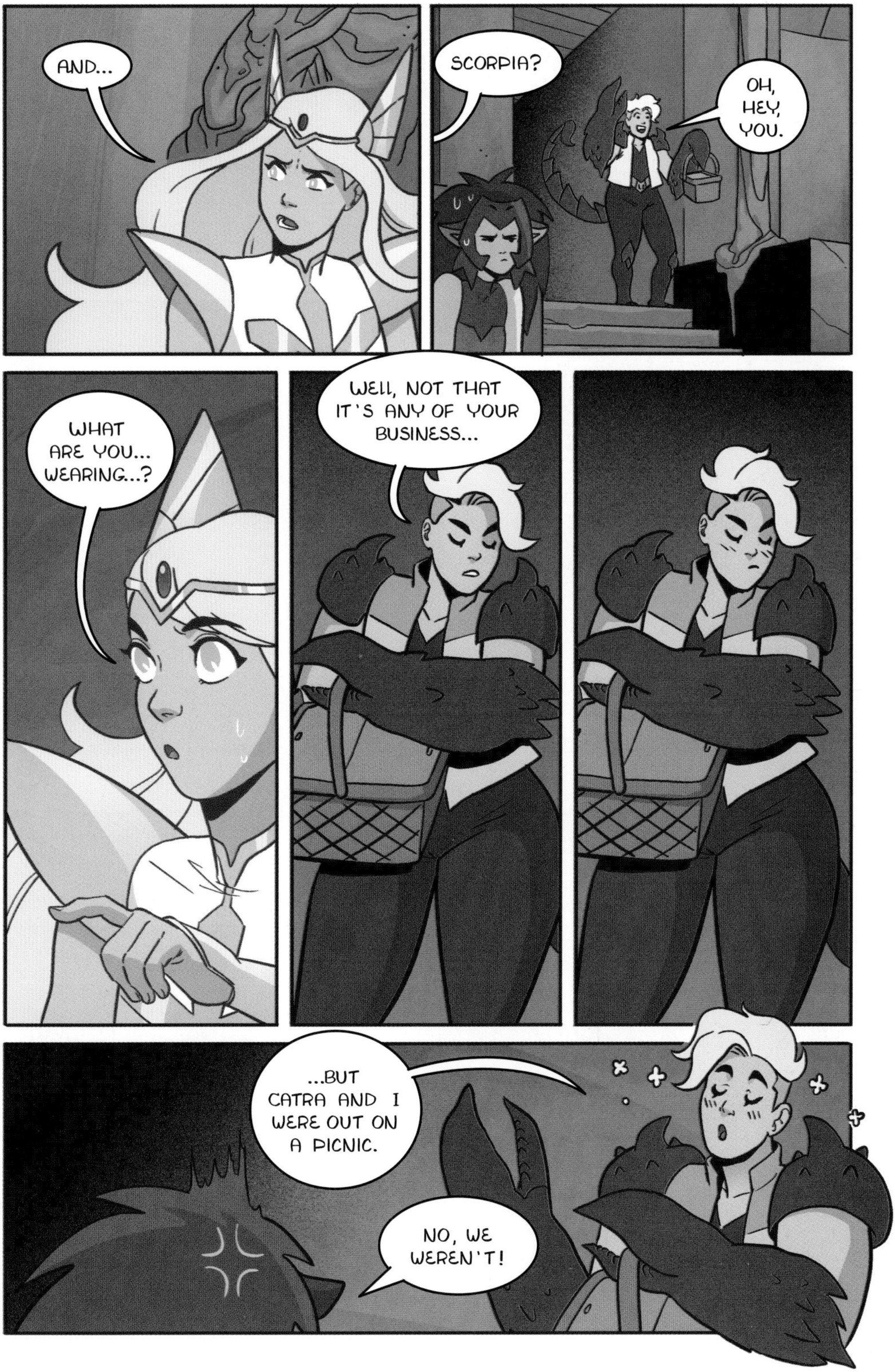
AND...
SCORPIA?
OH, HEY, YOU.
WHAT ARE YOU... WEARING...?
WELL, NOT THAT IT'S ANY OF YOUR BUSINESS...
...BUT CATRA AND I WERE OUT ON A PICNIC.
NO, WE WEREN'T!

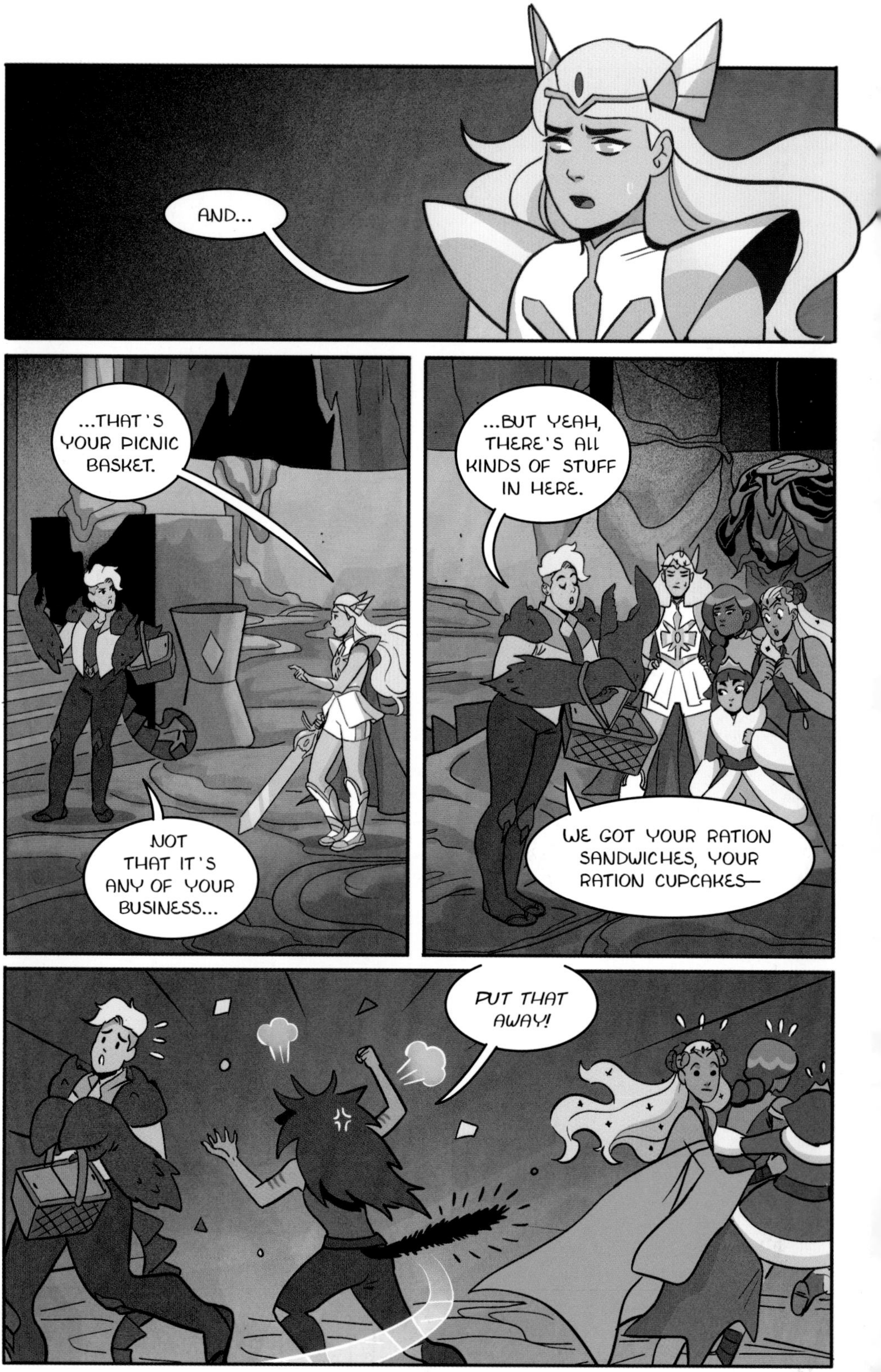
AND...
...THAT'S YOUR PICNIC BASKET.
NOT THAT IT'S ANY OF YOUR BUSINESS...
...BUT YEAH, THERE'S ALL KINDS OF STUFF IN HERE.
WE GOT YOUR RATION SANDWICHES, YOUR RATION CUPCAKES—
PUT THAT AWAY!

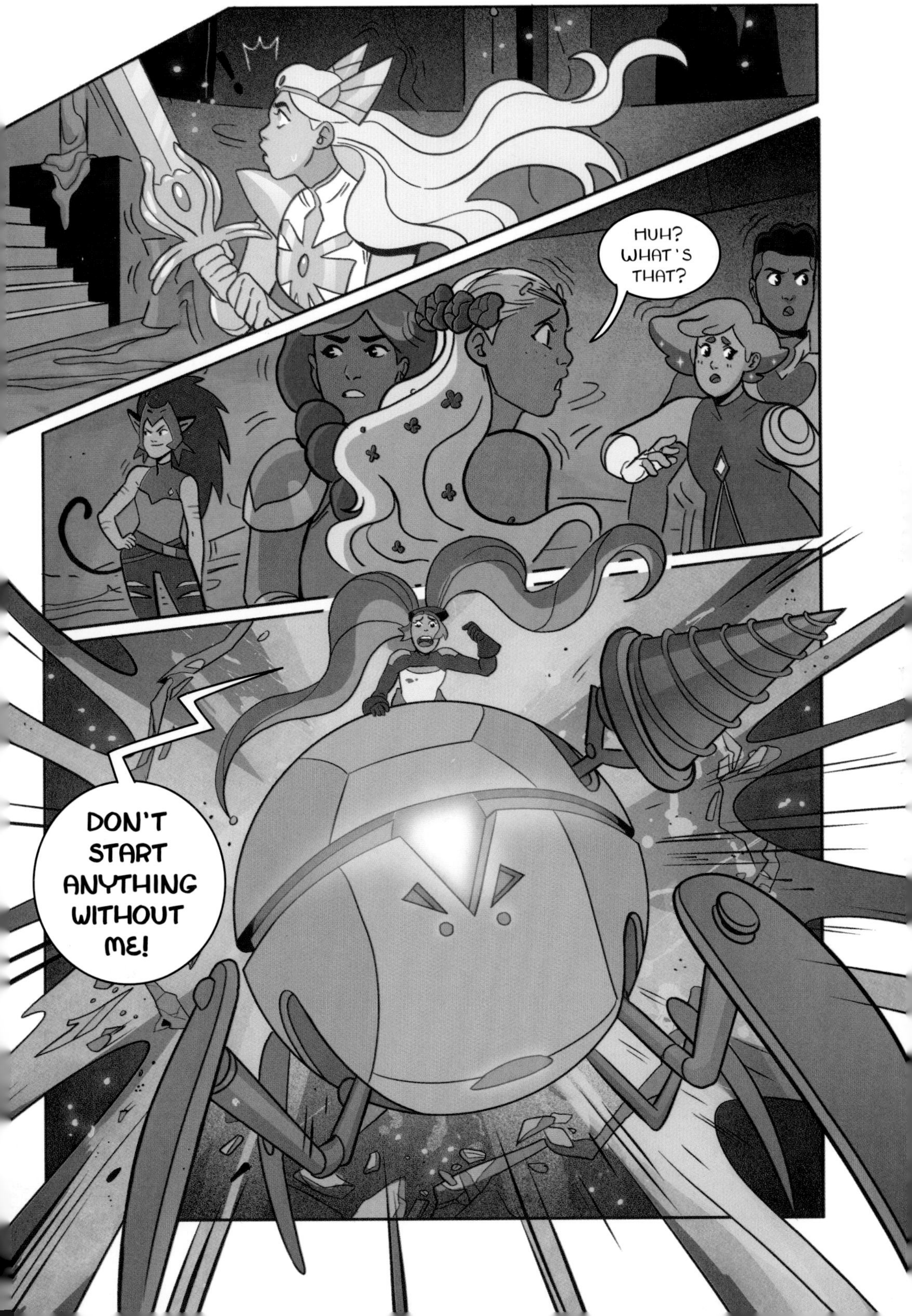
HUH? WHAT'S THAT?
DON'T START ANYTHING WITHOUT ME!

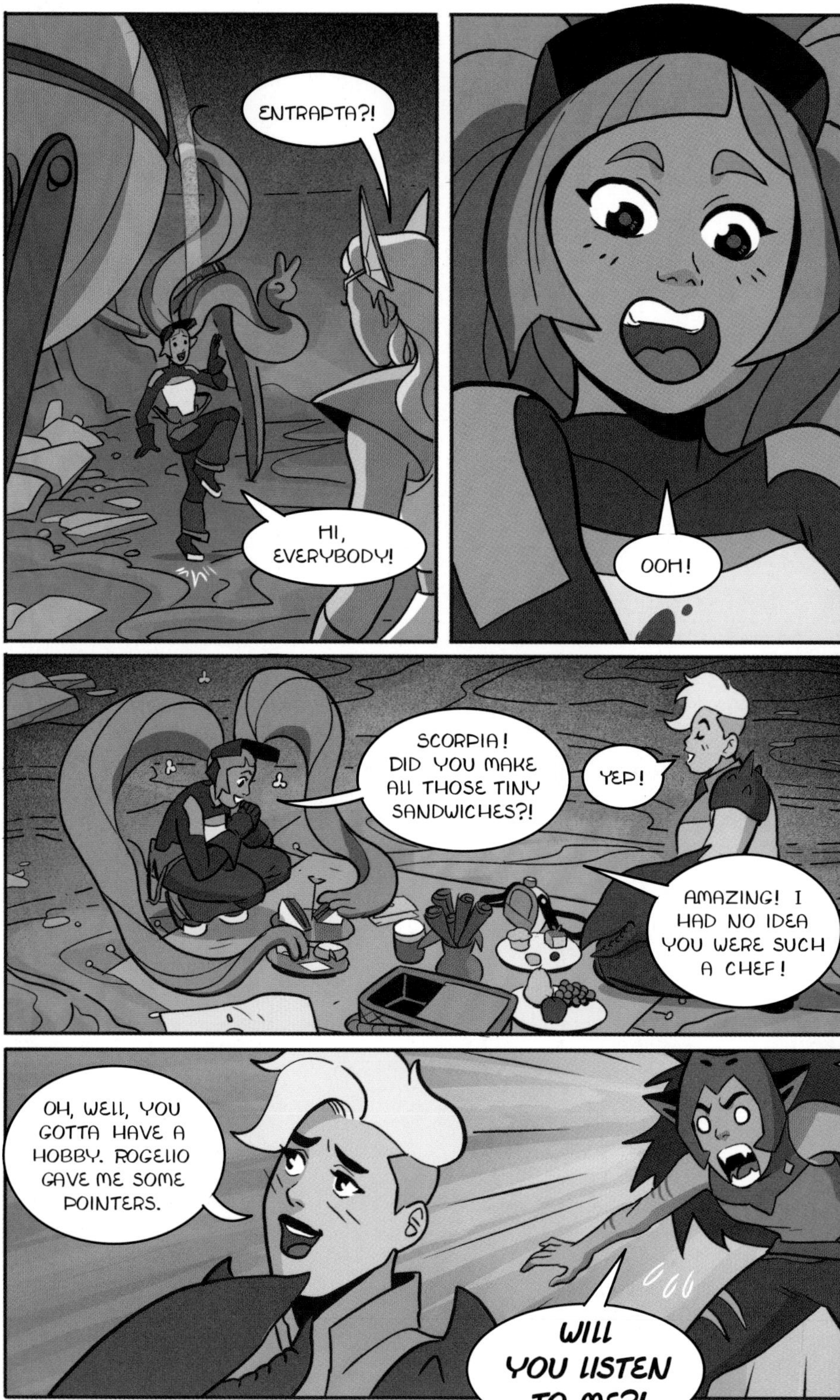
ENTRAPTA?!
HI, EVERYBODY!
OOH!
SCORPIA! DID YOU MAKE ALL THOSE TINY SANDWICHES?!
YEP!
AMAZING! I HAD NO IDEA YOU WERE SUCH A CHEF!
OH, WELL, YOU GOTTA HAVE A HOBBY. ROGELIO GAVE ME SOME POINTERS.
WILL YOU LISTEN TO ME?!

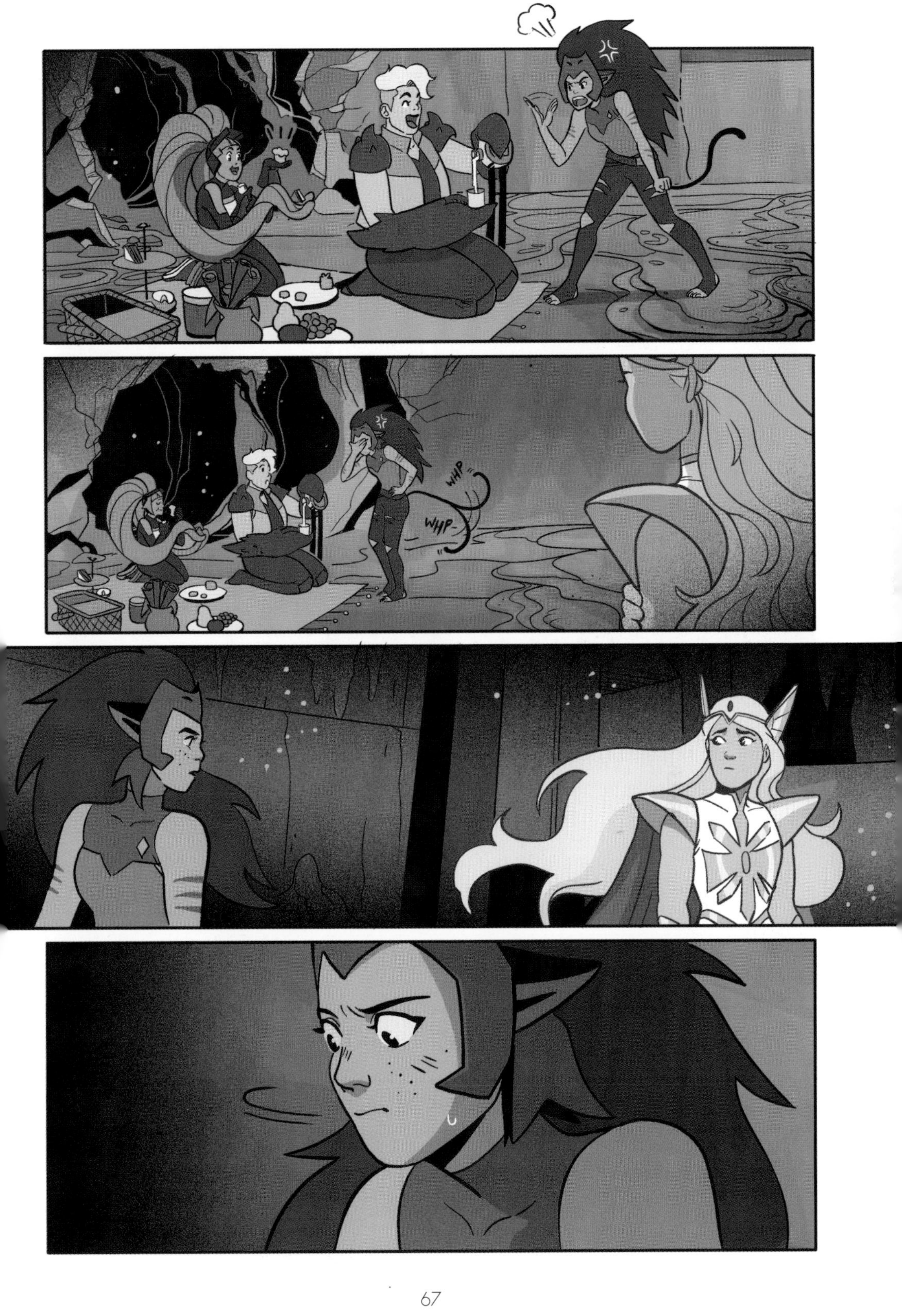
WHP
WHP_

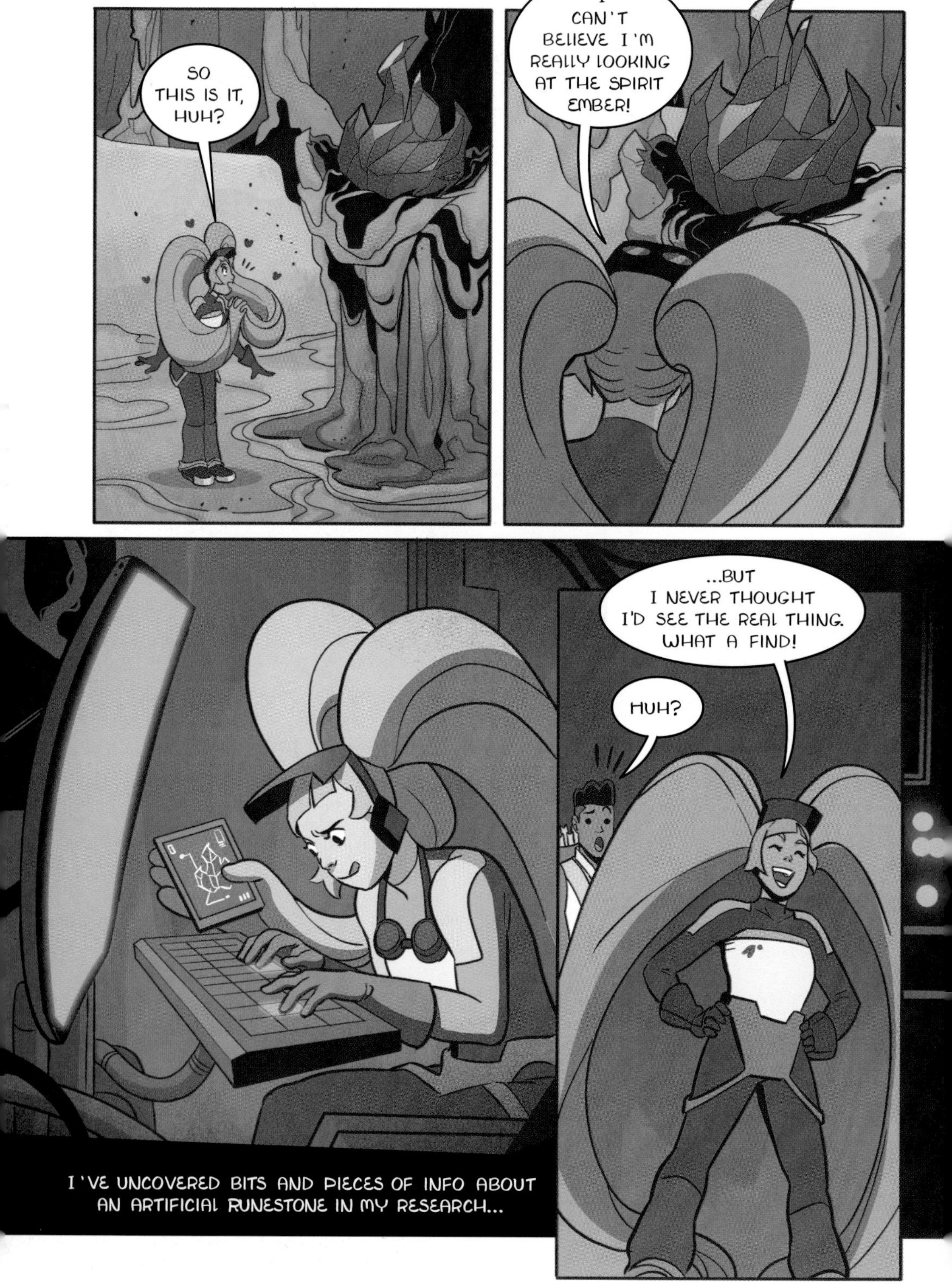
SO THIS IS IT, HUH?
I CAN'T BELIEVE I'M REALLY LOOKING AT THE SPIRIT EMBER!
I'VE UNCOVERED BITS AND PIECES OF INFO ABOUT AN ARTIFICIAL RUNESTONE IN MY RESEARCH...
...BUT I NEVER THOUGHT I'D SEE THE REAL THING. WHAT A FIND!
HUH?

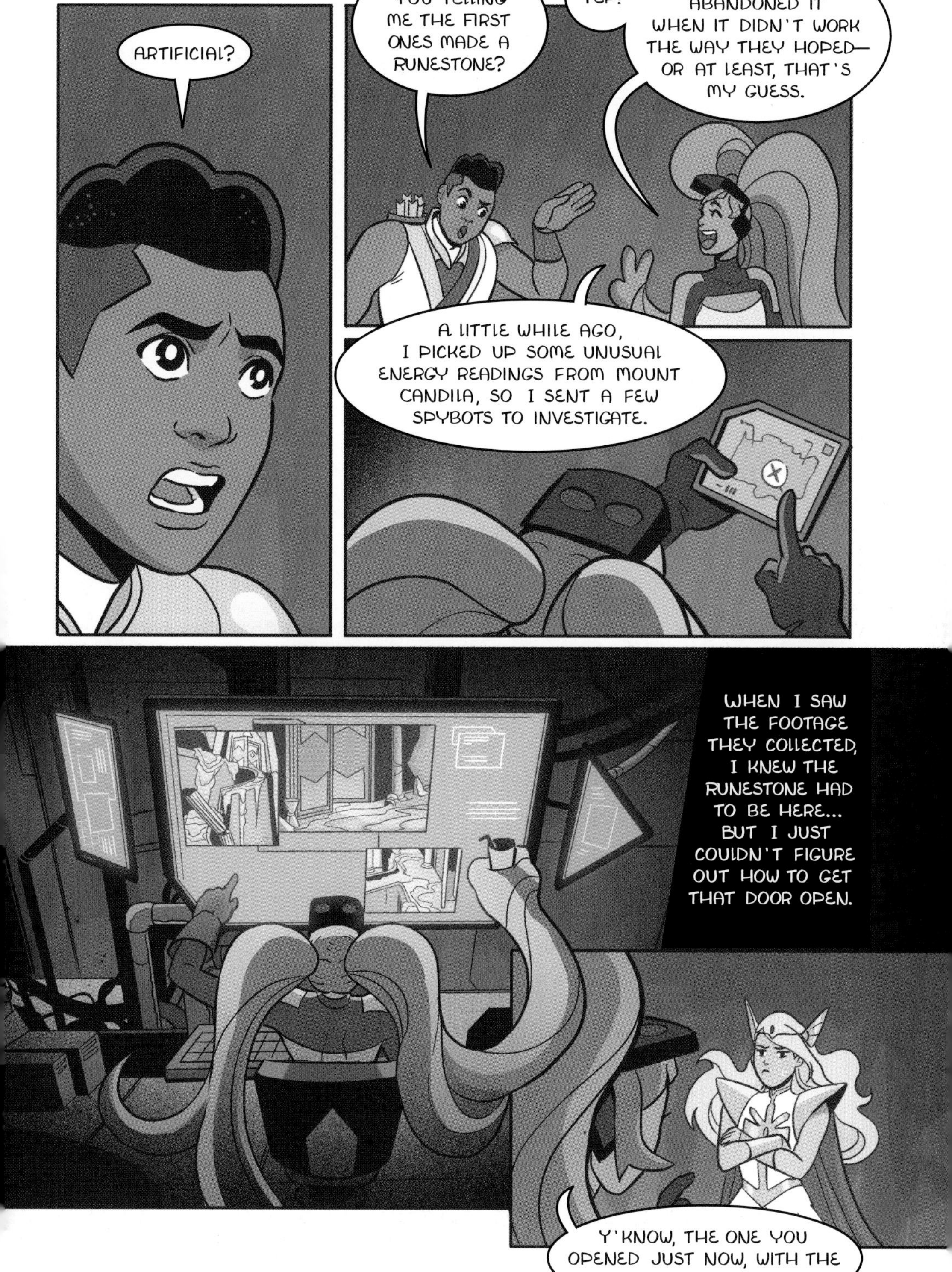
ARTIFICIAL?
ARE YOU TELLING ME THE FIRST ONES MADE A RUNESTONE?
YEP!
AND ABANDONED IT WHEN IT DIDN'T WORK THE WAY THEY HOPED— OR AT LEAST, THAT'S MY GUESS.
A LITTLE WHILE AGO, I PICKED UP SOME UNUSUAL ENERGY READINGS FROM MOUNT CANDILA, SO I SENT A FEW SPYBOTS TO INVESTIGATE.
WHEN I SAW THE FOOTAGE THEY COLLECTED, I KNEW THE RUNESTONE HAD TO BE HERE... BUT I JUST COULDN'T FIGURE OUT HOW TO GET THAT DOOR OPEN.
Y'KNOW, THE ONE YOU OPENED JUST NOW, WITH THE SHE-RA SWORD.

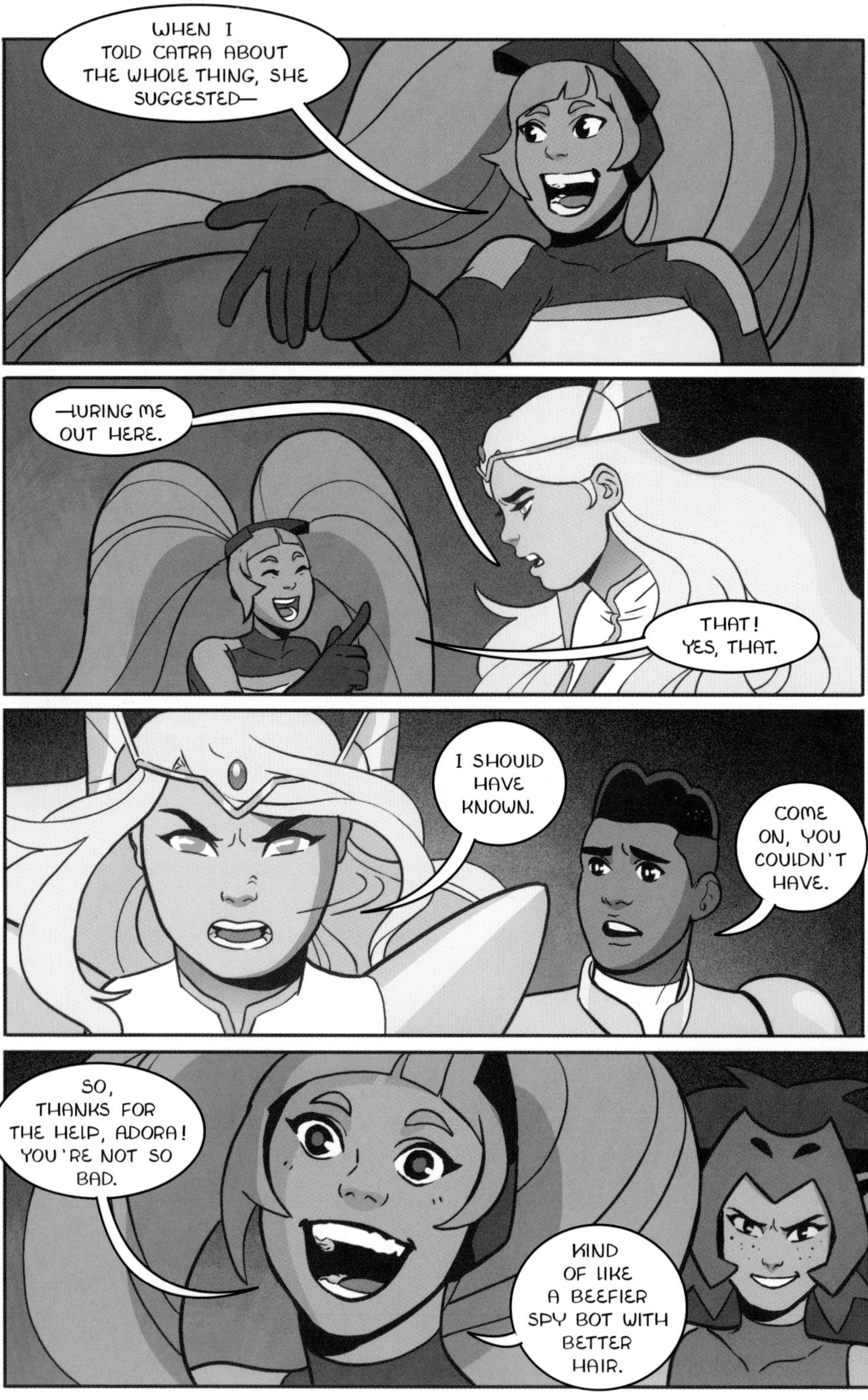
WHEN I TOLD CATRA ABOUT THE WHOLE THING, SHE SUGGESTED—
—LURING ME OUT HERE.
THAT! YES, THAT.
I SHOULD HAVE KNOWN.
COME ON, YOU COULDN'T HAVE.
SO, THANKS FOR THE HELP, ADORA! YOU'RE NOT SO BAD.
KIND OF LIKE A BEEFIER SPY BOT WITH BETTER HAIR.

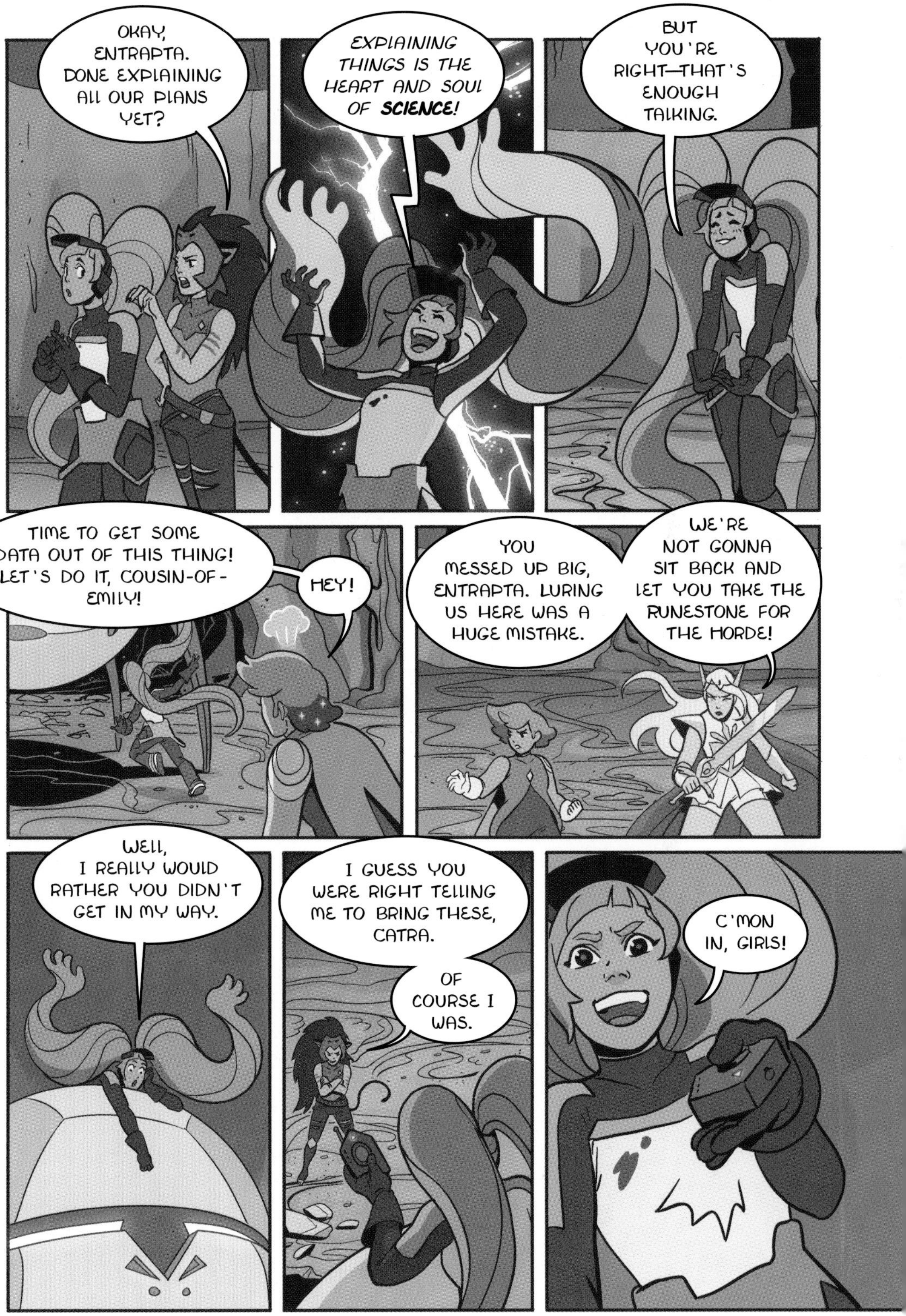
OKAY, ENTRAPTA. DONE EXPLAINING ALL OUR PLANS YET?
EXPLAINING THINGS IS THE HEART AND SOUL OF ***SCIENCE!***
BUT YOU'RE RIGHT—THAT'S ENOUGH TALKING.
TIME TO GET SOME DATA OUT OF THIS THING! LET'S DO IT, COUSIN-OF-EMILY!
HEY!
YOU MESSED UP BIG, ENTRAPTA. LURING US HERE WAS A HUGE MISTAKE.
WE'RE NOT GONNA SIT BACK AND LET YOU TAKE THE RUNESTONE FOR THE HORDE!
WELL, I REALLY WOULD RATHER YOU DIDN'T GET IN MY WAY.
I GUESS YOU WERE RIGHT TELLING ME TO BRING THESE, CATRA.
OF COURSE I WAS.
C'MON IN, GIRLS!

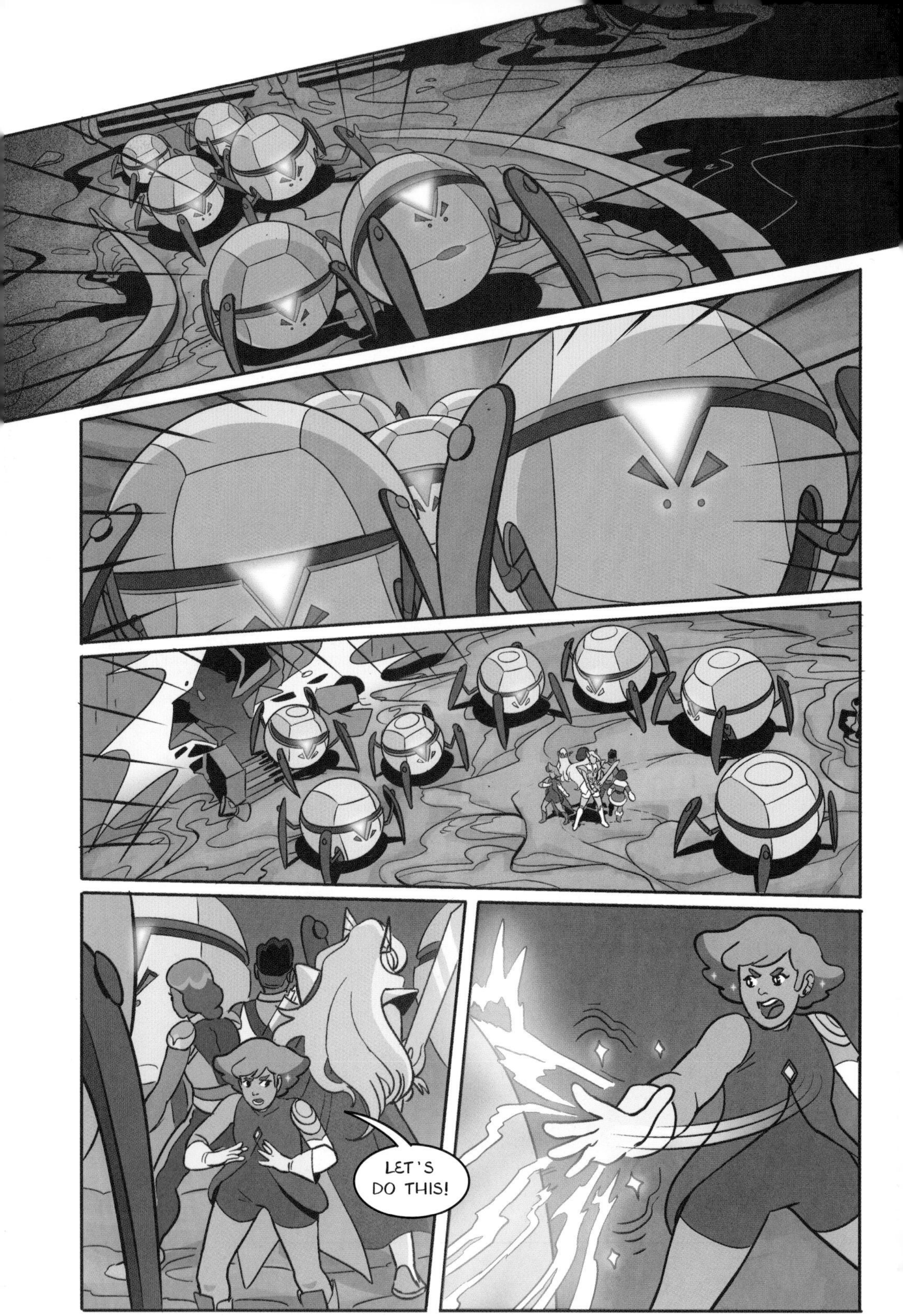
LET'S DO THIS!

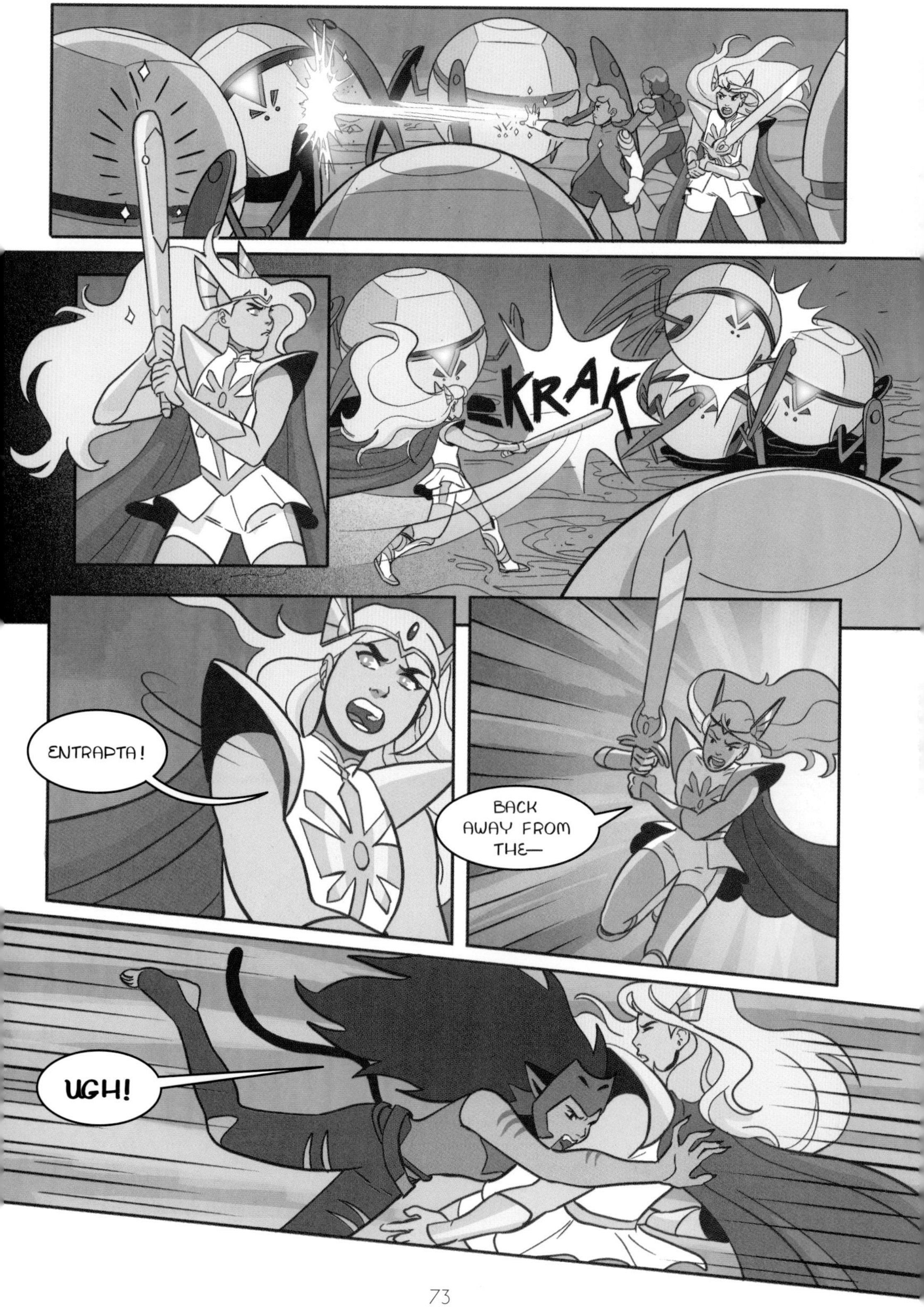
KRAK
ENTRAPTA!
BACK AWAY FROM THE—
UGH!

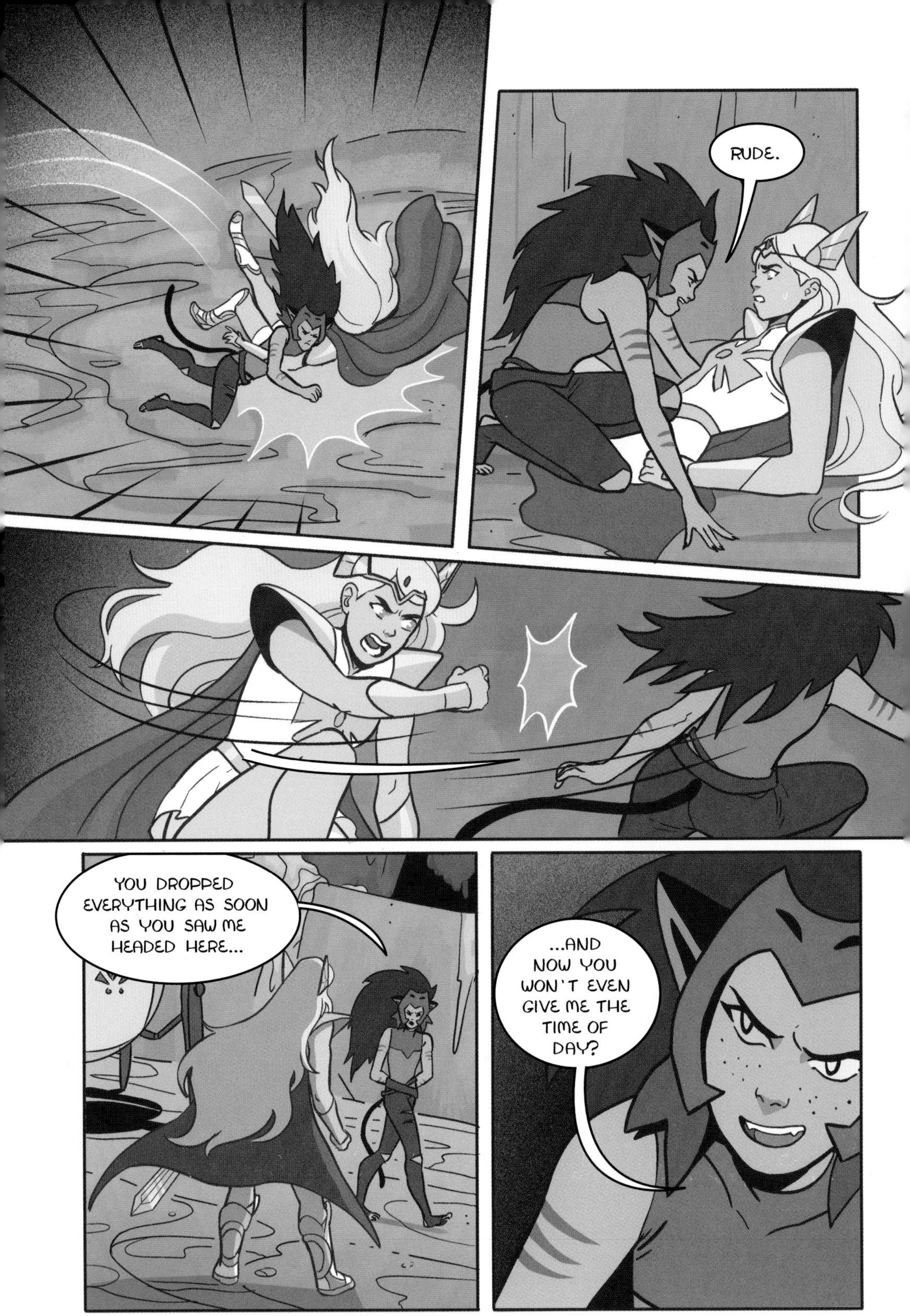
RUDE.
YOU DROPPED EVERYTHING AS SOON AS YOU SAW ME HEADED HERE...
...AND NOW YOU WON'T EVEN GIVE ME THE TIME OF DAY?

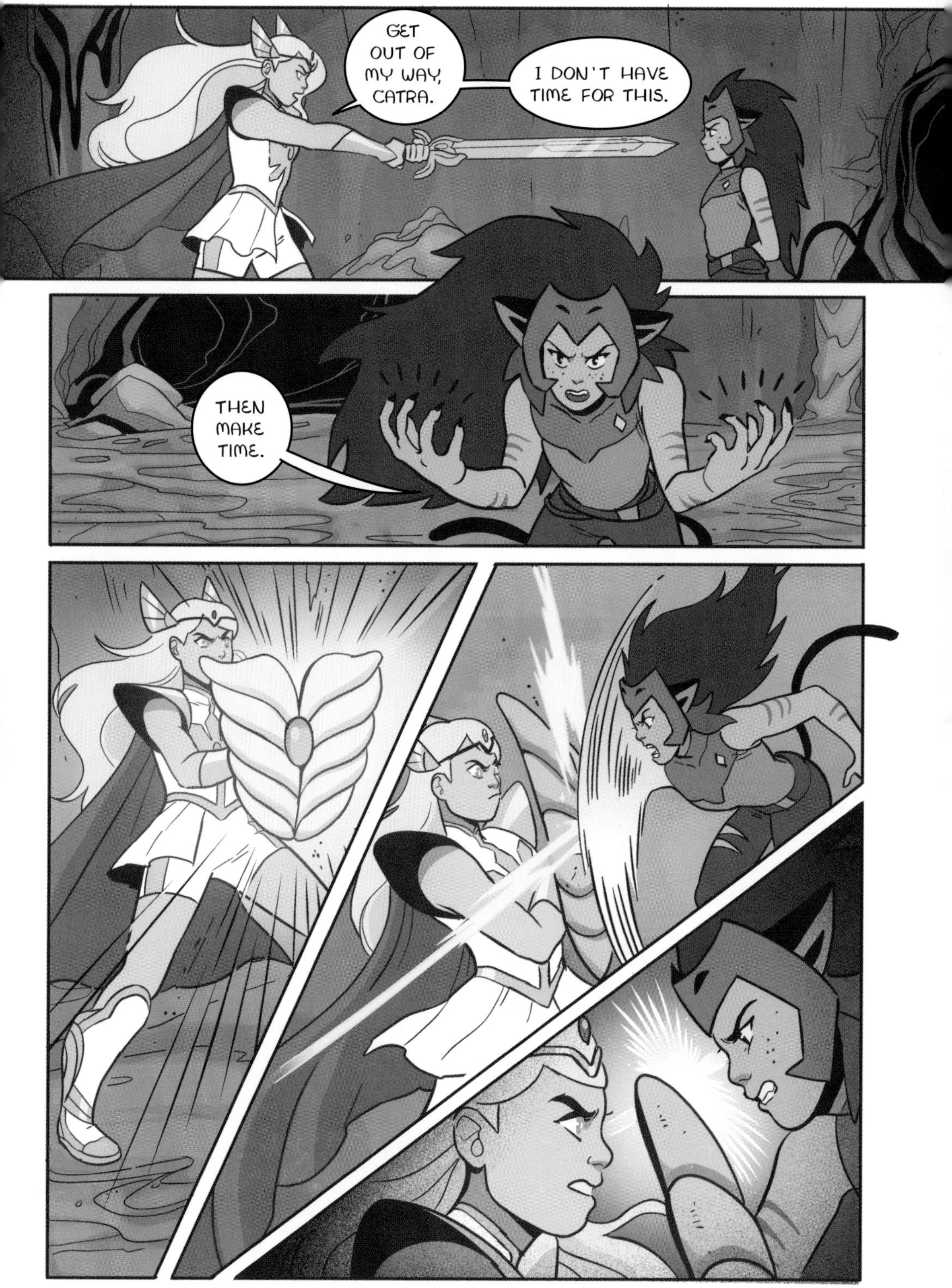
GET OUT OF MY WAY, CATRA.
I DON'T HAVE TIME FOR THIS.
THEN MAKE TIME.

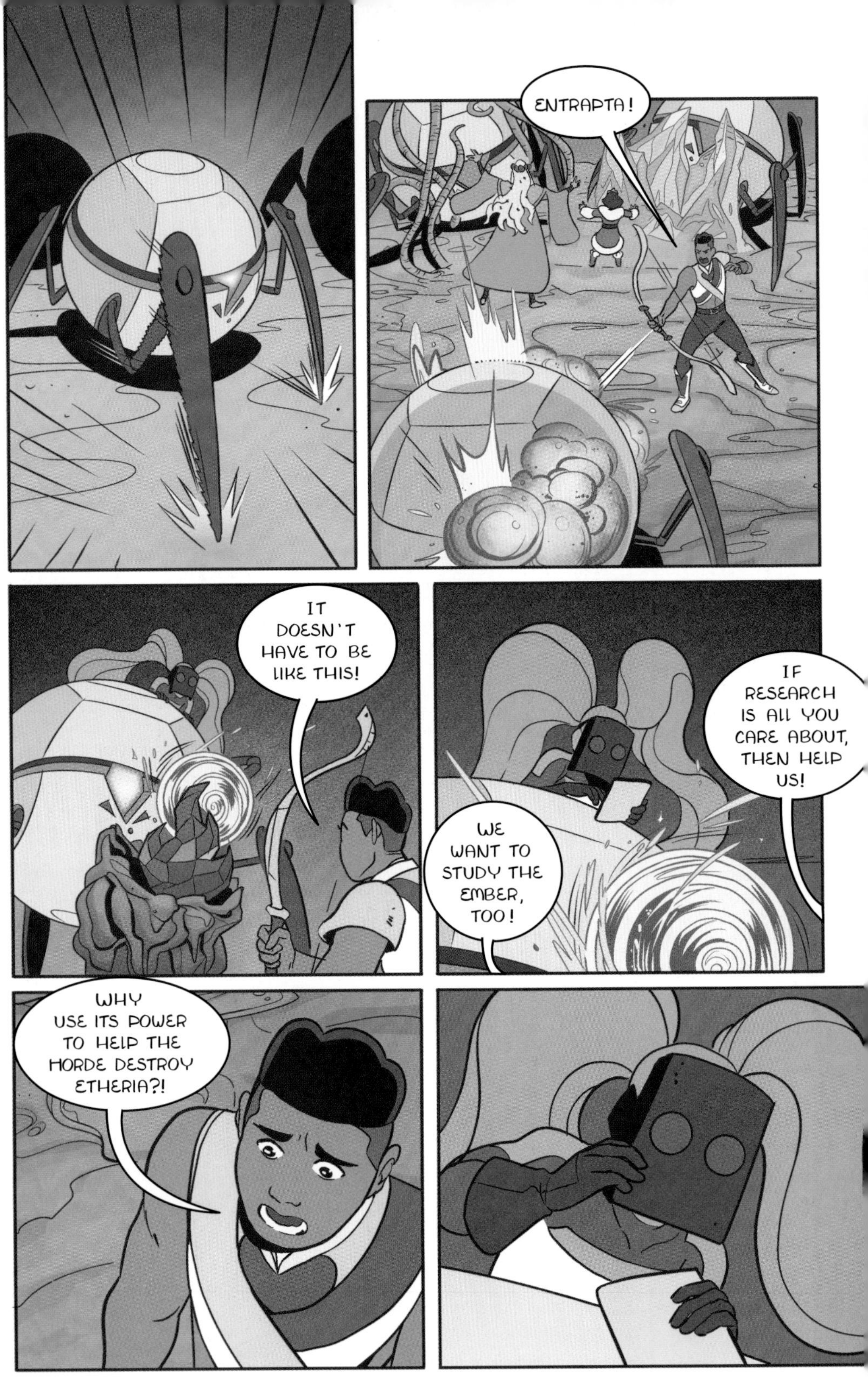
ENTRAPTA!
IT DOESN'T HAVE TO BE LIKE THIS!
IF RESEARCH IS ALL YOU CARE ABOUT, THEN HELP US!
WE WANT TO STUDY THE EMBER, TOO!
WHY USE ITS POWER TO HELP THE HORDE DESTROY ETHERIA?!

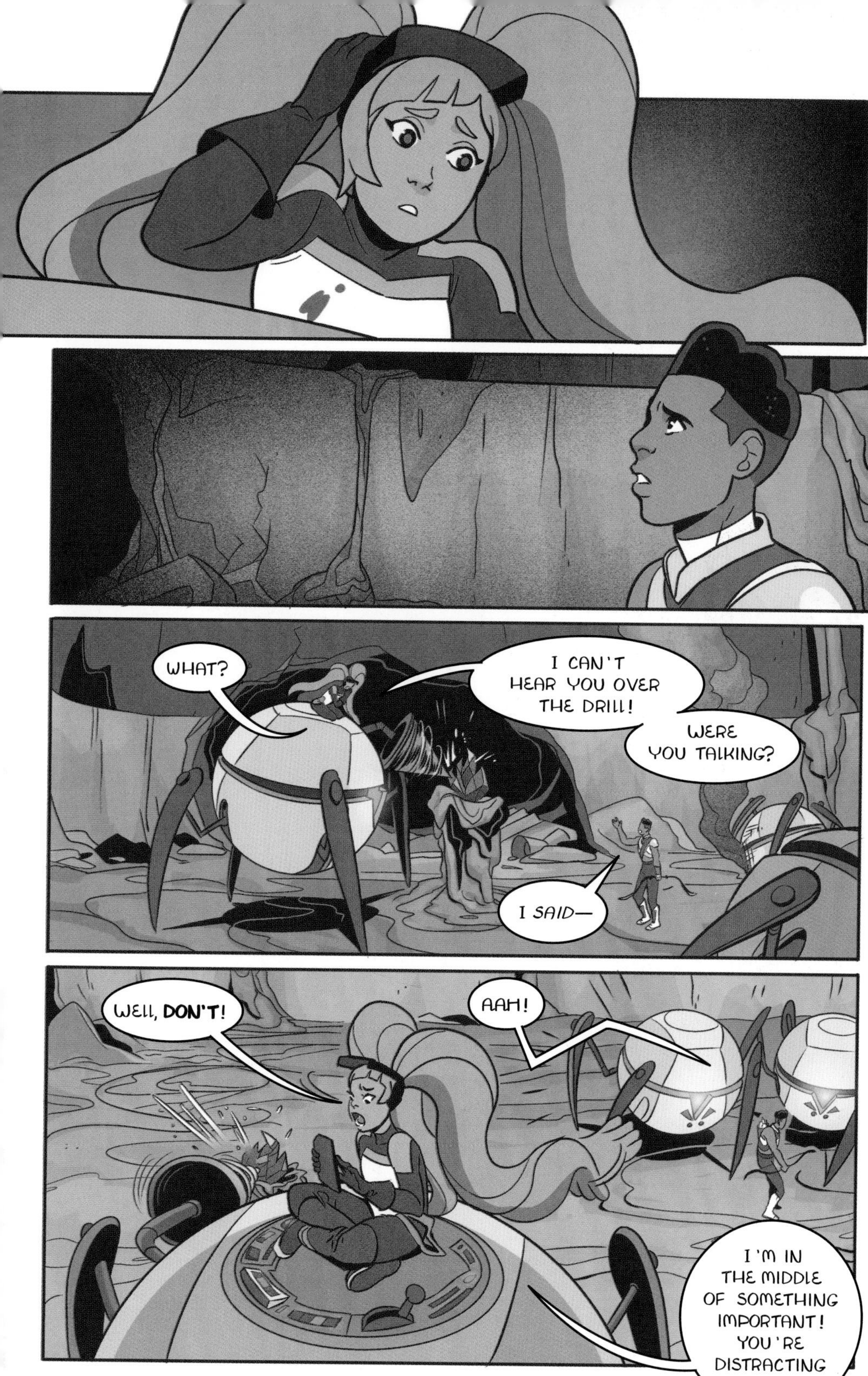
WHAT?
I CAN'T HEAR YOU OVER THE DRILL!
WERE YOU TALKING?
I SAID—
WELL, **DON'T**!
AAH!
I'M IN THE MIDDLE OF SOMETHING IMPORTANT! YOU'RE DISTRACTING ME!

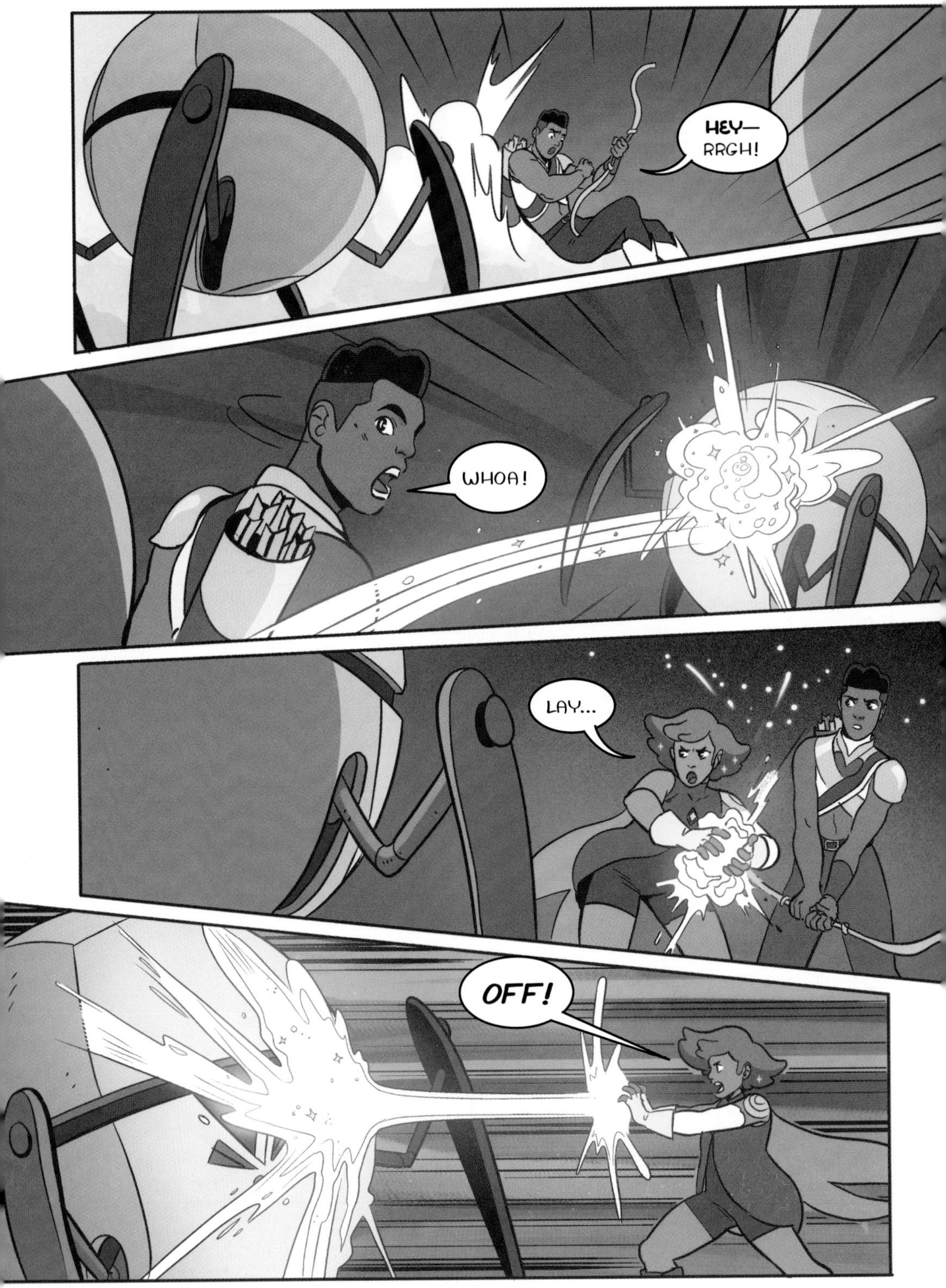
HEY—
RRGH!
WHOA!
LAY...
OFF!

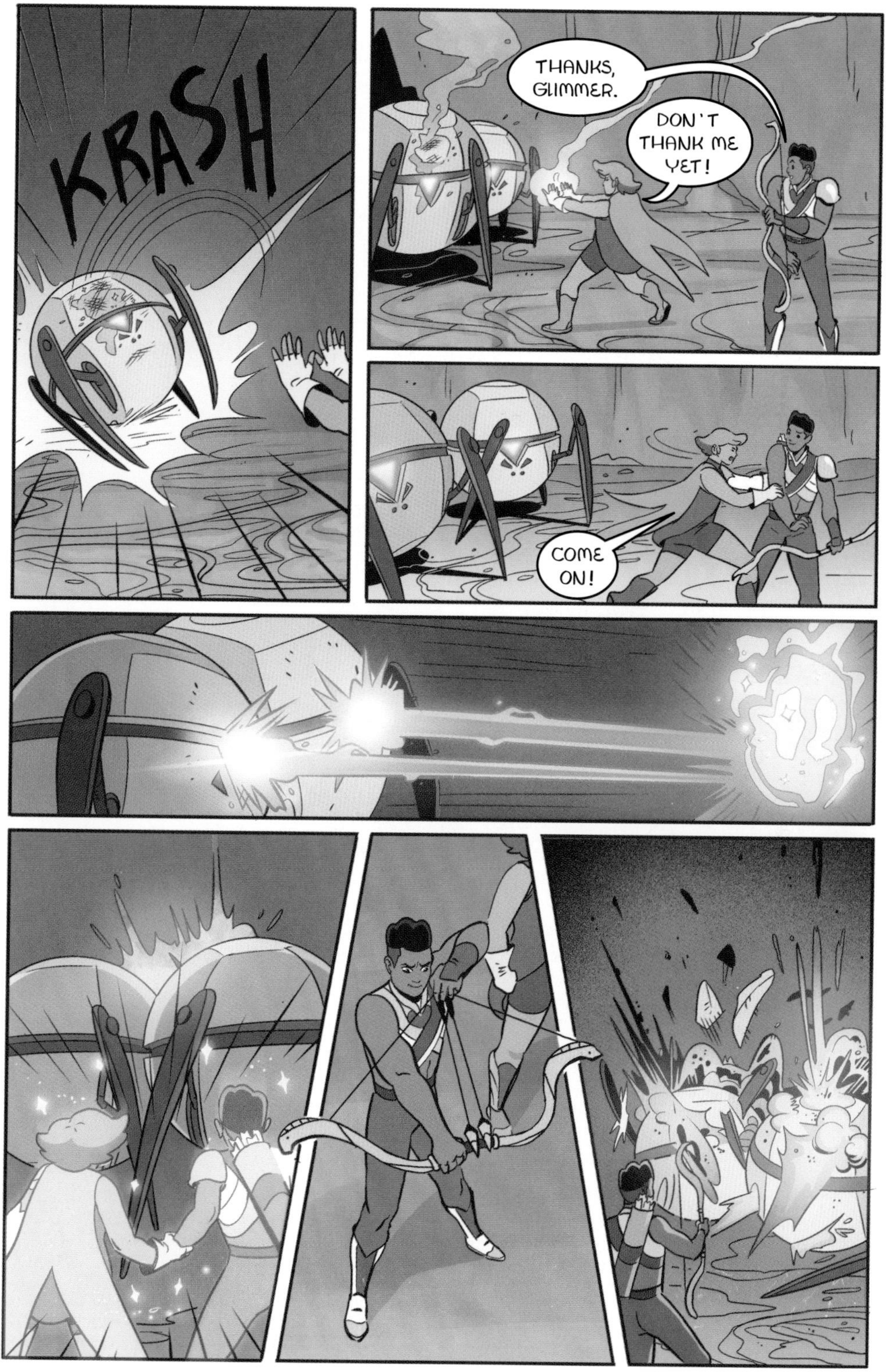
KRASH
THANKS, GLIMMER.
DON'T THANK ME YET!
COME ON!

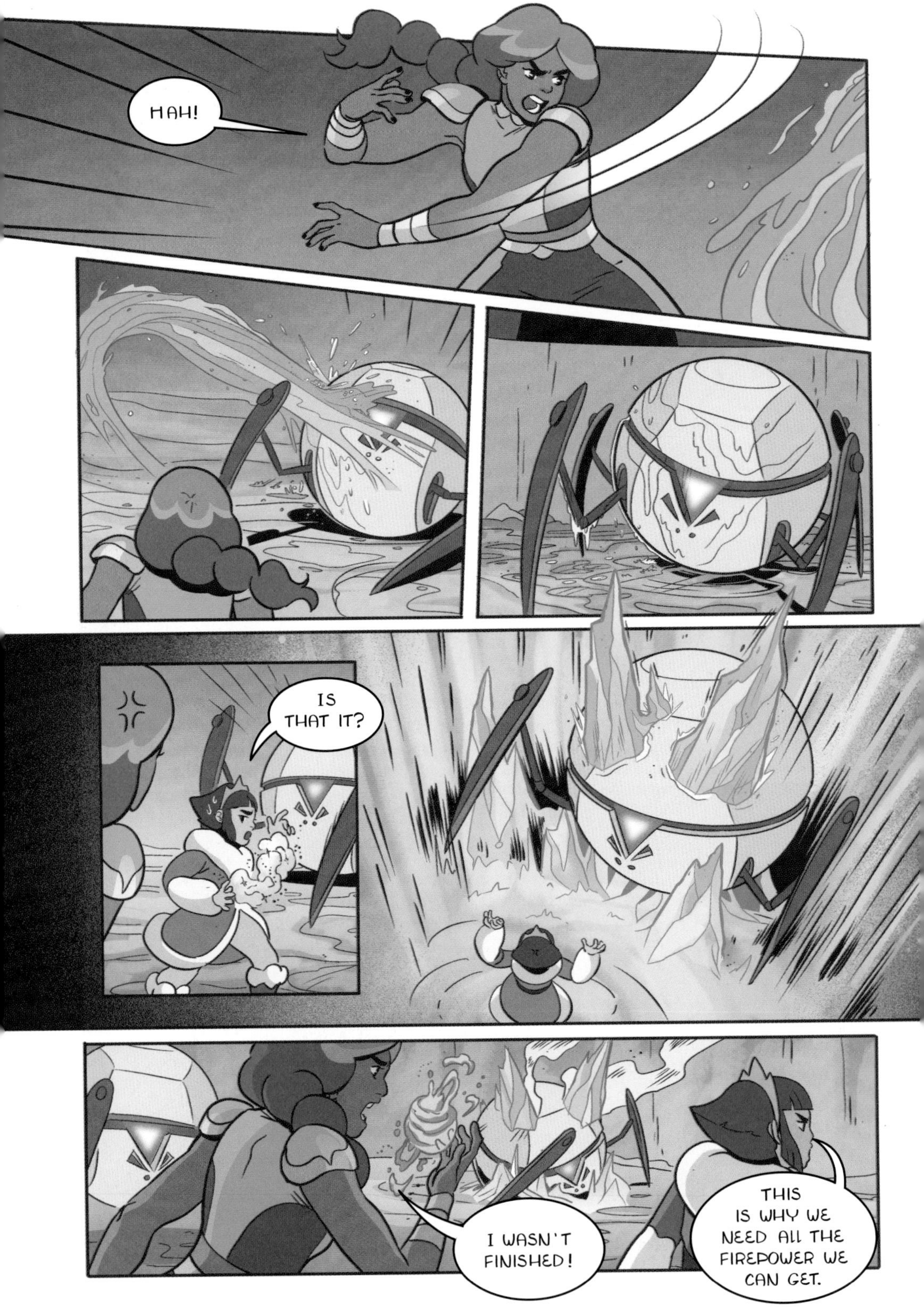
HAH!
IS THAT IT?
I WASN'T FINISHED!
THIS IS WHY WE NEED ALL THE FIREPOWER WE CAN GET.

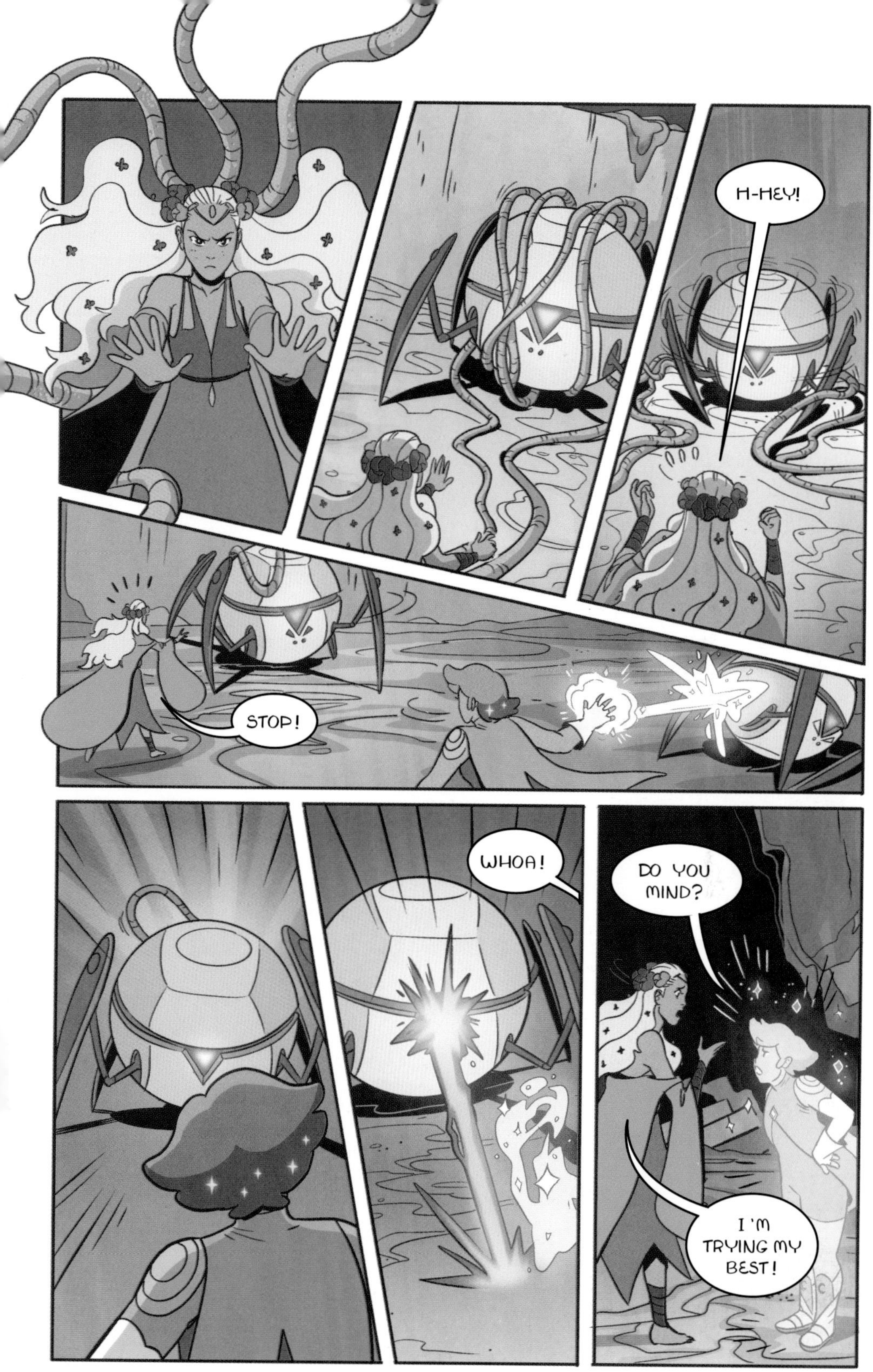
H-HEY!
STOP!
WHOA!
DO YOU MIND?
I'M TRYING MY BEST!

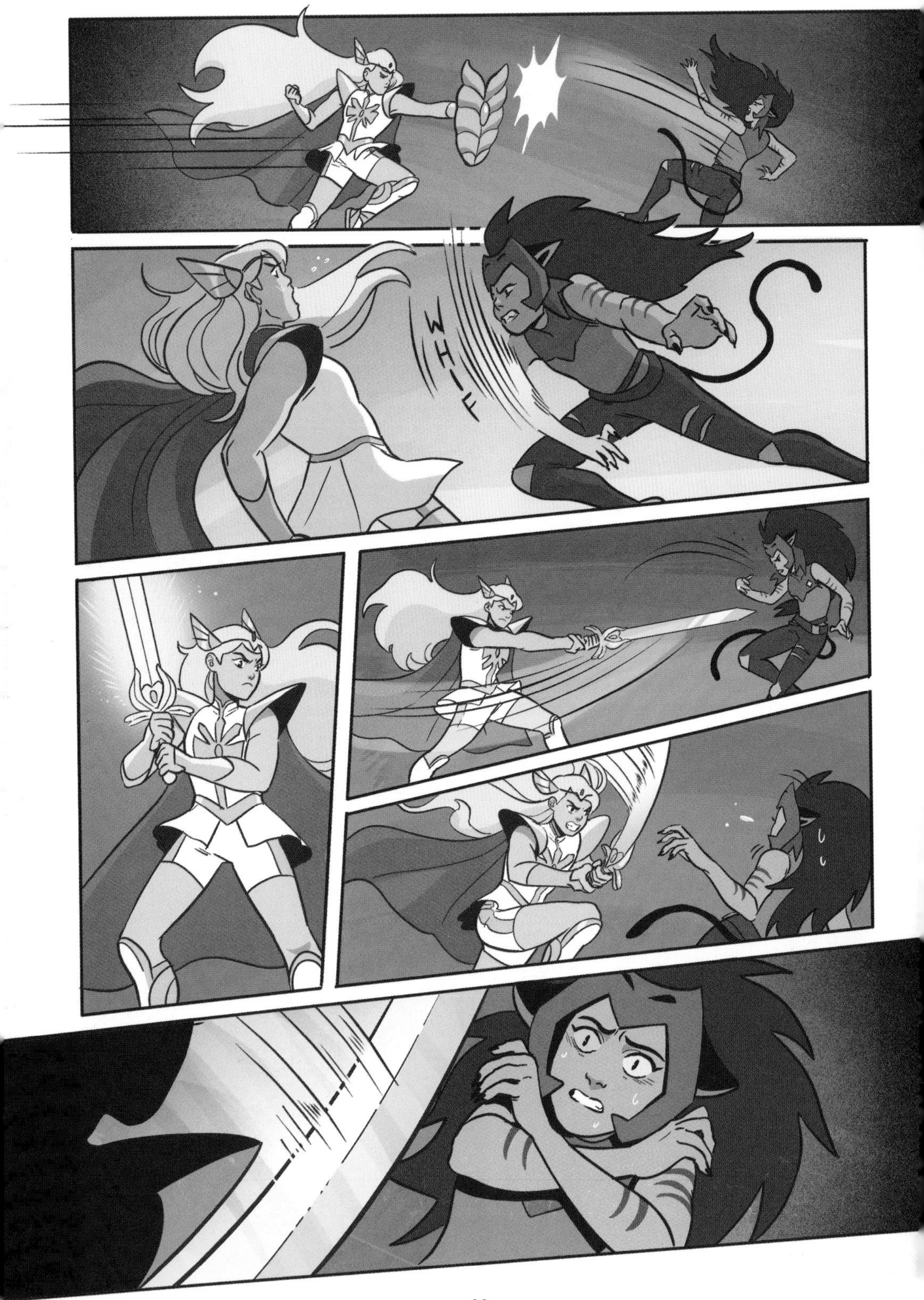
WHIFF

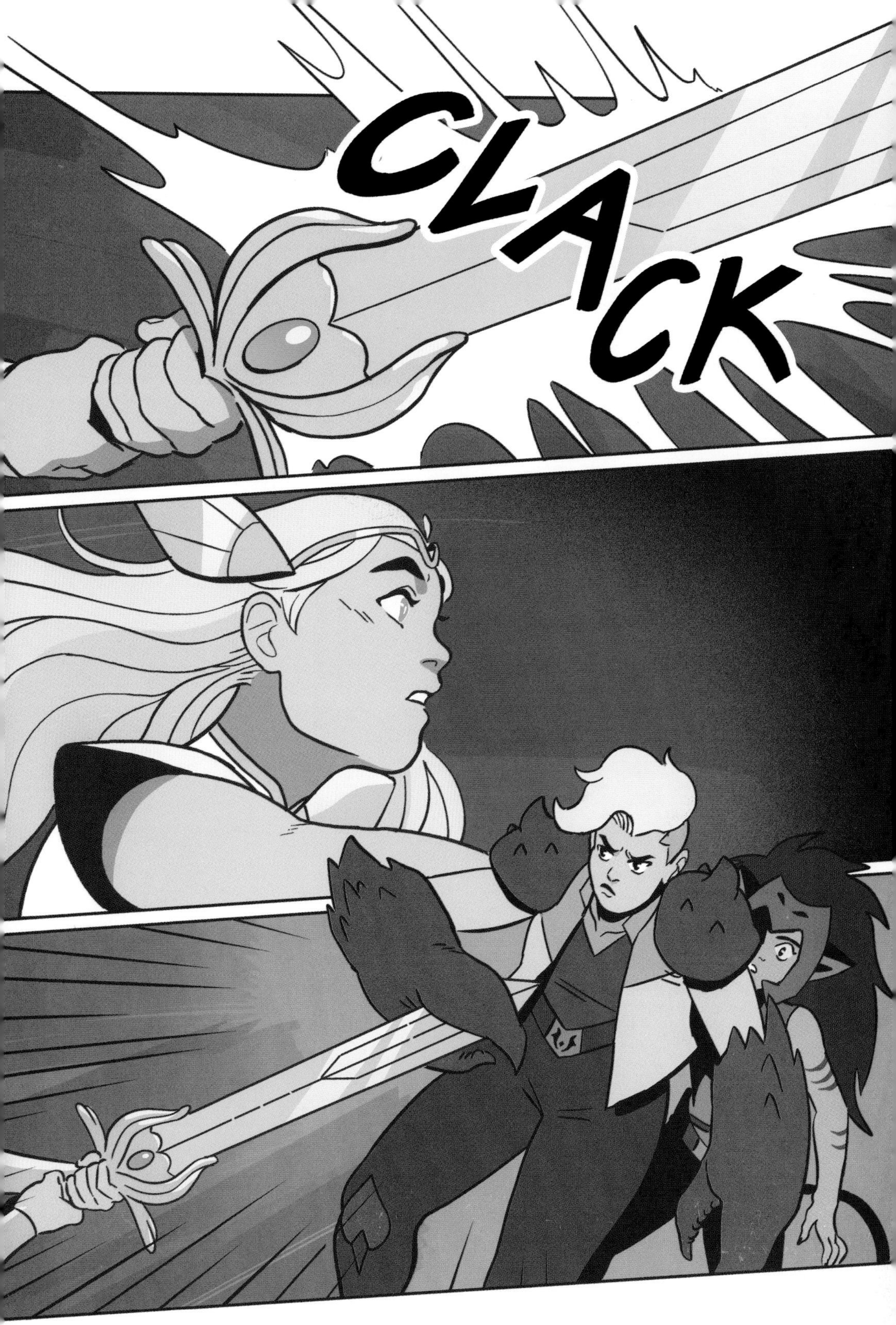
CLACK

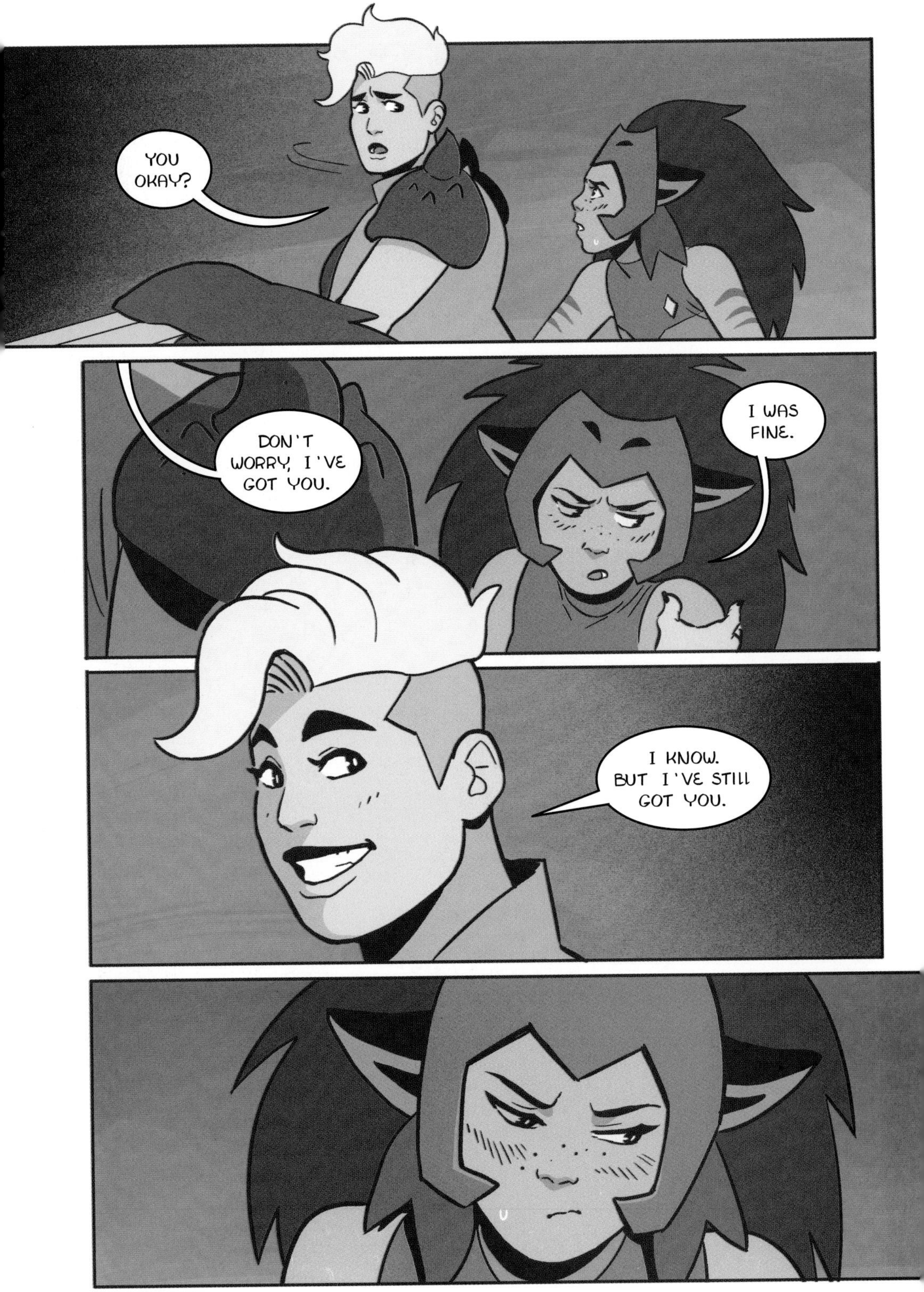
YOU OKAY?
DON'T WORRY, I'VE GOT YOU.
I WAS FINE.
I KNOW. BUT I'VE STILL GOT YOU.

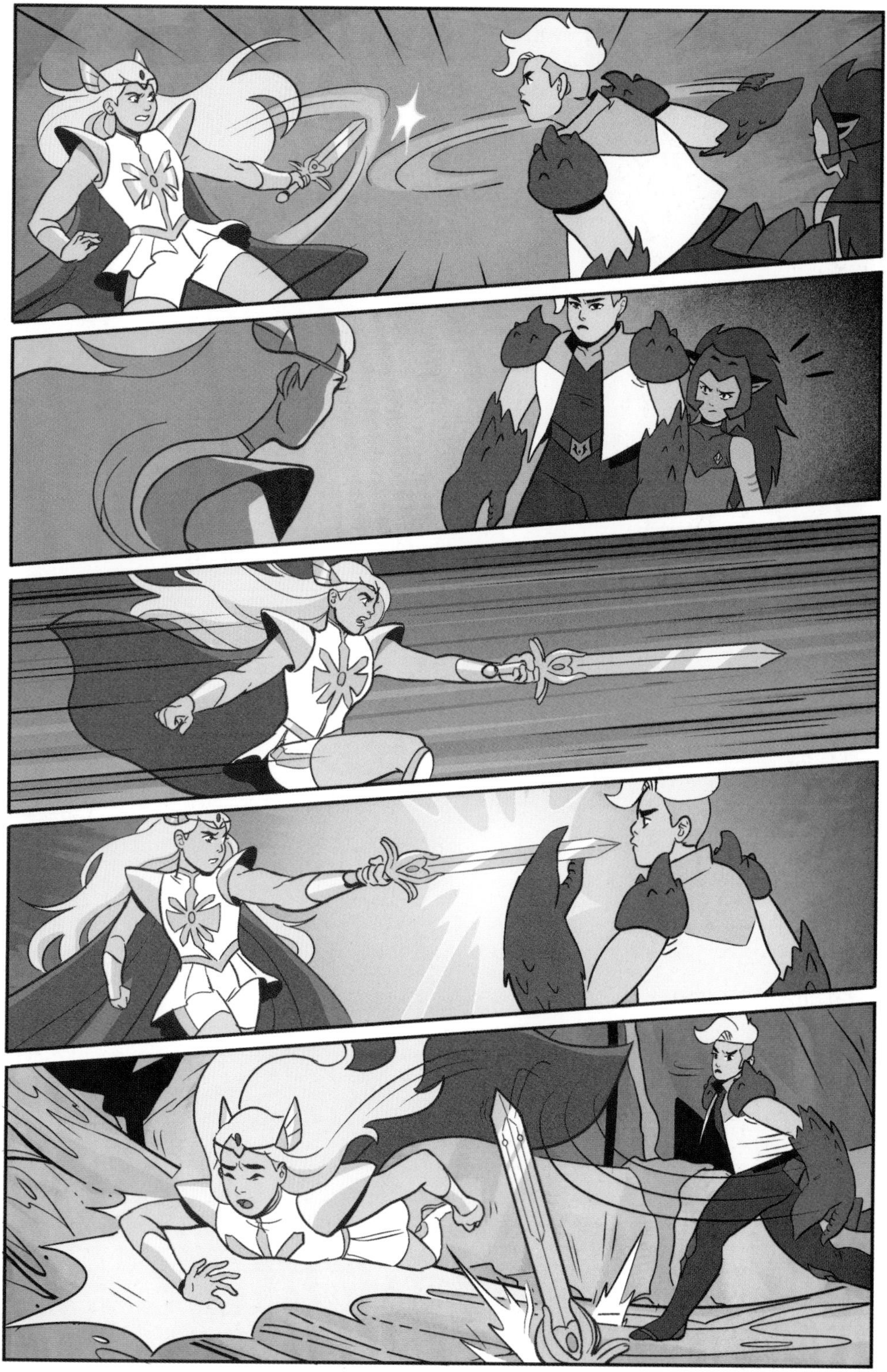

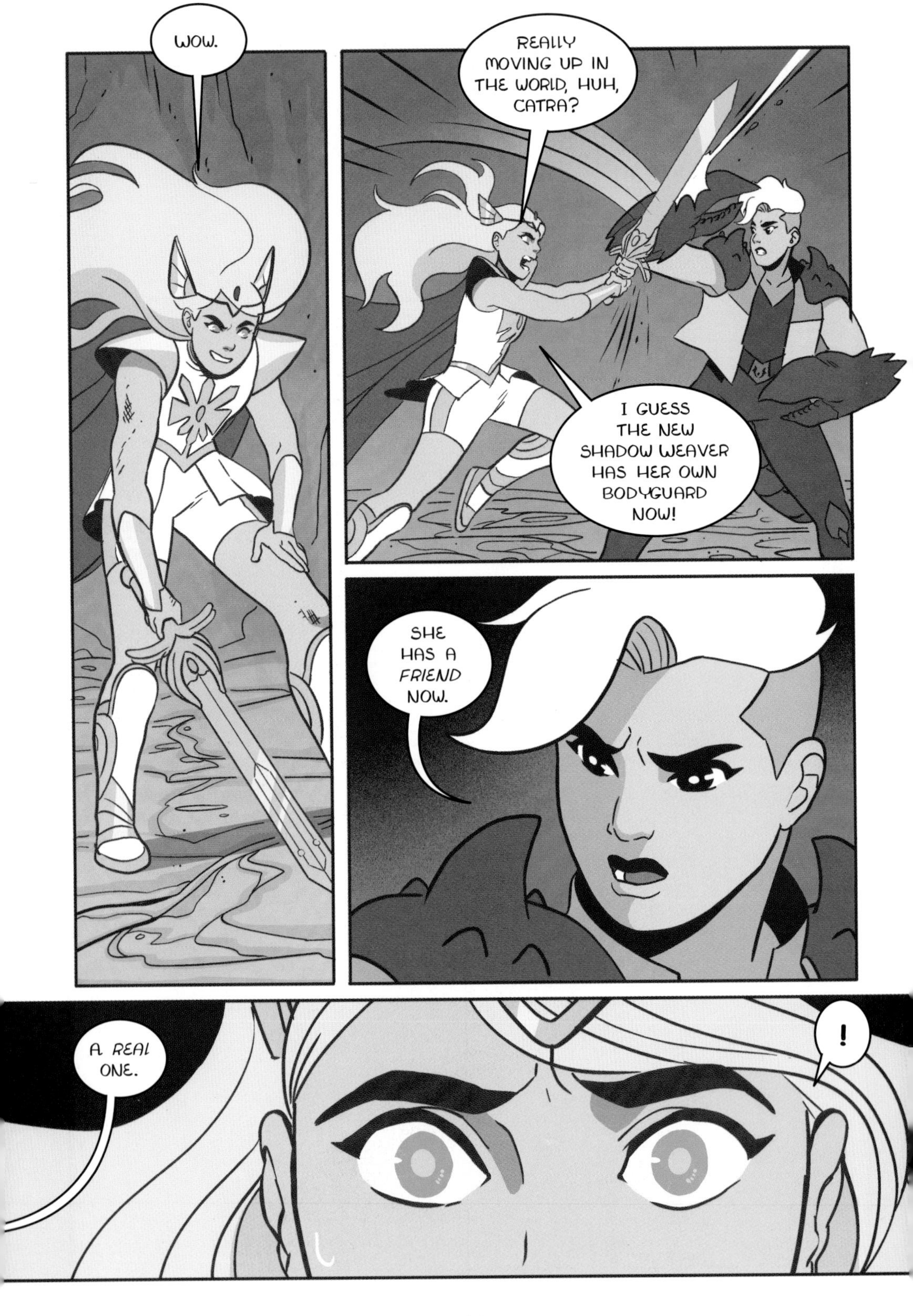
WOW.
REALLY MOVING UP IN THE WORLD, HUH, CATRA?
I GUESS THE NEW SHADOW WEAVER HAS HER OWN BODYGUARD NOW!
SHE HAS A *FRIEND* NOW.
A *REAL* ONE.
!

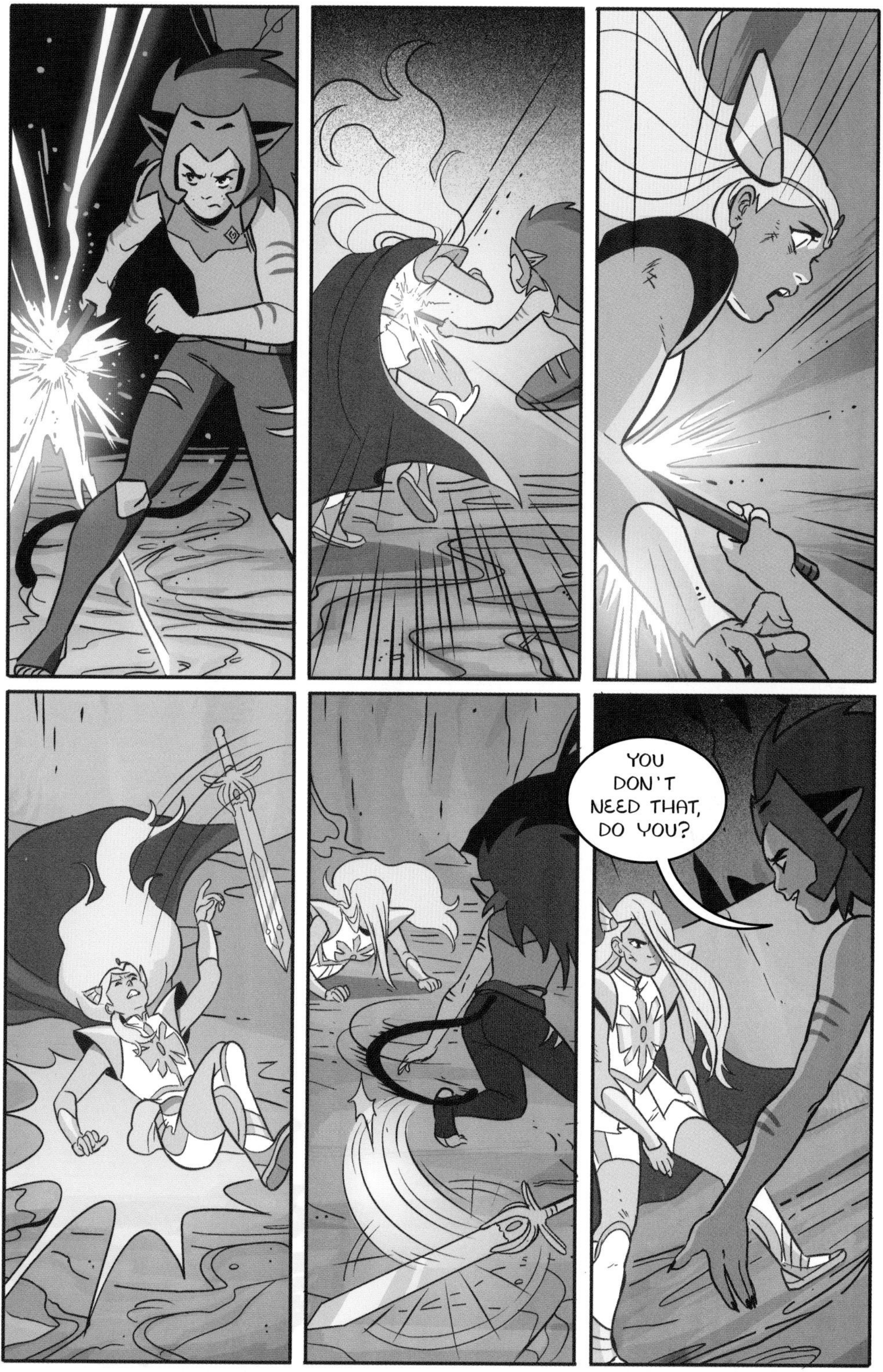
YOU DON'T NEED THAT, DO YOU?

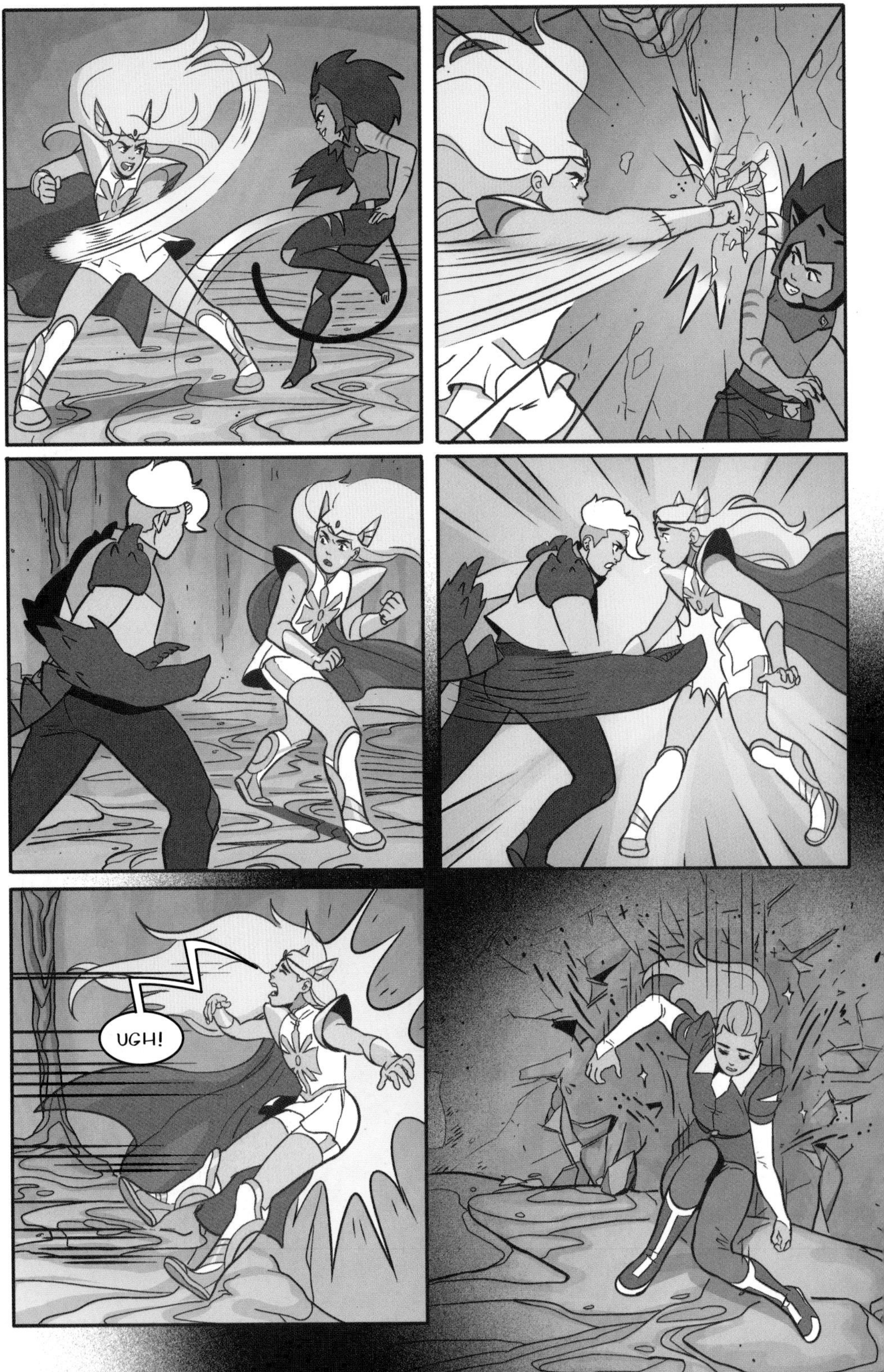
UGH!

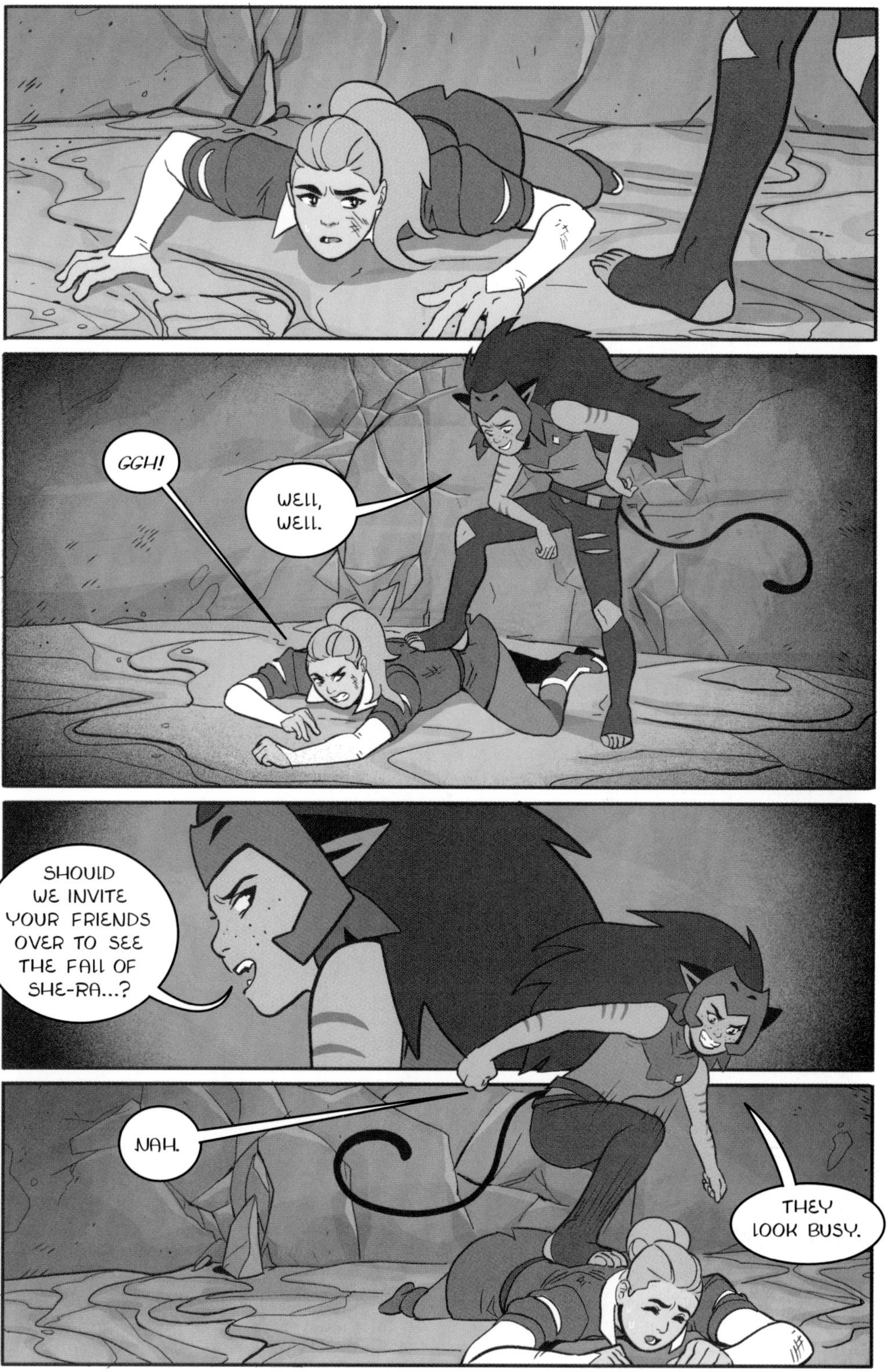
GGH!
WELL, WELL.
SHOULD WE INVITE YOUR FRIENDS OVER TO SEE THE FALL OF SHE-RA...?
NAH.
THEY LOOK BUSY.

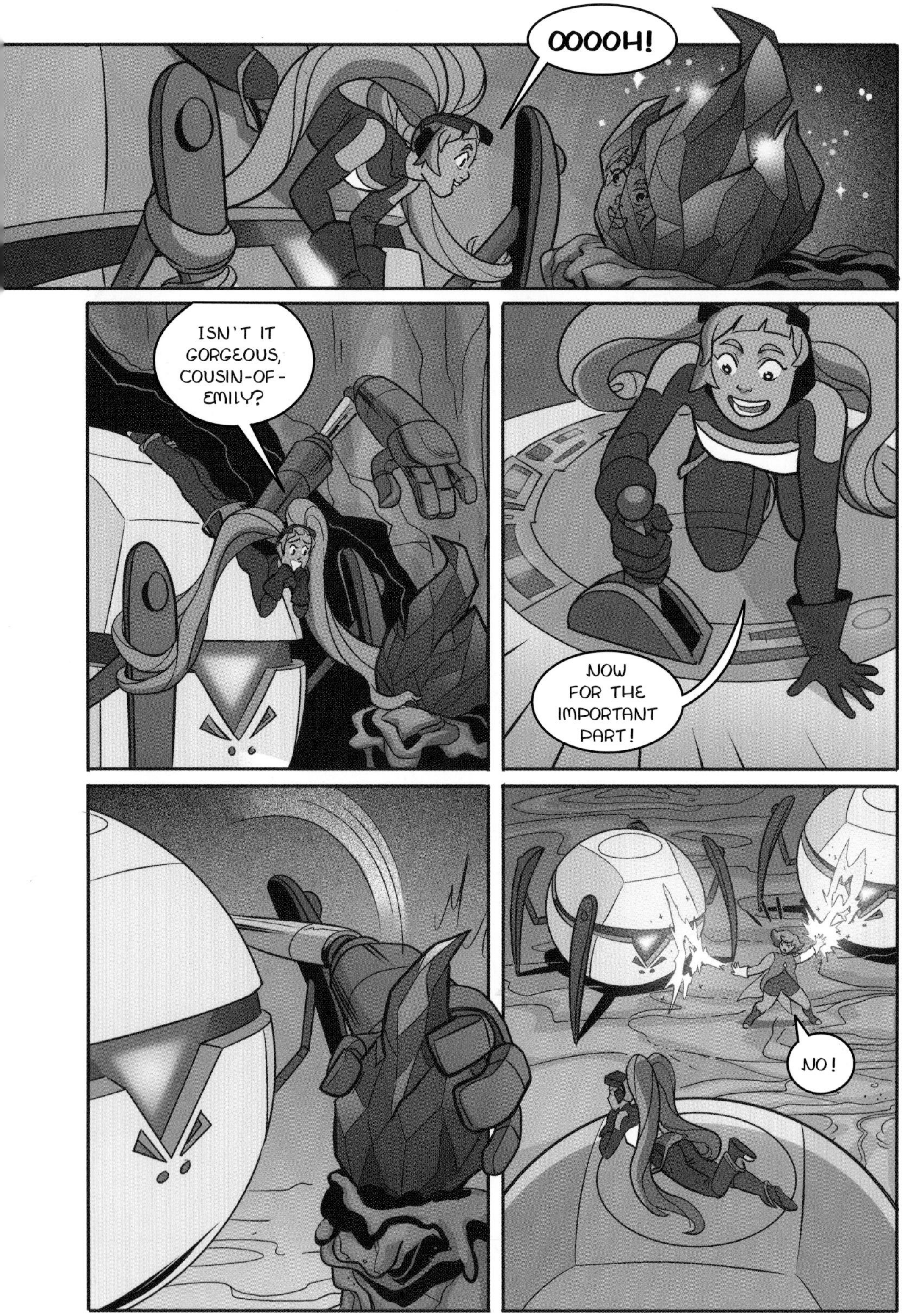
OOOOH!
ISN'T IT GORGEOUS, COUSIN-OF-EMILY?
NOW FOR THE IMPORTANT PART!
NO!

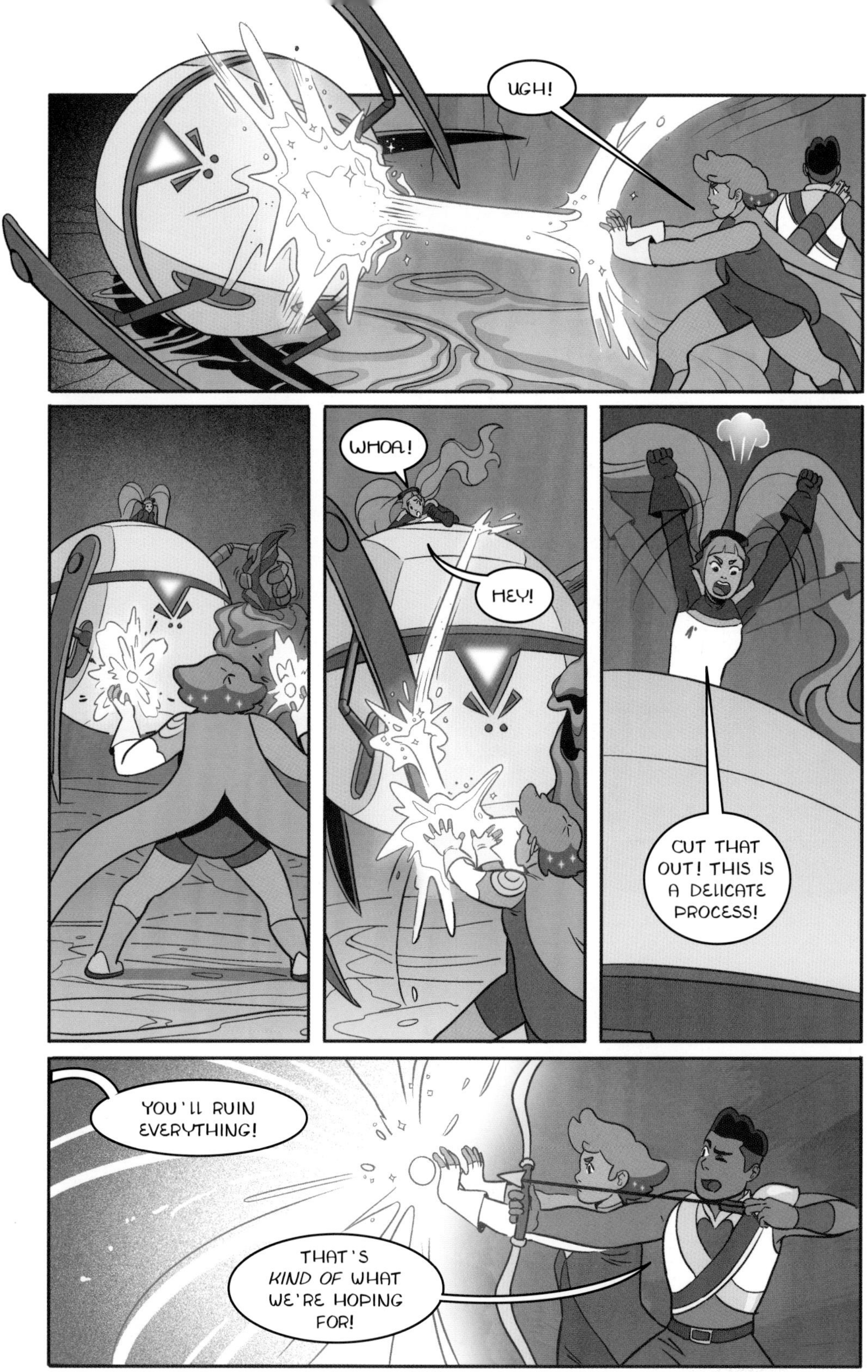
UGH!
WHOA!
HEY!
CUT THAT OUT! THIS IS A DELICATE PROCESS!
YOU'LL RUIN EVERYTHING!
THAT'S *KIND OF* WHAT WE'RE HOPING FOR!

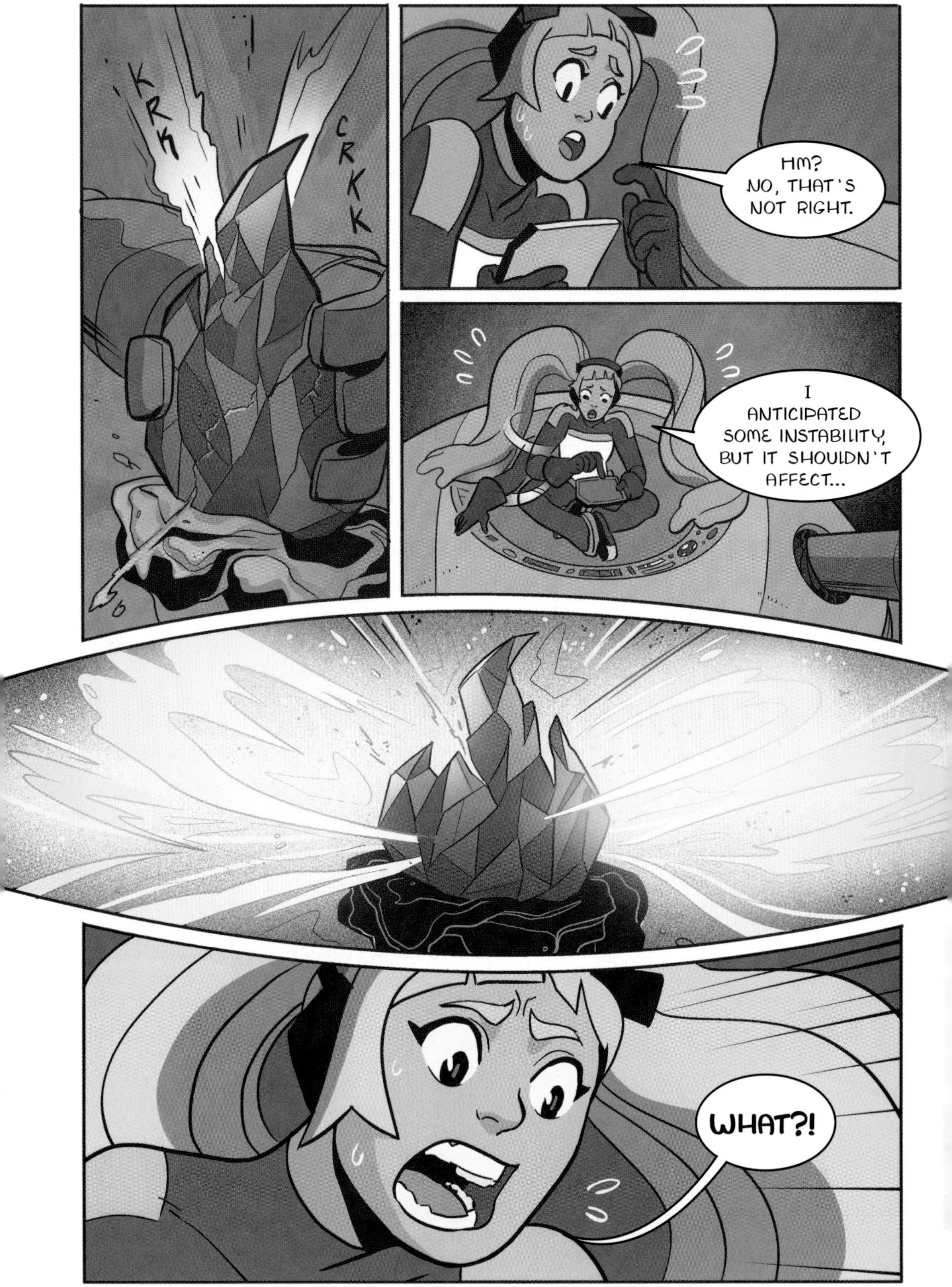
KRK
CRKK
HM? NO, THAT'S NOT RIGHT.
I ANTICIPATED SOME INSTABILITY, BUT IT SHOULDN'T AFFECT...
WHAT?!

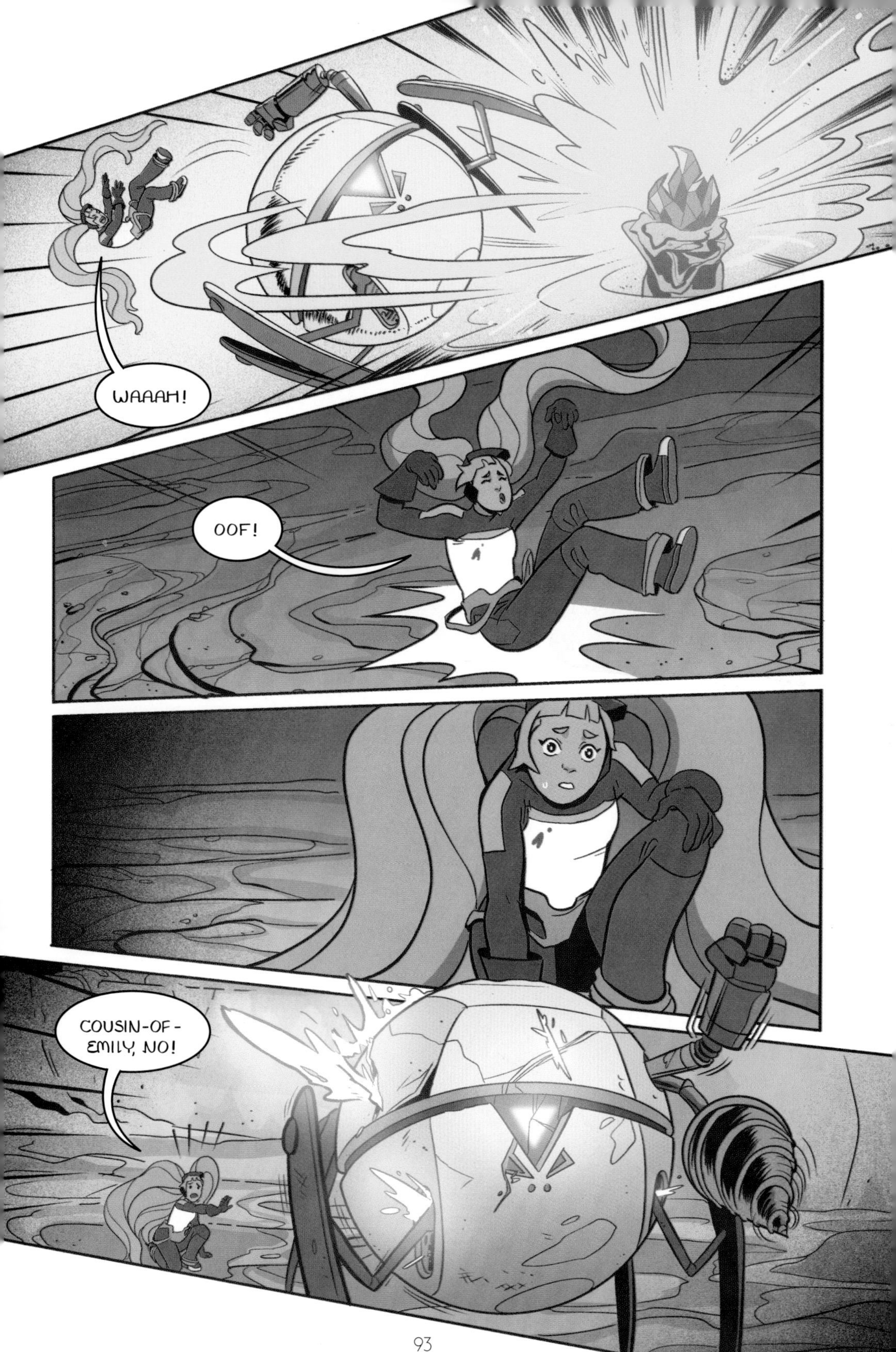
WAAAH!
OOF!
COUSIN-OF-EMILY, NO!

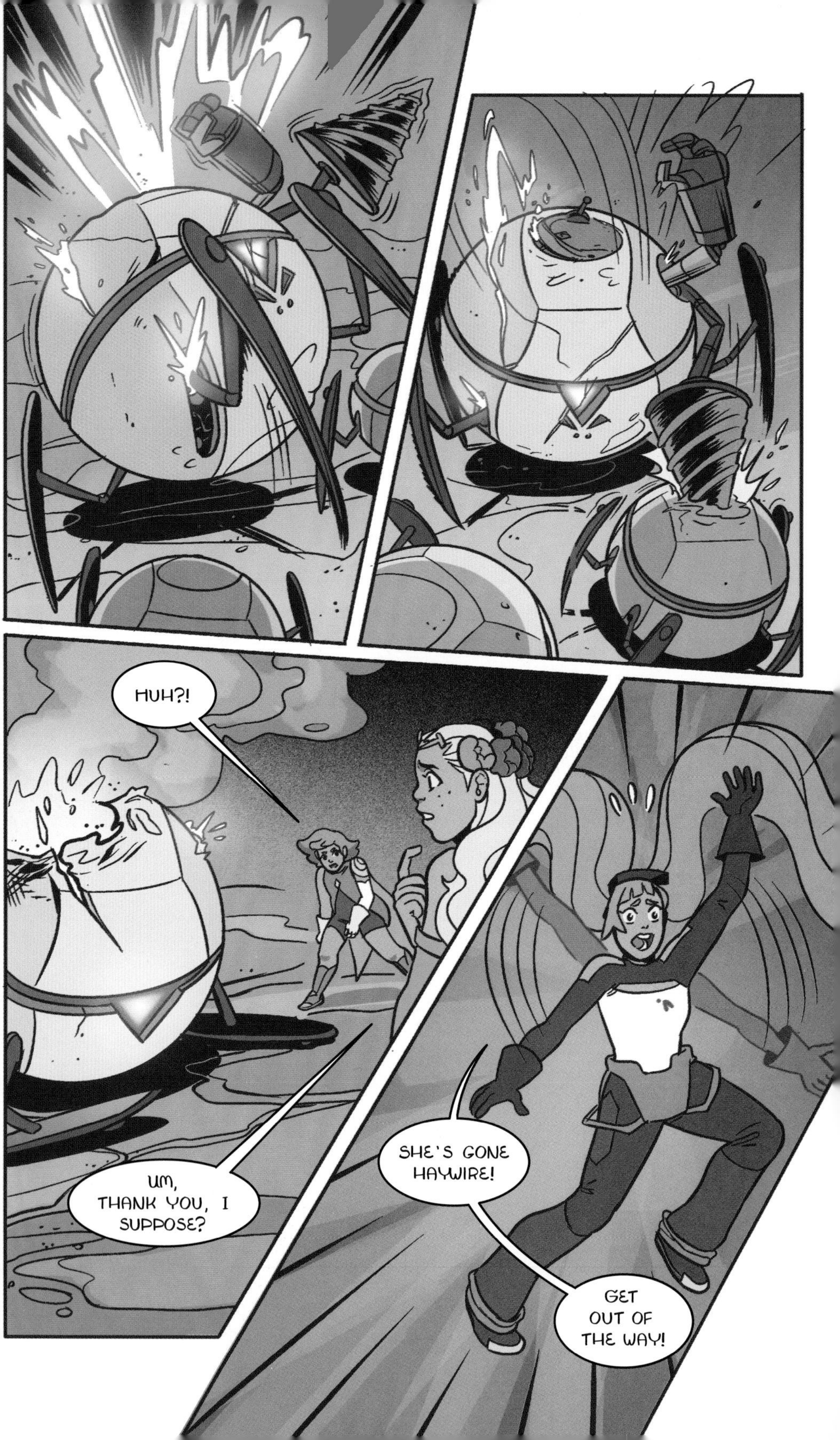
HUH?!
UM, THANK YOU, I SUPPOSE?
SHE'S GONE HAYWIRE!
GET OUT OF THE WAY!

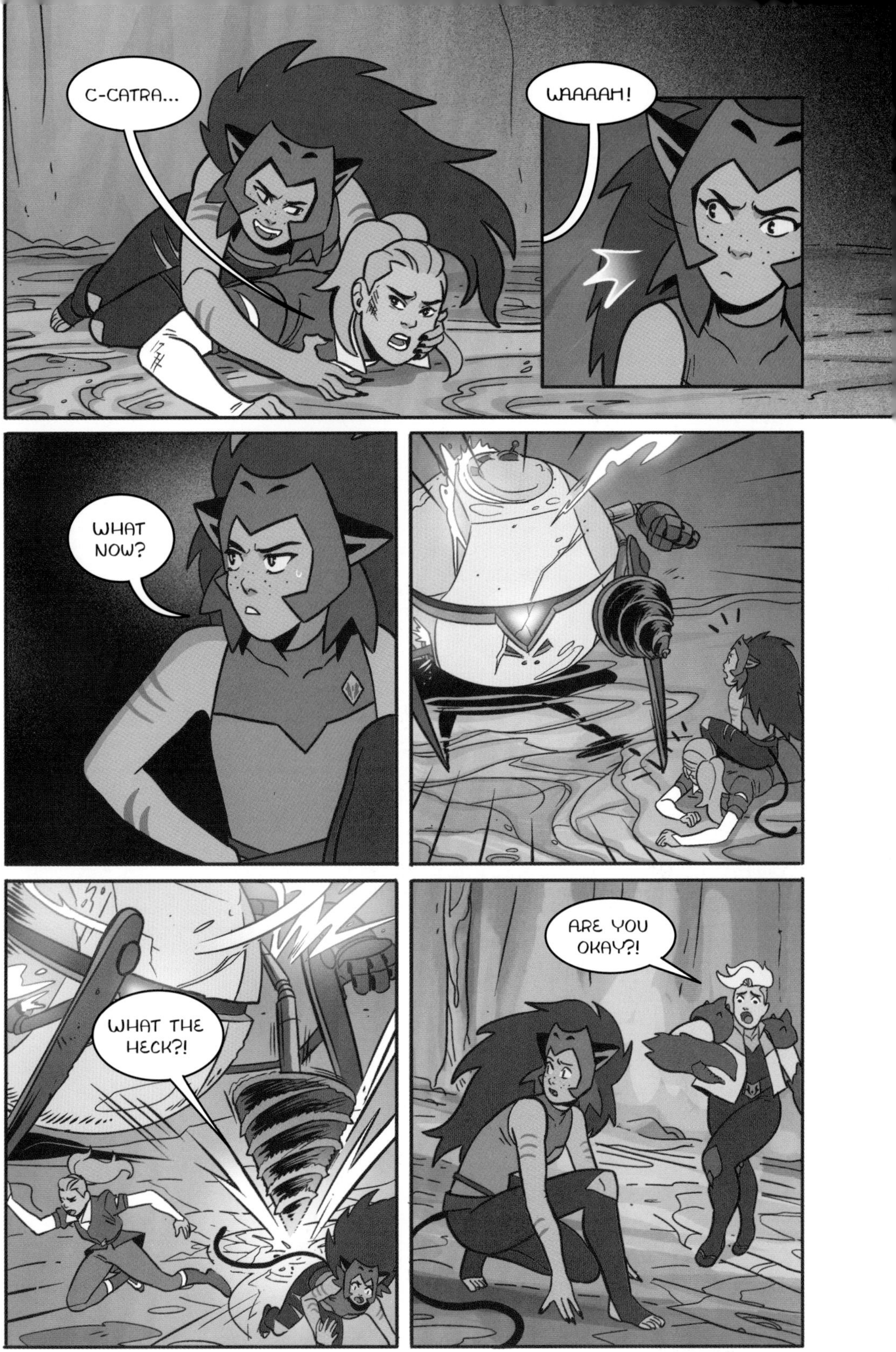
C-CATRA...
WAAAAH!
WHAT NOW?
WHAT THE HECK?!
ARE YOU OKAY?!

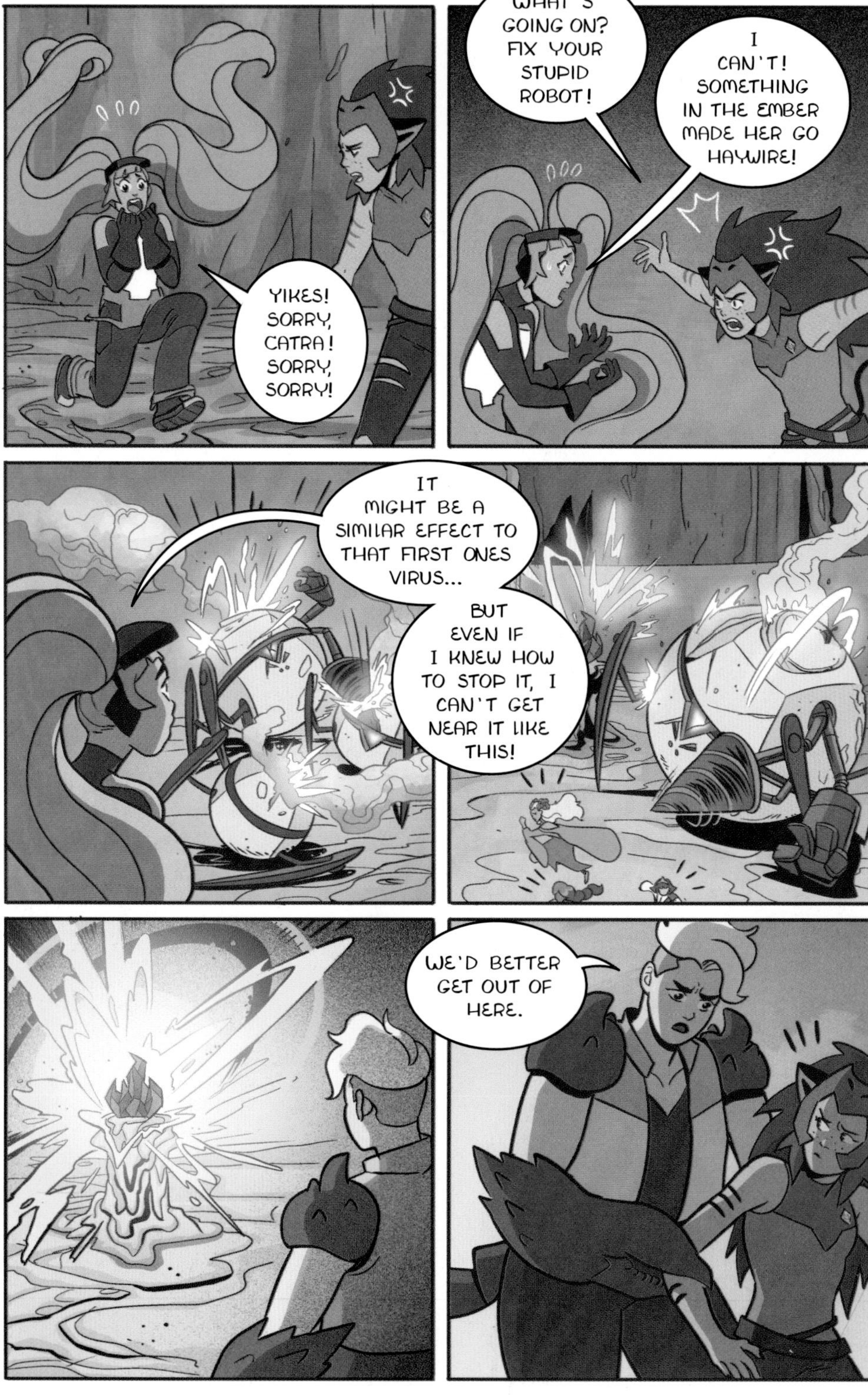
YIKES! SORRY, CATRA! SORRY, SORRY!
WHAT'S GOING ON? FIX YOUR STUPID ROBOT!
I CAN'T! SOMETHING IN THE EMBER MADE HER GO HAYWIRE!
IT MIGHT BE A SIMILAR EFFECT TO THAT FIRST ONES VIRUS...
BUT EVEN IF I KNEW HOW TO STOP IT, I CAN'T GET NEAR IT LIKE THIS!
WE'D BETTER GET OUT OF HERE.

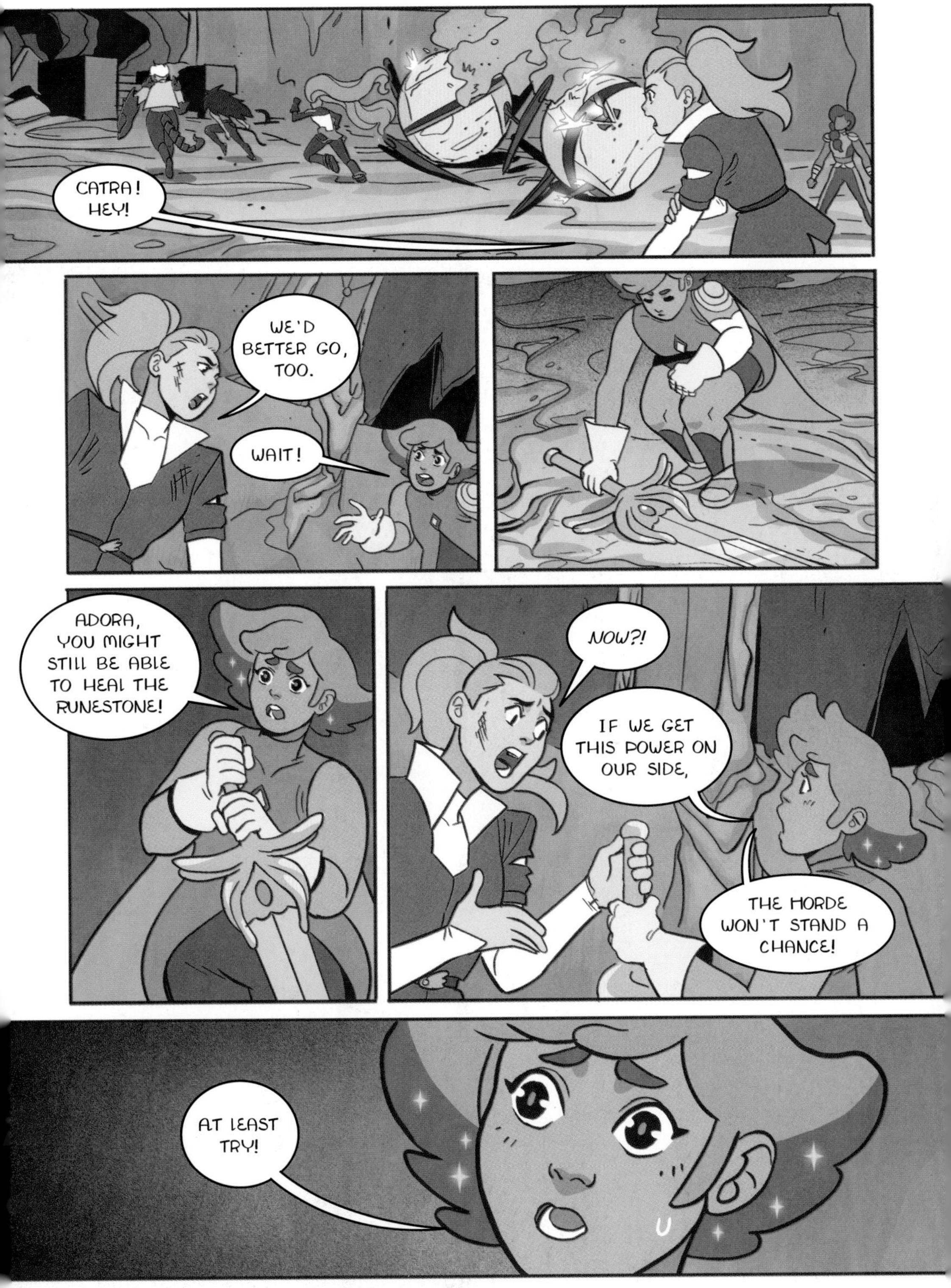
CATRA! HEY!
WE'D BETTER GO, TOO.
WAIT!
ADORA, YOU MIGHT STILL BE ABLE TO HEAL THE RUNESTONE!
NOW?!
IF WE GET THIS POWER ON OUR SIDE,
THE HORDE WON'T STAND A CHANCE!
AT LEAST TRY!

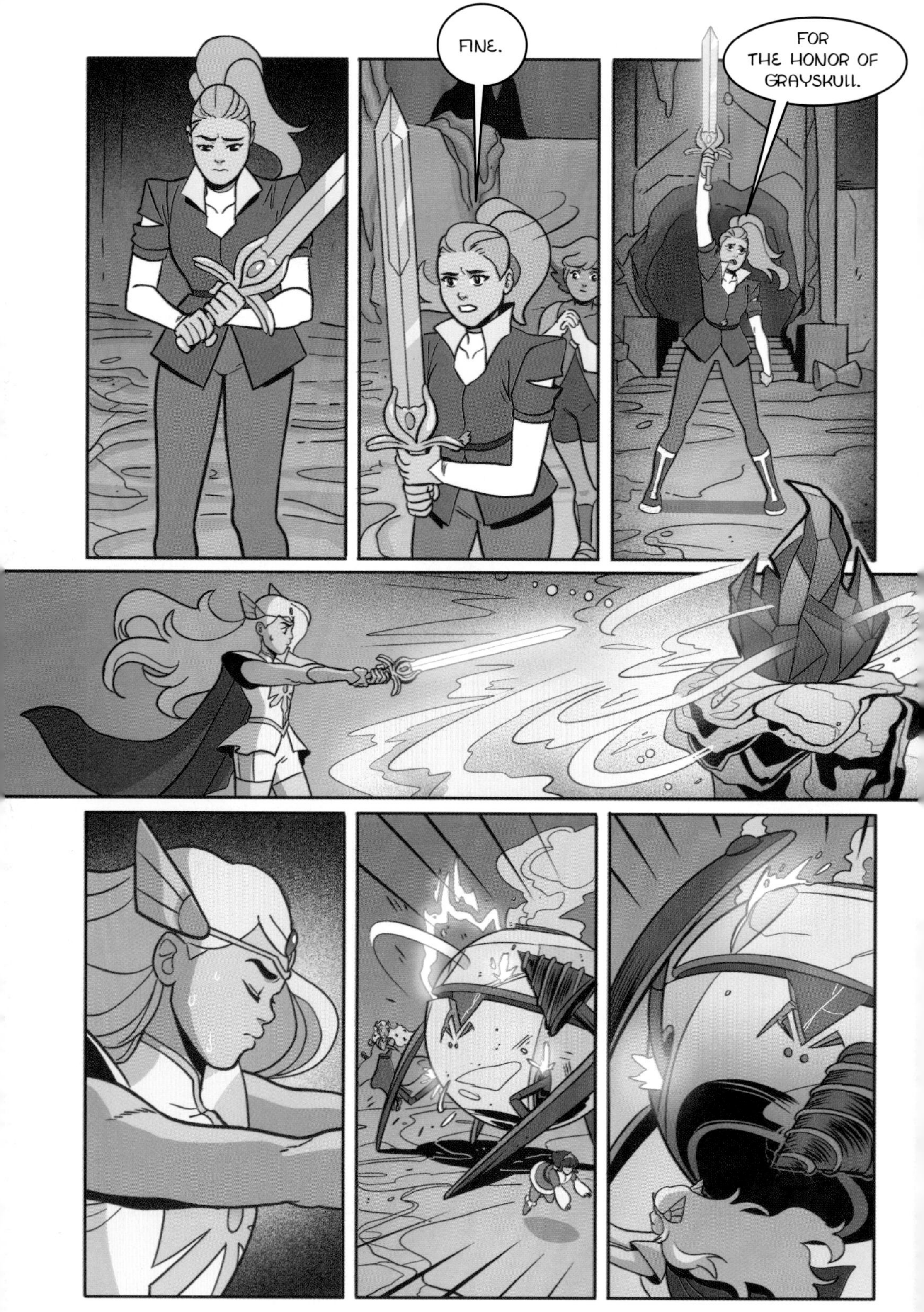
FINE.
FOR THE HONOR OF GRAYSKULL.

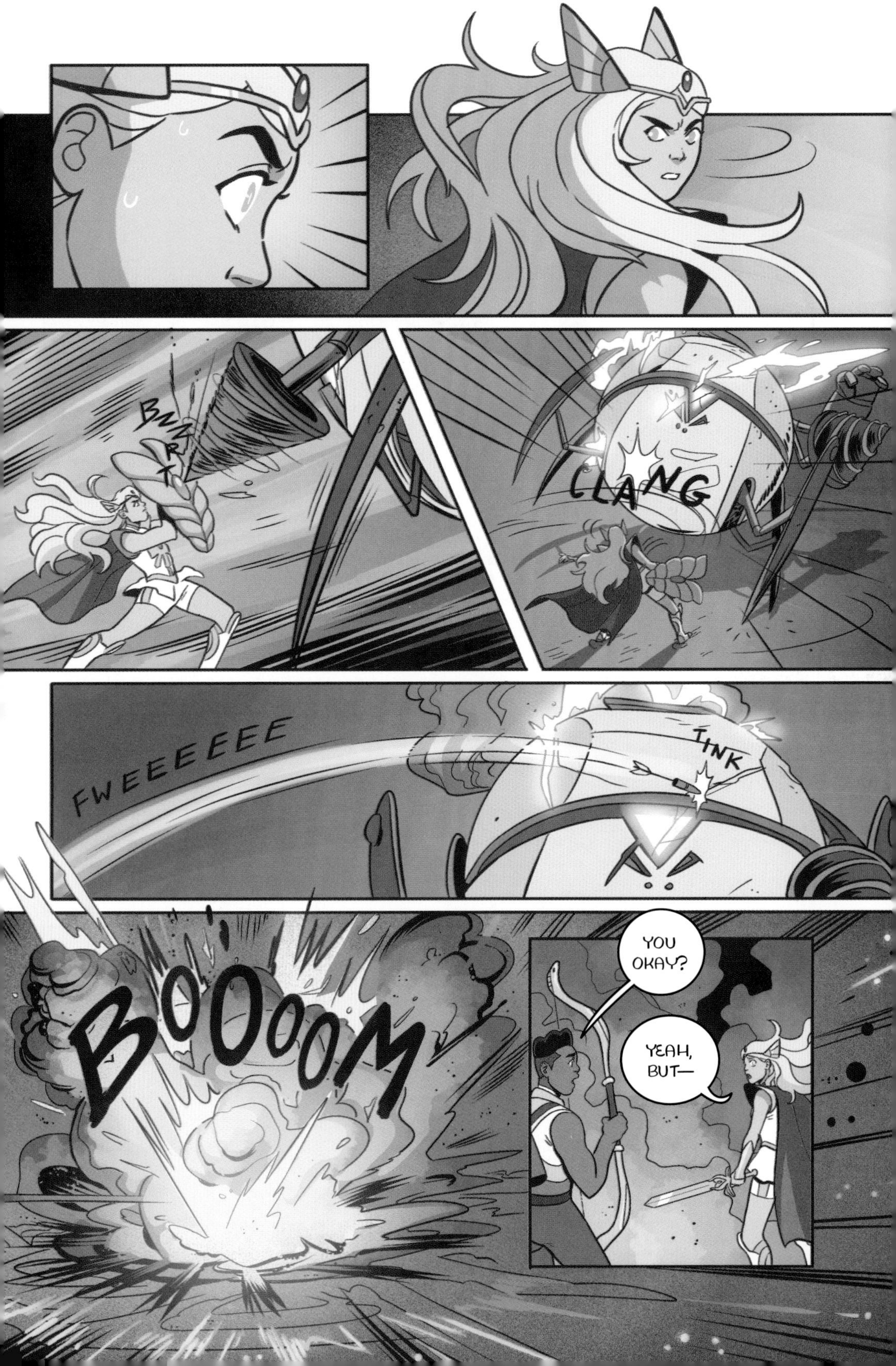
BZZZRT
CLANG
FWEEEEEE
TINK
BOOOOOM
YOU OKAY?
YEAH, BUT—

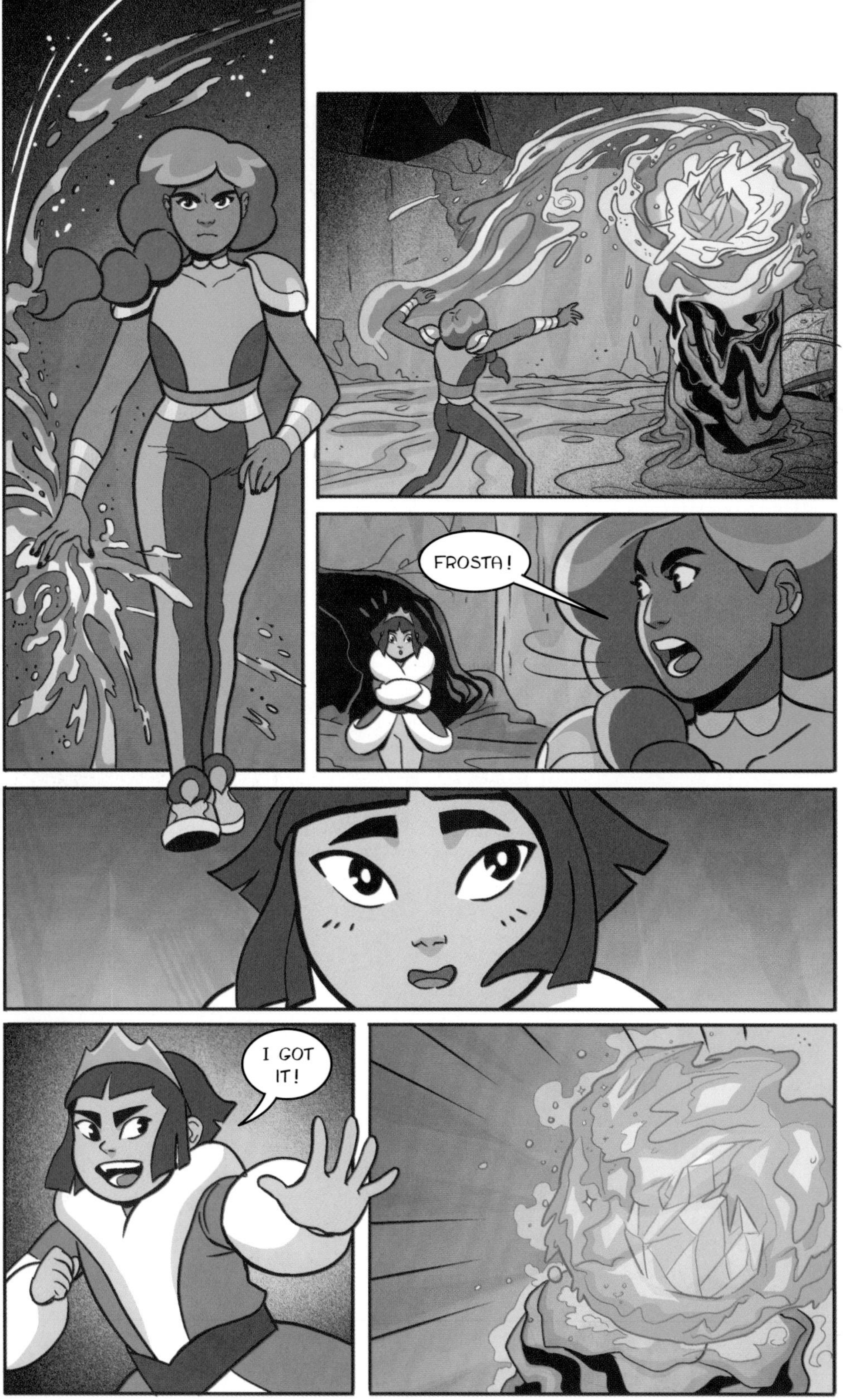
FROSTA!
I GOT IT!

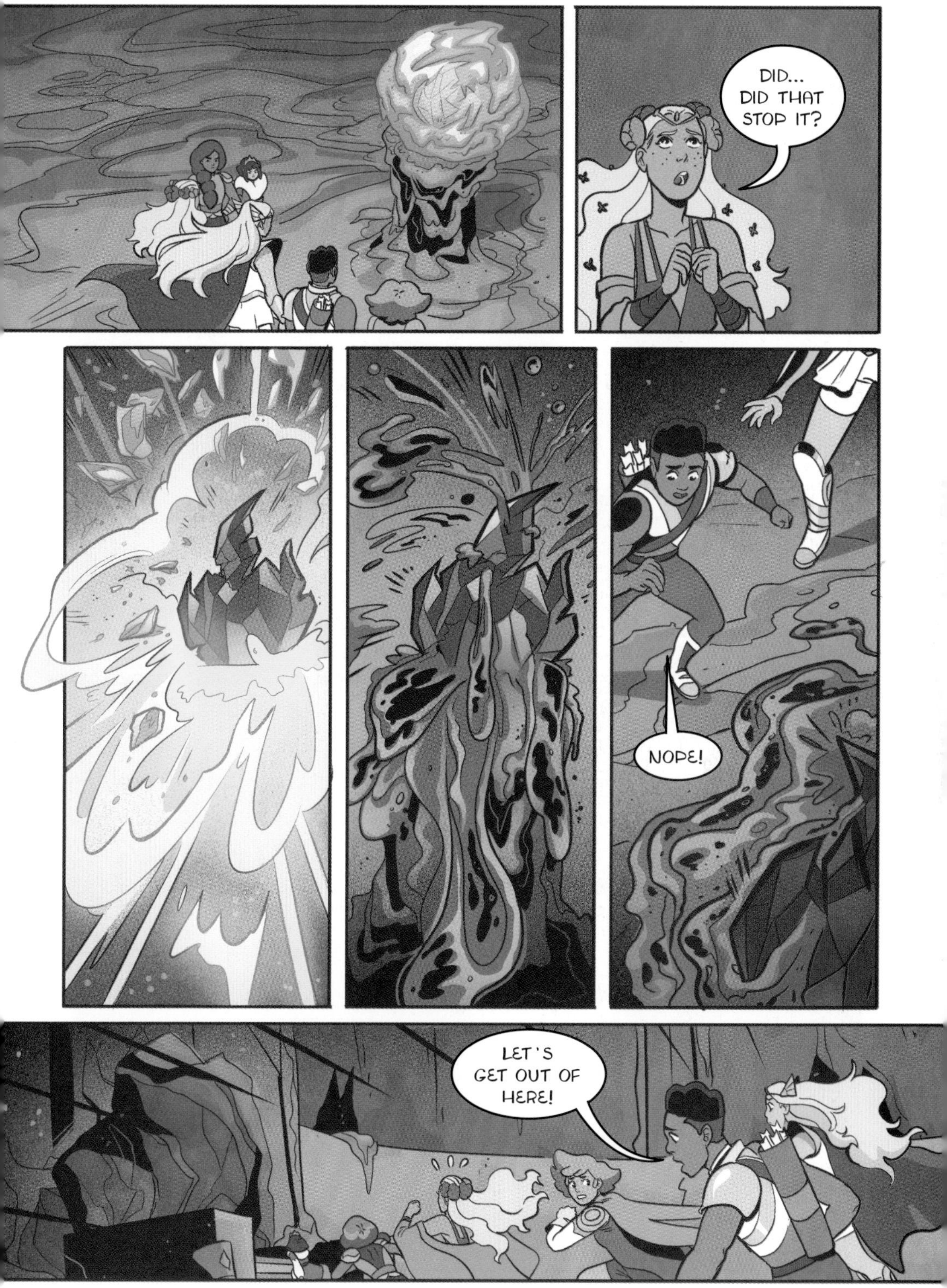
DID... DID THAT STOP IT?
NOPE!
LET'S GET OUT OF HERE!

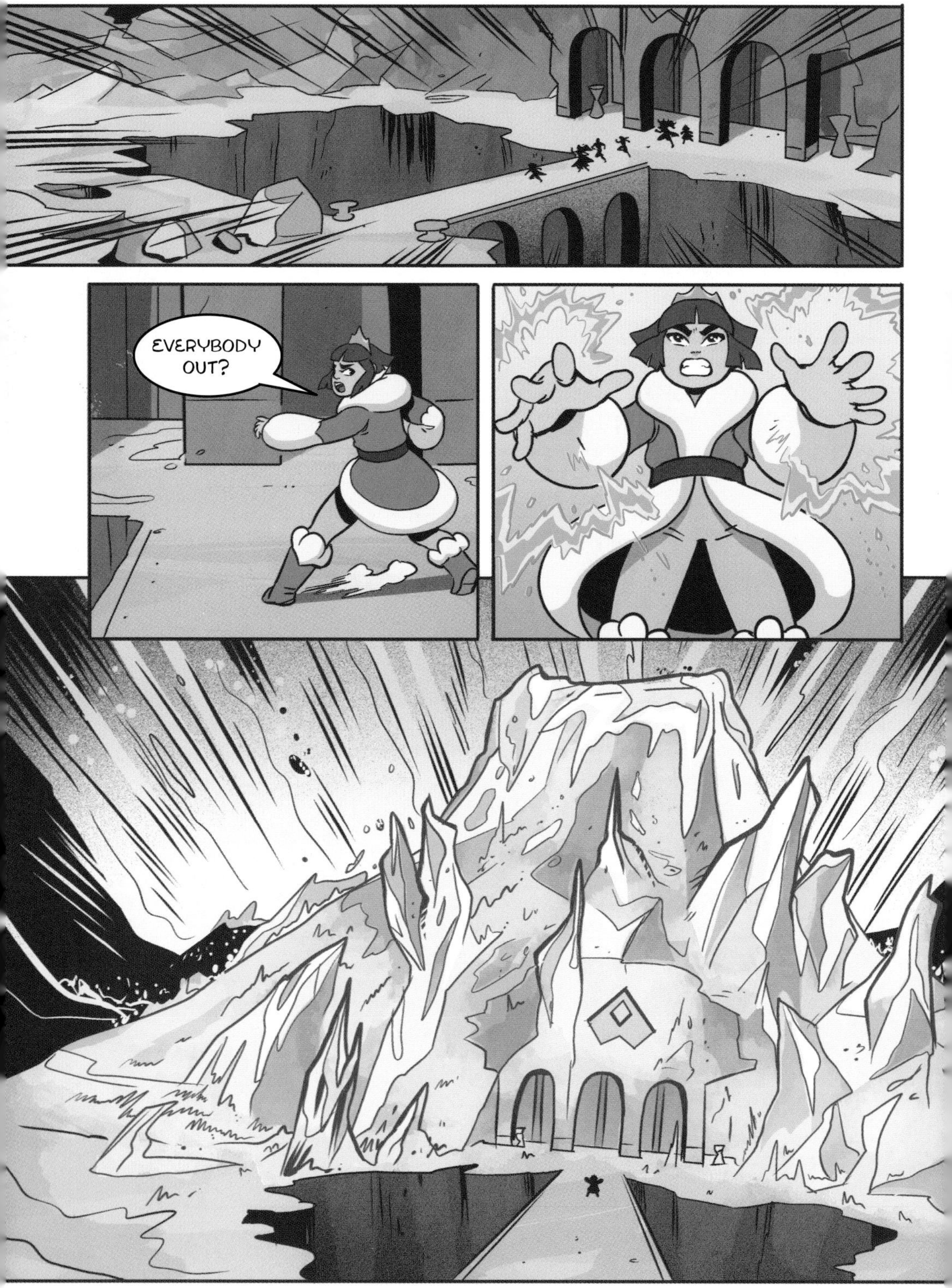
EVERYBODY OUT?

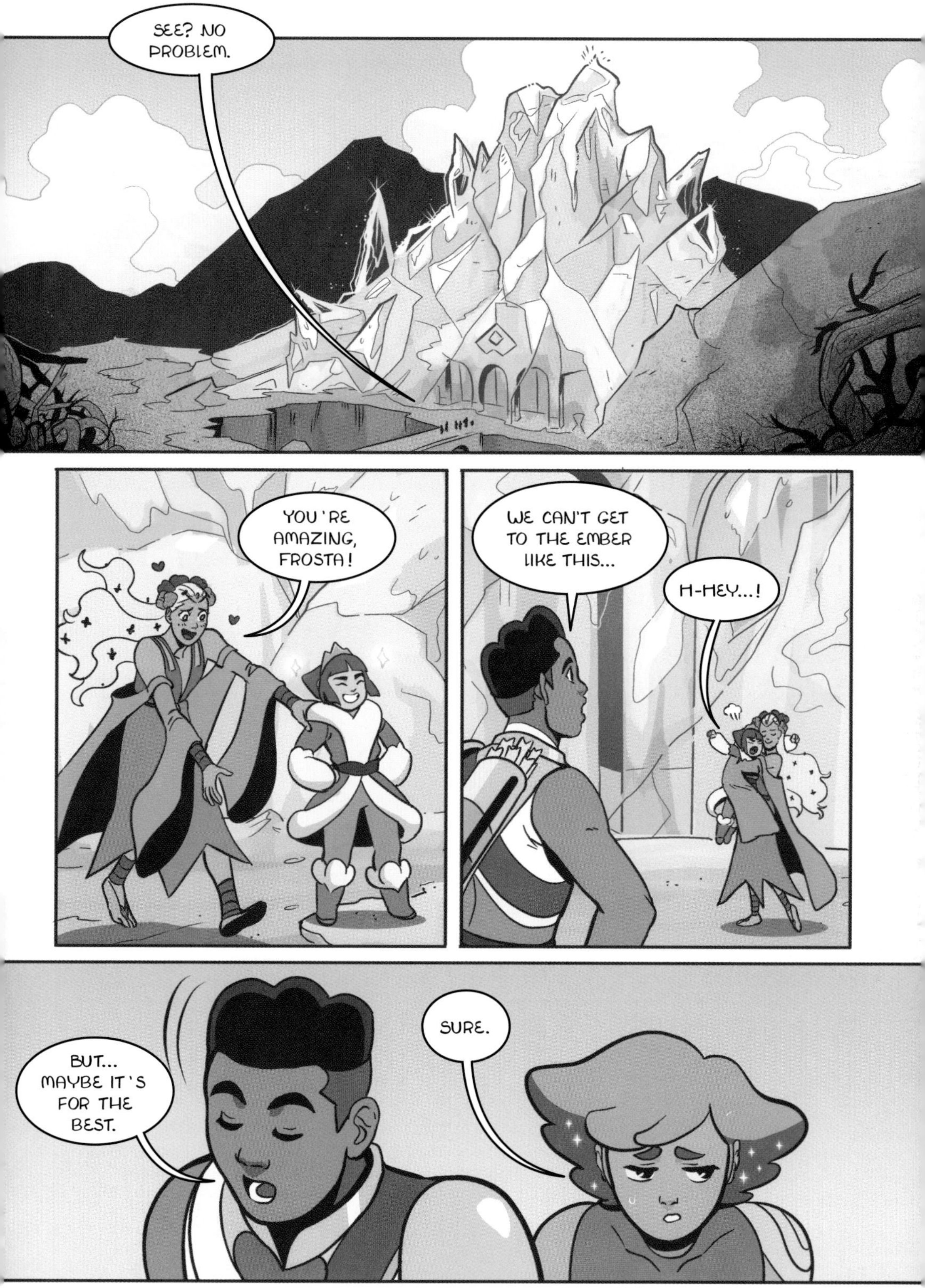
SEE? NO PROBLEM.
YOU'RE AMAZING, FROSTA!
WE CAN'T GET TO THE EMBER LIKE THIS...
H-HEY...!
BUT... MAYBE IT'S FOR THE BEST.
SURE.

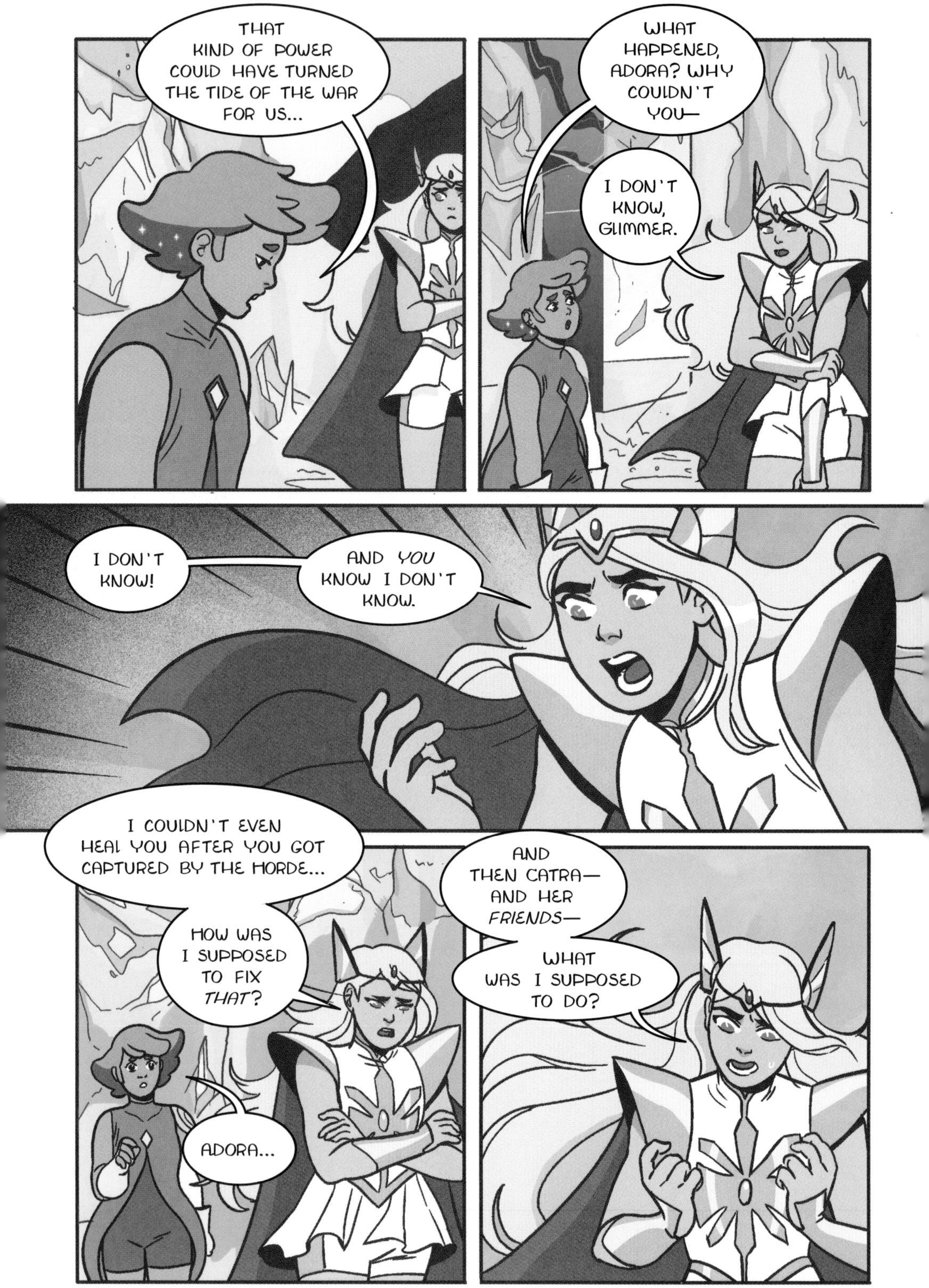
THAT KIND OF POWER COULD HAVE TURNED THE TIDE OF THE WAR FOR US...
WHAT HAPPENED, ADORA? WHY COULDN'T YOU—
I DON'T KNOW, GLIMMER.
I DON'T KNOW!
AND *YOU* KNOW I DON'T KNOW.
I COULDN'T EVEN HEAL YOU AFTER YOU GOT CAPTURED BY THE HORDE...
HOW WAS I SUPPOSED TO FIX *THAT*?
ADORA...
AND THEN CATRA— AND HER *FRIENDS*—
WHAT WAS I SUPPOSED TO DO?

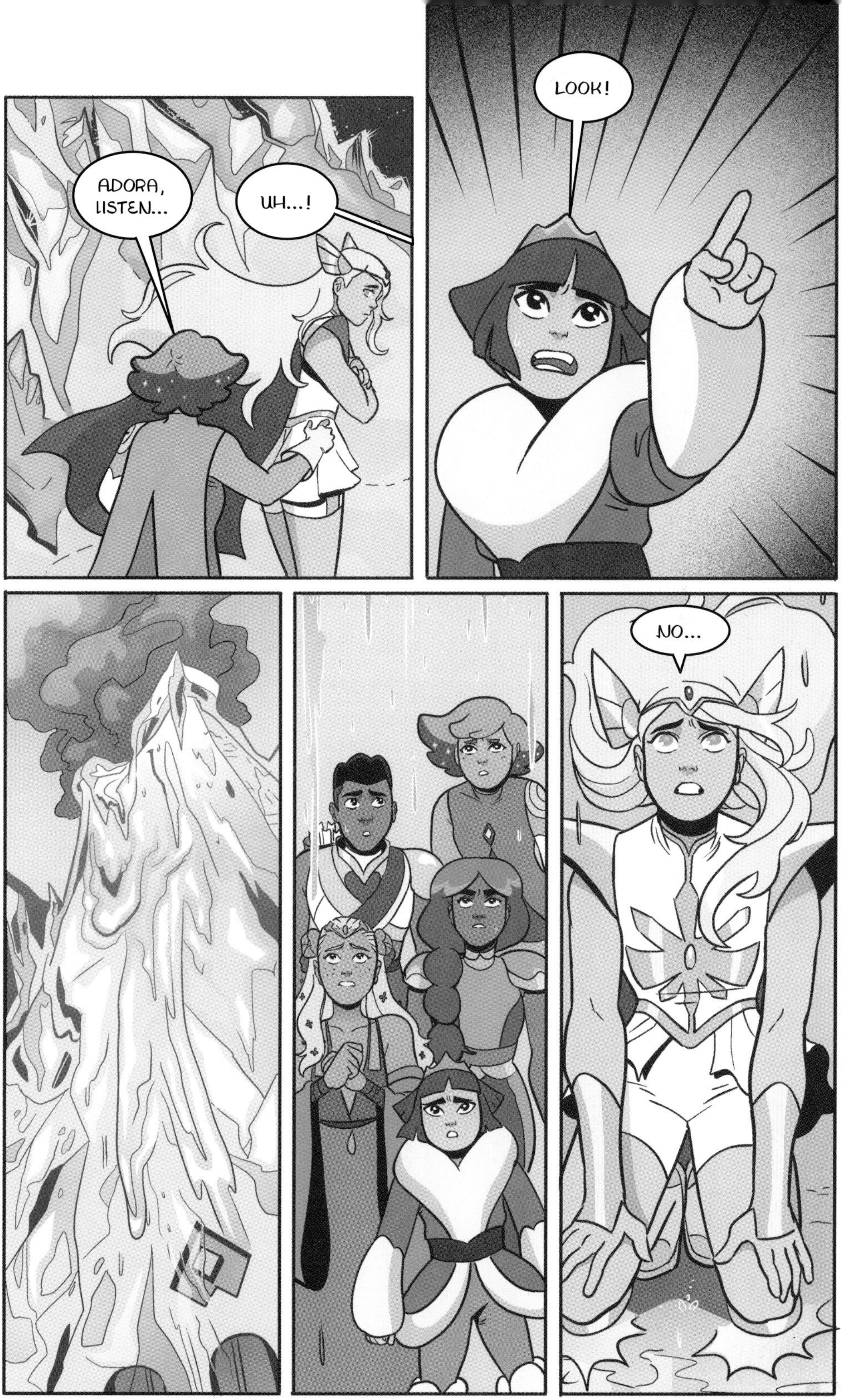
ADORA, LISTEN...
UH...!
LOOK!
NO...

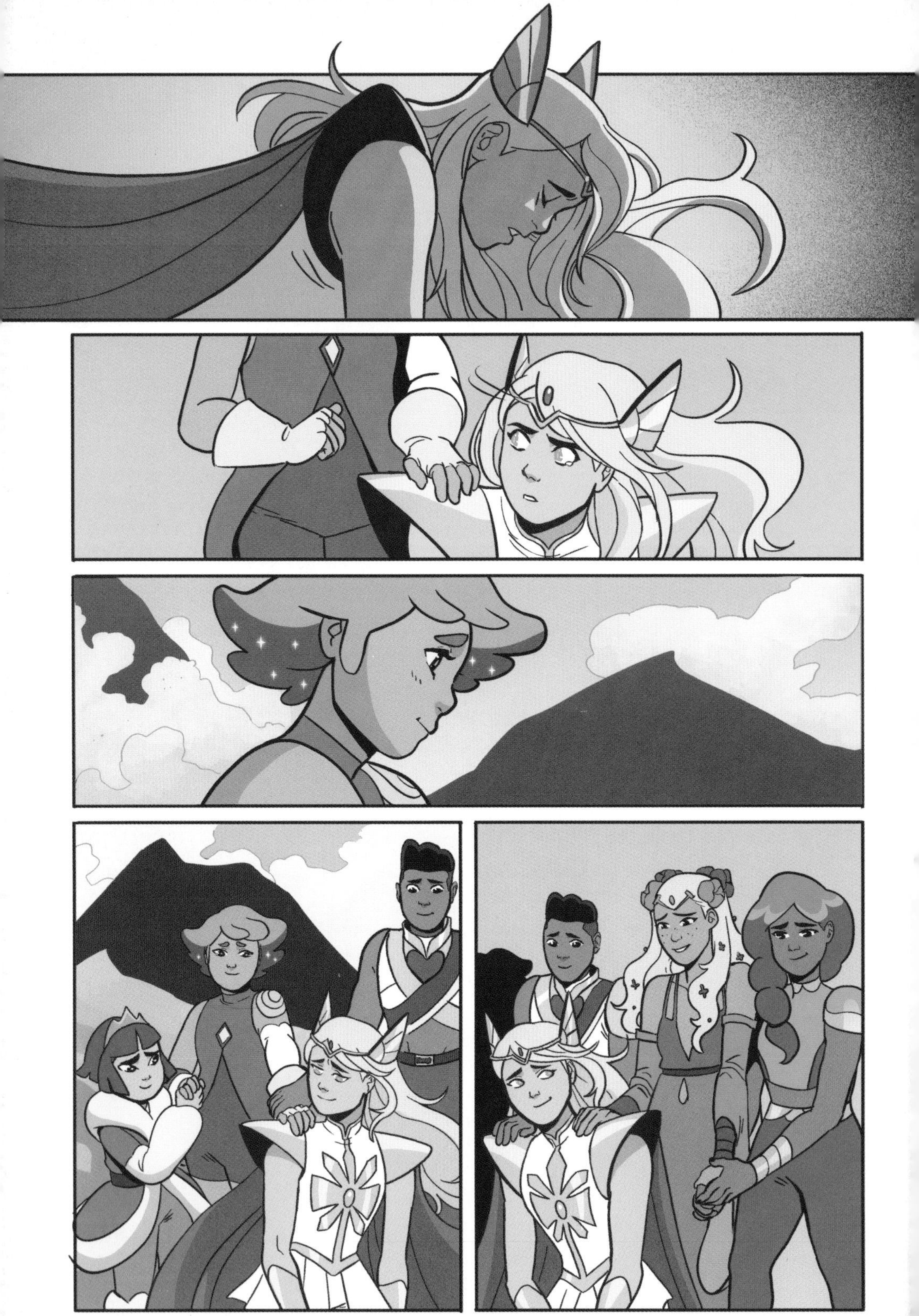

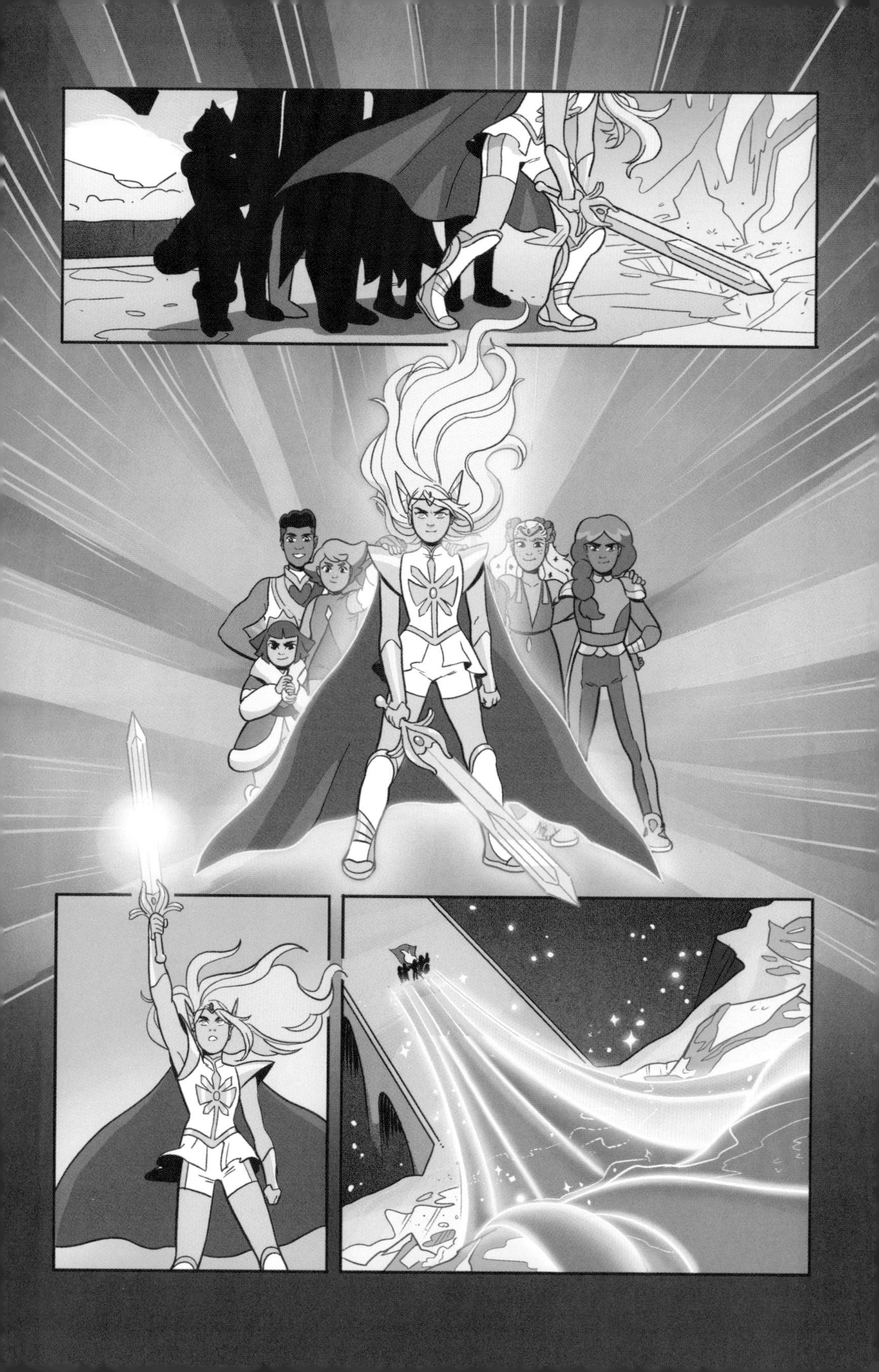

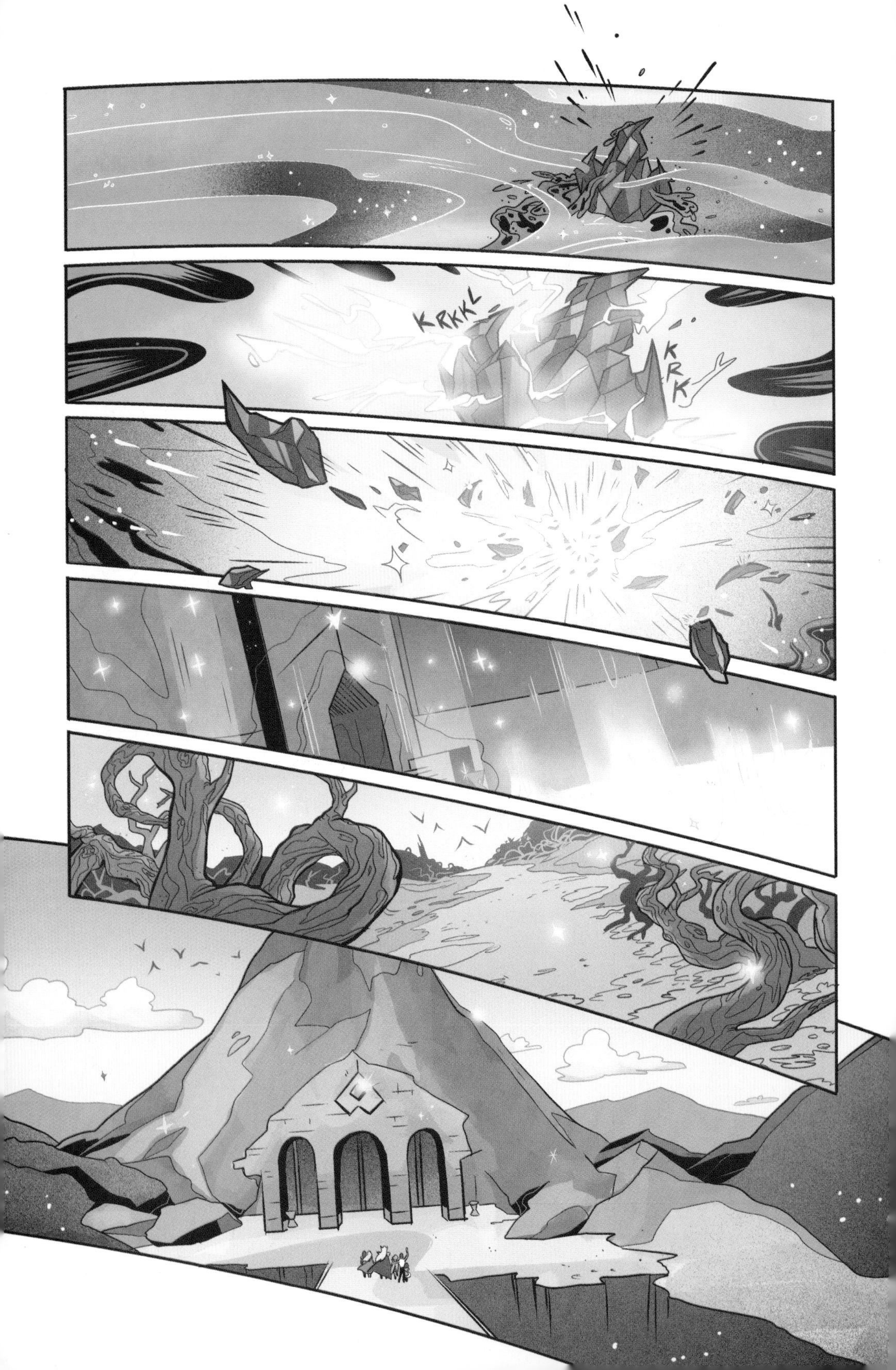
KRKKL
KRK

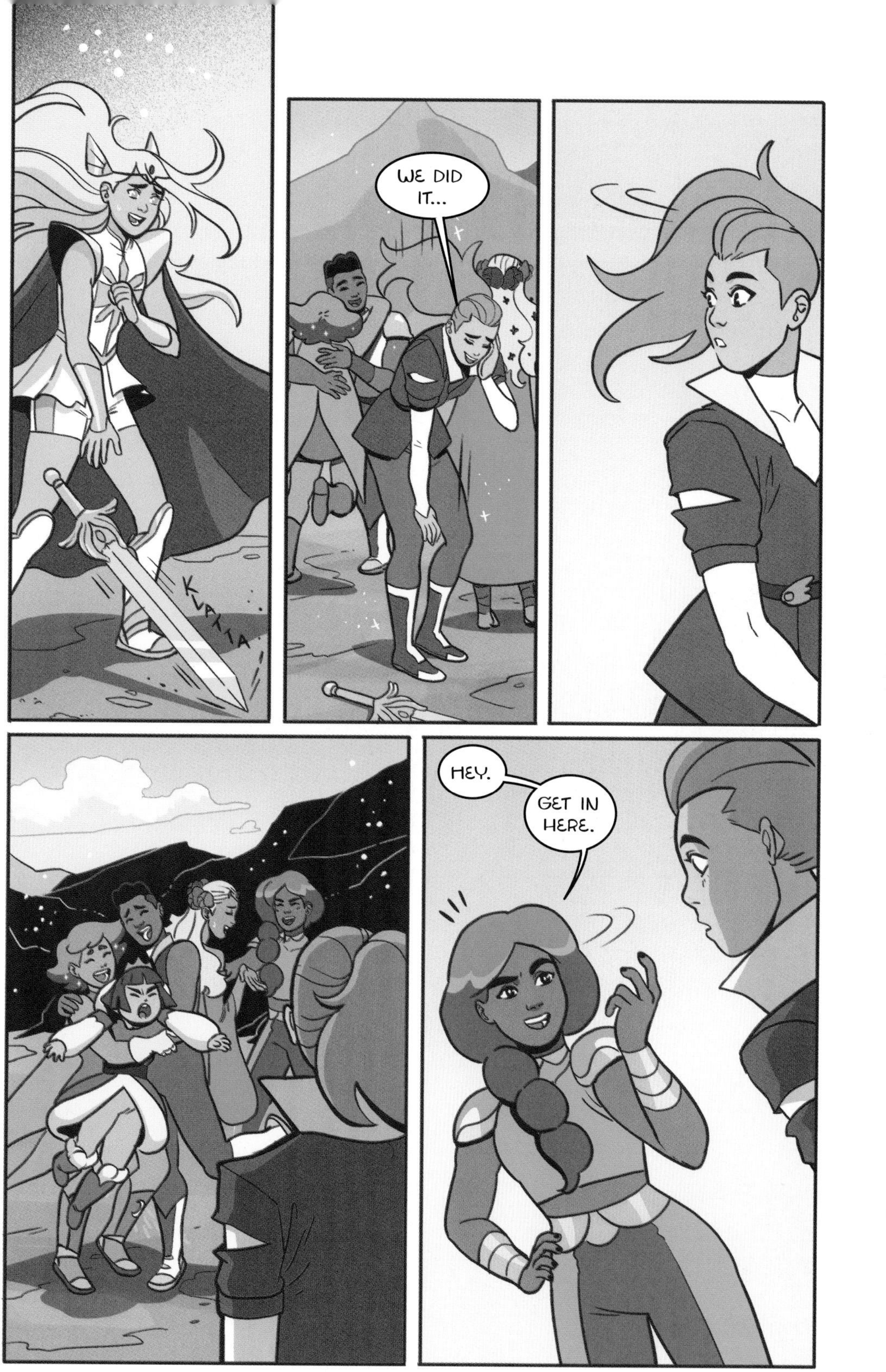
KRAKKA
WE DID IT...
HEY.
GET IN HERE.

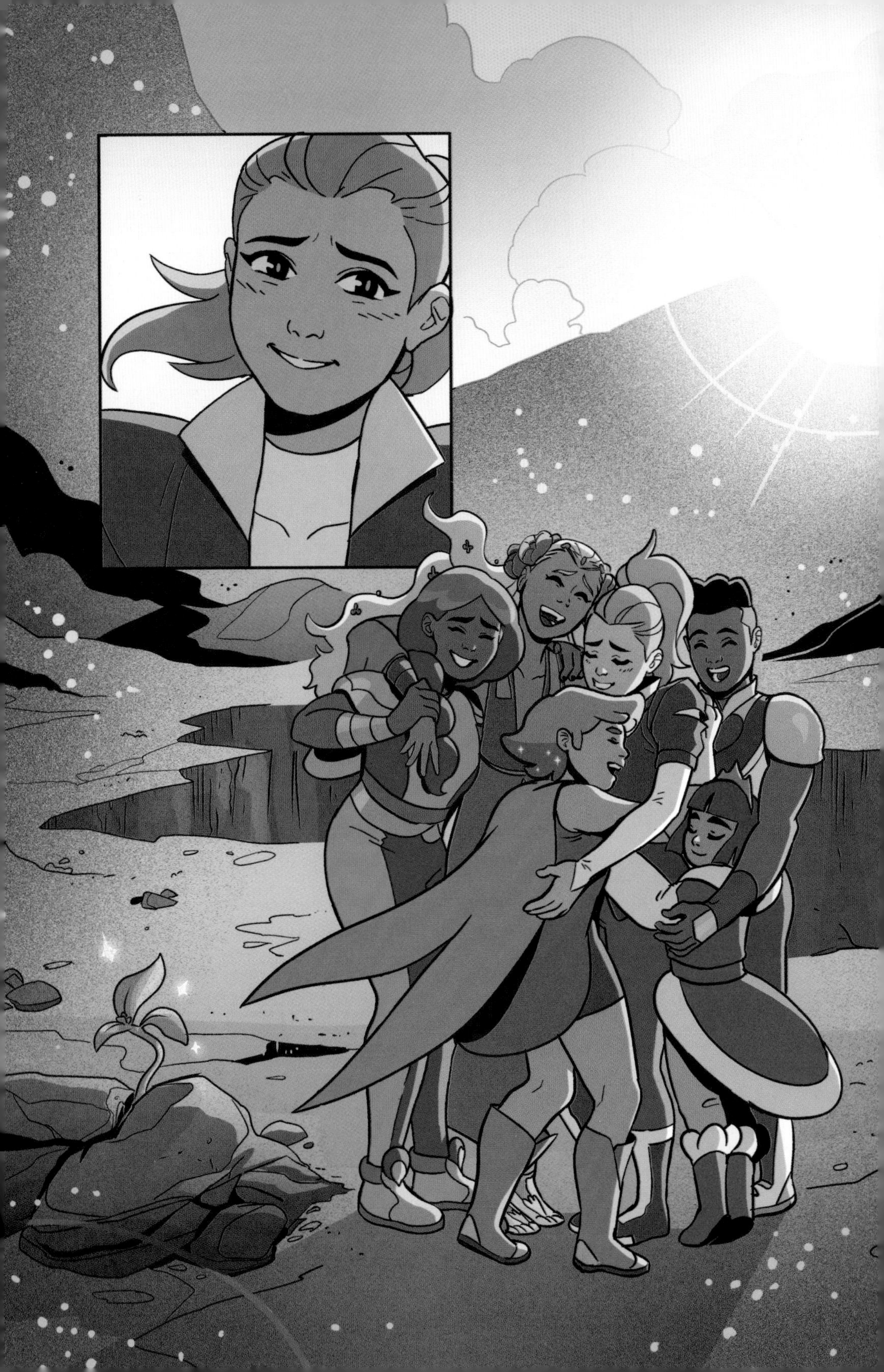

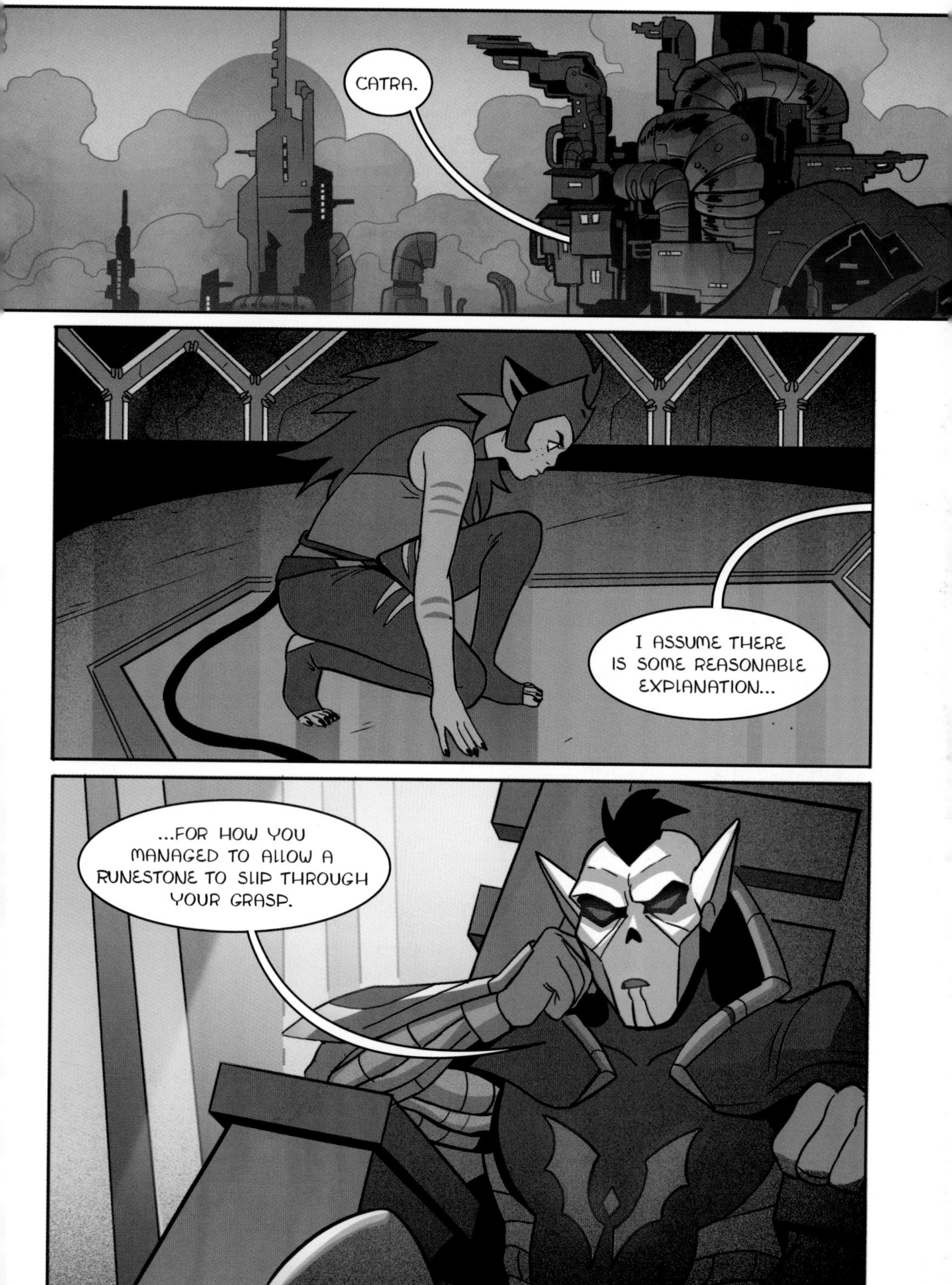
CATRA.
I ASSUME THERE IS SOME REASONABLE EXPLANATION...
...FOR HOW YOU MANAGED TO ALLOW A RUNESTONE TO SLIP THROUGH YOUR GRASP.

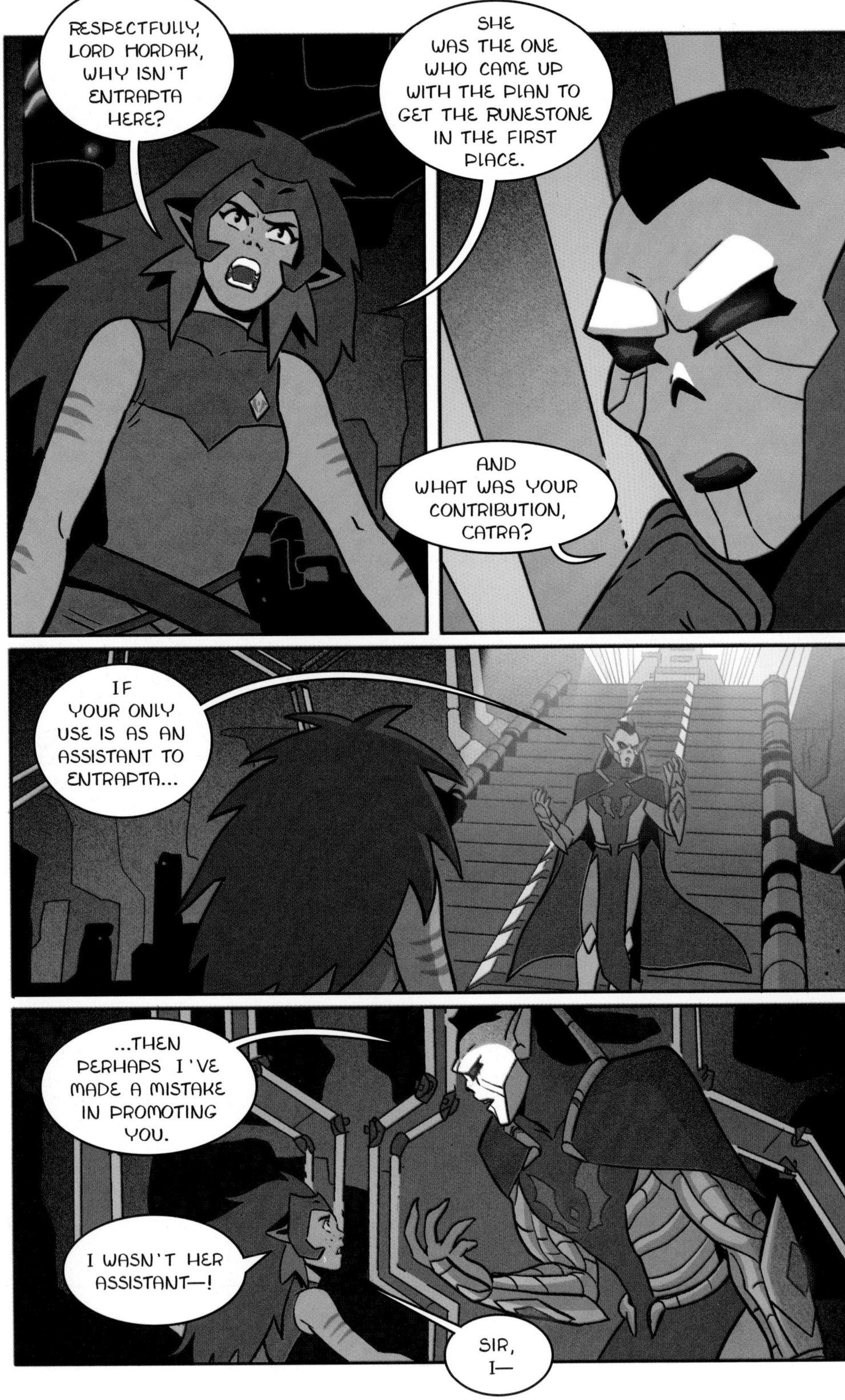
RESPECTFULLY, LORD HORDAK, WHY ISN'T ENTRAPTA HERE?
SHE WAS THE ONE WHO CAME UP WITH THE PLAN TO GET THE RUNESTONE IN THE FIRST PLACE.
AND WHAT WAS YOUR CONTRIBUTION, CATRA?
IF YOUR ONLY USE IS AS AN ASSISTANT TO ENTRAPTA...
...THEN PERHAPS I'VE MADE A MISTAKE IN PROMOTING YOU.
I WASN'T HER ASSISTANT—!
SIR, I—

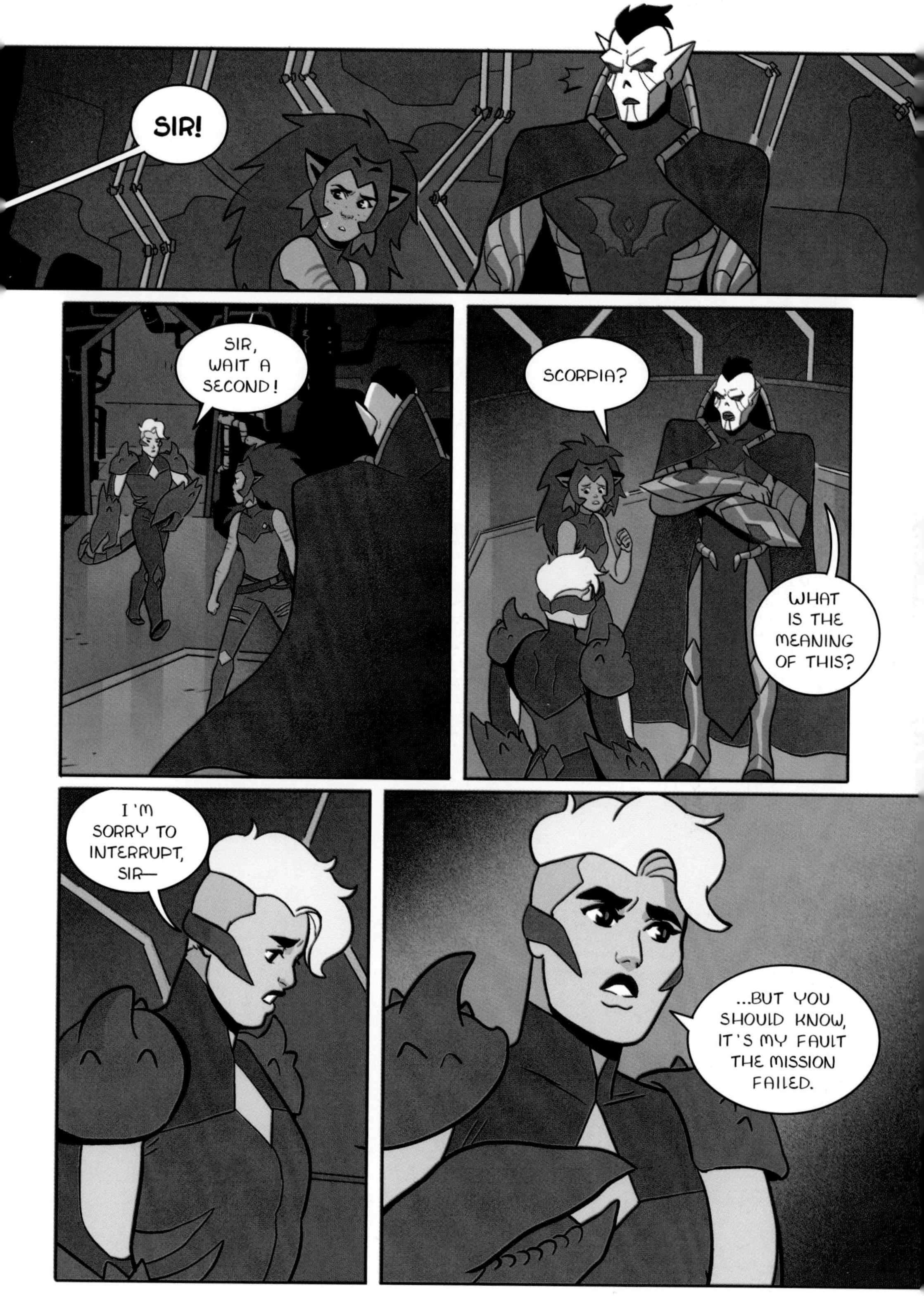
SIR!
SIR, WAIT A SECOND!
SCORPIA?
WHAT IS THE MEANING OF THIS?
I'M SORRY TO INTERRUPT, SIR—
...BUT YOU SHOULD KNOW, IT'S MY FAULT THE MISSION FAILED.

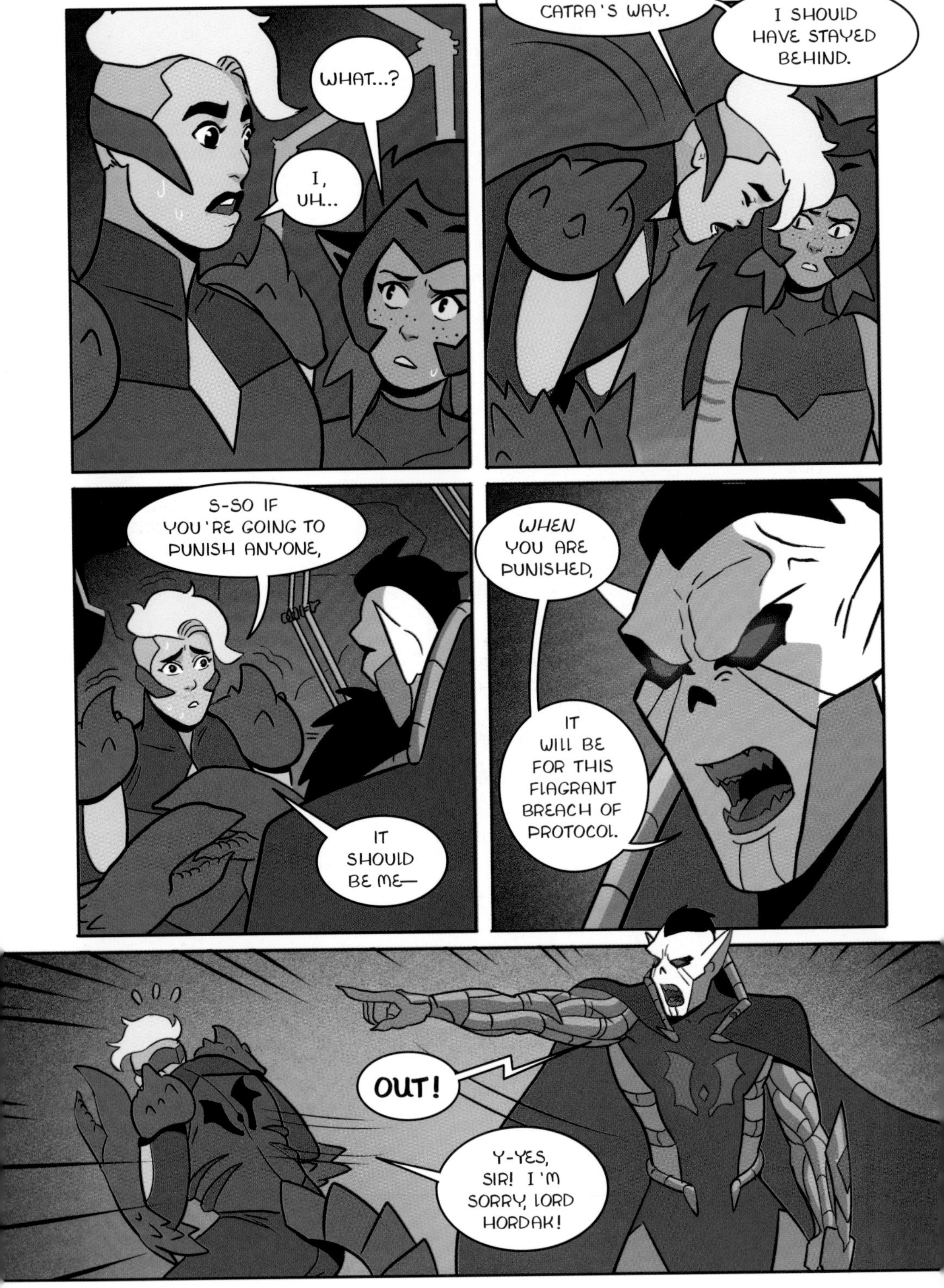
WHAT...?
I, UH...
I GOT IN CATRA'S WAY.
I SHOULD HAVE STAYED BEHIND.
S-SO IF YOU'RE GOING TO PUNISH ANYONE,
IT SHOULD BE ME—
WHEN YOU ARE PUNISHED,
IT WILL BE FOR THIS FLAGRANT BREACH OF PROTOCOL.
OUT!
Y-YES, SIR! I'M SORRY, LORD HORDAK!

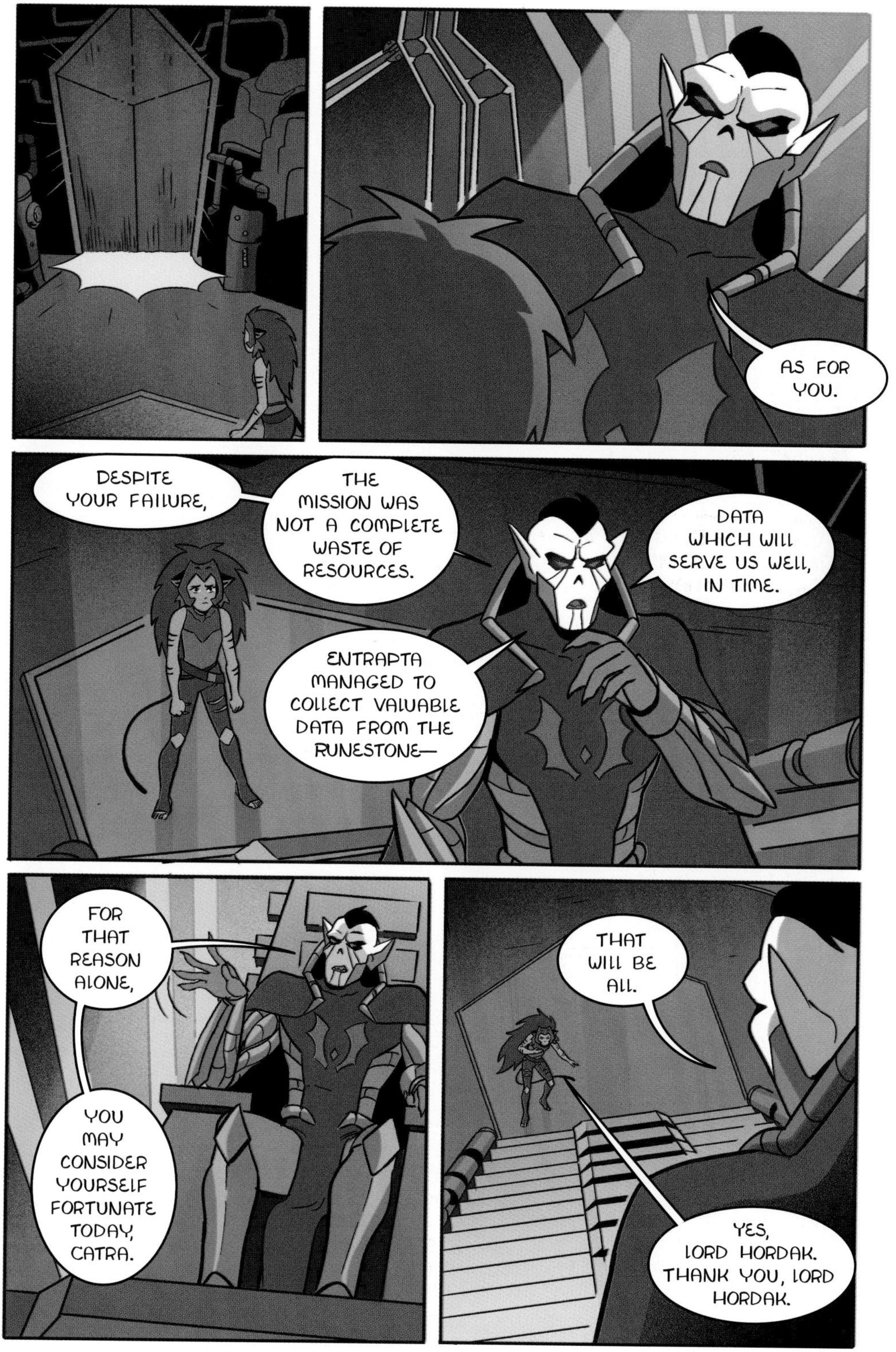

AS FOR YOU.
DESPITE YOUR FAILURE,
THE MISSION WAS NOT A COMPLETE WASTE OF RESOURCES.
ENTRAPTA MANAGED TO COLLECT VALUABLE DATA FROM THE RUNESTONE—
DATA WHICH WILL SERVE US WELL, IN TIME.
FOR THAT REASON ALONE,
YOU MAY CONSIDER YOURSELF FORTUNATE TODAY, CATRA.
THAT WILL BE ALL.
YES, LORD HORDAK. THANK YOU, LORD HORDAK.

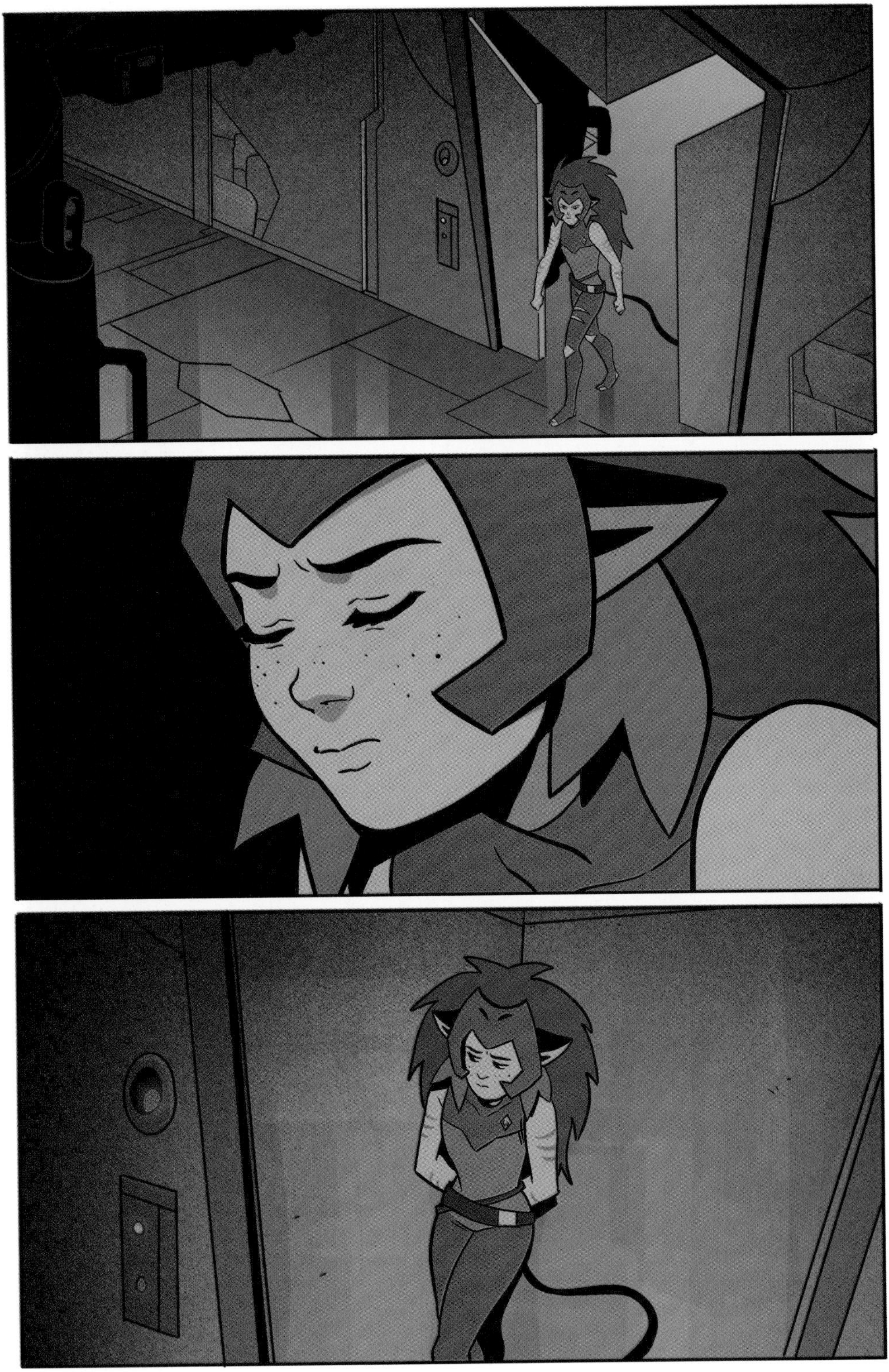

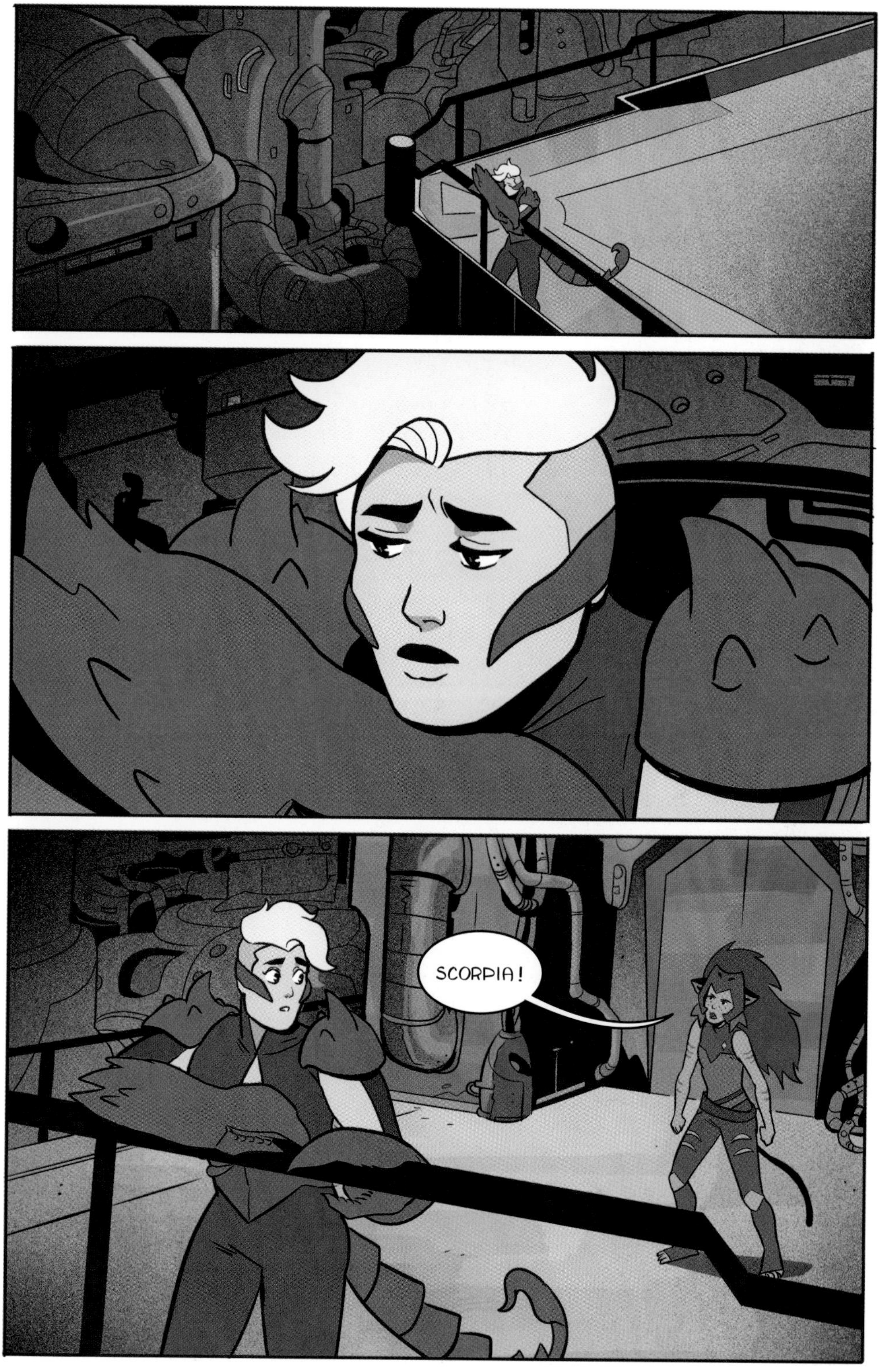
SCORPIA!

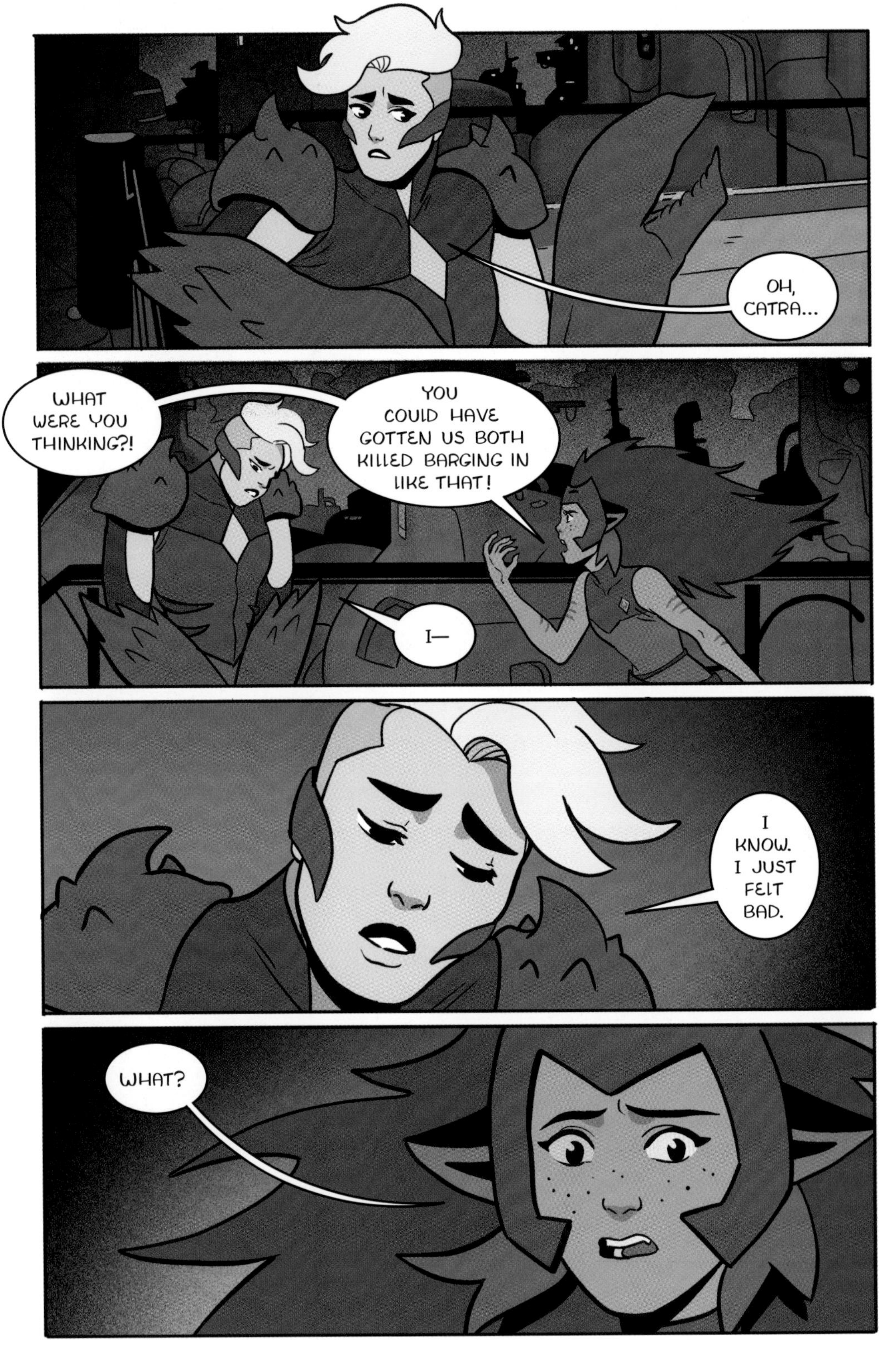
OH, CATRA...
WHAT WERE YOU THINKING?!
YOU COULD HAVE GOTTEN US BOTH KILLED BARGING IN LIKE THAT!
I—
I KNOW. I JUST FELT BAD.
WHAT?

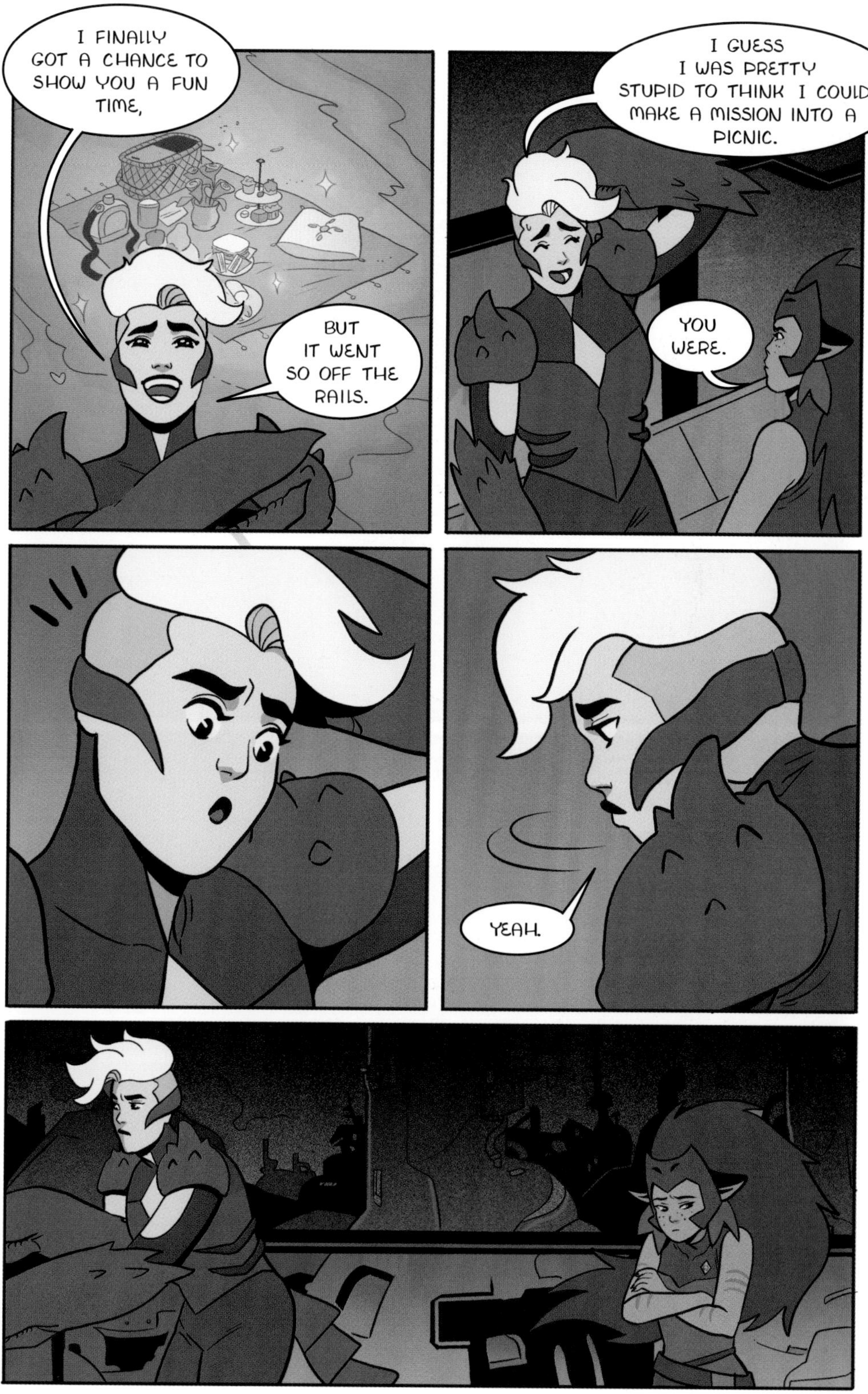
I FINALLY GOT A CHANCE TO SHOW YOU A FUN TIME,
BUT IT WENT SO OFF THE RAILS.
I GUESS I WAS PRETTY STUPID TO THINK I COULD MAKE A MISSION INTO A PICNIC.
YOU WERE.
YEAH.

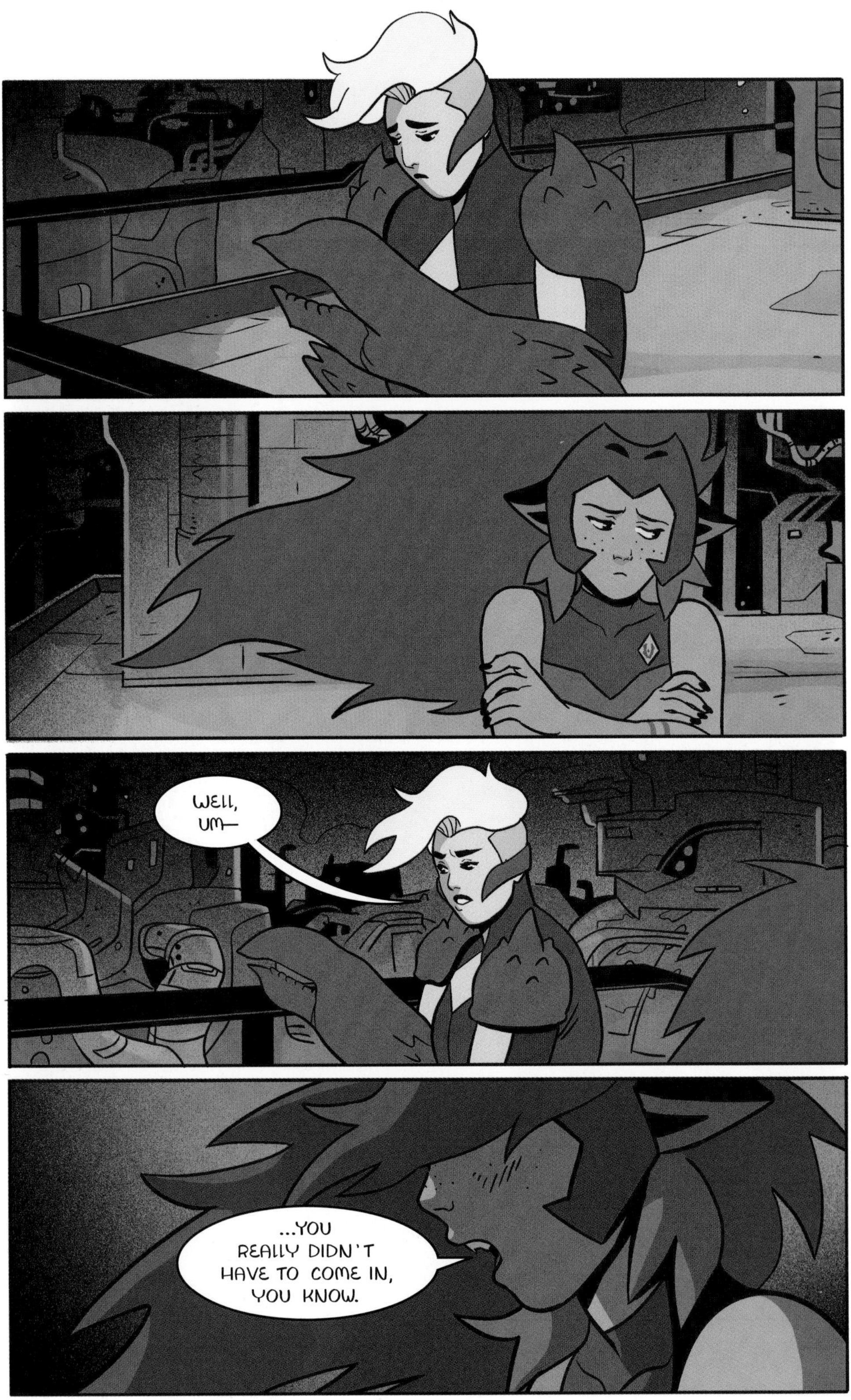
WELL, UM—
...YOU REALLY DIDN'T HAVE TO COME IN, YOU KNOW.

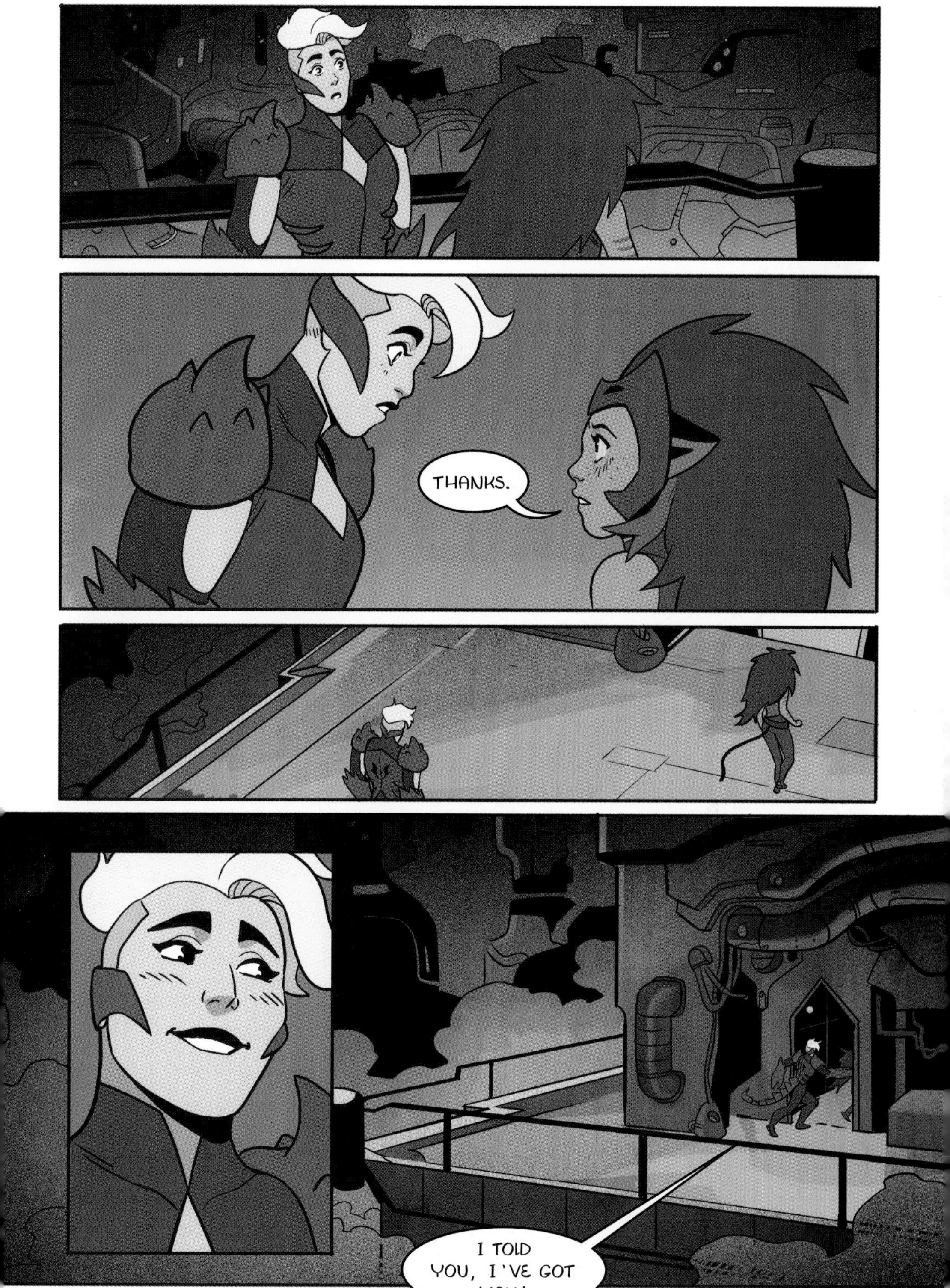
THANKS.
I TOLD YOU, I'VE GOT YOU!

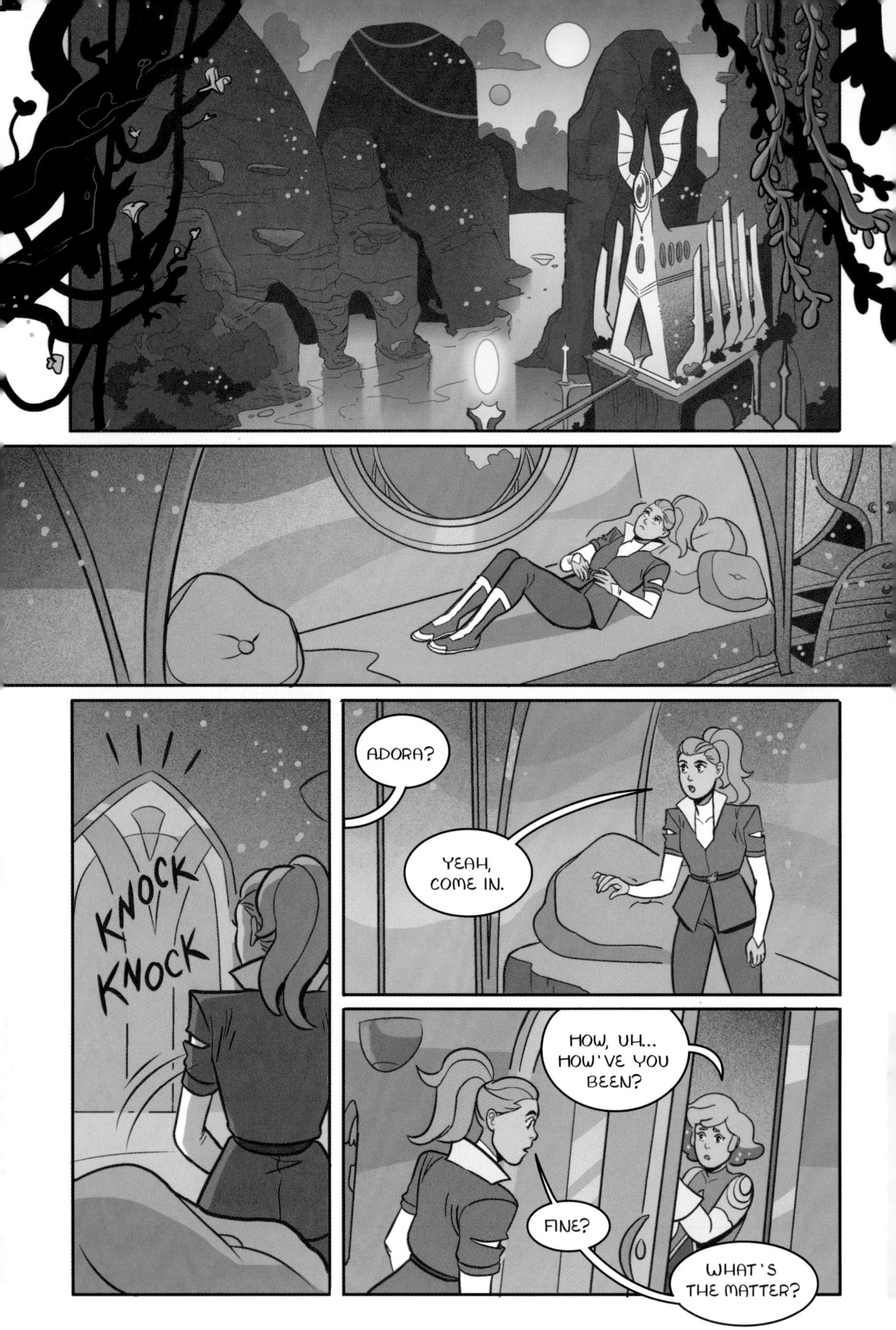
KNOCK KNOCK
ADORA?
YEAH, COME IN.
HOW, UH... HOW'VE YOU BEEN?
FINE?
WHAT'S THE MATTER?

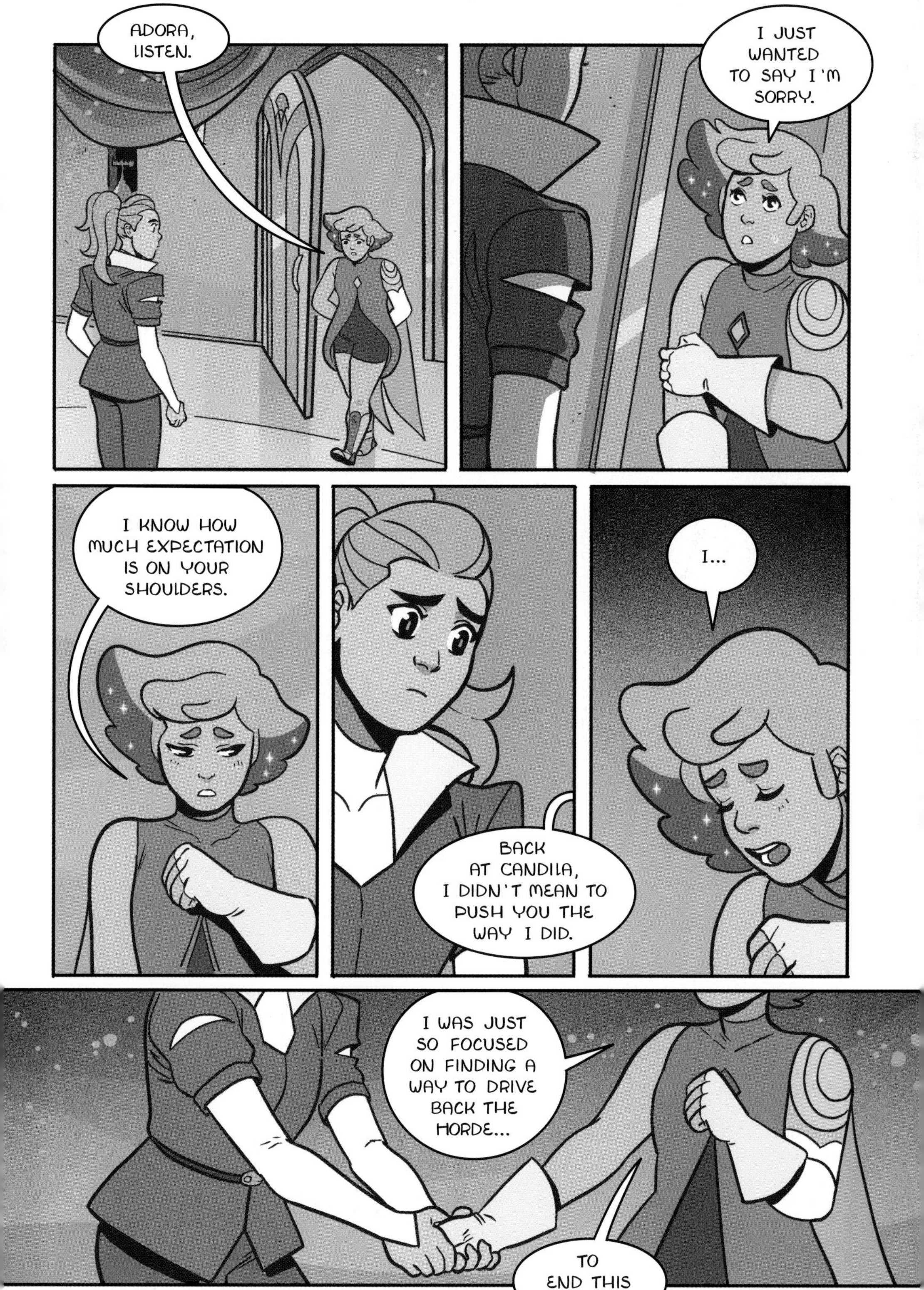
ADORA, LISTEN.
I JUST WANTED TO SAY I'M SORRY.
I KNOW HOW MUCH EXPECTATION IS ON YOUR SHOULDERS.
BACK AT CANDILA, I DIDN'T MEAN TO PUSH YOU THE WAY I DID.
I...
I WAS JUST SO FOCUSED ON FINDING A WAY TO DRIVE BACK THE HORDE...
TO END THIS WAR...

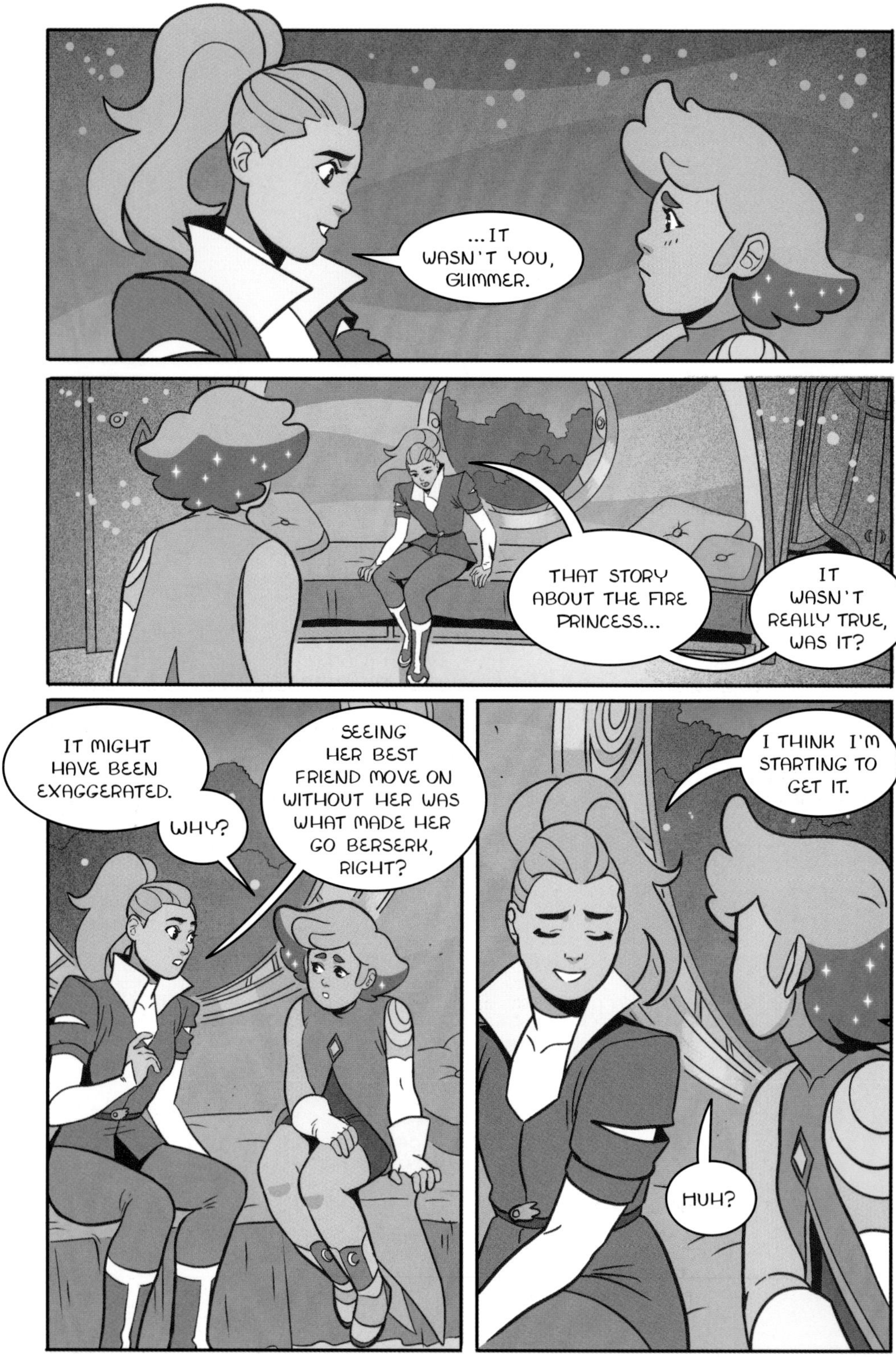
...IT WASN'T YOU, GLIMMER.
THAT STORY ABOUT THE FIRE PRINCESS...
IT WASN'T REALLY TRUE, WAS IT?
IT MIGHT HAVE BEEN EXAGGERATED.
WHY?
SEEING HER BEST FRIEND MOVE ON WITHOUT HER WAS WHAT MADE HER GO BERSERK, RIGHT?
I THINK I'M STARTING TO GET IT.
HUH?

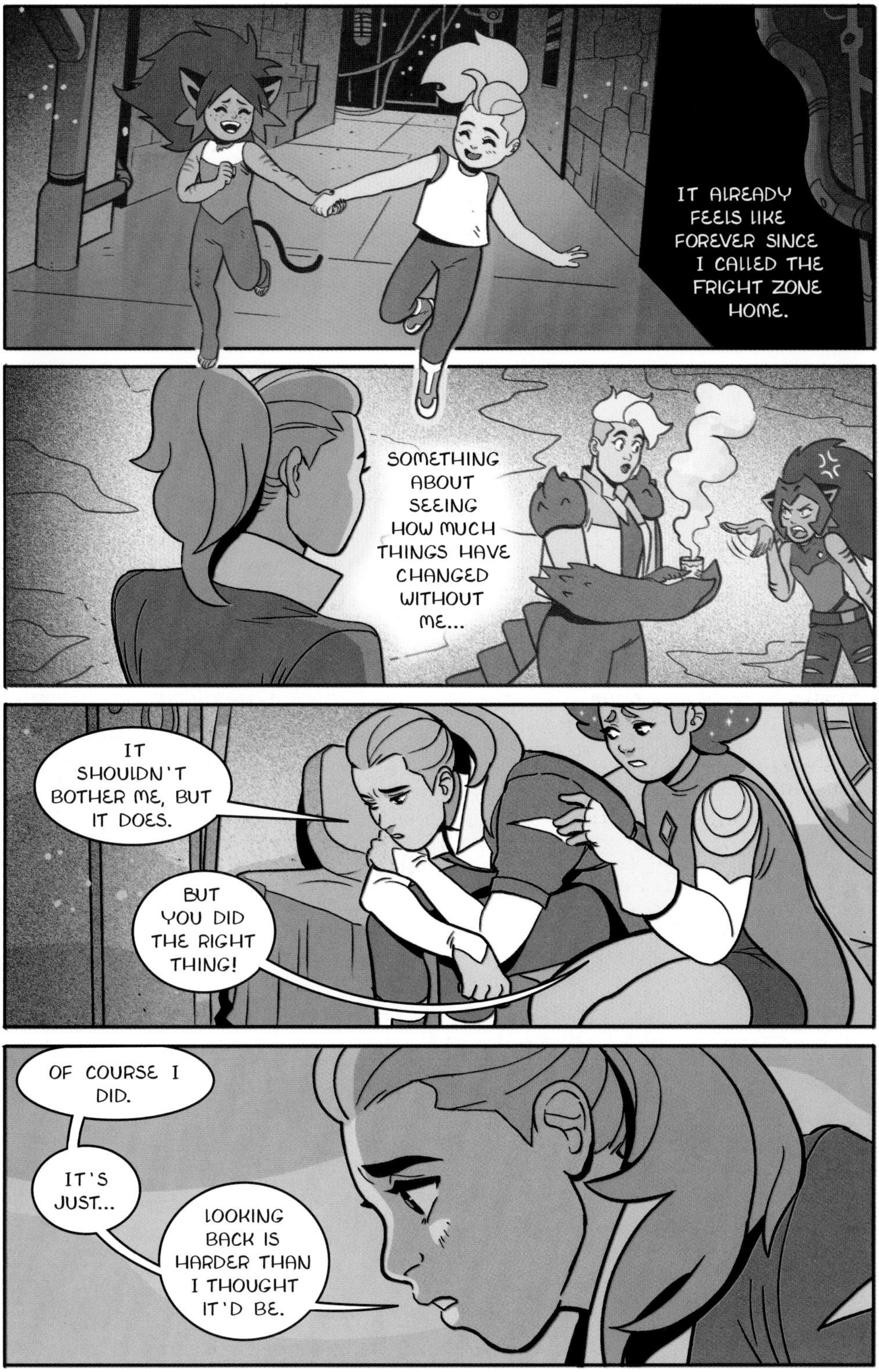
IT ALREADY FEELS LIKE FOREVER SINCE I CALLED THE FRIGHT ZONE HOME.
SOMETHING ABOUT SEEING HOW MUCH THINGS HAVE CHANGED WITHOUT ME...
IT SHOULDN'T BOTHER ME, BUT IT DOES.
BUT YOU DID THE RIGHT THING!
OF COURSE I DID.
IT'S JUST...
LOOKING BACK IS HARDER THAN I THOUGHT IT'D BE.

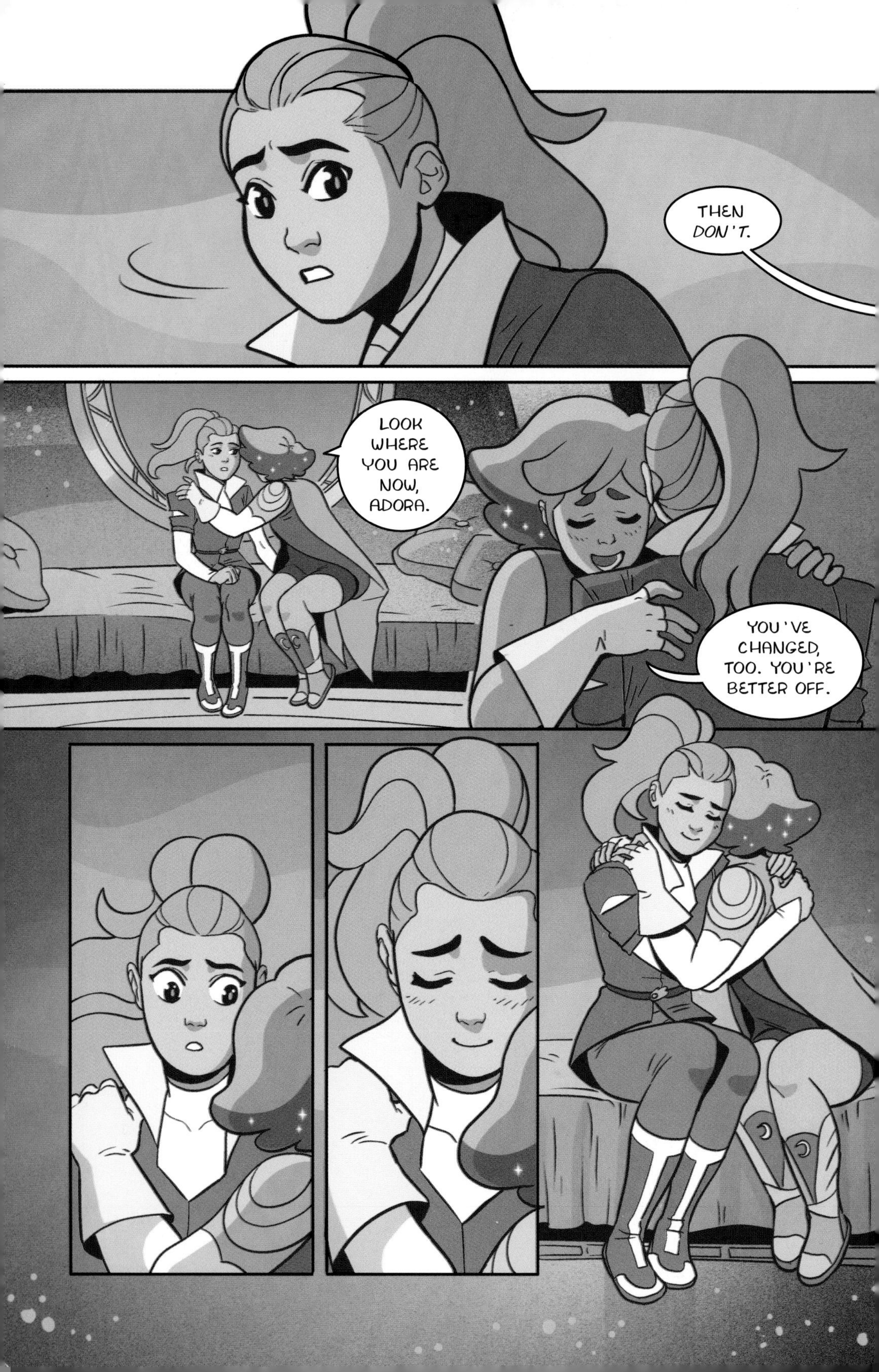
THEN DON'T.
LOOK WHERE YOU ARE NOW, ADORA.
YOU'VE CHANGED, TOO. YOU'RE BETTER OFF.

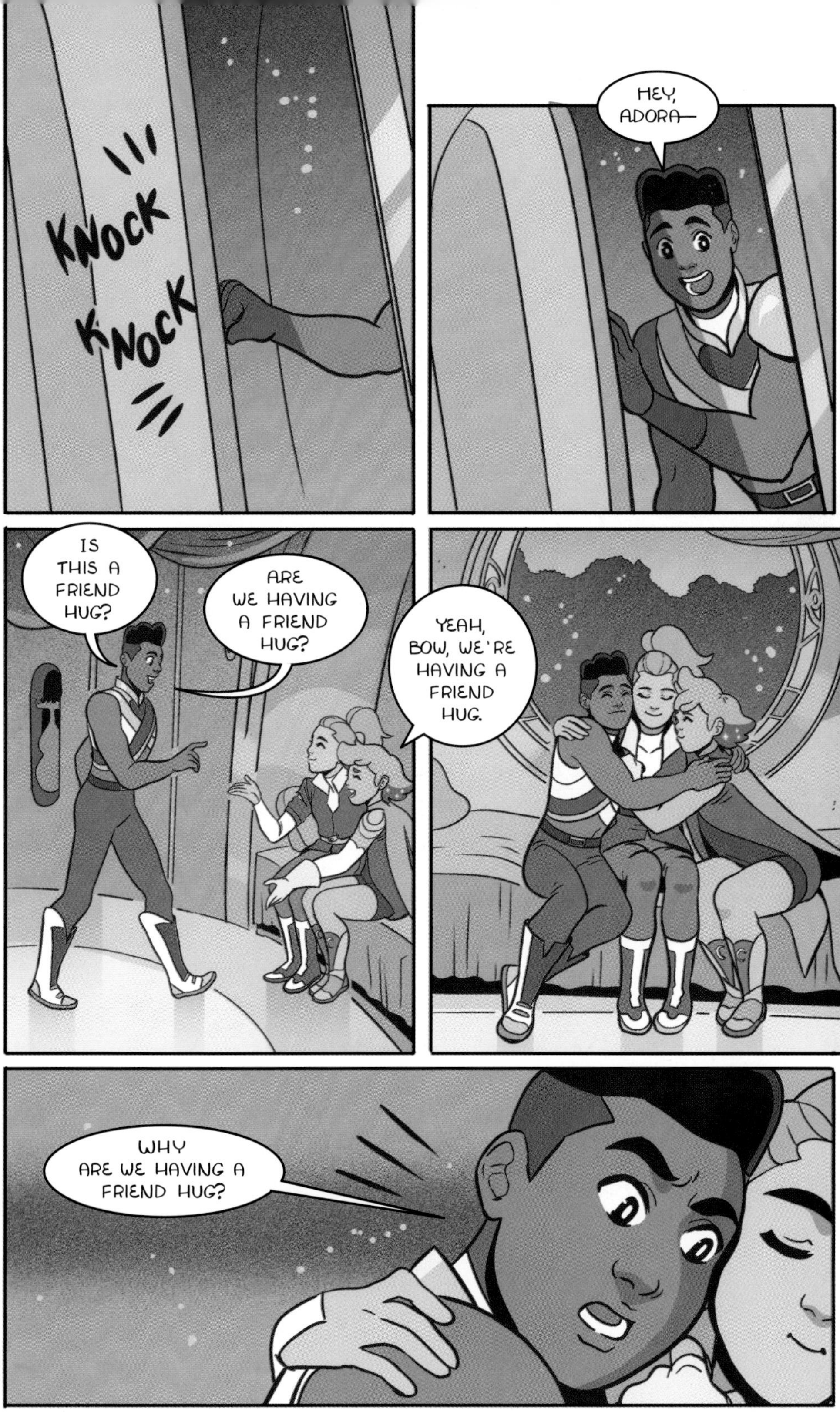
KNOCK
KNOCK
HEY, ADORA—
IS THIS A FRIEND HUG?
ARE WE HAVING A FRIEND HUG?
YEAH, BOW, WE'RE HAVING A FRIEND HUG.
WHY ARE WE HAVING A FRIEND HUG?

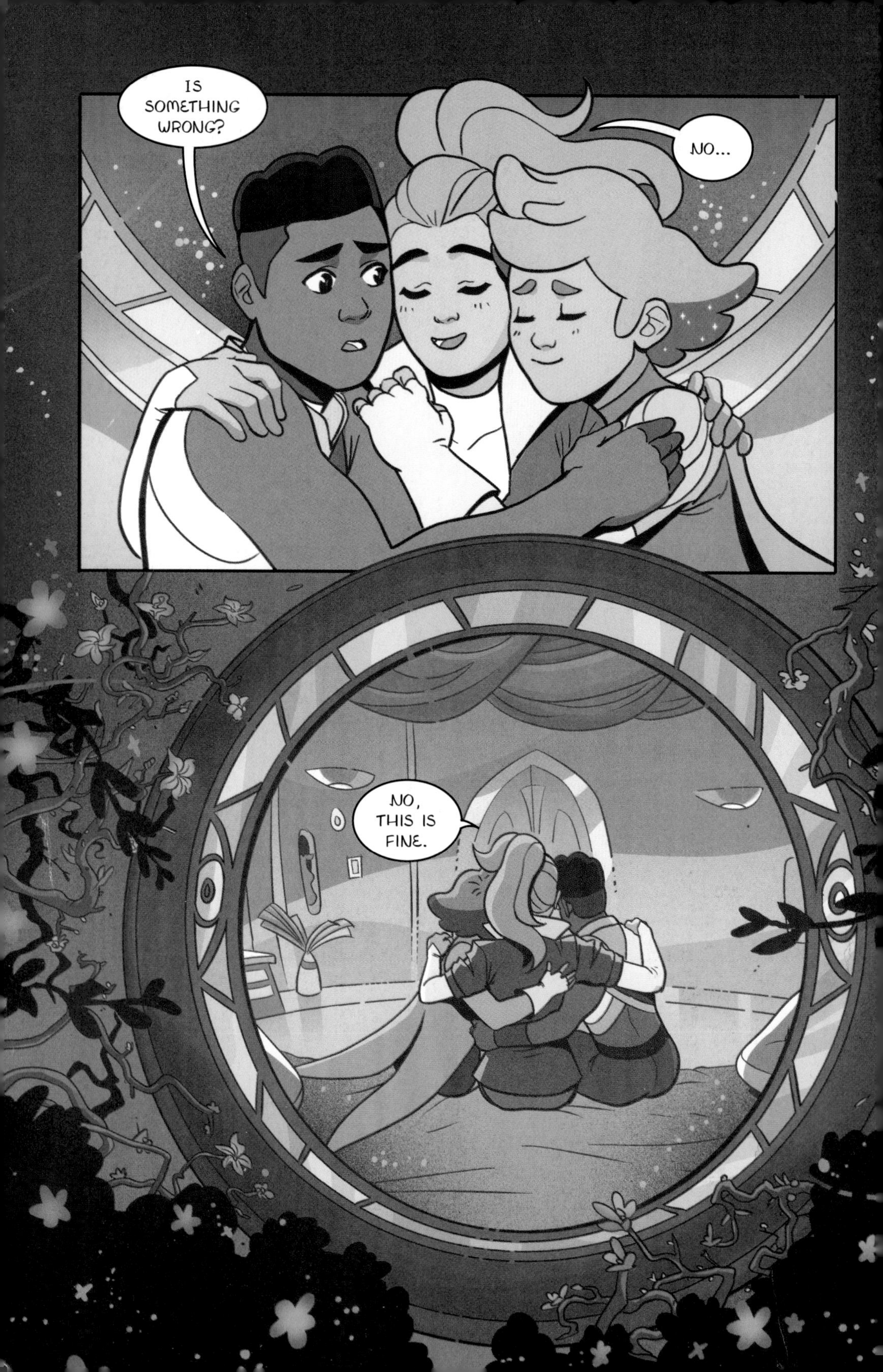
IS SOMETHING WRONG?
NO...
NO, THIS IS FINE.